The
WING
of the
FALCON

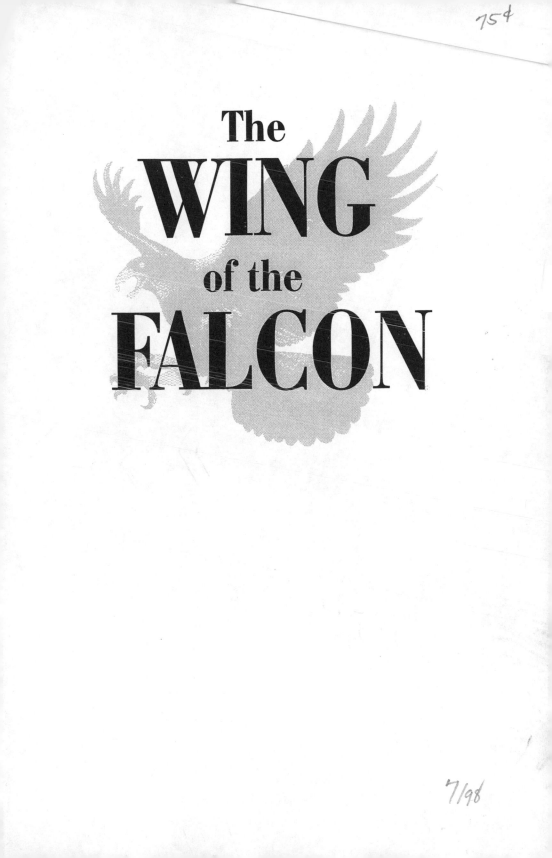

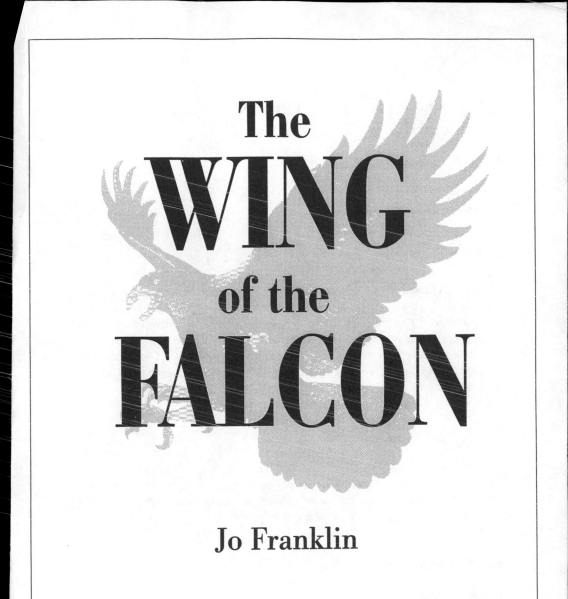

The
WING
of the
FALCON

Jo Franklin

Atlantis Press

THE WING OF THE FALCON
A Novel by Jo Franklin

Published by Atlantis Press

Distributed to the trade by
Associated Publishers Group
1501 County Hospital Road
Nashville, TN 37218
(800) 327-5113

The *Wing of the Falcon* is a work of fiction set during the recent war in the Persian Gulf. Some American, Saudi, Iraqi and other public personages both living and dead appear in the story under their right names. Their portraits are offered as essentially truthful, though scenes and dialogue involving them with fictitious characters are of course invented. Any other usage of real people's names is coincidental. Any resemblance of the imaginary characters to actual persons living or dead is unintended. The simplified map is intended only to illustrate the narrative.

First Edition, July 1995

Library of Congress Catalog Card Number: 95-94263
ISBN: 0-9645459-0-X

Cover photo used with permission of Sygma.
Manufactured in the United States of America
10 9 8 7 6 5 4 3 2 1

Book Design by Carolyn Porter. Jacket and map Design by Carolyn Porter and Todd Meisler. Falcon computer-illustration by Adrian Catarzi. Marketing by Alan Gadney, One-On-One Book Production & Marketing, West Hills, California.

This book is dedicated to those with courage—the courage to hope, to love, to fight, to extend their hands in peace.

V

ACKNOWLEDGMENTS

To acknowledge everyone who contributed substantively to this book would require another book. There are those with whom I have worked at the Department of Defense, the State Department, the Persian Gulf Embassies, the CIA, the Brookings Institution, and the Air Force, whose input has been enormous and without whom this book could truly not have been done.

In the end, however, there are a small handful of people who must be named: When all is said, I simply offer my most profound thanks to Captain David Frazee and Captain Mark Long of Special Operations. They are truly men of courage whose help continued down to the end of the line. My work with them and all of the other people of Special Operations with whom I worked before and during the War in the Gulf is a memory I will long hold.

I also want to offer my deepest thanks to General Norman Schwarzkopf. He once told me that he thought a film I had made, **Days of Rage: The Young Palestinians**, had helped to change the course of history. I know he helped to change the course of history. Always a tough negotiator, he said he had written a quote for my book jacket but would only give it to me if I gave him copies of all my films for his library. I hope, as the cassettes now reside upon his shelf, that they somehow emanate the tremendous affection and admiration I have for him.

I would like to thank Dick Cooper, of the Washington Bureau of the *Los Angeles Times*, for all of his thoughts regarding the manuscript, and to thank Ann Patty, a brilliant editor from whom I learned a lot. I would also like to extend the same thanks to Margaret Franklin—one of the world's great readers and editors and to Marcy Posner, vice-president of the William Morris Agency, for her endless help. To Ashley and Hugh Trout IV, thank you for your endless patience over piles of paper and terrible hours starting before dawn.

Finally, I would like to thank Alan Gadney and Carolyn Porter, the *sine qua non* of this publication—true friends whose support and guidance have kept us all going and on the right track.

A resounding thanks to Rugged who literally helped me ride through the rough times.

PRINCIPAL CHARACTERS

THE AMERICANS

Ray Holt: CIA Chief in Saudi Arabia

Elaine Landon: CIA Specialist in Communications Security

General Norman Schwarzkopf: Commander of the Allied Forces in the Gulf War

THE SAUDIS

Tarek Al Saud: Royal Family member, Director of Saudi Foreign Intelligence

Naila Al Saud: 28-year-old doctor, Royal Family member, sister of Tarek's wife, Nura

Nura Al Saud: Tarek's wife, former brilliant student educated at the Sorbonne

Musaid Al Saud: Young Saudi technocrat, brother of Naila and Nura

Osman: One of the non-Royal Family "Merchant Princes"—a leading Saudi investor and entrepreneur

Said Gharash: Head of the Gulf Bank, friend of Tarek

Badr: Tarek's main aide

Walid: King Fahd's main aide

OTHER CHARACTERS

Antar: Saddam Hussein's inner circle, Head of Iraq's Covert Operations

Yusif Khalidi: Renowned Palestinian archaeologist working in Iraq

Yasmina: Iraqi artist and mistress of Yusif Khalidi

Hamid: Tarek's mole inside Iraq

بِسْمِ اللهِ الرَّحْمَنِ الرَّحِيمِ

يَسْأَلُونَكَ مَاذَآ أُحِلَّ لَهُمْ

قُلْ أُحِلَّ لَكُمُ الطَّيِّبَاتُ

وَمَا عَلَّمْتُم مِّنَ الْجَوَارِحِ

مُكَلِّبِينَ تُعَلِّمُونَهُنَّ مِمَّا

عَلَّمَكُمُ اللَّهُ فَكُلُوا مِمَّآ

أَمْسَكْنَ عَلَيْكُمْ وَاذْكُرُوا

اسْمَ اللَّهِ عَلَيْهِ وَاتَّقُوا اللَّهَ

إِنَّ اللَّهَ سَرِيعُ الْحِسَابِ

صَدَقَ اللَّهُ الْعَظِيمِ

سورة المائدة

In the Name of Allah, the Compassionate, the Merciful

They ask you what is lawful to them. Say: "All good things are lawful to you, as well as that which you have taught the birds and beasts of prey to catch, training them as Allah has taught you. Eat of what they catch for you, pronouncing upon it the name of Allah. And have fear of Allah: swift is Allah's reckoning."

'The Table', Holy Koran

PROLOGUE

The old bedu beckoned the boy to him. The harsh desert light burned the sand spilling silently, endlessly around them. The child approached, fascinated, as the old man stretched out his arm with the hooded falcon. The strong talons of the falcon gripped the leather band on his arm. The bird's head, blinded by the tiny leather hood, turned slowly toward the sound of footsteps approaching.

The old man bent over the boy. "Now, watch." He gave a sign to another man who opened a bag, and a small bird flew upward. The bedu stood absolutely still for a moment and then pulled the hood from the falcon. Its head swerved instantly. With a piercing scream it flew into the air and sank its talons and beak into the prey, devouring the flesh midair.

The child watched the falcon slowly curve in the sky and return to the bedu's arm.

"They are all different, you see, all different," said the bedu, stroking the blood-flecked wings of the falcon. "Some, they attack midair. Others circle and circle in the air until they tire the prey, then they attack. Others strike while the prey is on the ground; they use devious maneuvers to intimidate, to demoralize the prey, then they pounce and kill. They are all different." The old bedu stroked the wings and looked down at the boy. "You must learn how to hunt the falcon, how to train it."

1

The boy sat down beside him while he put the hood back over the falcon's eyes and gently placed it upon a wooden perch.

"To hunt a falcon you must begin in the early morning," said the old man. "You must look for the traces of his talons in the sand, search for remains of its food in the desert. Then, when you know this, you plan the strategy. Dig a deep hole in the ground so that you may stand but the falcon can't see you. When you are ready, release a pigeon tied to a long string. The falcon will see the pigeon and swoop." The boy looked up, startled, when the bedu suddenly clasped his hand down on the child's shoulder, "The falcon will see the pigeon and begin to eat it."

"And then," the old bedu cackled, eyes dancing, "you begin slowly, slowly to pull the pigeon toward you. Quietly, quietly until the falcon is within your reach. And," he clamped a hand down on the child's other shoulder, "you catch him by the legs. You must be very careful or he will try to kill you, to pluck your eyes out. But," he brought his old brown leathered face down to the child's, "if you are clever, you will have him."

"Then, you must train him to hunt for you." The old man looked down for a moment while the boy gazed at him in fascination, and then took the falcon, hooded and silent, back on his arm. "You cover his head with the small hood, and you talk to him. This bird who hates humans, you talk to him until he becomes used to your voice. In time, he will become used to your voice."

The old bedu called the bird's name, and the bird turned toward him. He began to stroke the bird's deep brown wings. He picked up a piece of bloody meat and handed it to the child. "You stroke his wings," the small fingers moved forward obediently to gently touch the massive wings, "and you give him the food." The child stretched out his hand and the bird seized the bloody morsel from him. "He will grow used to you."

"And then you train him to kill for you." The bedu picked up a

long piece of string. "First you only let him fly with this, so he will not escape. You bring him some lure. It is good for the falcon to eat small live birds and their feathers while in training. And you train, again and again you loose the lure in the desert in the early morning, and in the evening. Until finally he knows you are the master." The old man dropped the string onto the ground. "Then he will hunt for you. He is a killer and he will hunt for you."

I

JULY 1990—THE PERSIAN GULF

Captain John Roberts, U.S. Naval Intelligence, felt the sweat drip down his face. The ship lurched slightly beneath him. He kept his eyes on the waters of the Gulf, steadied himself against the gray metal siding of the ship, and continued to walk down the deck toward the control room. In the distance, toward the Arab coast of the Gulf to the north, he saw the slow movement of an oil tanker silently lumbering south toward the Strait of Hormuz. Then he heard the faint creaking of wood. To the right, the hull of an old wooden fishing dhow drifted alongside his ship. The American watched the old man on board the dhow—a face lined and creased, baked by the sun—mending the soiled fishing net while a younger man at the hull slowly drew the nets back into the boat.

Roberts closed his eyes for a moment. The heat, silence, and slow rolling of the water beneath him moved through his body like a drug. He hated the Gulf. He breathed in the deep humidity of the air, struggling against lethargy, and kept walking toward the control room.

He glanced at the coast of Saudi Arabia. It seemed a dense, impenetrable world, a closed country, where people lived lives

5

in ways that were beyond his understanding, indeed almost beyond his curiosity. He glanced north toward Iraq and then to Iran, the coast on the other side of the Gulf faintly discernible in the distance. He thought about the horrors of a revolution that had seemed a descent into the dark ages. Slumbering now, quiet, but still not over. Yesterday, a small boat had come from Iran to Dhahran. They had stopped the boat loaded with figs to check the captain's entry papers and had discovered the young men hiding, a few more refugees in an endless stream escaping to any port in the Gulf that would take them. Roberts shook his head and walked toward the control room, past other seamen barely moving in the stultifying heat. A plane sounded in the distance from Iraq.

Roberts opened the door to the control room and saw the puzzled faces watching the bootleg monitor they had installed to pull down the images from the KH-11 spy satellite.

"Iraq is moving troops to their border with Kuwait," murmured one of the men without turning. Roberts, went quickly to the monitor. He peered at the images, then instantly sat down and shot off the cable to Ray Holt, CIA Chief in Riyadh, Saudi Arabia.

He walked back out on the deck and looked down at the dhow now starting to move away from the side of the ship. Inching its way to the north, toward the sliver of coast along the Iraqi border, then up the narrow Shatt al-Arab waterway closer inland toward Basra and drifting toward the movement of the Iraqi troops with the sound intercept equipment he had installed quietly at Ray Holt's instructions last night. He glanced down, the little WJ-8990 Tactical Intel System MANTIS, the minute, 24 kilogram receiver/processor stowed below the hull in the radio pouch of an innocuous backpack.

The dhow seemed to move one foot, then two. Roberts

started to walk back to the control room. For a second he felt a shudder to the ship's rail on which his hand rested. He turned around. And as he did, he saw the dhow explode.

In an instant, the dhow, with its two men and little MANTIS unit, burst into a screaming flame of fire on the water beneath the hot sun of the Gulf.

❋ ❋ ❋

Washington, D.C.

Elaine Landon, asleep, heard the phone ring once, then twice in her Washington apartment. The voice on the other end seemed a whisper in the night.

"Holt in Riyadh has requisitioned you. Defense says it's nothing. He says it's an emergency. The car will be there in thirty minutes."

She moved quickly. Her training, like a separate creature took over, she hung up the phone, stood up, flicked on the light, brushed the long sand-colored hair back, wordlessly pulled clothes from the closet and put them on. And then she waited. She walked toward the window, her face caught for a moment in its reflection offering a momentary glimpse of the pale aqua eyes, the high cheekbones, the elegant aquiline features. The beautiful young woman of about thirty who came and went from the apartment nestled in the center of Georgetown. She glanced down at the street; the car was not there yet.

Elaine looked back at the lovely old high-ceiling apartment with its yellow walls, deeply beveled oak doors, the myriad windows that in the day flooded it with light and in the night watched the parade of humanity unfold itself up and down M Street.

She moved back toward the desk by the antique wooden bookshelves, gathered together the papers she had been working on, and put them in her briefcase. The tiny antique clock she had brought back from the Middle East ticked along steadily next to the picture of the even-featured man whose gaze seemed distant. She felt her hand stiffen as she looked past both and toward the window again. She walked over to it, staring, waiting.

Below her walked a homeless brown man of no age, any age, wrapped as he was night after night in his swaths of cloth, turbans of debris, wheeling, as he did night after night, his shambled assortment of possessions in a metal cart. He walked past the last well-dressed people emerging from Georgetown restaurants open until 2:00 A.M. Patrons who in the day would disappear and be replaced farther up the street, where M turned into Pennsylvania Avenue, by the picketers with their signs of God, love, and government, jostling like mimes against the journalists, secretaries, bureaucrats, rushing in and out of the White House and Executive Office Building complex. Blocks that seemed a world away. Insular.

Her eye moved to the darkened marquis of the little Biograph Movie Theater across the street, then down to the art gallery below her, its sign illuminated by the street light that hung over it. "You were gone again," said the young woman who owned it, "so the phone company dropped your new directories off with us." The woman had smiled and invited her for a coffee, some conversation if she ever had the time. The woman had walked back down the stairs with a pleasant shrug. "Come anytime, we artists, we painters lead a lonely life."

We artists, we painters lead a lonely life, Elaine whispered to herself as she heard the sound of the car approaching below. *And my medium? I paint pictures that you will never see. They are made of thousands of tiny strands and filaments that connect everything. Sound that curls, bends, and moves noiselessly across the air to finally whisper in another country. Invisible words that will appear only later. Tiny chips that upon being touched, like the political impulse that formed them, activate, inform into an enormity that is no longer containable. I look for sounds that don't sound. Words that write themselves and disappear. Languages that mean nothing but to the mathematical decoder. Webs of voices that don't want to be heard.*

We artists lead a lonely life. Holt in Riyadh has requisitioned you. She felt her hand stiffen, the tenseness moving all the way up her arm. *Maybe it could be done from here....* Her mind was grasping, reaching now. Unconsciously she began to pace, moving from the window back into the library with its intricate moldings, the brass lamp on the desk catching pieces of the street lights outside, the sign of the art gallery below. Her eye moved back to the picture of the man on the desk, the small antique clock. *I may know, my painter friend, a level of solitude you never dreamed of.* Her gaze wandered back to the darkened movie marquis across the street. "Visions of Light," blinked the title under the street light. The car pulled up. *Was hers a vision of light? Rarely,* thought Elaine walking down to the car. *More often of darkness.*

he car moved along the canal road leading out of Georgetown into Virginia to CIA headquarters just a matter of miles away. The lights were on in the small conference room at Langley, nestled in the assemblage of gray buildings. The three men waiting for her drank coffee as she was stopped by the guards, cleared the checks at the gate, then passed through the building entrance. She entered the room and nodded at James Turley, the section head. Turley's languid frame, the always slightly insidious slant of his body leaned against the back of a chair while he listened to the stocky attaché in uniform from the Defense Department, and the aide from the State Department who seemed to incessantly, compulsively take off his wire rim glasses, clean them, put them back on. Turley glanced up and focused on Elaine standing there. Turley, effete, the last of the legions of Ivy League products that had once populated the Company. Whippet thin, with ferret-like eyes, wearing an expensive tie, he thrust a package of materials at her. "Holt in Riyadh. You know about him?"

"Everybody knows about him," Elaine said in a clipped tone. The liaison from Defense appeared momentarily taken aback at the abruptness of her reply and then wrote it off to the overwhelming possibility that people who have to work with Turley might grow to detest him. Turley seemed not to notice. Unruffled, he continued.

"Holt wants you get on a flight to Riyadh today." Turley moving as though voice and hand were synchronized, picked up a brown envelope, opened it, and dropped the images in front of Elaine. Grainy images, dots, like thousands of ants on an anthill.

"The imagery," droned Turley with his usual ennui, "was processed at the National Photo-Interpretation Center in Washington. It was then evaluated by DIA watch officers in the Pentagon, who duly noted the positioning of Iraqi troops along the Kuwaiti border." The Defense attaché started to say something, but Turley drawled over him. "It has since been evaluated by our team here, the White House as well, and we have all decided that this is of little interest to us."

"What does this have to do with me?" asked Elaine tersely.

"That, love," his voice hovered in mock despair, "you'll have to ask Holt when you get to Riyadh." His eyebrow arched. "Something vague—about communications. Holt doesn't explain. He's the only person on the face of the earth within this establishment who can get away with that, but…"

"Because he's usually right," muttered the aide from State, now apparently absorbed with adjusting the frames of his glasses.

"Usually. Not always; that's the part I try to remind him of." Turley handed Elaine the information on her flight, the initial directions from Holt on how to meet him.

"Why does he want me in particular—I've never met him," puzzled Elaine.

"He seems to know about you," Turley shrugged. He buzzed for the car and handed her a second package. "General briefing material, a little night-time reading for you." He stood up, the meeting over.

Elaine left the room, exited through the security checks, and drove in silence, scanning the material Turley had given her. Curious for a moment at the thought of meeting the legendary Ray Holt, even more curious about why he wanted her in particular.

The driver deposited her back at her apartment, and she rapidly began packing. Once again she scanned the papers she had been given, then walked to the window, gazing down at the sign of the painter's art gallery below. She recalled Turley's comments, the final one. "Holt…he seems to know about you." Finally she stopped.

The small clock on the desk offered up a chime for the hour. And with it came the realization of what she had been asked to do—return to the Middle East. Suddenly the reality of going back after what had happened seized her. Her hand froze midair. *Holt in Riyadh …he seems to know about you.* She looked once more at the picture on the desk. *How very little he must know about me or he would never have asked me to do this.*

The driver knocked hastily on the door. She closed her suitcase and left.

※ ※ ※

Riyadh, Saudi Arabia

Ray Holt got Turley's message that Elaine Landon would board the flight to Riyadh that day. He strode through his Riyadh office, past the machine spewing out urgent communiqués from Washington, past the monitors, past the imagery from the National Photo-Interpretation Center showing the incessant movement, flecks that meant human beings, thousands of them—Iraqi troops moving towards the Kuwaiti border. "The assholes back in Washington wouldn't know if a bomb dropped on them," he thought. He pushed his hand through his once-red hair, now flecked with white, and scanned her dossier once again.

Elaine Landon, thirty-one years old, prior work assignment, Operations, U.S. Embassy Beirut, Classified Information: Communications Intercept and Computer Security Operations. He flipped the page. London: Detailed to U.S.-British Operation to Intercept Materials for Iraqi Nuclear Plant. He dropped the heavy folder. The small photo attached fell out.

Long blonde hair, crystalline blue eyes. Interesting, he thought, that a woman like that would go into this kind of work. He looked at the photo for another moment—the eyes, something dead about the eyes. His hand, tanned to the color of the desert he'd been stationed in so long, flicked the picture back into the file. Something to think about later when he had time. He looked out across the city and thought about why he wanted her specifically. A small shudder passed down his back.

2

▲▲ The flight to Riyadh is now boarding."

Elaine looked at the seat number on her ticket, then made her way to her seat on the plane for Riyadh, which was rapidly filling up. Exxon and Mobil Oil workers returning to Aramco, U.S. businessmen, military personnel, and finally, practically at the end of the boarding line, a beautiful young Arab woman in her twenties who seemed to be by herself. She glanced about tentively at the plane full of men and then noticed the empty seat by Elaine.

"Would it be alright?" she asked hesitantly.

"Certainly." Elaine moved her overnight bag and the young woman gave her a lovely grateful smile. Elaine was struck by the soft luminous quality she radiated. Her large dark eyes, framed by her long dark hair seemed to emanate gentleness. She put her briefcase in front of her, then glanced shyly at Elaine's books on Saudi Arabia, which headquarters had rushed over to her.

"This is your first visit to Saudi Arabia?"

"Yes," said Elaine. "Is it yours?"

"Oh no," she said softly. "It is my home. I am going home." She stopped suddenly.

Elaine wondered for a moment at the silence and then let it go, returning to the book in front of her and finally closing her eyes, hoping to get some sleep as the night flight took off.

As the plane headed east, the very sound of the engine agitated the apprehension she was struggling to block out. She tried to clear her mind to sleep, but the tiny night lights of the plane seemed to blink, fracturing the vague images that unrolled in her mind while the plane flew toward Riyadh. Vague, chaotic images moving in flashes across her mind. Last night's drive into Virginia, to Langley, to see Turley surfaced, then like a broken kaleidoscope, pieces of the past spun disjointedly before her. Elaine twisted in her seat.

"Our flight path over the Middle East will change slightly due to turbulence."

Elaine pulled awake briefly at the sound of the pilot's voice and then, realizing they were far from landing, closed her eyes again. Her mind drifted back to Turley, to the ride into headquarters and then finally much further back.

Now in her mind, she was traveling down another road, heading deeper into Virginia, past Williamsburg. She was driving through snow on the ground, passing deer that darted in and out of the thickly wooded forest, startled by the headlights of her car traveling in the night toward the high chain-link fence topped by barbed wire. The entrance was a plain-looking gate house posted with military police. The entrance, like many plain-looking things, was deceptive. The Farm was large, with distinct sites for training in border-crossing, sabotage, weapons, air and maritime operations, ambush, evasion and escape, clandestine meetings. The training at the Farm, being selected for Clandestine Collections, seesawed through her mind like scenes from a black-and-white movie. The memory dissolved into the interview with the man from the Company as she would learn to call it. She could still hear his voice. "Most of you have been selected from the Universities because of your outstanding technical abilities," he coughed and then went on, "and because you've indicated interest in a life dedicated to protecting the security of your country while helping others to preserve their freedom." For an instant she smiled, recalling it. The speech about the secret warrior—the man's voice in the welcoming speech to her group and the other recruits from Cal Tech and MIT, rolled across her mind like the echo from an old gramophone, replaying a refrain, stuck. A life of sacrifice, of silent courage as secret warriors in the battles of our time. Her voice in her mind, like a second sound track over his, *I thought I could make a difference.*

"Clandestine Collections" the voice reeled along in her head, "headquarters here with field stations and bases in almost all countries, the Near East, headed by a Division Chief and Deputy Chief. Collections is running agents, producing finished intelligence. At no time will you be openly connected to the Company. You will learn to live your cover...your number in the State Department will ring at the agency...your fictitious 'superiors' at State will be handled by voices on the phone at the agency who will be assigned to play them."

She felt herself lurching deeper into the memory. Running in her fatigues, the physical training, the classes in tradecraft. She saw herself, heard them. *Hold it like this...place the paper like that...the ink will become visible only when treated with...audio penetration is the key to...the sabotage instructors 'the burn and blow boys' will instruct you...a listening device attached to....* "Correspondence, Miss Landon," the instructor's tone seemed alive for a moment, "between CIA stations, bases and head-quarters is the lifeline of Agency operations. CIA Counter-Intelligence begins with the Office of Security, protects build-ings and documents...." Her hand now is on the computer installation as his voice goes on, "The best system for storage

16

and retrieval that IBM can build. It has a numbering system for topics, subjects, intel reports for the different agents and different phases of each operation. Microfilm is automated for instant document retrieval. Yes, your file begins with #201—all agents begin with #201—real and cryptonym."

Suddenly the memories seemed to speed, to spin, the kaleidoscope now out of control. The flight into Beirut. She was there again. He was there again. The face in the picture on the desk now seemed alive. Safe houses, foreign agents of always dubious allegiance. Covers beneath covers, operational reports, field reports, the fears of a cover blown. A reality that made the classes seem almost sweetly naive. She thought of how they had gotten deeper and deeper into Beirut...the information, the networks. Suddenly she jerked awake as she felt the image surfacing again—the explosion, that hideous light.

Elaine opened her eyes and quickly picked up the package of reading material to steady herself and conceal her agitation. She glanced at the young woman beside her filling the margin of the publication she was reading with notes, then at the title. It was the *New England Journal of Medicine*. The young woman felt Elaine's eyes on her. She looked up and smiled, the same shy smile that had so struck Elaine earlier.

"You are a doctor?" asked Elaine somewhat surprised.

"Yes," she nodded. "I went to medical school in Riyadh and then on to intern one year in obstetrics. Then I decided it was really child care I loved, so I did a year of pediatrics at Children's Hospital in Washington. I have two more years to go...." she stopped again, the same pause that Elaine had noticed earlier.

The young woman looked back up at Elaine. "What about you? You're something of a surprise here," she said with a small nod of her head toward the rest of the plane filled with men.

Elaine smiled. "I've just been assigned to our embassy in Riyadh as cultural attaché. The assignment came rather quickly. To tell you the truth, I really don't feel prepared. I was stationed once before in Beirut, but that's quite a bit different from Saudi Arabia. I've been trying to read these history books to catch up."

The young woman nodded sympathetically and glanced down at the page where Elaine had left the book open. It was a picture of the mud brick walls of an ancient turreted house. A soldier stood guard at the carved wooden entrance. The picture seemed to strike something inside the young woman, her eyes became suffused with a softness, something of sadness.

"You know the place?" asked Elaine watching her.

"Yes," she said softly. "That was King Abdul Aziz's house. He lived there until he died in 1953. It seems like another world, doesn't it?" Her hand reached out and traced the picture, the long corridors of Murraba Palace leading into one of the King's sitting rooms. "He used to hold his majlis here." Her finger moved across the old black and white photo of overstuffed chairs upholstered in faded velvet and lined up against the walls. "The tribesmen, the bedu, whoever wanted to see him came during the day to talk to him, ask him for help, more sheep, camels, money for a dowry, whatever."

"A dowry?"

"Yes," the young woman laughed, "The men pay a dowry to the bride's family. Now instead of camels and sheep, it's more often Mercedes Benzes and stocks." She pointed to the picture of the courtyard with doors opening onto it from all sides, balconies above. "This was the harem, the women's quarters. The King used to visit his wives in the afternoon. They were not to be seen by anyone other than family. Abdul Aziz himself did not see their faces until after the wedding. After that they spent their lives within the walls of the family. They used to watch what was going on by sitting behind those wooden lattices, where they couldn't be seen looking down into the courtyard." She smiled softly at the surprised look on Elaine's face. "My mother was married to my father in a traditional arranged marriage at the age of fourteen. She lived almost her entire life secluded in the women's quarters." Elaine listened, fascinated, and waited for her to go on.

She continued shyly. "My mother was known as Um Musaid, the mother of Musaid, since giving birth to a son is considered a woman's highest achievement. She suckled him until he was three, and nursed her daughters until they reached the age of one, since girls are weaned earlier. The focus of the family was of course on my brother, since he would carry on the family name." Elaine realized the young woman had stopped and wanted her to go on. Elaine pointed back to the picture.

"You said 'they' when you mentioned Abdul Aziz's wife. How many were there?"

"Oh, by the end, I think he had about three hundred, four at a time as the Koran allows. He had about one hundred children by the time he died—the last are in their forties now, governors of some of the regions, like Prince Mugrin up in Hail. You might meet him—an Air Force Captain born in a tent." She stopped, seeming lost in thought.

"You seem to know a lot about him, King Abdul Aziz?" asked Elaine.

"Yes," the young woman said simply. "He was my grandfather."

Elaine, more than a little surprised, looked at the young woman. Her deep brown eyes were lost somewhere, she seemed isolated, far away. Finally she looked at Elaine, talking as though to herself, her voice soft.

"Family is everything here. Everything."

"Still?" asked Elaine, gazing back at the picture of the empty courtyard, feeling something terribly vulnerable in the young woman that she wanted to understand.

"Oh, yes," said the young woman. Elaine heard the young woman's voice subtley shift. She continued quietly. "I myself will have to marry within the family."

"What do you mean, within the family?"

The young woman looked back at the picture of the courtyard, the fountain at the center, water falling softly into the pool. "I mean that as a member of the Saud family I am supposed to marry another member of the family. The men may take spouses from outside if they choose. Not the women." She focused her large dark eyes on Elaine, almost painfully. "I'm something of an embarrassment to the family. Twenty-eight years old, not married. I have declined each marriage my brother Musaid has tried to arrange for me. Since my father died he is now the head of the family. But now," she said, "but now, I guess...."

"You don't want to marry?" Elaine asked, surprised at how close she somehow felt to the young woman.

"I want to marry, but not this way." Abruptly, she turned the conversation. "And you? You haven't a ring on, but somehow you don't seem single." The innocent comment hit Elaine like a blow; she drew back visibly. The young Arab woman was startled at the response to her question. Exhausted and surprised at what she herself had said, she smiled shyly again. "Perhaps it is a good idea to get some rest now."

Elaine opened her eyes hours later to the sound of the landing announcement. Through the plane window she saw torches of gas flares from the oil fields, then the desert slowly rising beneath the body of the plane, undulating rivers of red sand flowing in the hot sun. Elaine continued to stare out the window while the young woman next to her marked "Saudi Citizen" on her disembarkation card and wrote in her name, Naila Saud. She said goodbye to Elaine and then slowly stood up, smoothed her silk dress, and opened the compartment overhead from which she took a voluminous black silk cloth. She hesitated then placed the black silk over her head so that it covered her face, her back, shrouding her to the floor, until she had become a column of black, breathing through the black silk as her eyes caught the gleam of sunlight on the gold mosques of Riyadh.

Elaine watched, fascinated. The lovely young Arab woman with whom she had boarded the plane in Washington seemed erased now, anonymous, thought Elaine. For an instant she considered herself with a clarity that was painful. Detached, distant, a person who had constructed her own walls. *Were you always this way? No. Are you this way now? Yes. And why. Yes, there is why, isn't there?* Her mind snapped shut. Elaine pushed the thought aside, stood up and touched her khaki-colored suit, wishing for a moment that she too could erase herself before meeting the man waiting for her. Always another man, eager, curious, an offer she didn't want. And memories that seemed to live and breathe in the night. The plane door opened.

Elaine's last glimpse of the young woman shrouded in black was on the runway below. There a man in a black limousine with a small green flag blowing in the desert wind waited impatiently. When the young woman descended the steps he quickly pulled the car up to the ramp. The heat seemed to swim in the air. Wordlessly she stepped into the back seat of the car, and it turned from the gleaming new airport onto the road to Riyadh. Elaine lost sight of her as the man from the Embassy, holding her name aloft, rushed over through the din of the

21

airport. She followed him toward a car, barely looking at the hajjis bowing, praying toward Mecca.

❈   ❈   ❈

Elaine gazed at the desert surrounding the road from the airport, its great emptiness broken only by an occasional bedu camp.

The car picked up speed, passing a bedu woman in black, seated in the doorway of her tent. She sullenly eyed the long dark limousine. The woman, her hammered silver and carnelian bracelets glinting in the sun, brushed the dust from her abaya and called to a small naked child. The bedu woman stared again at the sleek car and then closed the flap of the tent.

Elaine saw dark faces along the side of the road, the poor Egyptian laborers in their trousers, the pale green pants of the Pakistanis smeared with dirt, the dusty white thobes of bedu whose eyes peered through red and white kaffiyehs wrapped around their heads.

The car sped on toward the city, blowing up a cloud of desert dust behind it. It plunged into the heart of Riyadh, a sprawling city, toward the labyrinth of the old souk. Elaine scanned the crowded sidewalk where merchants sat in front of their shops, surrounded by their wares. An old man smiled up, toothless, amidst bags of spices. A woman beside him hawked fish laid out in front of her on a cloth. A young man behind a shop window filled with rows of gold bracelets waited impassively while two women, covered in their black abayas, examined gold belts from India. Elaine opened the window slightly. Heat flowed in along with the smells of lamb and chicken cooking in the food stands. The pungent odors so familiar from the streets of Beirut brought a rush of memories that she struggled quickly to submerge.

Elaine breathed deeply and looked up to see the gleam of the gold, ivory, and deep blue of the Mosque, wrought together in a design as intricate as the babel of voices below it. Suddenly the voice from the top of the minaret called out to the city. Like an echo from the ground came the sound of shops closing, long metal doors rolling shut with a clang. The men moved to the square, bowed quietly and prayed.

The driver sped on past the enormous new steel and glass government buildings. Elaine watched the guards close the building doors for the midday prayers; the bedu boys of the National Guard changed their patrol before King Fahd's gleaming marble city palace.

The car stopped at a building with nothing more than a number to identify it as Ray Holt's offices.

3

Ray Holt picked up the phone and called Tarek as he heard Elaine Landon's footsteps coming down the hall. He opened the door and focused on the beautiful young woman with the long slim legs and pensive eyes whom the driver ushered into his office. He motioned Elaine to sit and spoke brusquely.

"Welcome," he said. "Flight all right?" He did not wait for an answer. "Listen, I am going to have to make this quick. We've been called into an emergency session. You were in Lebanon for three years as a specialist on computer security?" he asked, looking at her folder.

"Yes, I was working on computer security operations and intercepts. Systems, basically."

He nodded, closed the folder. "We've had some problems with information flow."

The signal lit up on the telex machine from Washington. "Obviously we don't want to give the impression that we can't run a shop without a secure communications system. And so, your cover is cultural attaché. I want you to move around the society a bit, just make it look good, you know how to do it. Spend time with the women, whatever..." Elaine nodded and waited.

"Look," he said, "I understand that you have no background

in this part of the Middle East. Just look interested; don't say too much; you'll probably only be in Riyadh and Jeddah, maybe Dhahran. The rest," he smiled, "is only a lot of small villages strewn around the country where they've put in some electricity and water in the past few years. Beyond that you have the great deserts—the Nafud and the famous Rub al Khali, the Empty Quarter, where the bedu tribes still roam."

Elaine took out a pen and notebook, but he waved them aside.

"I'll give you some stuff later, I'm just skimming the basics now."

He looked her up and down. "If you don't have any long skirts—to the ground—get some, because otherwise you're going to be the only pair of legs in Saudi Arabia, male or female. Long sleeves, high necks for blouses. You're not expected to conform to all the rules for Saudi women—you don't have to wear the veil. The people, in the cities at least, are sophisticated and understand that is a Saudi custom that doesn't apply to outsiders. In fact, a lot of these Saudi women are now highly educated, speak three languages. Some of them will really surprise you beneath those abayas."

He sighed, "Before all of this fundamentalist shit started coming over from Iran, the Saudi women started to get out of the goddamned thing themselves, but now everything has clamped down again. Things have gotten pretty tense here lately. In any case, you can't drive a car and I would suggest you not wander around without an escort."

He stopped, his voice relaxing a bit. "This is a very different world. And it's easy to judge these people harshly, the sins, the failings. But you'd make a mistake to do so. They have lived through an upheaval of reality that you and I will never be asked to cope with. The old ones who remember the grinding poverty that was here, isolated with only the few traditions that kept them alive. The young ones overwhelmed by so many possibilities, so much wealth. All of them trying to pick through this cataclysm for an identity, some reality."

A secretary stuck her head in the door. "The conference call from the National Security Council is supposed to begin in ten minutes."

He shot her a look of complete irritation, muttering, "The Ambassador truly believes this is just another bluff on the part of Saddam to get the Kuwaitis to the bargaining table on oil prices. He's irritated because 'goddamned Ray has got everybody worked up.' " He glanced up at the clock and continued more hurriedly.

"Alright, you won't have any trouble with communications—the place is run with the most sophisticated satellite phone and wire transmissions that exist. It was all installed new, the latest high tech, just a short time ago. You also won't have any problem with crime—the penalties are pretty stiff and quick. If you leave your purse in the middle of the sidewalk you can go back one week later, pick it up exactly where you left it, and find that nothing inside has been touched.

"Who are all the foreigners in the street?"

"Foreign workers from the poorer countries in the Mideast—Jordan, Egypt—others from Pakistan, India. Then there are the pilgrims, the 'hajjis,' the ones with bundles of stuff strapped to their backs—Arabs, Africans, Asians—Muslims from every country on the map. They come into the country to make the Muslim pilgrimage to the holy city of Mecca. Mecca, as you probably know, is the most important city in the Islamic world, the holiest of shrines, and Muslims feel passionately about it. Boatloads of them dock in Jeddah every day, planeloads from the East arriving in Riyadh and Dhahran. All these people streaming into an otherwise tightly closed country, headed for Mecca. A logistical and security nightmare."

"It sounds fascinating," said Elaine. "I'd like to see Mecca."

"You won't," he said bluntly. "Mecca is a closed city. Only Muslims are allowed in, and they are very strict about it. With your blonde hair and embassy affiliation, it would be hard to convince anybody you are a Muslim." He closed her dossier and continued abruptly.

"Our embassy here in Riyadh has instructions that you have been sent as an instructor from the CIA to improve their computer programming operations. While here you will publicly use the cultural attaché cover they have created for you. The embassy staff will devise whatever cultural activities you want to maintain this front."

Elaine nodded, shifting slightly.

"They are, obviously, unaware that this is a cover beneath a cover, the computer instructor guise, and I want you to keep it plausible. The embassy staff is to have no idea whatsoever of the nature of the work you are doing with me. Don't misunderstand me, they are a well-meaning bunch, but information leaks out of that place like a sieve. Some of it is just people getting a little loose with what they say. But it goes beyond that." He turned brusquely. "Which is one of the reasons you're here."

His voice trailed off when he caught sight of paper churning out of the computer. He quickly ripped the sheet off. "Oh god, this is great," his eyes rolled upward. "Rumors of Iraq invading Kuwait should be discounted. Iraq assures allies these are simply training maneuvers."

Ray wadded up the paper and threw it in the shredder. "Shit, whoever wrote this should be out of a job."

Her eyes stayed focused on him. "And my job? Why I'm really here?"

He turned back to her, "I'll tell you in a sentence why you are here. Every communication we move is being tapped into." Elaine started.

Ray nodded, " 'Secure' communications, embassy transmissions, military communications. I, for one, believe that Iraq is going to invade Kuwait first and then try for the rest of the Gulf. I don't have to tell you that a tap into our computers, our communications, could single-handedly destroy our ability to check this guy, to fight him. Our every strategy, surprise tactic—blown. At the same time I'm tracking major fundamentalist cells, uprisings ready to blow across the map—Tunis, Khartoum, Cairo—here. Not exactly the time to be leaking like a sieve."

His buzzer went off. Ray put on his jacket. "Sorry this is so rushed. I'll drop you off at operations set-up." He moved her through the security checks, then toward the control room where his men were monitoring the transmissions from the Kuwaiti border. Elaine followed him down the hall past a tall man hurrying into a conference room.

"The Ambassador." Ray tilted his head. "He speaks absolutely fluent Chinese."

"Chinese? You mean Arabic."

"No," said Ray rushing down the corridor. "He's a China expert. Doesn't speak a word of Arabic. This post is the first time he's ever set foot in the Middle East."

Her eyes never left him, he noticed, pulling it all in. What was it he saw in them? Beautiful eyes, brilliant, and yet dead.

Yeah, he mused in a moment's insight, with an inaudible laugh, and what the hell do I look like to her? Ray, the legend, the fixture, practically grown over with sand. A workaholic to be sure. Personally straightforward, lies when he has to professionally. On a good day a sense of humor. Even on a bad day a deadly accurate eye for the situation. Knows the Kingdom inside and out. Mandate simple: In the morass of Middle East politics, Saudi Arabia is a key U.S. ally—do whatever it takes to keep it afloat. Ray the old desert hand, utterly American, does everything but fly the flagpole up his ass. Money, only a moderate interest. Women, doesn't chase them. No, he thought, I buried that part of myself when I buried Kitty. Her image flashed for a second. The face of the young wife he had brought out to this outpost years ago. She had learned to love it as much as he. Helping bedu women deliver babies in tents, feeding their children. They had mourned her as he did when she died. He had simply put that piece of himself in with her when he lowered her into the grave. Finally, totally.

He pushed the elevator button. And this woman? Christ there were more walking dead in the intelligence world than in the graveyards. Burnt out, busted up. So long since they could say anything real to anybody that they died from the inside out. Human starvation of another sort. A disease of the soul, a spiritual Molokai.

Ray opened the door to the computer operations room, filled with the sound of static. Elaine pulled up a chair. The lieutenant was replaying radar scans in sync with the monitor while another logged the satellite feeds from the Iraqi-Kuwaiti border.

"Damn," muttered the lieutenant nervously, "these guys just keep streaming toward Kuwait."

Suddenly the monitor to the left went blank. All heads turned instantly.

The AWACS surveillance feed was black. The lieutenant wiped the drop of sweat from his eye and adjusted his uniform nervously. "Maybe it just malfunctioned, but this is the third time in two hours."

He shot a look at Elaine, who was already timing the blackout on the second hand of her watch. He continued anxiously, "Someone tampers with its program, slips it a trojan horse, a daemon? Taps into it with new commands to go to black, we lose our surveillance. It's possible—all you need is one clever guy with some access. The Ambassador thought I was crazy when I mentioned this to him earlier."

"I want the computer logs on the precise timings of the previous blackouts," said Elaine.

The lieutenant's gaze was now openly curious.

"You're here to check the leaks in security, aren't you?" His voice was uneasy. "We all know something's wrong, but nobody talks about it publicly." He wiped his brow, "God, the panic that would spread if it got out. That's really why you're here, isn't it?"

Elaine offered no reply. Her silent assessment of the stunning task before her was interrupted by Ray's voice.

"What do you need?"

Elaine stared at him, for a minute not comprehending.

"I'm no technocrat, so just tell me what you need," repeated Ray.

"Charts, diagrams, specs, installation records." she said, now understanding what he meant. "After I go over them I'll meet with the people, check the equipment. First, I need to develop a picture of the systems, the design, the possibilities."

Ray was already walking out of the room. "The Ambassador wants to speak to me for a moment. Meet me back in my office when you're finished."

Elaine turned around to the sound of Ray's voice disappearing. She was startled to see another man standing behind her.

He clearly had been there for some time. The light from the screen cast a shadow along his white thobe and the striking features of his face. Dark eyes set in olive skin, an almost liquid depth to them above the strong cheekbones, the finely chiseled nose. Tall, broad-shouldered, lean, age somewhere around forty. The man looked at the radar screen again, then back to her. There was something startling about the directness of his gaze. A man making an instant, unhurried, totally professional calculation. He looked at her for another moment, then walked out of the room.

Elaine made a few more notes from the lieutenant's logs, then walked back to Ray's office. The man in the thobe was standing casually inside the room alone. Elaine, disconcerted by his unexpected presence, introduced herself.

"I'm Elaine Landon, the new cultural attaché—I was looking for Ray Holt."

"A new 'cultural attaché,'" he smiled, a faint touch of amusement about the eyes and mouth.

She was about to speak again when he extended his hand, "And I am Tarek bin Ahmed al Saud." It was an elegant movement, the fluidity of a hand moving toward her as his eyes continued the assessment, intent, cool, detached. The door opened behind her.

Ray walked in. "Elaine's a specialist; satellites and computers, sent to work with us. She's signed into the embassy as 'cultural attaché' but what she's really doing is working on coordinating the intercept operations on Iraq's communications—trying to get some of theirs, and keep them from getting ours." Ray suddenly stopped seeing the alarm on Elaine's face at this information he so casually divulged.

"Did he tell you who he is?" Ray looked up inquisitively at Tarek. "Director of their Foreign Intelligence, he's...." Ray stopped again, exasperated as the buzzer went off. "God-dammit, it's the Ambassador. Look, we're going to have to talk later. Tarek, let me know how to find you later. Elaine, I'll have

31

the driver take you to the house they have set up for you in the embassy compound."

Elaine nodded to the two men still standing in the room and followed the driver down to the car. He drove the short distance across the embassy compound in silence and dropped her off.

Elaine stood motionless and looked out the window at the embassy enclave around her. The sentry, the iron gates that opened onto the white concrete walls of what amounted to a little town. The main embassy building structure stood at its center, housing the Ambassador's office, the big reception area, smaller office cubicles for the various attachés. One-story flat-roofed houses on palm-lined streets spread out around the new sleek embassy, all functional, and tidy, except for the occasional gaudy plastic tricycle indicating the presence of a family. *And I*, she thought succinctly, *am alone.* She walked through the living room, bedroom, and small kitchen, refrigerator stocked with basics, including two bottles of California Chardonnay. The furnishings were modern, anonymous, the colors muted. It made no difference. She had no intention of making her imprint on this place.

She felt the dark pull of the depression she struggled against, always lingering just below the surface. There was a darkness to it, but it was more merciful than the horror-filled nightmares of Beirut that woke her in the middle of the night. She breathed deeply. She could see her life for a moment, a pale thread becoming paler, a loner becoming ever more isolated. She gathered the papers Ray had left her and tried to study the charts of the communication system. Finally, she put them down, unable to concentrate, the memories getting too close. She lay down on the bed trying to close her eyes, but relentlessly the flash, the explosion came again, the sounds of the sirens in Beirut.

She sat up, breathing deeply, and knew she would start to break if the scene replayed itself one more time. At what point, she wondered, did the mind stop torturing itself? The face in the picture frame back on her desk in Washington now floated through her mind.

He is dead, she whispered to herself. *They are all dead. Holt in Riyadh seems to know about you. Holt in Riyadh doesn't know the whole story, does he? Or he never, never would have asked me to come back.*

Agitated, she looked at the phone and thought of calling Ray, telling him he would have to find somebody else. Today she knew what he had seen—a beautiful young woman who was reputed to be brilliant at what she did. A woman who hid behind her work and the distance it offered. What he didn't know was that there was nothing left inside. She thought of the agents who had cracked, who should have seen the signs. She quickly picked up the phone and dialed the driver. He appeared within minutes.

"Where do you need to go, ma'm?"

"Just anywhere, just drive." He asked no further questions.

Elaine's eyes took in the streets of Riyadh. Each sight that came before her seemed to breathe up the deep conservatism that ran through everything here, a country breaking through to the twentieth century in odd disjointed spurts. As The car lurched through the traffic, her mind was swerving, veering from the images that kept rushing up. The Arab streets, were different from those of Beirut, yet similar enough. All of it unsettled her. Something about the face of thar man, Tarek al Saud, unsettled her.

She forced herself to focus on the street they passed through, then closed her eyes. The face of the young woman with the long dark hair on the plane flashed across her mind.

She wondered for a moment what had become of her. The thought of the girl disappeared as she got out of the car and returned to her silent living quarters. She closed the door behind her and stood absolutely still, staring at herself in the mirror.

She should have never come here, she whispered to herself, she should simply have said no, and never returned to this part of the world.

4

Tarek made a mental note to himself about Elaine Landon and drove back to his office a few miles away in the heart of the city. He stood by the window and watched the men in long white thobes filling the square in Riyadh. They bowed in a sea of white, and their words hung like silver in the air. "Allahu Akbar," whispered Tarek. They knelt now, hands outstretched beneath the hot desert sun. "Allahu Akbar...."

Tarek turned from the window in his office and glanced at the communiqués flowing in from the rest of the Middle East marked to his attention. His aide Badr walked in behind him as Tarek adjusted the monitor, watching the AWACS flying low over the border with Iraq. The Iraqi troops were moving steadily. Badr stared at the screen.

"What do you think, Tarek?"

Tarek lit a cigarette. "The same thing as Ray Holt. It has started."

Tarek moved back to his desk, picked up a surveillance video cassette of the underground fundamentalist cell meeting, and put it in the VCR. The image came on the screen, a tan car moving through the Riyadh traffic pulling up to the building. A young man in a white thobe, a red and white gutra on his head, got out. A woman covered in a black abaya followed him into the building. The camera jerked for a moment. Tarek glanced down at the list that accompanied the cassette describing the subjects. "Engineering graduate Dhahran University, 22 years old." The camera showed another man from the sidewalk turning to enter the door. "Student at Riyadh University, 19 years old." As the members massed for the fundamentalist cell meeting, a white Mercedes pulled up to the curb.

Tarek moved closer to the screen while the camera panned the dark, even features of Osman's second son. "Abed bin Osman, 24, graduate of University Southern California." Across the list Tarek wrote CONTINUE SURVEILLANCE. He turned the tape off and spoke to Badr.

"Contact Hamid, tell him I want to meet tonight. Same place. Notify the helicopter."

Badr closed the door of the Director's office behind him and walked quickly down the corridor, the long warren of unmarked offices of the intelligence unit. He glanced at the clock on the wall, thought briefly of their mole Hamid, who had been attached surreptitiously to Antar, head of covert operations in Iraq, and hurried on, mentally sorting the tasks before him, as Tarek went quickly to the car below.

※ ※ ※

Tarek's driver wove through the city, past Korean bulldozer teams, half-finished buildings, power lines lying all over the road, massive television antennae and phone installations, and the computer terminals that ran everything from communications to the air conditioning in the desert city.

The car pulled to a stop at the hangar. The pilot started the engine and threw the switch as Tarek climbed into the helicopter.

The sound of the helicopter beat through the silence of the

desert stretching below. Long pale slopes of sand shimmered in the red reflection of the sun. The bedu in fluttering white, by their black tents, looked up as the helicopter blades punctuated the desert stillness. Below wandered a small goat, a herd of wild camels, and then nothing but the endless sands, breathing up their heat to the descending night.

The helicopter headed northeast toward the coast. As they approached, the pilot extinguished the running lights; the helicopter dipped toward a rocky ledge and landed amid swirling sand. Tarek got out, and the silence descended. The wild beauty of the place stung him. Its deserted sands dropped to the liquid blue serenity of the Gulf. Across the Gulf was the coast of Iran. Only a few miles to the north lay the borders of Kuwait and Iraq.

Tarek walked across the rocky plain toward a ledge of the low cliff that faced down onto one of the small coves. He found the path and slowly, while the small rocks beneath his feet chipped off and fell to the sea, made his way down to the opening in the side of the cliff. Tarek brushed a few twigs together for a fire and then returned to the entrance of the cave and listened.

He could make out the sounds of a small engine, and saw the black motor boat approaching the cove in the moonlight. A young man pulled alongside the bank and stopped the motor, and an old wooden dhow hidden in an inlet appeared and glided toward the boat. The voices of the men wafted up in the stillness while the young man loaded the guns into the dhow, which drifted off into the night with its cargo from Iraq.

Presently came the sound of small rocks falling, and Hamid appeared, hands cut by the cliff's edge. Tarek embraced him.

"Salaam Alekum."

"Alekum Salaam, Hamid." Tarek searched Hamid's young

dark face as he sat down by the fire. Hamid wiped the blood from his hands with his thobe, exhausted.

"Hamid," said Tarek softly, "you are all right?"

"I'm all right. Neither Saddam, nor Antar suspect anything." He glanced up, irony flickering across his face, "I'm only another faceless 'assistant' to them." His voice was tense.

Tarek nodded, the risks of these meetings for Hamid always in his mind. "The plan?"

Hamid spoke quickly, "Saddam's going to move swiftly. He's going to make his move now. His aim is to take over the Arab countries of the Gulf. He's banking on the premise that Kuwait has no defenses to speak of, and the other Arab countries will never pull together to take a stand against him. The U.S. will make noise but hasn't the will to fight. The Soviet Union is in a state of collapse and won't be able to act."

Hamid looked at Tarek. "The strategy is simple—roll into Kuwait, take it over, threaten the other Arab countries not to intervene, paint the U.S. as infidels from the outside if they try. Saddam feels he can easily frighten the Americans with terrorist attacks on their posts and facilities here, and that the U.S. will pull out like they did in Lebanon."

Tarek listened, face taut, while Hamid continued. "Once Saddam has Kuwait he simply rolls into Saudi Arabia and the rest militarily. If there is international opposition, he'll go a more covert route—hit Saudi Arabia with a series of ongoing terrorist attacks to unnerve the populace, frighten and discredit the current leaders, make them look like they've lost control. The cells seeded throughout the country will be positioned to rise up, work up the general population, then oust the government in what will appear to be an indigenous movement, so that no one outside can legitimately intervene. Saudi Arabia will be left with a government based ostensibly in Riyadh with the strings actually being pulled by Baghdad."

Hamid moved closer. "I know part of the plan. But not all yet." The light from the fire showed the frustration on his face. "Saddam's tapped into some of the old Iranian revolutionary cells—the 'people's revolution' to rid the Middle East of the old corrupt monarchies and return it to the people, the discontent of the 'haves' and the 'have-nots'—Palestinians, poor workers. A lot of these people are deeply buried within the society, in place, ready.

"Antar's orchestrating covert operations for Saddam. Connections from when he was a diplomat in the U.S., Europe before that. He's set up an entire network of fronts, safe houses, agents, cells."

Tarek stood up to go.

"There's something else, Tarek." Hamid paused for emphasis.

"Saddam is working with someone inside, a member of the Royal Family. Antar's working the agent."

Tarek looked at him, stunned.

Hamid nodded tensely. "I don't know who yet. The operative within the Royal Family is either highly or extraordinarily well placed. He's been delivering incredible information from within both U.S. and Saudi operations and communications."

Hamid threw a twig into the fire. "One last thing." Tarek waited. Hamid looked dead at him. "The agent inside has orders for assassination."

"Assassinate the King?"

"If he fights back."

Hamid stood up to go. "There's another name on that list. The person they're most afraid who will counter their plans. Yours."

The silence of the desert night held only the sound of water lapping hungrily at the shore. Tarek remained absolutely motionless for a moment, then turned. "Take care, Hamid," he said quietly, "take care."

Hamid looked back at him for one last minute, his voice strained. "Tarek, I found out what happened to Khalid when Antar discovered him." His voice dropped, he shook his head. "It was brutal."

With those words, Hamid eased his way down to the water's edge. Tarek listened to the small boat start its journey across the passage of water to Iraq. He walked quickly toward the helicopter. The pilot, seeing Tarek's dark figure approach, started the engine.

As the ground disappeared below, Tarek leaned his head back, breathing deeply. The faces of the members of the Family played in front of him while the helicopter blades cut across the desert sky. The many faces, their many reasons. Hamid's words echoed in his head.

"...a member of the Royal Family." It is someone in the Family.

✩ ✧ ✧

Tarek's helicopter touched ground in Riyadh. He entered the waiting car.

Tarek leaned toward the driver. "Take me to the King."

The car moved through the dark streets of Riyadh and stopped at the palace gate. The guards raised their guns, then recognized Tarek inside the car and motioned it through the high iron gate. Another guard at the entrance swept back the tall wooden doors. Tarek walked down the long marble foyer and then up the winding staircase until he arrived at the second door of intricately worked brass. An old attendant was seated on a small chair.

"He is sleeping?" Tarek asked.

The attendant shook his head and rose on unsteady legs to open the door. In the dim light of the vast bed chamber Tarek saw the oud player sitting in the corner on a thick pillow strumming a melancholy refrain more to himself than for the man for whom he played night after night. He nodded at Tarek and then toward King Fahd who was sitting at a small mother-of-pearl card table. Slowly the King reached out, picked up a card, thought for a moment, and played it, his dark hooded eyes glazed with insomnia, the pallor from his diabetes casting a waxen shadow along his jowls. His thick short fingers tapped thoughtfully on a small round tea cup, then reached toward the deck again. He was oblivious to the person standing in the dark. Tarek walked over and sat down beside him.

"You should sleep."

Fahd looked wryly at him, "I should, but I don't. And you?"

"Only during speeches."

Fahd leaned toward him, amused. "I have a joke for you. King Hussein of Jordan gave it to me—he said be sure to tell Tarek. American, Israeli, French, and Syrian intelligence are all talking about who is the best. And so one says—let us make a bet. We will each loose a gazelle in the desert and see who is able to track theirs the fastest. So the first one is for the Americans. Instantly they mobilize the Marines and the AWACS. After a day they bring their gazelle back. The second is for the Israelis. Mossad sends in the surgical strike force and undercover agents, and in a day they bring theirs back. The third is for the French. The French president sends in a man with four weapons sales contracts, three blank passports, and they bring theirs back in a day. And the fourth is for the

Syrians. One day goes by, two, three days go by. The American, the Israeli, and the French begin to talk. What has happened to him? Finally they decide to go find him. They wander in the desert searching and come upon an old villager who points—and there stands the Syrian—beating a donkey to death trying to get it to confess it is a gazelle." Fahd chuckled when Tarek laughed. "Hussein loves that one."

He turned from the card table. "What did you come to talk about?"

"I met with one of my key agents stationed inside Iraq."

"And?"

Tarek recounted Hamid's report.

Fahd gazed at him evenly and then chose another card, "We have a deal with Iraq. Oil price negotiations, bluffs, there is always talk." His eyebrow arched up for a moment and then dropped. "But we have a deal."

"Maybe you had a deal," said Tarek.

The King dropped the card in irritation. "Saddam may ultimately have visions of taking over the Arab world, but he is still too weak. He wouldn't fly in the face of the rest of the Arab countries now. Besides, I have his assurances, his word."

"His word means nothing."

"I realize you consider diplomacy tedious," King Fahd's eyes flashed in anger. "But you will see. He can be dealt with. With patience, a little give on our part. He's years away from being able to do such a thing. You should not confuse public words for mass consumption with private diplomacy."

"The man's like an animal who smells blood. He moves by instinct."

"Smoke screens, bargaining," Fahd's voice was annoyed.

"He's never done what anybody's expected."

"He can be talked to. This will disappear."

"Or perhaps," said Tarek. "We're what's going to disappear. First Kuwait, then us."

Fahd's hand shot up in exasperation, "We have agreements."

"You believe that?"

"I believe that."

"You want me to do nothing?"

"Nothing."

"And the someone in the Family . . .?"

Fahd swung around angrily, like a man suddenly goaded to life. "Why," he breathed sarcastically, "would someone in the Family...?"

Tarek did not yield. "Belief, ambition, fear, greed, madness, anger, confusion. They are all there. Everything that has ever raised a gun through history, moved the knife that stabbed a brother through the heart, toppled a government. It is all there. All the elements ready to explode—fundamentalists, angry technocrats, women, bedu, reformers bent on ending corruption. Someone in the family, Hamid said. But who, how many, maybe there is more than one... ."

Fahd swept the cards from the table, angry, then frightened at Tarek's words. His eyes closed, and he withdrew again. He opened them when he heard Tarek stand to leave.

His voice sounded oddly distant when he spoke, "There is no one in the Family."

Badr heard Tarek's footsteps coming down the long, empty corridor at midnight. He pulled up the chair by Tarek's desk.

"Tarek, we started the surveillance on the cell members

you ordered—Osman's son Abed, and the rest. We're identi-
fying a number already."

Tarek scanned the list, thought briefly of Abed, the son of
his friend Osman, a leading Saudi businessman, and dropped it
on his desk.

"Badr, I want you to set some new agents in place. I want
you to run them personally. Nothing on paper, report to no one
but me, bypass the regular channels. No information to Sultan,
Naif, Abdullah, Saud.

I want the best. I want them going in as valets, maids,
drivers, the rest. Behind them I want devices, taps, going into
all the residences, offices, cars you are going to cover. I want you
to monitor these personally, drop nothing, pick up every
sentence for analysis."

Badr listened, intrigued. "You want to give me a clue who
this onslaught is designed for before you go? Our targets?"

Tarek stopped at the door. "The top members of the Family
below the King. Abdullah, Sultan, Naif, Saud. I'll be adding
more names shortly."

Badr's eyes widened at the names of Crown Prince Abdullah,
Minister of Defense Sultan, Minister of the Interior Naif, and
Foreign Minister Saud. A small involuntary whistle escaped
below his breath.

"Tarek, I should brief the King?"

"The King doesn't know about it."

Tarek turned as he walked out of the door. "You sent the car
for Naila?"

Badr, still stunned, merely nodded. "Musaid asked that she
be driven to his house."

5

The young woman with whom Elaine had boarded the plane sat facing her brother. The conversation throughout the small dinner with his wife and two children had been tense, strained, one superficiality laid over another.

Naila watched Musaid while the servant brought the tea. He settled himself into his living-room chair and motioned for the children to leave them. His thin face looked back with irritation as they slammed the door. The servant, ever fearful of his temper, hastened away. He faced Naila.

"The marriage I've arranged for you is quite suitable. He is of course part of the family and a first nephew of King Fahd; that will be quite advantageous...."

Naila listened to him as though the voice was coming through a long wind-swept tunnel. She sat in silence, her eyes gazing at the window that now looked out onto nothing in the night. For a moment it seemed almost surreal that she was there. That the conversation she had struggled against for a lifetime was unfolding around her. She closed her eyes for a moment as anguish shot through her.

Her gaze drifted toward the school across the city. The ten-foot high walls surrounding the girl's school stood unchanged since her own time there. The sound of young voices carrying up into the sky when they had driven by on the way from the airport had filled her with an unexpected flood of feelings. Little girls in freshly pressed uniforms, the strict order of the classrooms, the rigidity of the lessons, the blinding glimpses of the world outside—she remembered the excitement, the dreams that had begun to grow in that dry school yard. Her throat tightened at the ashes those dreams were about to become.

"We will," Musaid continued, "have the engagement party in a matter of weeks, I am making arrangements for it already and will let you know the exact date shortly. Naila, you're not listening to me."

She stared at him, the thin features, delicate, beautiful in his sisters, somehow gaunt, stunted, under-grown on his face. A weakness in the mouth, a self-absorption to the eyes. He looked at her for a moment, then motioned for the houseboy.

"I'll have the servant take your bags up to the room, I…"

"I'm not staying here."

Musaid's head shot up, his eyes narrowed.

"I'm going to live with Nura and Tarek," her voice was quiet. "Nura and I have discussed it and… "

"You didn't discuss it with me."

Her voice remained quiet. "There is nothing inappropriate about my living with my sister and her husband. I lived with them through the years I was going to medical school here, and I am quite comfortable there. It is not that far from the hospital."

His eyes stayed on her, "Well, that won't be of consequence since you're finished with all of that."

"I'm going to continue to work in the hospital."

A red flush of anger covered his face. "I don't see any reason why you…"

"I am going to continue to work as a doctor in the hospital," her voice now was low.

His hand brushed out querulously striking the cup before him, "I will decide…"

Her voice silenced him, her eyes fixed on him. "Unless, Musaid, you let me continue to work in the hospital, I will refuse the engagement. I have few rights, but I do have the right to refuse." She stared at him, anger pouring from every fiber in his body. He abruptly stood up and walked out of the room.

Finally he returned, the tension of control taut on his face. He motioned her irritably toward the door.

"I will take you to Tarek and Nura's house."

※ ※ ※

They drove in silence, Musaid's wife Khadija, frightened, huddled in the back scat. Naila stared wordlessly out the window as they approached the high white walls of the wealthy family compound surrounded by orange trees and bougainvillea. The guard at the gate ushered them in.

The tall wrought-iron gates opened onto a long driveway that led up to the house, a sweeping two-story white design that was at once architecturally modern with its clean flowing lines, white marble steps, elegantly vaulting windows and arches, and yet beautifully antique, with intricately carved wooden balustrades and latticework saved from the old homes in Jeddah. The entrance opened onto an atrium, the house divided into two wings. The general living quarters were to the right. To the left were the private women's quarters, sitting rooms where the women would entertain one another secluded from male visitors on the other side. The graceful winding staircase led up to the second floor, where bedrooms overlooked the gardens, and from behind lattices and white walls to the city in the front.

As Naila emerged from the car the servant started to motion her towards the women's sitting room, but Naila shook her head and walked quietly up the stairs into the room that had been hers throughout medical school. She shut the door behind her.

Naila listened to the final call of the muezzin and looked down at the gift awaiting her. She picked up the emerald pendant and held it to her throat. Light caught the clear deep green facets of the nearly flawless stone the size of a pigeon's egg. She held one of the matching earrings surrounded by diamonds up to her ear. Naila looked down at the small note: "With love from your sister Nura—welcome home."

She closed her eyes and heard the sounds of the palms brushing against the window and the walls of the villa, moving to some ancient desert metronome. Tears now started coming down her face. She watched her brother Musaid get into his car, his words about the arrangements for the marriage still ringing in her ears.

The servant opened the door hesitantly. "They are waiting for you in the women's quarters. Will you be going back down or retiring for the evening?" Naila whispered she would sleep now.

The maid behind her crossed the vast bedroom with the white marble floor, the Baccarat chandelier, the pale blue silk covering the bed, unpacking Naila's clothes. The little housegirl went on to draw Naila's bath, turning on the water in the adjoining bath suite, meticulously testing the flow into a marble and gold bathtub. She poured in a half bottle of rose scent, then began polishing a silver hair brush and comb while she waited for the tub to fill.

Naila looked at her, distracted for a moment from her own sorrow, and thought sadly of the girl's life. She had been sent to the household from Pakistan at the age of thirteen. Here, when the family awoke, the girl appeared with a tray of coffee, roses and toast. She drew the curtains, opened the tall wooden shutters, fluffed the pillows, and then waited outside the door until the small silver bells rang again to indicate the tray should be removed. She went home for two weeks a year on the PIA flight to Karachi. Packed in with sweating Pakistani laborers and servants, their clothes torn and dirty, carrying cardboard boxes for suitcases, one of the stream of thousands of foreign workers, poor Indians, Pakistanis, Egyptians who swept Saudi streets, carried the trays, chauffeured the cars, and tried to send some money back home.

Naila watched the maid's dark head bending over to check the water, laying out her lingerie, humming an Indian melody. The gold phone in the bathroom rang. The girl picked it up, spoke to the butler downstairs in Urdu, then handed her the deep blue velour bath towel.

"Thank you," said Naila, "thank you very much."

The girl smiled and said shyly, "Welcome home, everyone has missed you."

Naila waited for the girl to go, then walked over to the stairs. She looked down the long stairwell at her sister Nura, then at Tarek's mother, the long silk folds, of her traditional dress highlighted by the ancient wrought gold of her necklace. Musaid's wife sat next to her, while the servant poured tea. Khadija's small frightened face withdrew into the shadows as she pulled at the long sleeve of her dress. Her voice, barely a whisper as she reached for her abaya. "Musaid is waiting for me, I must go, but please…" She stopped, looked at Nura and then whispered. "Please, I know it is Musaid's right as her brother, but tell Naila I am sorry. I am very, very sorry for what Musaid has done. I have always admired her so much. Her work, her strength, her talent, maybe because I don't have these things myself. Please, I am sorry." She bowed her head, adjusted the abaya, and left.

Naila tensed at the harsh jarring feelings that overwhelmed her now. She walked quickly back into her room and sat down on the edge of the bed. Her silk dresses from the west seemed to jeer from the closet. She struggled against her tears, got up and closed the closet door. On the floor stood the small black medical bag with her initials, N.S., embossed on the leather. Naila bent over, opened the case, and picked up her familiar stethoscope, her throat choking. She placed it back in the case and closed the latch. The I.D. card on the bag had her picture on it: "Dr. Naila Saud. Children's Hospital, Washington, D.C." She looked at the picture on the badge, her long dark hair spilling over the open collar of a white shirt. Trembling, she bent her head and prayed silently toward Mecca, begging now for the strength to do what she had come to do. The words barely audible—a whisper, a plea.

"Bismillah, al Rahman al Rahim..."

She looked up. Nura stood before her.

"You can always say no."

Nura stood watching her, then stretched across the bed in her cream silk robe. She seemed to wait for the night breeze to cool the heat, to listen to the soft sounds of the palms brushing against the shutters, the tiny noises of the desert beginning to move at night. She lit a cigarette, gazing at the blue smoke curling up into the sky.

Naila was struck as always by the beauty of the woman in front of her, the sensuous elegance, at once finely controlled and abandoned, by the intellect behind the penetrating green eyes. Effortlessly, fascinatingly, Nura's mind seemed to flow between abstract and concrete, past and present, philosophy and passion, moving with a languor and a heat that seemed of the desert.

"I can say no, but..." Naila's voice trailed off.

"You will," asked Nura, watching her closely, "agree to it?"

"To the marriage, or to the person Musaid has chosen for me to marry?"

"Any of it," said Nura and drew in the smoke.

"Does it really make any difference?" asked Naila.

"You can say no."

"I can say no," said Naila. She stopped. "But I can't say yes to what I really want. You have what you want, but I..."

"What is it you really want?" asked Nura quietly.

"Someone else."

"Someone Musaid will never agree to."

"Yes."

"And so?"

"And so," said Naila quietly, "I will do what I have to do. I really have no choice, have I?" She frowned. "I have delayed it, run from it in my own way, as long as I could. But we know that Musaid ultimately has control over whether I can stay or go. The permission to travel, to study. And he has said I must return. And so," she looked about the room. "My choice?" She looked at Nura sadly. "My choice is to refuse and then never be allowed to return again to my home, my family, to lose everything I love, to live my life as a castaway who has disgraced her family." Her voice broke. "And so I am here."

Nura rose to go. Then she paused, "Naila, the man you have left behind, is he someone you only think of, or is he your lover?"

"He was," said Naila, and heard Nura's breath catch, "my lover."

Nura, frightened, went over and touched her sister's face. "Be careful my little one," she whispered, "be careful. You must leave it behind." Naila nodded.

"Nura," she said. "Nura, you make love to a man you desire, don't you?"

"Yes, for me there has never been anybody else, always Tarek."

"You are very lucky."

"Yes," she said softly. The compassion of the single word held in the night air as Nura left. Naila sat still on the bed thinking of the last night with him before she had left. The love they had shared now seemed to mock her in the emptiness of the silent room. And within it the quick fear darted through her mind once again, that in the passion of the moment she had forgotten to take any precautions against pregnancy. She pushed the thought back, overwhelmed by the grief, the loss that engulfed her. She closed her eyes and prayed for the strength to go on.

Nura walked down the long corridor, which circled around the atrium, to the other side of the house. She opened the door to the bedroom and took the small journal embossed with her initials out of her drawer. She wrote until she heard the sound of the footsteps. Tarek opened the door of the bedroom. Nura stopped writing and put the small journal down.

"Naila is here?" he asked.

"She is sleeping now," said Nura. "Tarek, I'm worried about Naila, I…"

She stopped and watched his face, then drew him down to her, "You look exhausted, where have you been?" she whispered.

He did not answer but leaned over her, looking at the

exquisite green eyes, her full breasts and the soft mound of her stomach beneath the cream silk. A woman whose body and mind drew him as a flame draws the eye in darkness. He had never been near her without feeling desire rise up in him. He remembered the first time he had made love to her. She was barely more than a child then, and yet she burned into him, drawing him deeper and deeper into the luxurious sensuality that emanated from her, deeper into the complexities and perceptions of her mind that so intrigued him.

"Nura," he said, "I want you to go away for a while, to Paris, somewhere, anywhere it is safe. Take the children. Saddam is moving troops to the Kuwaiti border. I am worried it is going to get worse."

Nura brushed the idea away. "What does Fahd plan to do?"

"Nothing."

Nura looked intently at him.

"Nura, I want you to tell me everything you hear within the Family, I want you to listen..."

"Listen?"

"Somebody from inside is working with Iraq."

Nura's face and body were suddenly motionless. "You know who it is?"

"No."

For a moment she stood watching his eyes. Then she put her hand along the back of his neck and pulled his mouth down to hers. "I'm not going," she breathed, tracing his mouth with hers.

She leaned over on one elbow, her long black hair falling across her shoulders. She scanned the dark outline of his body beneath his thobe. Then she reached over to open it. "I want you," she murmured, rising to kneel above him. She smiled when the silk of her robe fell open. "I want you."

She moved the silk back so the light of the small lamp fell

across her breasts, the full nipples a pale soft mauve in the low light. She took his hand and put his fingers in her mouth, wetting them with tiny licks of her tongue, slow pulses of wetness, and then brought his fingers down from her mouth onto her nipple. She brushed them slowly around and around, her eyes closing, as they stroked toward the center. Her thigh brushed against him, and she brought his fingers back to her mouth. Wetting them again, she opened her legs.

"See," she whispered, "what you do to me." She drew his fingers into the soft folds of the lips between her legs, stroking the pink flesh within so he could feel the wetness already flowing around the tiny firm ridge. Stroking and then suddenly bringing them up inside her so that her breath caught and her eyes closed.

She leaned down over him. "Naila asked me," she whispered, brushing her full breasts against the hardness of his dark chest, "if I made love to a man I desire." Tarek closed his eyes. Her hands moved across his body. "Did you know that even as a young girl I wanted you?" She breathed and moved her leg between his. She traced her fingers along his face and then down his body, slowly stroking until she softly curved her palm around the thickness of his penis and then brought her lips to it. "Shocking," she whispered and put her mouth around it, "if they had known what such a young girl was thinking."

He watched her for a moment, then stood up. She reached up for him standing over her, gazing at her lying on the silk beneath him. Gently he took her hands and pinned them over her head. He brought his tongue down along the soft inside of her arm and his hand pulled the silk strap from her shoulder; it fell from her breasts. He pushed her legs open wider with his; she gasped and he slowly brought his hard penis inside of her. She moaned. He reached for the glass of wine next to her and spilled some of the warm liquid over her breast and then brought his mouth over her nipple. "And what was it you wanted," he breathed. He felt her body moving beneath him. "This?"

He slowly moved his tongue over her nipples. He felt them getting harder and she moaned again.

"Or maybe this?" He drew back from her; her body arched up to his, begging him now. He whispered down to her. "I know how I want you."

He parted her legs, drew his hand along the inside of her thigh and then reached for the silver flask of perfume by the bed. He stroked the hard silver along the inside of her leg, slowly turning it, her skin flushed beneath it, warming the pale metal. He gently stroked it between her legs, soaking it in her moisture. He pulled her head back, kissing her, and then moved the wet cylinder from the lips to within the cheeks of her buttocks. She gasped as he slowly slid it inside her, slowly turning it, pulsing it.

"Or maybe this." He removed the top of the jasmine cream flask and let some of the cream seep between her legs. His hand began to stroke again, moving his fingers along the outside of the flesh and then within her. His tongue played over her nipples. She moaned again, her body beneath him, hypnotized with pleasure, whispering up to him, begging him.

"Or maybe," he said as he felt her fingers tighten around his arm pulling him toward her, inside her, "it was this." Slowly, then roughly, he opened her legs and rose up above her, then thrust deep into her while her body shook and her climax circled around him.

While the palms brushed lightly along the wooden shutters, he moved inside of her and then lay close to her until sleep came.

6

Through the night Elaine struggled to sleep, but the confusion of the dream played itself out again. Brilliant orange gas, a bomb exploding, the dark face in the car speeding toward the barricade, and a thousand tiny sounds, static-covered messages and fragments of paper, each with a word, a phrase, lying on the desks of the decoders, falling on the floor in disarray when she tried to reach for them. She forced her eyes open and looked down at her hand clutching the sheets on the bed. She made herself look at the room, the curtains, the light, focus on the small things, the hair brush on the dresser, the comb, until she felt steady. She put on her robe and looked in the mirror. Her haunted eyes stared back at her. The silence of the room now seemed a reverberation, a dimension.

She quickly gathered together the charts, specs, installation designs, usage schedules of every element of the communications system, details of the system, and began to lay them out. Tracing every element of the system, the interlocking designs, she began sketching out the possibilities. Forcing herself to focus, she poured over the material, making copious notes, becoming immersed finally in the myriad systems.

At 4:00 P.M. a messenger appeared and handed a schedule to Elaine. Ray's note was hasty. "There's a reception at the Ambassador's tonight. Start with this for your 'cultural attaché'

show. The Ambassador
quite enthused you're he
cultural events for you
connect with Tarek ton
the rest of the charts th
hours she worked thro
finished the diagrams.
clock, changed into a si
across the compound to

She entered the lar
suits, men in thobes, women in cocktail dresses, a journalist and a senator she recognized along with one of the oil company executives who had been on the flight to Riyadh. A cacophony of conversations spilled over one another about defense contracts, oil installations, airline franchises—bejeweled women gesturing, embassy functionaries dutifully circulating. The butlers moving about the arms merchants, ex-ambassadors brokering deals, with trays of hor's d'oeuvres and champagne. The Ambassador's wife greeted Elaine.

"Welcome, there are so many people here I want you to meet." A plump, pleasant woman, she seemed delighted at Elaine's arrival. She took her arm as she continued talking. "I've made arrangements to take you to a Saudi wedding tonight—but that won't start until midnight. Also, I want to introduce you to Osman, one of the leading Saudi art collectors. He's here tonight. Perhaps you can arrange an exhibit with him. First come meet the Ambassador."

She led Elaine over to the Ambassador, who stood beneath the chandelier of the U.S. Embassy reception room absorbed in conversation with a chunky man in an overly expensive suit, who was discussing defense contracts he hoped to conclude with Iraq. He started to greet her, then stopped short at the

val. Elaine watched Tarek come in, struck
nce that seem to emanate from him.

e's a man I'd like to talk to," mused the defense

n't bother," said the Ambassador dryly, "he already
ws more about what you've got to sell than you do."

Before the Ambassador could turn his attention back to
Elaine, the Senator from Wyoming strolled up to him,
attempting to continue a conversation he had obviously started
earlier. "Saddam Hussein is an impressive man. I've just come
down from a stay in Baghdad, an important ally…"

Elaine watched Tarek move on, scan the faces, take a drink
from the passing waiter while the Ambassador's wife sighed at
the endless interruptions and finally took Elaine by the arm.
"Come, let's go find Osman." She nodded toward a middle-
aged man, casually elegant in a white thobe, standing on the
other side of the room. As they started across the room, Elaine
was surprised to see Tarek walking over toward him. Elaine and
the Ambassador's wife came up behind Osman just as he
moved forward to embrace Tarek.

"Tarek, the antique Nura brought me back from Paris is
beautiful. Tell her again my thanks—she always finds my best
pieces." Osman turned to peruse the crowd, his eye resting on
former Oil Minister Yamani. "He was under house arrest for a
while, wasn't he, Tarek? I heard Fahd fired him when he argued
with him. I guess the lesson simply is never disagree with Fahd.
It is a shame really. I liked the man, he was very talented," said
Osman, in a tone of simple decency and natural generosity.
Osman's gaze wandered back to a young secretary who had
been watching him. "You know, Tarek," he confided, "I realize
now that it is only in a woman's body that you can truly think.
It is like the quiet in the night when you can finally hear the

sounds of your thoughts." He sighed, the sigh of a man at ease with himself and the endless tiny foibles of the egos around him. Osman, a man who had moved through money, through intellect, to arrive ultimately at the world of the senses. An elegant voluptuary, a man who breathed in the feel of the body the same way the old men filled their lungs with the smoke from the long-stemmed pipes. Freed by all of the money his investments had made over the years to be what he truly was, a man with an equal love of philosophy and the senses. He amassed his art collection, enjoyed his women through the hot torpid afternoons, accrued more money effortlessly, built another lavish new house, and loved his sons.

Osman glanced back, smiling at Tarek. "Tarek, there is a beautiful woman, blonde, lovely blue eyes, being ushered around by the Ambassador's wife. Who is she?"

"The new cultural attaché the embassy just brought over. She's standing behind you," said Tarek, now amused.

Osman turned around, startled at Tarek's words. Tarek gracefully ushered Elaine forward as the Ambassador's wife allowed him to do the honors.

"Miss Landon, I'd like you to meet someone."

Elaine watched what seemed to be the same sense of amusement she had seen earlier when she had introduced herself as 'cultural attaché' playing across Tarek's eyes. "Osman is one of our leading art patrons." He looked at Osman, affectionately. "Actually he truly does have one of the most extraordinary collections, and is genuinely one of my favorite people. I'm sure you 'll...

Tarek started to say something else, then stopped suddenly at the sight of a butler motioning him over to the phone. He walked off without a word and spoke on the phone. A moment later, Elaine watched him go out the door, brushing past Ray who was on his way in.

The Ambassador's wife chattered on with Osman as Ray headed toward Elaine. He paused nonchalantly for a moment, then whispered in her ear.

"Say good-bye to the Ambassador's wife—we've got to go somewhere. I'll meet you in front."

Before she could even turn around, Ray was moving toward the door. Elaine muttered a hasty good-bye to Osman and the Ambassador's wife, who looked somewhat confused by Elaine's rapid departure.

"You have to go somewhere? Well, have a nice time and I'll have the driver pick you up in time tonight for the wedding," she said waving her hand and turning back to Osman.

Elaine got into the car, and Ray began to drive hurriedly through the streets of Riyadh. "Tarek said he wants to ask Walid about something before we talk. Trying to get to Tarek is like trying to hit a moving target sometimes. The man moves like a bedu in the night half the time, so I figure we go to Walid's."

"Who's Walid?" asked Elaine.

"Walid...the king's adviser, manages his schedule," muttered Ray to Elaine while barreling along the maze of streets. "Yes, you are in for a dubious treat." He wound the car toward Walid's 'city house.' "How does one describe Walid? Small, wiry, agile, the perfect linguist, the perfect cynic. One of the most politically skillful men around. He survives everything, slides through identities like a chameleon. Endlessly decent and helpful, beyond reproach to Fahd, then like a stiletto with his competition. Plays unsuspecting foreigners off against one another on contracts and becomes richer as every day passes. Acts highly religious before the old Sharia Court judges, then goes back to his 'city house' for an evening of drink and whores.

In this country where alcohol is strictly forbidden he has gallons of Black Label Scotch for the protocol entourage after hours. Seems to be able to get up every morning and do it again. The man survives brilliantly. Tarek hates him," concluded Ray, pulling into the driveway.

A servant opened the door for them, and they entered Walid's house. Twenty or so people milled around, some stretched out on cushions, head covers laid aside, sipping scotch in a room decorated in a garish marriage of Beverly Hills rattan sofas and desert camp Bedouin hooked rugs, the portrait of a tired camel on the wall. Standing in the foyer was Walid, holding a telephone receiver to his ear, his eyes wandering lazily about the room. Arch disdain laced his reply to the man on the other end of the phone. "My dear sir, His Majesty has been rather busy lately, but of course I will present your contract to him at the appropriate time. Certainly, certainly. Yes, of course, it is important to move on this at once." He sipped at the scotch in his hand and nodded to Musaid who was coming through the door.

"Perhaps, Mr. Johnson, your people have forgotten the additional paper I have requested on this—the note guaranteeing a five percent 'commission' if this contract goes through." Walid's eyelids lowered for a moment.

"Ah, I see, I see. 'This is not your practice.' " A slow, mocking smile slid across his face. "Your attorneys in New York don't feel that... Such a pity, really. Perhaps, Mr. Johnson, you could consult with them again. It is so difficult really to ask His Majesty to look at everything. You can, appreciate, I'm sure, how very pressed his time is. Certainly, certainly. Perhaps we will talk again, when you've been able to consult your attorney again." He hung up the telephone.

Walid turned to Musaid with a look of disgust. "We don't

have a policy of paying commission fees," he mimicked. "Can you imagine? This ignorant fool thinks I'm going to let a multi-million-dollar airplane parts contract go through to Fahd without a commission? We don't do that in the States," he mimicked again. "Sir, perhaps I should have said... They are so very naive aren't they? Perhaps I should have said, 'Sir, this is the Middle East. Not only will your contract not ever be presented if you don't, but you, sir, will never do business anywhere else in the region again. I, sir, will not only kill the contract but your entire corporation's future with our neighbors.' " He clucked his tongue. "So naive, so naive," he shrugged. He held his hand out for a refill of scotch, eyes now fixing upon Elaine just as Ray spied the car and took her arm.

"It's Tarek," Ray said quietly. "Just fade into the woodwork for a while."

Elaine saw Tarek enter the room, immediately pick up on Ray's gesture to meet him afterwards, and then move toward Walid. "Tarek, I am sorry we kept missing one another today. Fahd had more insomnia. It's really problems with his stomach, I think. In any case, after staying awake all last night, he slept through the afternoon so we only just finished. Here, have a drink," he waved the servant over. "We did finish the schedule. Let me know what you need, O.K.?" Walid took another long drink of scotch.

"Walid, the information you sent me wasn't clear," Tarek said.

Walid turned quickly to face him; looked at him curiously for a moment and said nothing.

"Walid, what was the sense of the meeting I missed with Fahd, Abdullah, Sultan, Saud? Their reaction to the information I sent?"

Walid looked vaguely about the room, then shrugged. "That

we don't want to get involved." Walid turned with a languid smile, "The only thing I know is that quite simply Sultan does not want to get involved. Fahd does not want to get involved." He focused his eyes narrowly on Tarek's.

"I also know you might want to leave it alone. Just simply leave it alone."

Abruptly, Walid walked off across the room toward Elaine. She listened coolly to Walid, stepping back ever so slightly while he pressed on in a conversation that was clearly making her increasingly uncomfortable. Walid, now drunk, reached out for the Arab call-girl standing behind him. All of a sudden he called out in a loud voice. "Just remember what I said, Elaine. If you change your mind and want somebody to sleep with tonight, just call."

A hush fell over the crowd. Elaine looked stung. She searched the room for Ray and then, not seeing him, walked quickly to the door. Tarek walked out behind her. She turned, flushed. "The driver, the driver isn't here."

Tarek spoke softly. "Would you like me to drive you?"

She gave Tarek a look of exasperation. He laughed. "It's all right; Walid and I are not alike. Besides," his smile was amused, engaging, "the Ambassador keeps very close tabs on me."

Tarek opened the car door. He watched her, elegant, reserved, silent, while they drove along the winding Riyadh streets.

"I am sorry about Walid," Tarek finally said quietly. "He gets drunk. He's a vulgar man, I suppose, drunk or not. Useful but vulgar." She seemed to listen. "You will meet many nice people here. Walid, however, is not one of them."

She looked at Tarek's handsome face, and smiled uncertainly.

"You have spent a lot of time in the U.S., haven't you. Your

English…" she stopped when she saw Tarek's amusement.

"Yes, I am a product of your educational system from the time I was thirteen years old—Princeton, then Washington."

She was embarrassed. He gently shook his head and smiled at her. "May you have better luck in finding Saudi culture than you had tonight at Walid's." He stopped the car in front of Ray's office.

✠   ✠   ✠

Ray looked up, overwhelmed by the mass of papers on his office desk when Tarek and Elaine came through the door. "Look at this," he muttered, frowning, "why the hell don't I ever get any good news?"

He pushed the papers aside and glanced up matter-of-factly. "Walid really is an animal, isn't he? I don't know why I forget. I got beeped and came back. What a mistake on my part. I shouldn't have left you there." Ray's voice dropped as he pointed to the intercepts they'd gotten so far from Baghdad.

"Tarek, so far we're getting shit. Christ, it's chaos out there—all these fishing dhows, little speedboats darting around, tanks moving along the border. Anybody could be anything, they're crawling out from every cave, every piece of sand along the fucking Gulf. And Baghdad is loving it—you should see the stuff they send across for us to pick up—we've got crates of this mindless crap." He wadded a piece of the paper and threw it in the trash can. "They must be doubled over laughing in Baghdad while they write this stuff. Picking through it for anything real is like trying to find a feather in a ton of chicken shit." He dumped the pile of papers back in the carton.

"Tarek, I've just gotten a communiqué. The White House

truly doesn't think this is going to blow, but if it does, and I think it will, I believe Bush might be persuaded to send in some forces. But we're going to need backup from you. We've got to get it arranged—quickly. Assurances you'll let the Air Force, the troops operate out of Saudi Arabia."

"Fahd won't agree."

Ray stopped pacing the floor and stood still. "What do you mean, he won't agree?"

"He won't agree."

"Tarek," Ray breathed menacingly, "he's got to. This country is like a sitting duck out here. They'll blow Kuwait right out of the water and then head here. They'll drop mines from every little dhow and speedboat in the Gulf, they'll launch Scuds, chemicals, troops out of every point on the map in Iraq and laugh as they blow the Kingdom right into the fucking sky."

"He won't agree."

Ray sat down at his desk.

"Tarek, for Christ's sake, what do you want us to do, how can we..."

Tarek swung around, "Damn it, Ray, what do you expect? You drag the man down a rat hole with this stupid Iran-Contra mess. Your people think up that ridiculous scam, bring him into it as a middleman and then leave him there publicly embarrassed in front of the whole Arab world. You make him look like some stupid stooge of the U.S., working with the Israelis to deliver arms to Iran."

Tarek paced the office floor. "Now, why does he do that? Why? Because he's afraid of Iran. He's trying to buy a little time underneath the table, but you blow him out of the water. Now he's afraid of Iraq—but he also doesn't trust your people. He's also terrified of the fundamentalists breathing down his back. He's not going to get close to this with a ten foot pole."

"He's just going to leave us out there?"

"Same as you left him out there on the last one. He thinks your people are inept and he thinks they've been lying to him for a long time."

Tarek stopped pacing. He pulled out a cigarette. "It is," he said slowly, "very difficult, very, very difficult for him to believe a lot of what you say. The Shah, for instance. Everybody in the Gulf knew that the Shah was dying of cancer for over a year before he died. Everybody knew the son was too weak, too young to be accepted in his place. So Iran has a succession problem. They also have serious unrest in the country. We all knew this. But your people, they profess ignorance. Only months before the Shah dies your president calls Iran 'this one great bastion of stability in the Middle East.' The intelligence you pass on to us says there is no great problem, this ignorant mullah Khomeini; he is nothing, the Shah is fine."

Tarek watched the curl of smoke from his cigarette.

"So Fahd says, 'why are they giving us this disinformation?' Because that's what it must be—after all, they couldn't be that stupid. The U.S. has access—they helped the Shah set up his whole intelligence system, helped him equip his secret police squad, SAVAK. So the U.S. can tap into information they want there. A blind man could see what's happening—and they try to tell us the Shah is fine? Why?' "

Tarek stubbed out the cigarette. "So suddenly the Shah, your old ally, is dumped, and Khomeini is in. And the U.S. now professes amazement. Who are these people, where in the world did they come from? And Fahd listens to this next round of amazement from your people. And you know what he thinks?"

Tarek leaned forward. "He thinks it is unimaginable that a superpower could be so ignorant, could be walking around dealing in world foreign policy with such a level of stupidity. He thinks to himself, 'clearly that can't be.'"

He sat back. "And so for him the only logical conclusion is that you've been lying to him. That you've known all of this all along. Didn't want to have to engineer publicly getting rid of the Shah, so you helped Khomeini covertly. I mean a Muslim Shia leader in your pocket wouldn't hurt, would it? You could play havoc with the Soviets—they're frightened to death of the Muslims in the southern part of their own country. And you'd still have Iran."

Ray shook his head. "He really thinks we helped put Khomeini in power? That's crazy—how does he explain the fact that the man became a thorn in our side ever since, hated us?"

"Simple. He used you, then turned on you." Tarek shrugged sarcastically. "Selling arms to them didn't do anything to lessen that impression. No, all it did was to destroy Fahd publicly when you used him for the middleman stooge. In Lebanon, the first shot is fired and you cut and run. He figures he can't trust you."

"Tarek," Ray leaned toward him, "we can't sit back and let Iraq take over the Gulf."

"I know."

"So what's the answer?"

"I don't know."

"Fahd's going to have to make one last leap of faith, Tarek."

"And I should push him?"

"Yes, Tarek, there's another reason why Elaine is here."

He handed Tarek the usual overnight ream of paper.

"Four More Palestinians Killed as Intifada Continues, Israeli Crackdown on West Bank Following Death of a Jewish Settler in Fire Bomb Attack." Tarek leafed through the pages.

"Nothing too new, right? I'll tell you what is new," Ray said.

"You know how Israel is starting to crumble a bit from within? Something is starting to happen here. We're seeing these little 'dislocations,' 'interruptions.'" He waved his hand, "Christ, I'm not a technocrat, I don't really understand how all this equipment works. But our guys are finding some unexplained glitches in the phone systems throughout the country, the computer operations that run the country's electricity, water, oil systems. Also, our info in the Embassy is being tapped into. That's one reason why Elaine is here." He paused. "And there's another reason.

"Tarek, I've spent practically my entire career here. You and I have seen a lot. But I'll tell you what we've never seen before. Not only is our information getting out but also information from the closed-door sessions of the Royal Family. It's being leaked. And it's showing up in Iraq. There's no way," he waved his hand at the electronics equipment around him, "or we'd find it. It has to be a person, a someone from within passing it to a person outside. In short, a member of the Family."

Tarek watched Ray.

"And so," Ray concluded, looking wryly at Elaine, "that is why we have another 'cultural attaché.' Elaine's going to scour our systems until we find out what's going on. But it's got to be someone inside."

Tarek said. "I know."

Ray looked startled. "You know who?"

"No," Tarek walked to the door. "I'll be in touch."

Elaine watched him leave and turned to Ray. "Does he really believe we put Khomeini in power?"

"Fahd does." Ray sighed. "Tarek probably doesn't. He probably knows how stupid we really are."

Ray kneaded the muscle at the base of his neck. "Christ, and now Iraq. Do you know we slipped a CIA base into Iraq a few years ago—not to spy on Iraq, but to share information with them? Gave them our satellite photographs of Iranian troop positions during the Iran-Iraq War so that..."

Elaine finished the sentence for him. "So that now they know our capabilities and how to use adverse weather and night to move units and equipment to avoid our monitoring operations." She paused thoughtfully. "You know, they probably figured out a bit of our signal intelligence capability as well, and could have changed a lot of their communications doctrine to avoid our intercepting their plans."

"Jesus," muttered Ray. "And our intelligence!" He emitted a disgusted laugh. "Shit."

He pulled open a drawer. "You want to see what I've got here?" He pulled out ream after ream. "This one, about Khadaffi, how he likes to dress up in high heels and skirts." He dumped it on the desk. "This one about Sadat, how he used to have anxiety attacks and smoke dope and wander off into the desert." He pitched it on the desk. "Mubarak, every boring detail about any conversation or phone call the Egyptian president ever made or is going to make, the most extensively bugged human being on the face of the earth." He dropped it on top of the others. "And underneath it, just these occasional little commentaries on how Saddam is building up his Republican Guard, setting up ever so many new little missile manufacturing operations, how nice it is that Iraq is buying so much stuff from the U.S., description of Saddam that adds up to the portrait of a megalomaniac that nobody wants to notice."

"He's an interesting man, isn't he?" said Elaine.

"Saddam?" Ray turned to her, surprised.

"No. Tarek."

"Ah, Tarek," he smiled, still rubbing the back of his neck. "Tarek is probably one of the most fascinating people I've ever met—a really intriguing mix of pieces. He's their Chief of Intelligence, but he's much more than that. I've known him since he was a kid. He's incredibly smart, and by virtue of his job and his rank in the Royal Family, he's rich forever. So he's incorruptible and a straight shooter, not something that's all that common around here. He also shares everything he gets with us, at least everything we're interested in, and we essentially do the same with him. If I hadn't told him what your specific assignment was, he'd have figured it out anyway within a week."

"He had it figured on sight."

Ray nodded, amused. "His number-one aide, Badr, is out of the same cloth. We work well together, and we damn well better, because this situation looks like it's going to be bigger than all of us.

Elaine asked, "You knew him when he was a kid?"

Ray smiled. "His family sent him to private school in the U.S. when he was thirteen, and then on to Princeton, with King Faisal's sons. And in the summer when he came back home, his mother sent him out into the desert with her father, an old man who heads one of the tribes in the north. That old man taught him how to hunt and track like any Bedouin who ever came out of the desert. I can see him now, coming back from the desert, tough like a piece of leather, getting dressed to go back to Princeton." Ray stretched out his legs.

"You know," he mused, "I went to visit him one time. Climbed the dormitory stairs to find him, at one in the morning, hunched over a backgammon game with Saud, the foreign minister now, while this gorgeous girl sat waiting for him, enthralled. Christ, he did always seem to be a virtual magnet for women. Musaid was sitting there working on his math problems."

70

"Musaid?"

"His wife's brother. He never amounted to much. I think they found him sort of a middle level technical job. Well, hell, with a few thousand princes, not half of them are going to be superstars. There's quite a distinct layering of the stratospheres, an actual meritocracy to some degree. Many of them are totally inconsequential or at least so far off to the sidelines or down the totem pole that they really don't count—Musaid and about a thousand others. In any case, he went to school somewhere in California. He's one of those kids who did a hundred and eighty degree turn. You see them, used to chasing everything in skirts, although there's really an unattractive quality about him, so I wonder how successful he ever was, but anyhow when he finally returned home, he became very conservative. He's the one who dragged Naila back. Jesus, these poor women; they only get so far out there, and then they get pulled back. About the only option she had was whether to move back into his house or Tarek's. But you want to know the biggest irony of those years in Princeton?" continued Ray in the same vein. "You know who else was there at the same time with Tarek and Saud?"

Elaine shook her head.

"Antar." It was a sudden physical reaction at the mention of Antar. He watched Elaine's eyes go dead; something shut inside. "Yes," Ray went on, curious at what he'd just seen, "Antar, Iraq's head of covert operations. He and Tarek were great friends back in school, spent long hours together talking about the Middle East, how to change things. Then Antar became more and more involved, in the Baath Party, Saddam's more radical inner circle."

He glanced up at the clock and stood up to go. "You'll find out Tarek is a man of many, many pieces—one of them is

71

Princeton, one of them is Royal Family, and one of them is bedu."

Elaine closed the folders. "You have any idea who it is in the Royal Family that's working with Iraq?"

Ray hesitated. "As Boris, the old Russian agent who was here for many years, used to say," he mimicked the accent. "There's old Russian saying." He paused, "In the dark all the cats look gray."

Elaine attempted a smile, but it was clearly strained. The phone rang.

"It's the Ambassador's wife. She says she'll be by now to take you to the wedding—it starts at midnight. The chauffeur will be downstairs to pick you up." Elaine nodded.

Ray watched her go, then turned back to the empty room.

"And so, Tarek," Ray said aloud to himself. "I wish to hell we'd never seen this, because if you start to fall apart from the inside, you're going under and then," Ray picked up the little American flag on his desk, "so does a whole lot of American power and presence in the Middle East."

He looked back at the final report from the KH-11 satellite. A hundred thousand Iraqi troops were moving toward the border—triple the number from yesterday. A new "logistics train" that could give Saddam everything he needed to invade.

The ambassador's limousine, the small American flag flying on the front, waited for Elaine outside the door. The chauffeur opened the door for her, and the ambassador's wife greeted her warmly. The car sped on toward Sultan's palace. When they reached the walls around Sultan's palace, the guards peered in, then swung open the palace gate to admit Elaine and the ambassador's wife.

They walked up the wide marble stairs and entered a vast silk-walled reception room where the women handed their abayas to the servants. Beneath the chandeliers, the gowns and jewels of the Arab women reflected the facets of the prisms above them while they chattered about the bride's dowry, the husband's money, and his place in the Royal Family hierarchy. Elaine watched the mothers and sisters perusing the other young women, discussing their money, their family merits, their personalities as potential matches for their sons and their brothers, while they waited for the bride.

The ambassador's wife whispered to Elaine. "As cultural attaché, you should get to know the various groups within the Family, and then of course, the other big merchant families around. My god," she stopped short and nodded her head toward a little girl all dressed up. "Look at that jewel around her neck; the child can hardly stand up it's so heavy." She shook her head, "You know, I never get used to it really—this incredible wealth. That's one of Sultan's daughters. Sultan, the minister of defense. They say that Sultan is the richest member of the Royal Family now. All of the arms deals, his commissions from them I guess. Actually they say that Fahd also made a lot of the commissions in the name of his favorite son, the little boy they call Abdul Aziz. Somebody told me the other day that he was now the richest kid on earth. I suppose Crown Prince Abdullah is rich enough too," she shrugged. "But he's the real straight shooter in the group. A real bedu—rooted in the 'Arab' world."

She pointed Elaine in the direction of a young woman dressed in blue with lavish sapphires on her throat and arm. "Look at her ring finger." Elaine looked down curiously at the ring turned oddly on the young woman's hand. "It means," whispered the ambassador's wife, "that the marriage has been consummated. You know these marriages are all arranged by the family. Some of them work, some of them don't," she shrugged. "The families marry them off to consolidate fortunes, or sometimes to strengthen ties between various factions of the Royal Family that have been bickering. God knows there are enough splits below the surface these days."

Elaine looked across the room and to her surprise caught sight of Naila, the lovely young woman from the plane. She started to say something when suddenly the crowd hushed and faced the entrance.

The massive doors opened, and King Fahd entered, followed by Crown Prince Abdullah and Sultan, robes rustling. The crowd bowed. Upon cue an array of female musicians and dancers burst forward, dressed in brilliantly colored chiffons, striking the ancient chants and rhythms on their tablas. They whirled through the room before the tables laden with silver, crystal, food, ice sculptures and orchids. And then, amidst the applause, the groom and the bride entered, draped in diamonds, pearls, and billowing white taffeta.

Elaine once again spotted the young woman from the plane. The young woman seemed to stand absolutely still, looking at the bride moving through the crowd. Then she turned around and silently walked out of the room—she was gone by the time the Ambassador's wife returned with their drinks.

I t was 2:00 A.M. before the driver returned Elaine to her small embassy compound house. Elaine thanked the ambassador's wife and then opened the door to the house. She walked in, then sat in silence.

She put her head in her hands. Ray had seen her react to Antar's name. She stared at the wall. She should tell him now. She should tell him she couldn't do this. She should tell him why. She should leave. Before another day passed, she should leave. The images started careening again, colliding. She started to pick up the phone, but put it down. "Oh god," she whispered to herself, "how could they have asked me to do this? How could they have asked me, of all people, to do this?"

At the end of the day, she would tell him. She would go through her review to help him, and then at the end of the day she would tell him. And then she would get on the plane and go as far away from this place as she could.

7

arek sat in the darkened office, the halls empty, the clock striking 3:00 AM. He put on the small audiotape and listened to the voices of the cell members, praying, chanting. He turned off the tape and picked up the sheaf of reports that Badr had left for him. The first was from his desk man in Tunis assigned to trail Arafat, detailing the PLO chairman's usual wanderings and histrionics. Cairo reporting on its taps on President Mubarak coupled with the report of Tarek's agents inside the Muslim Brotherhood operations in Cairo and Alexandria.

He thought for a moment of the world of lies he inhabited. Lies, shadows, half-truths. Sifting them, he had become a man who took nothing at face value. He picked up the second folder and rapidly thumbed through the reports from his agents in Bonn, Rome, the Islamic Center in Morocco. He signed off on Badr's note for fabrication of documents for some new agents to go into Yemen, a "porter" to be placed in the foreign minister's home there, a new "chauffeur" for the defense minister's mistress. He went back to the satellite photos, the convoys of Iraqi troops and trainloads of tanks moving south from Baghdad to Basra and from there on to assembly.

And finally he picked up the video cassette that one of Hamid's couriers had delivered the day before. Tarek looked at it—thinking of Hamid and finally of Khalid, his agent in Iraq who had preceded Hamid. He wondered sadly how the end had really come for Khalid. He leaned his head back in his chair as Khalid's face filled his mind. Khalid had been brilliant, talented, agile. The perfect agent. When Tarek had told him years ago that his assignment would be to insinuate himself into Saddam's small entourage, he had done it beautifully. He became one of the small corps that Saddam trusted. Right up to the day that Saddam and Antar suddenly decided they didn't trust him anymore and had him killed.

Tarek felt an involuntary chill of fear for Hamid as he inserted the cassette into the player. The picture flicked on; an enormous scaffold appeared with empty nooses hanging above it. Off to the side young guards with machine guns stood by a group of dissidents, twenty or so terrified looking people huddled together. Kurdish women, some young children, middle-ged men, teenage boys.

He watched as Saddam entered the scene and raised his hand to indicate that the cameras should begin filming. He began to read a document, "For crimes against the Republic of Iraq." The camera panned guards with machine guns starting to herd the group of people up onto the scaffold. One woman screamed and clutched at the young guard pushing her. He raised the butt of his gun and smashed it into her chest, then kicked her toward the stairs of the scaffold.

The voice went on. "For crimes against Iraq..." Antar stood in the shadow behind him.

The guards began to put the nooses around the necks of the condemned and realized that the child was too small for the noose to reach. An empty crate was brought. The child, whimpering, confused, stood on it. The guard absently patted the child on the head and placed the noose around his neck.

Saddam finished the proclamation and told the camera crews to make final adjustments.

Suddenly the flimsy scaffold groaned and then collapsed beneath the weight of the people, part of it caving to the ground. Some of the condemned were killed instantly; others dangled half-dead, the child screamed, hanging in the noose still alive but with his neck broken. Saddam, infuriated, waved the guards over before the screaming, sobbing chaos. They opened fire. The shrieking ceased.

Tarek stopped the cassette and froze the picture. He leaned closer toward the monitor. In the far distance, behind the guards, behind Saddam, stood a young man. Trim, dark hair, intelligent-looking eyes, unmoving, simply watching the events. Tarek searched Antar's face for a trace of revulsion. He turned off the cassette.

Beneath the constant struggles for power in Iraq, Antar had not only survived but was standing behind Saddam—once a friend, now a shadow, a clever, clever mind. And now, thought Tarek, we stalk one another. Stalk one another across cities and deserts, with weapons, satellites, computers. Stalk one another in a hunt that neither dares lose.

He looked at the cassette, his mind turning back once again to Khalid. Khalid had been brilliant. Antar had been more brilliant. Antar knew ultimately who had sent Khalid, and now Khalid was dead.

He wrote a communiqué for Hamid, walked down the hall and handed it to the night transmitter.

The man moved it instantly through transmission. Recognizing who the communiqué was for, he thought of how long it had been since he'd actually seen Hamid. How many years now the mole had been in place. And how few survived this long.

Tarek returned to his office and waited. And knew, as though he were there, what Hamid would be doing as the morning unfolded.

✠ ✠ ✠

Hamid watched Antar's back disappearing down the long hall of the Iraqi Assembly Chambers. He waited until Antar entered the Assembly Chambers and the door had closed behind him. Hamid quickly picked up the sheets on the desk and ran them through the copy machine. He put the copies into his shirt and placed the originals back on the desk exactly as they had lain. He walked out of the office, nodded to the guard at the front door and stepped into the strong Baghdad morning light.

He walked quickly past the shopkeepers sitting bored in front of the rundown facades. Reaching the entrance to his apartment building, he nodded to his landlady, walked up to his room and closed the door. He turned on the television set to watch the 8:00 A M. Baghdad news. A young woman appeared at a desk. "In the Name of God the Compassionate, the Mighty...," her voice began the usual introduction before the backdrop of cheap footage of Saddam Hussein's motorcade. "President Saddam Hussein today..."

Hamid listened to the clatter of his landlady's pots and pans. He turned up the sound on the TV, then walked over to the edge of the tattered rug. Silently he pulled the rug back and then lifted the small plank of floor board below it. He reached in and took out the tiny camera. He took the sheets, covered with sweat, from inside his shirt and laid them out on the floor. He listened again for the sounds of the kitchen below and then began to click off the frames, shot by shot, moving precisely along the blocks, which delineated troop arrangements, and training installations.

He walked to the bathroom, lit a match, and watched the sheets of paper burn. He flushed the ashes down the toilet and then returned to listen to the newscast; he took the film out and put the camera back in the small space he had dug out below the floorboards, then replaced the board and the rug.

He glanced at his watch, went to his desk and turned on the radio to its faintest level, tuning it to the Riyadh frequency. He opened up the compartment below the bottom of the right drawer, took out the decoding pad, and waited with his pen, listening to the sounds of Radio Riyadh. At 8:04, an announcer began reporting the arrival of various Iraqi officials to Mecca to make their umrah. Hamid began marking as the newscaster went on about the airport and the medical facilities available to assist those on the holy pilgrimage. When the reporter finished, Hamid stopped and moved the decoding sheet over the first sheet, working silently while he read it. In the bathroom, he lit another match and flushed the ashes down the toilet. Then, he returned the decoding pad to the compartment in the drawer. He turned off the radio and put film back inside the opening hollowed in the bottom of the lamp.

He listened to his landlady bustling around the kitchen and thought about his drop now confirmed by Tarek. The sun was already hot above the Tigris River, while the fumes and the blares of the traffic spiraled up in cacophony. He stretched out on his bed as the sound of the muezzin began its call from the mosque. The sad familiar wail floated through the room.

B adr hurried into Tarek's office shortly after the clock struck 9:00 A.M. "Transmission from Hamid."

Badr hunched over Hamid's communication from Baghdad outlining Iraq's chemical plant capabilities, Scud missile production sites, nuclear elements and their assembly potential, biological weapons plants, tanks, and escalated Air Force training. Reference to a communication network set up with unnamed dissidents and cells located in Saudi Arabia. Terrorist training camps located throughout the Gulf, along North Africa.

"Ya Allah," muttered Badr as he rapidly scanned the data, "how the hell did he get this stuff? I don't even want to think about what he had to do to get it." He got up and headed down the hall for their computer ops on dissidents within Saudi Arabia.

Tarek pushed his chair back and looked at the map on his wall. His eye roved the tiny pins staggered across the map, each one, he thought wryly, with the potential to explode. The red ones on the east coast, circling the oil fields in Dhahran and Dammam where the Shia laborers sweated and pumped the oil for a predominant Sunni Saudi Arabia, for a Sunni royal family they viewed as heretical Muslims. The yellow pins spiraling through the entire country for the foreign workers. This sea of strangers now swarmed the streets of Riyadh, Jeddah, and every outpost between. The educated ones manned over fifty percent of the key economic sectors of the country—electricity, finance, trade, manufacturing, construction. All of this in the hands of people with no allegiance.

The blue pins, fixed solidly in the major cities, marking the political cells now under surveillance: young Saudi bureaucrats, engineers educated in the U.S., and Europe; the ones that now railed against Fahd, complaining that he was moving too slowly to allow them into the top of the power structure. Others, that he was too westernized. Young women, educated and angry at being excluded from jobs, infuriated at being confined, segregated, and denied privileges available to the lowliest Saudi male.

His eye roamed finally across the white pins strewn through the desert, the wild stretches of the Empty Quarter, the Rub al Khali desert in the southwest, the Nafud desert to the north. The trail of white pins marking, like a long white thread, the tribes of bedu who still roamed the desert. Tarek looked at the small red flags stationed by some of the white pins on the map. The country now seemed alien to the bedrock conservatism of these people. The fundamentalists were systematically starting to tap into some of the tribes, calling out that the country had lost the true way, that it was time to rise up.

Pins strewn like quake faults across the map. Liberals, conservatives, modern women, fundamentalists, all looking for an answer. Each one hearing what he or she wanted to hear. Looking for a star in the Arab world—embarrassed by the ineptitude of the Arab world. All hearing what they wanted to hear.

He picked up the line to Badr. "Badr, send the latest KH-11 reports on Saddam's troop movement to Fahd's meeting today." Badr shifted uneasily knowing the response to his appearance at the meeting.

8

Ray watched Elaine come into the office as he finished his morning coffee. He instantly took in the expression on her face, the distance, the eyes looking somewhere else.

"Ray," said Elaine, "I need to talk to you."

Ray put down his coffee cup.

"Ray, I'm not going to…"

Suddenly, drowning the sound of her voice, the control siren screamed an alert signal. Ray looked in alarm at the master control panel board for the oil facilities. The tiny lights went blank.

The tech burst in the door. Elaine whirled around. He thrust the computer logs at her. "It's a flash alert, a major unexplained outage at the oil terminal."

Ray and Elaine stared at the monitor. Then suddenly, just as unexpectedly and equally unexplained, the oil terminal functions, and the screen returned to normal, the tiny lights blinking.

Ray, unnerved, quickly took Elaine by the arm. "They are waiting for you in the 'expanded' —makeshift —intel unit I've set up to deal with the problem. I love that phrase 'the problem.'" Ray wasn't smiling.

Elaine hesitated for a moment and then walked rapidly toward the door of the signals intelligence unit. A guard stood by the vaulted room, constructed with wire wraps, tube shields, insulated connectors. She motioned to the guard to open the door and walked in.

The tension was palpable as the three men poised before computer consoles stood up. Elaine walked over and extended her hand to the older balding man. "I'm Elaine Landon, in from Washington." He shook her hand nervously and introduced himself as Captain Jefferson. She acknowledged the other two men then continued, "Do you want to begin with a rundown?"

Captain Jefferson nodded, instantly struck by the fact that she seemed highly efficient, totally focused, and also totally unapproachable on any sort of friendly level. He handed her a list of equipment. "The government has just spent a fortune installing all these new Tempest-tested teletype machines, the printers to control any electronic leaks that could be picked up on communications going out of here. Still they say the stuff is showing up in Baghdad. I'm damned if I know how they're getting it." He stopped suddenly embarrassed.

"I'm sorry about that slip, about being leery of Baghdad. The policy is that we have no problem with Iraq, I know. The White House says their troop build-up along the Kuwaiti border is nothing. But last night Ray Holt came in here with one guy from Marine Intelligence who is as alarmed as he is but says he's afraid to push his case. Bureaucracy, stepping out of line, that sort of thing. So Ray says to direct our communications intercept operations from here to Baghdad and, if asked, we should describe our operation as a 'practice maneuver.' He says if anybody lands on us, we can stick it on him. Says he's too old to give a shit if they fire him." He chortled quietly as he moved back toward the room, "I love that guy—practice maneuver." He became serious once again, "This scares the shit out of me, these leaks in security. If we end up bringing troops in here before this is all over these leaks could mean the death of every man we bring over."

He handed Elaine the report he had prepared for her. After a moment he spoke up somewhat hesitantly. "I understand you've worked with the NSA Tempest operations in Beirut." She nodded. "Maybe you'll pick up on something we're missing. As far as what we're getting from them...the poor son of a bitch next door is about to die under an avalanche of unprocessed data. You know," he sat back in the chair and sipped some cold coffee, "it's a nightmare really, code-breaking today. I mean, the microprocessors are giving everybody, even these dumb-shit Third World countries, the ability to make a good crypto system. Baghdad isn't as slick as the Soviet Union on ciphers—God, the Soviets have really gotten impossible to decode—but it's no piece of cake either dealing with this junk from the so-called Republic of Iraq." He turned to a man who had entered the room.

"Jack, meet Elaine. Elaine, this is Captain John Roberts with Naval intelligence, tried to help Ray, installed some sound monitoring equipment to send up to Iraqi coast. A bootleg operation using a dhow. Didn't go too well. The Iraqis had them nailed before they even moved out, put a mine underneath them in the night. Well, more on that later."

"Is this a good time for you to review?" asked Jack. Elaine nodded and followed him into the unit next door. "Collections operators are working the signals. We have the usual team monitoring telephone taps, bugs. Some stuff we get is helpful; the rest," he shrugged, "is the usual disinformation that they plant when they're onto the fact we're tapped in."

"Satellite telecommunications?" queried Elaine.

"Since most of these Gulf countries have installed all the newest satellite microwave-relay-station systems for telephone and telex over the last few years, it obviously makes that part of intercept a hell of a lot easier to get into. The diplomatic, commercial, political, military stuff that's done via telephone, telex, radio-telephone, radio satellite—you know you can intercept them from the antenna or the ground station beaming the stuff up to the satellites. So we tap into a bit of stuff that's worthwhile that way."

He grimaced. "But still, we're only scratching the surface of getting what we need, what's going on, directives from Baghdad. We get almost nothing of their communications with the cells we know are seeded throughout Saudi Arabia."

"The Iraqis have been known to use buried fiber-optic cable, which as you know is tremendously difficult to intercept," noted Elaine.

"Right, and maybe they're moving some of it on landlines we don't know about, or undersea cables. Those are a possibility, but they are hell to trace. Landlines, certainly, are the worst. To tap a landline cable requires physical access to the actual cable—we have to be able to operate and maintain our tapping equipment, hands-on, somewhere along the cable. It's clear the Saudis trust us to some degree, but it's also clear that they have never come clean on all the locations of their internal landlines, and that those lines have been used to carry a lot of high-priority secret command and control communications that they don't want us to see. It's possible that someone deep inside with a knowledge of those landlines could be using them to move this stuff to Baghdad."

He handed her a chart. "As far as anything else beyond COMINT operations, we're seeing what we can get on movement in the Gulf itself, picking up the stuff on SIGINT equipment, the Rhyolite satellite." He laughed as he picked up a sheet. "Here's the latest stock exchange report and weather broadcast in

Baghdad this morning—that's worth about the paper it's written on."

"I think it's highly likely," said Elaine, "that by sharing intelligence with them we exposed a lot of our SIGINT capability—so that they know how to move a good bit of their communications in ways that would evade our intercepts." Jack nodded.

Ray came into the room and quietly pulled up a chair, listening. "Jesus, we made it so easy for him," mumbled Ray.

"Him?" Jack looked curiously at Ray.

"Antar. We just welcomed him into Washington with arms extended when he showed up as a diplomat there. Nice little dinners with the secretary of state, the national security advisor. Cultivated by all the American bankers, businessmen, Cabinet members." Ray shook his head. "The U.S. Administration so desperate to have a power to balance Iran's, the businessmen so eager for a new client, the bankers so interested in a new customer. First they removed Iraq from the terrorist list, then made loans to Iraq. The President of the United States, during the years he was VP, made calls to insist that the Export Import Bank fund him at ever greater levels, and then we sold him technology, the very goods for their arms build-up. And Antar smiling all the while and playing them for everything they were worth. Until one day he disappears back into the bowels of Iraq."

Ray stopped then looked at Elaine. He pushed his chair back "Sorry, I get so frustrated. Look go on with your briefing, I just wanted to check that you'd gotten situated with the fellows." They watched him walk out the door.

Elaine turned back to Jack. "What's the status on current overhead coverage?"

Jack shrugged, "Washington is looking into shifting some orbits around to increase coverage."

"Why not launch a new 'bird'? Are they considering that?" asked Elaine.

Jack shook his head, "There are plenty of satellite systems in 'cold storage' since the Shuttle *Challenger* and Atlas booster disasters, but no way to launch them—unless you want to borrow a Soviet rocket." He laughed, a small attempt at humor. The small laugh faded. "And on the truly critical point—how Baghdad is tapping into our stuff—we're nowhere."

Jack looked momentarily startled as Elaine reached over and took his pen. "I'm going to sketch out a new breakdown here and outline the kind of team from technical operations back at headquarters that you'll need to help you," she explained.

He looked on, impressed at the rapidity with which she began to sketch the diagram on the paper she took from his desk. She glanced up at him, "I'm going to leave it up to Ray, how he's going to get them to fly the team in considering 'we don't have a problem'—I'm sure he'll think of something."

Jack smiled, unsure of whether she meant to be amusing or not. He took the flow charts she was handing him.

"We're going to need three units, let's call them Units A, B, and C to deal with electronic intelligence, covering radar information and locations," said Elaine. "Chambers D, E, F, G will house communications intelligence, people-to-people communications intercepts, communications traffic analysis, and code-breaking. Chamber H is for the NSA Tempest operation."

He stood back as she moved over to the control board. "In the meantime," she continued succinctly, motioning toward the console, "we can thwart some of their efforts at intercepts."

Captain Jefferson and the two other men from the signals intelligence unit joined them and watched her work through the frequencies on the control board. She glanced over her shoulder while they stared. "We're going to set up a system of false emissions. A system that's going to generate random frequency-hopping spread-spectrum signals that will force Iraq's crypto-graphers to expend incredible effort to break the signals. They're going to be decoy noises—and we're going to have one team member whose entire life is devoted to fooling listeners—to creating frequency-hopping, spread-spectrums along with an arsenal of other decoy techniques."

Captain Jefferson quickly sat down at the console and began to follow her instructions. After a few minutes he looked up, delighted. "There—the bastard monitoring noise information from us ought to go bat shit trying to figure that one out."

Elaine simply nodded and then listed the checks on their own system, ticking off each point of vulnerability. "Ready?"

Elaine and the three-man crew moved rapidly through the initial checks on the security of the computer systems. Tests on the sound frequencies emitted by the computer printers. Efficacy tests on the room vaulting surrounding the computer bank. Checks on cars and vans regularly seen outside the compound that could monitor the sound. She ran specs on the building materials in the Embassy walls. She opened up the computers themselves, scanning their insides for implanted listening devices. She searched for bugs in the obvious cavities of the machines, miniature bugs within the tiny crevices, or filaments of wiring. The young lieutenant on the team nodded in admiration at the sleek display of skill as he glanced up at the clock at the end of the day. But they had come up with nothing.

Elaine watched them leave, thinking of her instructor at Langley who had once said, "Finding a leak is like finding a short in an electrical circuit. You just have to test it, inch by inch. Like finding a short in one wire in a city the size of Minneapolis."

She walked back to Ray's office and stopped at the angry expression on his face. Ray held the phone, listening to Turley's voice flecked with static from CIA headquarters outside Washington.

"Ray, old man, they think you're crazy." Turley's voice droned through the static, edged with sarcasm. "They have, of course, gotten the information on Saddam's troops, but the reading here still is that it's nothing."

Ray hung up the line. He sat staring at the wall, then abruptly picked up the line again. "Fuck this."

Elaine, walking through the door, stared, "What are you going to do?"

"Possibly get myself fired." He dialed.

"Operator, I want you to place two calls for me—one to Secretary of Defense, Richard Cheney, the next to the Chairman of Joint Chiefs of Staff, Colin Powell."

9

Across the city in his office, Tarek continued to watch the monitors from the oil installations while he listened to Ray's report on Elaine's inconclusive findings for the day. Badr stood nervously by while Tarek dialed Naif, the portly Minister of the Interior.

Naif's voice on his car phone sounded with a crackle from the oil fields of Dhahran spreading around him. The tall oil derricks stood in the vast stretch of desert, their gas flames burning beneath the hot sun and the communications wires strung overhead. The pipelines stretched along the ground, thick metal cylinders of oil snaking towards the water terminal with its gray metal tankers lolling like dull whales drinking from the huge tubes that fed them oil.

Over the phone, Tarek could hear the AWACS plane climbing from the Dhahran airfield to begin its patrol over the enormous domes of oil.

"I got your call," Naif said, "but I don't have anything you don't know already. I'm only coming up with the usual. The same cells we've been tracking for a long time—disgruntled Shias working in the oil fields, foreign workers, the usual. The corrupt monarchy, rise up, overthrow the bastards, time for a new world, Allah."

Naif's voice was a study in frustration. "I've got guards on the ground, mine sweepers working the water here, waiting for some crazy person to try and blow up the oil fields. But there is, officially, no problem.

"Look, Tarek, I'm minister of the interior but I take orders like anybody else. And the orders are—we don't have a problem. So, I don't have a problem."

Tarek hung up the phone and stared at the wall. "You called Musaid and asked him to assemble a report for us on the outage?"

Badr nodded and handed him the last surveillance reports. "Musaid says he'll go to work on it immediately. He also says perhaps we should keep an eye on Abed bin Osman. Say's Abed's supervisor over there at Jubail mentioned he's getting a little concerned about Abed, says Abed takes off at odd hours, seems to make some odd trips."

"What about Abed, what are you getting on him?"

"It's coming in," Badr answered. "School in the U.S., vacations in Cannes, visits friends all over the Middle East, girlfriends in California, Berlin, Beirut. Sounds like a typical Arab playboy type. Except for after hours, when he spends his time at cell meetings. We've got him wired, tapped, and trailed twenty-four hours a day now. We should know a little more soon. Want me to bring him in?"

"No, we leave him out there, use him, follow him. Coming and going from Osman's he's an easy mark. Did you set up the taps on the Family?"

"I'm on my way now."

Badr strolled through the offices of the Ministry of Information like a man passing time on his lunch break. He went up to the third floor and looked in at an open door on the right, where a young man sat putting X's on the pages of a magazine laid out in front of him. Badr clucked his tongue in mild disapproval as he made another black X across a photograph at the top of a page.

"Ah, Rashid, leave that one in. She's so nice."

Rashid leaned back while both men gazed appreciatively at the blonde French actress in her bikini, smiling up at them from the latest edition of *Time*.

Rashid sighed. "Only the French girls…that sort of body like a fine foie gras, a golden Montrachet." Rashid picked up the black grease pen and finished the X across her. "Leave it in—and it'll be my ass." He flipped the page and marked the next across the advertisement for Black Label Scotch.

Badr sat down and put his feet up. "Does your job ever depress you?"

Rashid burst out laughing from behind the stack of magazines piled in front of him. "Think of it this way, Badr. I could be the poor bastards downstairs who have to actually cut this stuff out. Have you ever thought of that? That downstairs there are rooms full of Egyptians, Pakistanis, and broke Jordanians with scissors in their hands who have to sit there and actually cut the censored pictures, ads, stories out of every Time, Newsweek, Life, Economist, and the rest that goes on the news stands in the entire country? Now there is depression. Day in, day out, watching all of these gorgeous women, bottles of scotch, drop to the floor to be swept away in bins by an even more depressed Yemeni."

"What happened to the Koreans?"

"They fired them when they found out the poor slant-eyes were taking the clippings home and putting them on the walls above their cots." He peered back down at the picture of the actress. "Look at her Badr, just gazing at me. Do you think if she got to know me she might think of me as dashing, exotic? An Arabian lover, a Valentino-type mystery man, able to bring

93

the pleasures of the East to her bed? I could maybe be her dark thrill from the desert?"

Badr laughed. Rashid sighed. "Badr, remember the old Indian guy who worked here? He said I must have done something truly evil in my last life to be condemned to such an existence. Maybe in my next life I'll be a scientist. But I'd need some brains. Thank god they aren't necessary here."

He plopped the magazine down in the outbox and looked back at Badr. "So you came here just to harass me, or what?"

Badr chuckled, then pulled the wad of riyals from his thobe pocket. "Absolutely not. I always pay my gambling debts promptly. Why the hell does your horse always win? You pick these half-dead nags, horses that don't look like they could get to the other end of Riyadh and damned if they don't win."

"These bills are probably bugged or something. You probably have me followed to see if maybe I have some great sex life at night—after the horrible way I spend my days."

Rashid flipped him a copy of the Saudi Gazette as the paper boy dropped them on his desk. "There is a reason this paper is so thin, Badr. And money isn't it. Have you ever thought how truly terrific it would be if one day you picked up this paper and instead of all the inane pleasantries, they printed the real stuff. Think of it! Underneath this picture of the Gulf rulers in for the latest Gulf Corporation Council meeting it might say, 'Sheikh Zayed, Emir of Abu Dhabi, on the far right standing next to the ruler of Dubai with whom he rules the United Arab Emirates federation despite the fact that they loathe each other, has just planted four-thousand more palm trees on the grounds of his twenty-third new palace.' Sheik Zayed says, 'It's just another way to give the construction industry a boost.'"

Badr burst out laughing.

"Badr, you out of money or do you want to put something on Saturday's race?"

Badr flipped him ten riyals. "I'll call my bet on Friday."

"Badr, what did you really come for?"

He motioned for Rashid to follow him into the hall. "Time for the telephone man."

Rashid nodded. "I figured. When?"

"Now."

"Who?"

"Sultan, Abdullah, Saud, Naif."

"Bismillah," Rashid breathed deeply. "I bring anybody else? Who's in the loop?"

"No one else. You to me, me to Tarek. End of circle. Ready?"

Rashid stepped back into his office and picked up the phone. "I'll be out for the rest of the day," he informed his superior and followed Badr out of the building and into the back of the van.

※ ※ ※

A servant opened the door to Sultan's mansion and let the two telephone men in.

"Just a little problem on the lines. We'll check the various installations and be out of your way in no time. Mind if we start upstairs?"

The servant glanced at the credentials they held out and pointed to the stairs. The two men with their gear walked up the spiraling staircase.

"Shit, Badr, why don't I live like this? See that painting? I could live a lifetime with that."

"Just go to work."

In the study, Rashid uncupped the front of the receiver on the telephone. He took out a chip the size of a fingernail and inserted it, then fastened the top of the phone back on. He took a small filament from his bag and carefully wove it into the strand of carpet on the far end of the room. Then he moved to the picture on the wall and ran his hand along the heavy gold frame, then beneath the light hanging above it to illuminate it. "This ought to work."

He removed a tiny video camera the size of a penlight and drilled a small hole in the wall next to the picture, being careful not to damage the thin wire that emerged in a groove beside the camera. He attached the battery pack to the wire, removed the adhesive from the battery, and stuck it to the back of the picture frame. All that was exposed was a short segment of white wire that he rapidly covered with quick-drying plaster and a tint to match the wall color. The whole process took less than five minutes.

"Just check it once from the van, OK?"

Badr nodded and went down the stairs. In the van, he snapped on the video monitor. The picture of Rashid standing in the room appeared. He flicked off the monitor, and turned on the sound receivers as Rashid began to sing a little ditty. The sound came through. He got out of the van and went back upstairs.

"Fine. Now the bedroom. Then downstairs."

Rashid continued to hum as they moved along, one room after another.

10

Ray stared at the monitor from the KH-11. He picked up the phone.

"Elaine, I want you to come with me for an hour this morning." Ray's voice came jauntily over the phone before she'd even woken up. "I'll be there in thirty minutes."

Ray's car phone was buzzing when she got in.

"Sir, Turley's trying to call you from Washington," said a voice.

"When's he calling back?"

"At 10:00."

"Fine, hopefully the office line is still a little more secure than this goddamned car phone. I'll be there." He drove on through the traffic toward Fahd's palace, then parked at the curb. An entourage of the Royal Family was passing through the intersection ahead.

"And here before us," Ray quipped wryly to Elaine, who was sitting next to him, "are the key candidates for the member of the Family selling Fahd out."

Slowly King Fahd's limousine pulled past, his deep hooded eyes looking vaguely out the window. Ray shook his head.

"He's got to watch it," muttered Ray as much to himself as

to Elaine, who looked on, fascinated at the pomp. "He's right to be terrified of the fundamentalists—he's become an easy target. The bedu, whole parts of this country he's lost touch with. Some make comments about his personal life—talk about the women, drinking, the sons and their deals, the commissions. It doesn't take someone with his ear to the ground to hear it anymore. People everywhere are pointing with disgust to the palaces: Geneva, Costa del Sol, Jeddah, and the real atrocity in Riyadh, the one built to look like a replica of the White House. Jesus, how could a guy already fighting a reputation of being a stooge of the West, a hypocrite Muslim, make the mistake of building a duplicate of the White House?" Elaine listened as he paused and then continued.

"And the yacht, the plane with the pink bedroom and the staff of western women. What is the guy thinking about? Tarek's warned him about the deals, these contracts that he and his sons skim the cream from. 'Commissions' they're getting—in the billions." Disgust flashed across his face. "Some say getting one of Fahd's sons these days is like buying into the commodities market—a purchasable good with a big return. All the while Fahd seems oblivious to the discontent swelling around him." He pushed his hand through his hair glancing at Elaine. "The young technocrats deride him as a high-rolling potentate. The old tribes, with whom he lost touch long ago, see him as some sort of westernized creature. And the Royal Family? God, the verbal battles between him and Crown Prince Abdullah have gotten so bad I had a call one day saying Fahd had shot Abdullah in a fit of temper. Well, Abdullah lives on but God knows where that might still lead."

Elaine watched while the rest of the limousines followed Fahd's like so many circus elephants. Ray checked them off. "The Family," he mused wryly, "a family that runs a country with enough oil reserves and cash to shake up the international scene more than a bit. A family of now more than four-thousand princes, some of whom are quite distinctly more equal than others, plus un- counted princesses; nobody pays any attention to those."

"How does it work—the progression?" asked Elaine.

"A curious system, actually. The first-born is the heir, that is unless he doesn't quite have the talent, and in that case they move on to whoever is next. A hierarchy-meritocracy. It's worked for a while. They've hammered out their differences amongst themselves and stayed afloat. But now?"

He suddenly seemed oblivious to Elaine, lost in his thoughts. Quiet. All night long after he had left Elaine, the memories kept coming back to him of Kitty, of the old days when they had both come here, young, fascinated. God, the life they had led, the history they had watched happen. He turned back to Elaine who watched him quizzically, waiting for him to continue.

"When old King Abdul Aziz died, he left forty-two sons educated in falconry, desert lore and a bit of the Koran, and his first son, Saud, as king. That was a disaster and thank god they finally moved him out to pasture. Poor bastard shuffled around suites in Egyptian, Viennese, and Greek hotels dying of obesity and boredom still trying to figure out what had gone wrong.

"But Faisal, who followed Saud…Brilliant. Truly a man for the times. He saw where the world and Saudi Arabia were going and maneuvered deftly." He nodded to Elaine, "He saw the stuff in Tarek and brought him up like he was his own. Yes," he shook his head in admiration, "Tarek he taught well." He nodded back toward Fahd.

"Fahd in the early days handled the succession gracefully, did what he was supposed to. Educated himself, took on the jobs the Royal Family decreed for him, and carried them out thoroughly. And when Faisal was assassinated and Khalid, a nice man of no great talent, became King, Fahd became crown prince and did it well. He was nice to Khalid, never stepped in his limelight and did the work behind the scenes. And so finally Khalid died of old age and Fahd became king, and he liked it. But now he's gotten sloppy. Things have gone a bit beyond the bounds and he doesn't see it, doesn't feel it."

Crown Prince Abdullah's car inched up into the intersection. Abdullah raised his hand to wave, smiling at the people waiting for the procession to pass. Some waved back.

"Now there," said Ray, "is a real piece of work. A straight shooter, a bedu at heart. Abdullah goes out into the desert regularly to visit the tribes, a man more at home there than in his palace in Riyadh. And certainly more than in the West, which is alien, in fact fairly bizarre to him." Hell, thought Ray. Maybe it is. Abdullah had gone there a few times quietly to try to get treatment for his speech impediment. The man stuttered, and in the Arab world of leaders and orators, this could ultimately hinder him.

Sultan, the minister of defense, pulled up rapidly. "It wouldn't break Sultan's heart if Abdullah falters. Sultan wants the job, short of a battle in the Family. Maybe he'll get it. And then the remaining 3,997 younger princes will start queuing up. If the whole place doesn't blow into the sky first."

Ray realized with a start how much pain that thought caused him. He became suddenly quiet. This harsh and empty land had become more a part of him than he could usually afford to admit since being sent years ago as a young intelligence officer to keep tabs on the newly emerging country. Not so much the individuals. Most of them had made their own fate—and welcome to it. No, it was the country that mattered to Ray. The sheer beauty of the desert and the way a culture had developed—tough as brush and brutal as rocks, in some ways, but a culture that had enabled people to live here against long odds for generations beyond counting. It was adaptation and determination of an intensity that demanded respect.

And the fact was, Ray thought, it may have meant more to him than it did to some of these pale princelings. Certainly he had seen more of it, been part of it longer than some of them. As American civil servants went, he had pushed seniority beyond all known limits. And most of his career had been spent here.

Elaine had been watching him quietly. He finally turned back to her. "I want to show you something"

"Okay."

He headed the car out to edge of the desert that lay beyond the sprawl of Riyadh and sat there. The magnificent sweep of the brilliant desert terrain spilling before them, the silence almost preternatural. Ray looked at it for the longest time then turned toward her. His eyes seemed somewhere else.

"You know, I wasn't much more than a boy when I first came here." He looked back to the desert. "It was my first assignment as an intelligence officer." A small smile played across his face. "My extreme youth was a mark of how little importance the government attached to the assignment, coming as it did when the world was engulfed in war across all of Europe and Asia."

He thought of that old World War II plane dropping down in the night onto the dusty runway and his first sight of the people, of dark bodies clothed in rags lying on rugs, sitting on the ground, bending forward praying.

"It was like a descent into some nether-world, a warp of history. Tom Barger of the Oil Company met me. 'You should have been here a few years ago,' he said, obviously seeing my uncontrolled shock. 'They were all starving, they had nothing.

When we set up our first oil rigs we brought over a nutritionist to look into their diets. He concluded that they should all be dead.'"

Ray smiled at Elaine's expression. "Do you really want to hear about it?"

"Yes, I really do," said Elaine fascinated by the man, his life. He leaned back, eyes lost in the desert before him, and began the story.

He had gone with Barger and his bedu scouts, crossing the Rub al Khali, the famed Empty Quarter, with one of the tribes as Barger probed for oil. They had moved on camels across a desert sea of a thousand-colored particles, undulating mirages from the waves of heat, violent winds and sand storms, scorching days and cold nights. He had been stunned by the harshness of it and fascinated by the men around him. The bedu of the tribe were lean, spare men, stoic, yet with a whimsical sense of humor and abilities that amazed him. They could smell water and see another man coming miles away across the desert, or hear a twig drop a thousand feet away. They seemed to know the individual tracks of each of their camels. In fact, Ray had realized, most could remember and identify the tracks of every camel they had seen. They would study these tracks and tell him where the camel had come from—smooth tracks if it had come from the gravel plains; loose, soft skin tracks if it had come from the burning Rub al Khali. They could tell the breed of the camel, the tribe it belonged to, whether it had carried a rider. From the droppings they could tell where and when it had last been watered and fed. Their own births, deaths and lives were often remembered in terms of the lives of particular camels.

"The year the Black Camel died," Bin Salim had answered succinctly one morning when Ray had asked the boy how old he was, when he had been born. Bin Salim, his wild black braided hair flowing over the bandoleer strapped across his chest, had nodded thoughtfully and then gone on eating flat unleavened bread. Ray remembered the sounds on that cold desert morning as they sat there by the small fire. The camels lowed gently, lurching up from the sand of the desert floor when the light began to streak the sky. A voice called loudly, echoing across the cold of the desert to wake up to pray to Allah. People stirred in the black tents woven from camel's hair draped with weavings of brilliant reds and yellows, and began to grind coffee.

Bin Salim had looked at him with a combination of curiosity, amusement, and pity. Ray was shivering with cold. Bin Salim stood up and motioned him to follow. The boy pulled a coarse blanket from the back of one of the she-camels and wrapped it around Ray. He himself was dressed in nothing more than a white cotton cloth. He picked up a metal pan and crouched down below the camel's belly. Ray squatted beside the boy as he began to stroke the camel's udder with long, slow pulls. The warm camel's milk squirted into the pan. Bin Salim dipped a handful of figs into the frothing milk and handed them to Ray.

"Eat," he said, with enormous satisfaction at his English word. Ray ate the figs and bread and drank the thin, sweet milk.

Afterwards he had ridden behind Bin Salim and learned how to fill his skin flask with water, to use his cloak like a tent poled above him as he rode. They rode, often for days, between the wells of the central Rub al Khali, where the camels took water, and the bedu refilled their skin flasks. Traveling by some compass in their heads, laying out their black tents to camp, grinding bitter coffee with the mortar and pestle, baking the unleavened bread, and telling the news they had heard from the other tribes that passed.

Barger said that to the best of anyone's knowledge, these people and their ancestors had been moving along the edges of the desert for centuries while other civilizations had ascended and declined: Sumerians, Babylonians, Assyrians in the north; Minaeans, Sabaeans, Hinazarites in the south; Hebrews and Phoenecians to the west; Persians to the east; Pharaohs in Egypt. They had come and gone with almost no effect on the bedu who had a profound knowledge of the other tribes, knew little of the outside world.

One night, around the fire, they had asked Barger and Ray about Christians. How did they bury their dead? Were they circumcised? Did they just take women, or did they marry them? How were their tribes arranged? Ray was intrigued by the questions and the fact that beyond these simple matters they had no interest, nor did they ever doubt their own superiority.

One day while traveling with them, he met one of the most remarkable men in his life. As they came up over a large dune, he saw an encampment sprawling out in front of him across the desert floor. The black tents lay like flecks in a mirage. The heat seemed to shimmer, to float along the bodies of the camels standing still in the burning sun. He could see that the tents appeared to spiral out, surrounding one large white one in the center from which the bedu came and went. The guide next to him called out in Arabic to them and then rode on toward the encampment as they followed slowly. Ray and the others halted just beyond the edge of the tents when the scout returned, speaking briefly to his fellow tribesmen, then to Ray.

"Come, he wishes to see you."

The guards surrounding the white tent, bedu with daggers

at their waists and their red and white kaffiyehs wrapped around their faces, looked at him curiously. One motioned for him to stop. He took the bridle of Ray's camel and told him to dismount. He then waved Ray toward the tent's entrance.

As his eyes focused in the shadows of the tent, he saw before him a wild-looking figure surrounded by bedu sitting on a rug. The man seemed to be extraordinarily tall, towering over the surrounding bedu—probably as much as six feet, five inches Ray guessed. One eye peered keenly from a huge rough-hewn face; the other eye appeared blind. The man listened to the bedu speaking to him, then shot back a question in rapid-fire Arabic. The bedu answered and suddenly the large man leaned his head back and roared in laughter. He raised his arm, and another bedu instantly opened a large chest and began to put silver coins into a bag. He filled the bag, closed the coffer and handed it to the other bedu. The tall man continued speaking; without pausing he dictated something to a scribe, then turned to another bedu. He caught sight of Ray and without a word motioned for him to sit on the rug. A black bedu entered and handed small round cups of cardamom coffee to all, and the man waved for the coffer to be opened again. Once again the silver coins were scooped out and disbursed.

Suddenly the man waved his hand, and the entire assemblage stood up, bowed, and left. The man turned his eye on Ray, now alone with him. He stretched out along the cushions strewn on the rug, then noticed Barger standing by the tent door. He roared with laughter again and, in Arabic, directed him to join them. There was a brief exchange Ray that could not follow.

Barger translated. "He says to tell you he thought I was the only American who could survive in the Empty Quarter, but he sees now there are more." Ray looked at Barger in confusion. "It is Abdul Aziz. He's meeting with the tribes in the desert."

Abdul Aziz spoke again in a rapid guttural Arabic, unfolding a map in front of Barger, who took out a pen and began to make marks on it. "He wants to know if we are finding water anywhere while we are exploring for oil. He wants to have this information for the bedu as he moves about." Abdul Aziz began to pepper him with questions.

"He wants to know if you are a generalist, a spy like the British have been sending for years, or if you have a particular mission. He says he will be glad to be of help if he can." Ray was totally taken aback by the candor of the comment.

"Tell him," Ray said to Barger, "I am simply here to keep my government informed on the overall situation." Barger repeated the comment as Abdul Aziz nodded approvingly and spoke again.

"He says in the thirties, after he had captured the final piece of the Kingdom, Mecca, the Red Sea coast, the north along Iraq, the British were always worried he would go after their protectorates, Iraq, Kuwait, Bahrain, the other small sheikhdoms along the Gulf. He says he was always amused by the spies they sent. It was well known that he despised the Hashemite Kings the British had set on the throne in Iraq and that he worried about the British dealings in Palestine. He says that historically he could make a claim for taking over the sheikhdoms, such as Bahrain, but it would be foolish to threaten such a power as Great Britain. It would jeopardize the Kingdom. But the spies they came nonetheless. In the early days because of all the British trade with the East, now because of the oil."

Abdul Aziz leaned on one elbow and then looked inquisitively at Ray. Barger continued to translate. "Roosevelt, he wants to know your assessment of your President Roosevelt—whether he is strong enough, whether the allies are strong enough to win the war."

Ray felt the man's keen eye observing him. "Tell him Roosevelt is a capable leader, a clever politician. I think he has a chance of succeeding." Aziz nodded thoughtfully, and then spoke again to Barger. "He says he agrees, he wants to meet him." Ray looked up, surprised. "He wants to discuss what the Americans want here—is it just the oil or is it a political base as the British have along the coast? He wants also to talk to him about Palestine. He feels the British may be making a grave mistake there."

Suddenly Abdul Aziz stood up smiling and spoke once more as Barger interpreted.

"He says he is going to the desert to pray now, then to his harem. He would like you to return tonight to his tent to eat with him and to talk."

The enormous figure in his long white thobe with the carved silver dagger at his waist strode out into the desert. Three small boys ran into the tent and peered curiously at Ray and Barger, then ran out again.

"The sons," said Barger with a smile, "they wanted to see you. The older ones, like Faisal, he uses as his lieutenants—posts them in the provinces to oversee things. The younger ones he takes along with him to train."

"How many are there."

"About forty or so."

"Daughters?"

"God knows. Nobody counts."

"What do we do?"

"Stay. Finish the tea. Then sleep. He will kill a camel, and a sheep for a feast tonight for you and then talk all night. He sleeps only about four hours. He worries always about sycophants, that he's not hearing everything. He'll want to talk."

The two bedu guards ushered Ray and Barger to the guest

tent. "Frankly," said Barger as he stretched out, "it's a miracle that the country ever got pulled together. It's been constant warfare here for years between the tribes. But," Barger looked up at the small fly buzzing over him in the heat, "it looks like he's done it."

Ray leaned on his elbow as Barger shook his head in admiration. "Very, very clever maneuvering. This guy managed to capture Riyadh with a few bedu raiders when it was only a small town of mud brick buildings. That kind of moxie impresses the bedu. And then he managed to get some more men to join him by promising them that the spoils from whatever conquests they pulled off would be worthwhile. Very clever, this guy.

"He has a really astute psychological sense about how to appeal to them. They say even in the early days he was always generous with the booty. And when the odds were against them he'd appeal to their sense of nomad superiority and toughness. Finally, he added a dose of religious fervor, explained that they were not just taking the land and the goods of the tribes they conquered but bringing them the Wahhabi creed, the true way of Islam. Pretty soon," said Barger shaking his head again in admiration, "while the British and everybody else were looking to the Arab leaders they thought were going to be the powers, this guy was piling up victory after victory, pulling together long stretches of the Arabian peninsula, and a lot of tribes that used to spend their time fighting one another came under his command.

"Of course you know, his ultimate stroke of genius may have been the way he married the place together."

"Married the place together?"

"Oh God, yes," said Barger laughing, "you know to a bedu the one strong tie in life is family, and the closer the relationship, the closer the bond. Abdul Aziz would go out and conquer the tribes and then take in the children, the widows, marry one of them so they became family. Since the Koran says he can have four wives at a time, he'd marry a daughter, or a widow of a newly defeated tribal leader to cement the ties and then when it was necessary to take on a new wife from another tribe, he'd simply divorce one of the four and send her back to her tribe with gifts. Nobody saw any shame in it for the girl. Marriages have always been arranged, politics understood, in the desert. She'd go back a relative of the king, and if she had a son, all the better. Abdul Aziz would take him in, groom him for a slot, or if it was a girl for whatever marriage made sense to arrange next politically. It was brilliant."

Barger became quiet, and both the men slept in the heat of the tent and woke to the clear night sky of the desert. The bedu guards came to get them. Walking out toward the fire, Ray saw great mounds of food laid out, whole lambs on steaming beds of rice surrounded by dates, a camel roasting in a pit as the bedu from all the tents talked and ate, slowly, reaching toward the platter, rolling the rice between their fingers, pulling a piece of lamb from the carcass as they sipped tea. In the center sat Abdul Aziz, looming like a giant amongst them. He waved Ray and Barger over to him.

"He wants to know if you slept well." Ray nodded and sat down next to him. Abdul Aziz reached out toward the lamb's tail, where a great mound of fat stood, and handed it to Ray.

"He says this is the delicacy—you must have it." Ray took it uncertainly. Abdul Aziz watched in amusement.

"He says eat it with the rice." Abdul Aziz reached out and plucked the lamb's eye and handed it to Ray.

"This is the other delicacy. You must have it. He asks why you didn't bring your women with you. He says it is not normal for a man to be without."

Ray laughed. "Tell him she's back taking care of the children."

"He says you won't have any more at this rate. Maybe you need a second wife now." Barger leaned toward Ray in amusement. "He's teasing you—he knows the Westerners have only one. Thinks it's crazy, but knows. If you were a Muslim guest he'd give you one of the slave girls. But they won't give a Muslim girl to a Christian. We're considered unclean."

Suddenly Abdul Aziz leaned forward, speaking to Ray while Barger translated.

"He wants you to tell him more about Roosevelt, how he works, his leadership and management style. He wants details."

Ray began to talk of Roosevelt, operations now during war time as Aziz listened intently, uttering not a word for the next half hour, waiting in silence for Ray to continue every time he stopped, until finally Ray was exhausted. Abdul Aziz then leaned back before the fire with a satisfied nod of his head. He turned to Ray and began to talk again through Barger.

"Tell your people that Saudi Arabia has held as such since 1932 and it will continue." Abdul Aziz was relaxed. "Tell them that the Sabah family in Kuwait has ruled in one form or another since the 1700's and, with British aid, they will continue. Iraq has always been interested in taking the territory—but the British have control over the Iraqis and they can keep them at bay.

"The little island of Bahrain," he continued, "has been ruled by the Al Khalifa family also more or less since the 1700's, with the British behind them. Sultan Said bin Taimur rules Oman, as has his family for years. The sheikhs ruling the seven emirates down the coast, have all ruled for years with the British behind them."

He leaned back on his elbow. "Now, the question is this. The British came in years ago to police the piracy in the Gulf, to protect their trade coming from India. They worked with the local rulers, then took over officially after World War I, setting up 'protectorates' with the various thrones—the exception being this country, since we were considered too desolate to bother with.

"Now I see the allies winning this war—but with the Americans emerging with the power the British have had. And I want to know what you want."

Ray hesitated, admiring the man's relaxed, clever delivery. "That is an answer you should have from higher sources than I, sir," he said.

When Barger repeated this in Arabic, Abdul Aziz smiled. "Excellent. Arrange it." With that, he stood up. "We go now. It is better to travel at night. The other tribes are waiting. Come to see me when you have answers."

Ray looked back at Elaine who listened, fascinated, by the story. He went on "I can still see him in those meetings we had throughout the years that followed. Meetings in the desert, in the old palace in Riyadh. Meetings as World War II ended, as the oil money started to flow in. As the British began to crumble financially, as they finally pulled out of the Gulf, setting up the ruling families in Kuwait, Bahrain, the sheikhdom of the United Arab Emirates as independent states—as they packed up and went home, their Empire in India, the Middle East at an end.

"God, Abdul Aziz maneuvered brilliantly amidst the chaos of these small countries surrounding him, all of them trying to stabilize themselves in the new independence, the new oil-rich economy. And then I watched him grow older, saddened when he finally stopped having sons. To this day I can still see him near the end, sitting with Roosevelt, two old lions at the war's end deliberating the fate of the Middle East on the shipboard meeting they held on the U.S.S. *Quincy* in the Red Sea.

Roosevelt had developed an admiration for him, a man who had emerged as such a power in the Middle East and arranged to meet with him in what would turn out to be some of the final days of the American President's life." Ray looked back at Elaine and smiled.

"Oh, god, I can still see Abdul Aziz, traveling to the meeting as always in true desert fashion, his entourage of hundreds crossing the desert carrying sheep to slaughter for feasts, gifts, coffee servers, wives, sons, aides. When he finally reached the ship, they hoisted him—he was fairly crippled by then—upon his throne on board the *Quincy* where the equally crippled Roosevelt was waiting for him on the deck. The two men found an instant affinity and talked into the night, laying the plans for the Middle East that neither would live to carry out, mercifully oblivious to the chaos that now seems unending in the region."

Elaine, completely absorbed by the man's words, watched as he fell silent again. Abruptly he turned to her.

"I got through to Cheney. I'm trying to get him to fly over."

Elaine looked at him, startled. Ray nodded at what he knew she was thinking. "Yes," he smiled mirthlessly. "Called the Secretary of Defense, Cheney, then followed it with a call to the Chairman of the Joint Chiefs of Staff, Colin Powell. Turley back at headquarters almost detonated when he found out. I figure, fuck it. I'm also working on Tarek to try to get the king to meet with Cheney when, if, he comes. God, this is a nightmare." He now became dead serious.

"Elaine, as you know, I had to bring Jack and the fellows in on this, but so far the rest of the staff at the Embassy accepts the premise that you have been assigned to help monitor their computer operations, nothing more. They find you bright, good in briefings, and somewhat remote. They assume that's because you're a beautiful woman who doesn't want to get involved in embassy liaisons and affairs. I also," he continued quietly, "got a chance to catch up on the rest of my reading last night. On you. I didn't know the part about your husband being killed. I'm very sorry. That must have been rough."

"Ray, I don't want to talk about it..." She could hear her voice cut him off almost violently.

Ray stopped her. "Elaine, I know what you were about to tell me today. That you want to go."

She stared at him, totally caught off guard. He pressed forward. "I didn't know about your husband when I put the request in, or I probably wouldn't have done it. It's almost cruel. I admire you for having gone this far, and if you feel you have to go, I'll accept that. "But," he stopped. "I'm asking you not to. I'm asking you to stay and work with me." He shrugged. "What makes it so bad for you is precisely what makes you so good for us—you know too much, you're perfect for this."

She started to say something but he cut her off.

"Elaine, I know you can't give me an answer really. Just stay one day at a time, as long as you can. That's all I ask."

Elaine felt everything inside of her tearing apart, screaming to go, yet his earnest plea, the totally unexpected speech stopped her.

"One day at a time, that's all I ask."

She seemed unable to speak. Finally, with an almost imperceptible movement, she nodded, yes.

Ray started the car and began the drive back. They returned in silence. Ray pushed open the door and simply stared at the monitor from the KH-11. Just as he knew they would, the Iraqi troops kept moving. She turned to rejoin the technical crew.

"Are you going to be okay?" asked Ray gently.

"Yes."

Nothing more. She turned and walked out of the room. Closing, thought Ray, a conversation she still couldn't have. The clipped tone covered the kind of pain he could still remember. The kind of pain that had taken months and months, maybe years, to fade. And for her, an additional scar that ran so deep he could only imagine. He thought about the call he had put in to Turley at headquarters about her.

Turley's voice had been its usual concise self. "She's technically brilliant, Ray. Beyond that she's not only well trained but tough—she did some clandestine collections stuff in Beirut that was unforgettable. But what happened in Beirut—well, she blames herself."

"Do you?"

"Oh god, no," sighed Turley. "But did that ever make a difference when a person...?" His voice trailed off, then continued, "I knew how badly you needed her so I acted like it was nothing—her going back to the Middle East."

And finally Ray thought about his last words when he asked the question. "Has she talked about it—what happened in Beirut?"

"No. Never. Absolutely never."

11

At 3:00 P.M. that afternoon Elaine returned with the material she and the techs were coming up with. Walking into the office she saw Ray drop the telephone receiver after another fruitless call to Washington. His face was somewhere between despair and disgust. He looked at the materials she was carrying. Elaine's voice was low, "Ray, these are showing convoys of troops now encamped in Basra. Tents, armor, equipment, supplies back at the rear…"

Ray cut her off. "Take all the reconnaissance materials we have to Tarek."

She wheeled around rapidly to face him, clearly upset. "Ray we don't want to turn this material over to him—to give this to him."

"As of right now, we do."

"But Ray, normally we…"

"This isn't normal," he snapped. Then he looked at her apologetically, exhausted. "Look, I'm sorry. But I've just gotten off the phone with Turley. Washington still insists nothing will happen. Elaine, about Tarek, I trust him. What you've got to understand is that we have to trust him. Now," he muttered, "if we can only get him to trust us."

Her expression was completely distressed. Elaine started to say something else. Then Ray pointed up to the monitor of the KH-11. Elaine fell silent at the sight of the Iraqi troops moving, inch by inch, toward the border. Without a further word, she put all of the satellite reconnaissance photos, the intercepts they had been able to glean that seemed to have any potential, and the results of their technical review for leaks in a defense satchel and called the driver. Within minutes she arrived at Tarek's office. He was waiting for her.

He opened the door for her and then spread the material out before him on his wide desk. She watched for almost an hour as he moved over it, this man whom Ray trusted so. Dark, deep intense eyes pulling it in, his hand quickly making a note, a mark. There was a leanness, an economy to his movement. A rapidity that was followed by stillness. His face was a series of strong even planes; as the light hit it, it seemed to alternate between harshness and elegance. He scanned the report on Iraqi armaments first, then picked up the first and second shore radio intercepts, compared them to the sixth, and glanced at two points on the satellite chart locating the Iraqi missiles. He turned to her and fired off two questions that left her amazed at his absorptive capacity, and then went back to the printouts.

When he finished, he called for Badr, issued instructions for more analysis, and turned back to Elaine. For several minutes, waiting for him to speak, it occurred to her with a discomforting start that there was an intensity to him that drew her closer, a stillness about him that fascinated her. She had the feeling of a man layered so deep that no one might ever truly know him. She looked at him, wondering what was at the core. What drove a man so controlled? She was startled from her thoughts by another unexpected question.

"Why have they sent you for this job?" His voice was abrupt. "Tell me about your background. Ray mentioned Beirut, Washington."

Elaine watched his eyes, nearly motionless as they seemed

to absorb her. She hesitated, then remembered Ray's words, "…if we can only get him to trust us."

"I was assigned to Beirut in 1979 as a communications specialist working for the National Security Agency," she said. "Intercepts, decoding. The original assignment was to work on our operations regarding the PLO."

He waited for her to continue.

"The PLO was in control of Muslim West Beirut—they ran it like a separate little city. The Christian warlords held East Beirut. We were focused then on the Palestinians. The PLO." She stopped, looking at him curiously. "But you know all of this. Why…"

"I'm interested in your perceptions, not mine." His eyes didn't move.

"You knew Robert Ames in Beirut?"

Tarek nodded.

"Ames, the CIA, had set up extensive secret contacts with the PLO. Arafat passed him information his operatives picked up from time to time. He always used a Lebanese intelligence officer to deliver the information so everybody could deny the contact. Beyond that we got a lot of good information by taps on the Palestinians' phone calls. My job was to monitor them, make sense of them."

Tarek listened as Elaine continued. "What we weren't tracking very well, were the Shia. They were considered a relatively unimportant factor by our people at the top."

She stopped and shook her head. "It might have remained 'unimportant' if we hadn't blundered so badly from then on."

"What do you mean?"

"When Israel decided they wanted to drive the PLO out of Beirut in 1981, the U.S. said, essentially, we won't stand in your way." Elaine shrugged, "So the Israelis took that as a go-ahead.

They bombed the city, devastated it, cut off electricity, water, supplies. All of this carnage was inflicted with American-made weapons while the rest of the Arab world watched. They drove Arafat out—the Marines took him and boatloads of PLO off to Tunisia. A few weeks later Sharon and the Israelis communicated that there were still PLO and weapons in West Beirut and he wanted to clean them out once and for all." She stopped and looked up sadly.

"Sabra and Shatilla. They massacred seven-hundred men, women and children. Reagan acted horrified and sent in the Marines to 'protect' the citizens of West Beirut from the Israelis and the Phalange. But that was the final straw. The whole fundamentalist movement became stronger—and focused against us. We managed," she said with irony, "to unite all of these disparate pieces—Palistinians, fundamentalists—against us."

Tarek listened intently. "It was then that we began to work on intercepting the Shias' communications. But," she pushed her hair back over her shoulder in frustration, "our intelligence was so poor. We didn't know anything about Khomeini's people before they took over Iran, and we still didn't have agents in place when they began moving out towards new targets."

"One day I intercepted a cable and decoded it. It was from the Iranian Foreign Ministry to their embassy in Damascus. It indicated there was to be a major attack on the U.S., but it didn't have the date, the means. The multinational force in Beirut intercepted a second one. I showed it to my husband."

Tarek stared at her, "Your husband...?" But she raced on.

"That was the first bombing—the van loaded with explosives that drove into the U.S. Embassy with the suicide driver. It blew up and killed three of our best CIA operatives."

"And the second bombing? When they killed three-hundred Americans?"

She suddenly stopped. Tarek waited for her to continue, watching the tremor that ran up the line of her cheekbone. Her eyes involuntarily shut for a moment. "I don't want to talk about that." She was clearly agitated. "I'm sorry, I should go now."

He stopped her. "And what about London, Washington?"

She answered, her voice now dull, dead. "Intercepting communications and parts for the Iraqi nuclear weapons. They were moving trigger devices and other parts through London. We stopped a major shipment at Heathrow. It's quite possible, however, that they've managed to design their own." Tensely she moved to leave.

"And Washington?" he pressed on.

"A final run-through on technology for communications intercepts, computer security. They seem," she said with a twist of sarcasm, "to feel I have something of a talent for it."

"And now you are back," he concluded for her.

She halted, angry at being inquisitioned, interrupted, on edge.

Her words shot back at him, "Yes, you get the intercept and you can stop a nuclear bomb, an attack from being successful. They get it and you can lose a war and every man and woman fighting it." She looked at him. "Or lose a country." She stood up angrily to go. "Look, I don't have to answer questions from you."

He absorbed her anger with total equanimity. "No, you don't have to."

She stared at him. Suddenly he pushed his chair back and looked at her quietly. His eyes seemed to question, to look for something far below the surface. His voice matched the near silence that now surrounded them.

"Miss Landon, I have said something, asked you about

something that has upset you. I am very sorry. I did not mean to do that." His eyes took in the tremor that ran again through her cheek.

His voice continued quietly, "It was when I mentioned your husband, then the second bombing in Beirut. Your husband is also an intelligence officer? Tell me a bit about him."

For a moment she felt the walls of her defenses slide away and the almost overwhelming vulnerability of what he had touched upon engulf her. She looked at him, the dark intense eyes. She started to speak, at once upset and yet at the same time drawn to him, confused by the feeling that she could somehow trust him.

"I have difficulty," her voice was shaking "talking about…"

He interrupted her, his words now even more quiet, "You don't have to talk about anything unless you want to."

"I didn't ask to come here," she whispered up to heaven, to nothing, to the silence of the room. He said nothing, and yet there was a compassion to his stillness that reached her, leaving her the silence to compose herself. There was something about the man that came so close and yet didn't move. She now felt overwhelmed by confusion, and started to gather the papers she had brought.

"Leave those," he picked up the phone and spoke briefly in Arabic.

"I'm having a complete report drawn up on the oil terminal outage—I'll have it over to you in a couple of hours."

She stared at him, now completely surprised. His hand reached out and picked up a small cassette.

"I want you to listen to this. I want you to understand who these people are. It's a tap we have on one of the cells. I want you to understand completely what you're involved in here." There was almost a brutal directness to his eyes, now clocking every nuance on her face, every infinitesimal movement she made.

Elaine bent her head closer to listen with him. He watched her expression as the sound came on. The cassette scratched; then came the voice of a man whispering as he walked into the room. "We will pray."

"Allahu Akbar." The prayer swelled through the room, then stopped.

"This is the moment," the voice continued. "The cells, the tactics we will now turn on the corruption, the inequities, the injustices perpetrated by those who attempt to rule us. On the infidels from the West who support them. We are one now. We will succeed.

"Some of you will be operatives. Some will merely carry the messages. God will show us over time who is suited for which tasks. Some elements of our mission we will accomplish now; other elements may take years, but we will prevail. It is God's will, we will prevail." For a moment, the silence was eerie, an echo.

Now a second voice swelled up to fill the room.

"The basis of the power of those who rule you is fear. Your kings frighten you. Your bejeweled whores imitating western whores inspire in you a sense of awe. You are scared even of looking at those palaces where every imaginable act of lust is practiced day and night. You dare not cross the road when those huge, expensive limousines appear while the poor, their 'brethren,' walk in the dirt, working for them, begging help from them. You are scared of asking where all that money comes from—money gambled or spent on voluptuous blonde women." The men murmured; the voice on the tape rose to a cry. Elaine felt her nerves tighten.

"If terrorism, extremism mean defense of our religion and

honor, we welcome terrorism. Does not Allah command you to kill those who rebel against His will? Are you incapable even of using a simple knife or a simple shotgun? Think! Act! O infidels from the West, infidels from within, Jews—Islam, Mohammed's army is coming!" The voice on the cassette stopped. The sound of footsteps; the man had begun to walk through the room.

"Your names are secret here. But the road before you is not secret. It is your will that is to be tested, your strength. We know of no absolute values besides total submission to the will of the Almighty. People say: 'Don't lie!' But the principle is different when we serve the will of Allah. He taught Man to lie so that we can save ourselves. People say: 'Don't kill!' But the Almighty Himself taught us how to kill. Killing is tantamount to saying a prayer when those who are harmful to the Faith need to be killed.

"Deceit, trickery, conspiracy, cheating, stealing and killing are nothing but means. For no act is either good or bad isolated from the intentions that motivated it. Look at this kitchen knife. Is it either good or bad? With it a housewife can cut the meat she needs for food. A miscreant could use it to end the life of a true believer. And a soldier of Islam could use it to pierce the black heart of a harmful one."

Elaine could hear the sound of the knife touching the mike.

"The means are there. We need only," he breathed, "the will."

Now the sound only of footsteps leaving the room. And then a voice as the last one left.

"Allahu Akbar."

Tarek continued to watch Elain's expression after the sound had stopped. He picked up the tape and put it away.

"Miss Landon, this is what we are fighting. This and Antar.

This is what I am fighting. You may decide that you don't want to be involved." He then leaned closer to her.

"Miss Landon, I've asked you many questions about yourself. I've told you very little about myself. There are those of us who are struggling to create a new Middle East. Those of us who are desperately trying to pull our part of the world from the turmoil, the agony that has engulfed it. I am seeing far beyond the day in which there is an Arab-Israeli peace, I've worked throughout the years with every means I have to bring this about. We are struggling here to move from the past, to create a decent path to the future. I believe it is possible."

His words, their intensity, startled her. He paused, watching her closely. "I also believe that if you choose to help us, you could make a difference. I also think that if you don't, if you choose to walk away from it now, it will follow you to the ends of the earth anyway."

She stared at him, completely taken aback by the stunning brevity and power of his words. She stood up to go, shaken, every emotion in her body now at odds with the next.

He walked with her down to the car waiting below. He opened the car door for her.

"Miss Landon," his voice was then quite gentle, quite matter-of-fact. "Just an additional, small note. If you are going to use the cover of cultural attaché, you are going to have to move around the society a little more. It will hardly be plausible otherwise. Forgive me, but I have been tracking your movements—suspicions about you endanger us all."

She interrupted him, amazed. "You had me followed?"

"One has to be a bit ruthless in this job, a bit careful with whom one is working." He shrugged pleasantly. "I'm going to have someone take you around."

Elaine's eyes widened. And then she started to smile. She

looked at the man standing in front of her. Impressive, yes, very impressive. Fascinatingly agile. Elegantly ruthless. She liked him.

"Miss Landon, the report on the outage will be over to you shortly."

12

Tarek watched Elaine go, then returned to his office He picked up the phone. "Badr, get in touch with Musaid. He called to say that they were finished with the check on the system outage. Tell him to deliver a copy of the report to Naif—he should be back in Riyadh by now—one over to Fahd's office, one to Elaine Landon in Ray Holt's office. Our men went through the check with him—they found absolutely nothing."

Badr immediately reached for the second line and dialed.

Musaid listened to Badr's instructions, pleased to be asked to present the report to Naif, looking, as he always did for a way to enhance his position with the minister of the interior. True, the report had found nothing, but it was clearly a well-done professional piece of work that should make a good impression. He gathered the report for his meeting with Naif and scrutinized the computer monitor as the final spreadsheet appeared. Engineering schedules were complete for the week, the daily outputs summed up, even the new dollar fluctuations in gas and oil shipments. He glanced at his watch. It was a remarkably faster program. Over the past year it had made a tremendous impact on his level of efficiency as assistant director of operations for the sprawling new multi-operational industrial complex. He listened to the satisfying hum of the machines. The command structure was a near miracle. All of the functions, from the most minute to the most complex—electricity, water, air conditioning, communications, automatic conveyors, tank loaders, docks, now totally centralized, adjustable at the touch of a key, running the petrochemical operations and the basic functions of the whole complex on automatic pilot day and night. He liked the machines, felt a kind of personal affection for them. Their reliability, controllability pleased him; their predictability soothed him.

He switched the terminal off and leaned back in his chair, silhouetted by the young technocrats in thobes seated before rows of terminals outside his glass office. He saw them begin to gather in front of a small portable TV set. Curious, he went out to look. The face of Colonel Oliver North, defiant and self-righteous, filled the screen while his voice rose in response to a question by the CNN interviewer on the anniversary of North's congressional hearing. "The arms shipment to Iran was carried out."

Abed bin Osman mimicked North's mid-atlantic accent, "was carried out by making an asshole of Saudi Arabia. As usual, the U.S. not only bungled the job but compounded the damage by discussing it and Saudi Arabia's participation on worldwide television night and day. President Reagan, of course, slept through it all."

Musaid listened uncomfortably to Abed bin Osman. He left while the report and Abed continued amidst disgusted guffaws. On the dusty street below, a long-limbed dark foreign woman, leaning against a shop window, smiled up at him. His mind flashed for a moment to the moans of the American girls, girls who bedded strangers, sucking and screwing through the night. The images rolled uncomfortably through his head, along with Colonel North's face, until he pushed them back. He considered for a moment the level of hostility against Fahd throughout the ministry, rampant now among the young technocrats. It occurred to him that it might be time to say something, to indicate that these comments were not appropriate. Abed bin Osman's comments in particular made him uneasy—these kinds of things shouldn't be said in the office. He made another note to mention Abed again to Tarek. It occurred to him that he might also point out Abed to Naif.

He walked toward his car, passing the hajjis squatting on the ground, wrapped in rags, cooking dirty, greasy food. An endless stream of humanity flowing out of the bowels of Africa, Asia, the Middle East, disgorged from boats, planes, trucks onto the sands of Saudi Arabia, heading for Mecca.

He looked at the outstretched hand of one squatting in the dust, the amputated stump of another sprawling listlessly on the ground while a child peed in the dirt. To beg, to steal, to crawl toward the stone of the prophet. To sell rugs, trinkets, even their children to gaze upon the black rock from which the prophet had ascended. Past weary government bureaucrats checking them through to Mecca, past cars with paint smeared on the windshield, "Go home America," with pamphlets, cassettes stuffed in their pockets, the dirty, the disenfranchised, the disaffected, the thieves, the rich, moving toward Mecca day and night beneath the eyes of nervous officials. Moving toward the ultimate symbol, the seat of the Islamic world.

He entered a massive building in the center of Riyadh and opened the tall wooden doors to the reception room. Deep-blue velvet armchairs lined the sides of the room, forming a processional toward Naif, Minister of the Interior, who leaned uneasily in the throne-like chair. Clusters of old men in dusty white thobes with worn daggers at their waists and kohl along their eyes sat side-by-side with young, freshly pressed bureaucrats and university students, all with papers in hand.

"Talal bin Sultan," called an aide. A petitioner, a young man with a starched white collar on his thobe came up.

"Hamoud bin Khalid." Prince Naif's face settled into a look of exhaustion.

"There he sits," murmured the young man sitting next to Musaid, "imitating the majlis of old, like some lost haggard dinosaur stranded in a time warp in downtown Riyadh." The next paper was thrust into the hand of Prince Naif, son of Abdul Aziz, while the Riyadh traffic screeched outside.

Musaid waited patiently until Naif was finished with his majlis for the day. He stopped him, with a small apology, and handed him the report. "If there are any questions I can answer, Your Excellency, I'd be pleased to do so."

Naif smiled, glancing down at the gift Musaid had given him a few weeks ago. The handsome Boucheron watch had been enfolded in Musaid's note, "With deep appreciation for all of the support and help you've been to me throughout these years." Naif said a few words of warm thanks and disappeared down the hall.

Musaid knew what he thought. A nice boy, but without the real stuff, or for that matter the career path ever to make it big. Competent, but never really brilliant. Rigid, authoritarian to his subordinates—which had rankled more than a few over the years. Ah well, they had taken care of him as best they could.

Musaid moved on for the rest of his rounds, to personally deliver the report to Fahd's office. The guards stood armed with machine guns outside the Royal Palace. "Papers please," said one of the guards tersely. "Prince Musaid, sorry for the inconvenience, please." He opened the gate and let the Mercedes through. Musaid got out and climbed the marble steps between walls of armed guards with walkie-talkies. More guards checked his papers and opened the doors into the high-ceilinged entrance.

As Musaid started down the hall, the doors of the king's chamber opened and Crown Prince Abdullah emerged talking to Foreign Minister Saud while Defense Minister Sultan trailed behind with the king. They walked past him, without stopping. Musaid's mind went back to the TV earlier. The technocrats in his office and their comments about Saudi Arabia sucking up to the United States, pandering to the West, all the while being used by the West as a cash box, a milk cow, to fund dirty little projects they couldn't pull off themselves in the Middle East. Comments that they had become the laughing stock of the world—Saudi Arabia, the piggy bank, the puppet of the United States. No, he would have to put an end to such comments. It was one thing to make comments favoring a conservative social order, quite another to publicly deride the king and his government. Perhaps, in fact, he'd let Abed bin Osman go, just give the reason as "cutbacks in the staff." He made a note to let Tarek know of plans to dismiss Abed.

Again, he thought back to the television screen earlier. Once again the faces of the women and Colonel North all seemed to collide in flash-backs through his head. He got back into the car and headed for his modest house.

A woman without a veil stood outside the women's quarters. She looked up, startled to see him. She quickly put her head down and hurried back into the left side of the house, apologizing as she went. Another one of Khadija's friends, he thought. Sloppy of her to be seen that way, disrespectful. The door cracked open again and now two little girls looked out. "Baba," the little one in the frilly dress called. The smaller one tottered behind her. Musaid patted them on the head and shooed them back.

Khadija stood in the doorway behind them, looking apprehensively at him. He nodded but said nothing; they went back in and closed the door. He thought momentarily of going to look at the infant and then felt the lassitude creeping over him again. He walked over to the other side of the house and up the stairs to his private study on the far side of the house. He took the key from his pocket and unlocked the door. He opened the door to the dark green room with the long shutters drawn and lay down on the bed. He thought of something, pulled his pocket calculator out of his thobe pocket and began to work a few numbers on it.

Immersed, he was surprised to hear a small knock at the door. "Yes?"

Slowly the door opened. Khadija stood there holding the infant. "Musaid?" Her eyes looked at the floor. He said nothing. "Musaid," she repeated timidly, "The baby was born two weeks ago, and I thought," tears started down her face, "I just thought you might want to see her; she's very pretty. Musaid, it's been two weeks and you've never come to see us."

He looked at the frightened expression on her face. The baby made a whimpering sound. His wife disgusted him. Khadija waited, standing silently in the doorway. He motioned angrily for her to stop bothering him. Embarrassed, she walked away. He returned to the work he had brought home to finish.

He sat for a moment in the cool of the room. He opened his desk drawer and pulled out a small sheet of paper, turned on the computer in front of him and waited until it went through its start-up routine, then began to tap in the letters, the numbers. His fingers tapped silently back and forth as he scanned the sheet. He left a memo for the office regarding cutbacks, firing Abed bin Osman. He recalled the material and checked it for errors, then moved it and waited. The small signal sound came. He picked up his pen and jotted down the letters and numbers that appeared on the screen, double-checked his notes one last time, then turned off the computer.

He heard the distant echo of the muezzin calling the eternal prayer from the mosque. He placed one last call, leaving a message to let Naila know he would be by in the next day or two with details on the engagement party. Then he closed his eyes, sleep easing upon him.

13

Badr came into the office early in the morning. "Hamid just got through. The U.S. Ambassador's 'secure' meeting yesterday in the Embassy has already shown up in Baghdad. The rest is troops, arsenals, orders for escalated production of weaponry."

Badr continued, a look of concern flickering across his face. "Hamid says he's going to have to be careful for a few days. Saddam has become paranoid again about those around him. A whole new onslaught of purges are under way—his military, the guards..."

"Any word from Hamid on Osman's son Abed?"

"This," Badr thrust the sheet at him. "That Abed may have been up in Baghdad, may have met with Abu Nidal, done a few sessions with the terrorist operations. He's checking it out." Badr held out a small audio cassette. "I thought you might want to hear this. It's from a tap on the cell meeting a few hours ago. Abed was there."

Tarek put the small cassette in the tape player. The tape scratched for a moment and then they heard a man's voice.

"The plans are proceeding accordingly. Antar will notify you shortly about details." The voice stopped and then went on. "We could not do this without your help. Your access, information, is invaluable to the success of the operation."

Tarek strained closer, listening for the sound of a voice replying. There was none. Only the faint sound of footsteps leaving the room.

"Osman knows nothing about Abed's activities?"

"Apparently nothing at all."

Osman excused himself from his three guests playing cards on the verandah of his expansive ranch outside Riyadh, to get a bit of work done. He glanced at the small van driving down the long desert road that led to the ranch, and then continued on toward the study, to the sound of the telephone man working on the side of the house. He stretched, enjoying the feel of his trim body. On the way, he passed a little Pakistani serving girl carrying a tray of drinks. The Pakistani was a sweet thing really. He had noticed her before. He simply liked women, and women liked him. Each one fascinated him in her own different way. Sophisticated European women, strong-limbed American girls, this shy Pakistani. He enjoyed discovering how to please them as they gravitated toward him. He enjoyed their loveliness, like the art collection he had amassed. He gazed up at the paintings, and then turned to the business before him.

At his desk, Osman worked quickly through a sheaf of memos from Said, the head of the Gulf Bank. He went to work on them, initialing orders, signing letters, penning directions in the margins. He opened the summary of his portfolio at year's end. U.S. holdings: 6.8% of First Chicago Corp.; 5.3% of TransAmerica Corp.; 5% of Thermo Electron Corp.; 4% of Occidental Petroleum; 1% of J. P. Morgan & Co.; 1% of Chase

Manhattan. He turned the page to European Holdings: 20% of British Consolidated; 22% of Moorgate Investment Trust. He had four wholly owned Saudi companies: an investment house, plus insurance, construction, and transport firms.

He listened to the radio, the reports of the Iraqi troops. Listening closely now, he considered whether to move more of his money out of the Gulf. He sat back in his chair and picked up a small quartz paperweight. Now, he thought, despite what the Kuwaiti emirs and Fahd say, fear dances in the air like beams from a prism. For years, he had invested large sums abroad. The Saudi government itself had put so much money into the United States that it had become the largest single holder of U.S. Treasury notes. That had made sense, but now it was different. He looked at the amethyst tones of the quartz, then back at the flow sheets. Kuwaiti money flooding into Great Britain, the money that had gone into Bahrain when Beirut had collapsed as a banking center, was being wired straight into Switzerland. Now the fear was palpable. The computers moved money and stocks day and night. He would move a bit more money, to Switzerland.

An antique fan from his old family home in Jeddah turned in slow circles above him. He thought for a moment of the old days in Jeddah, when it had been a sleepy port town, water carried through the streets in barrels. Mail via cargo boats from India once a week. The world had seemed remote and far away then, before the flood of oil and money and the resulting chaos.

He listened to the radio again for a moment. Was it possible that someday as suddenly as it had appeared, it would vanish? Even he felt the unreality that hung over them, the deeply embedded psychological sense, even when times were good, that anything that came in such a way could disappear in the same way. No, he turned back to his portfolio, a calamity might befall the Kingdom, but private fortunes would survive—those that had been carefully hedged and diversified. As his had been, he thought with satisfaction.

Osman stopped by the paddock first before returning to his guests. He bent down to pass his hand along the white colt's long thin leg. With the touch of a connoisseur, he examined the finely chiseled head and the large eyes of the skittishly prancing colt, while the radio in the stable updated the news of Iraqi troops. On the other side of the paddock were several Arabian brood mares. Beyond, stretching away like a dark ribbon between white fences, was the exercise track. Osman's head trainer was bringing a promising two-year-old toward them at a gallop.

"This one is ready?" Osman asked the bedu boy holding the colt's halter.

"He's strong," the boy said. "And he likes to win." The boy wrapped his kaffiyeh around his face against the dust the trainer's gray horse kicked up when he flew by. "Rashid's son in the U.A.E. may have bought up a lot of horses in Europe last year, but he doesn't have one like that."

The boy rubbed the colt's neck, then led him past the other trainers, grooming and exercising horses in nearby paddocks, back to the stable. The boy and the colt quickly moved to the side of the road when a white Mercedes sped by them.

Abed got out, barely glancing at the horses, and approached Osman unsmiling. Osman tried to kiss the boy on both cheeks. Abed stiffened, held back almost imperceptibly. Osman seemed taken aback, then continued on as though nothing had happened.

"What a nice surprise, Abed," he said. "You come to visit out here so rarely. Look at this one, Abed—he's fabulous," Osman said as the gray horse circled back. Abed shook his head. "Ah," said Osman, "forgive me, you are in a hurry? Abed, at least you have time for a drink." He started to guide the young man by the arm, toward the verandah of the house, but Abed shook his head impatiently. "I'll be back in a few days."

Osman nodded. "That's nice—to see friends?"

"Yes," he shrugged. "Don't bother with any calls I might get. I'll take care of them when I come back." Abed crossed the verandah and disappeared into the vast house without speaking to the three women playing cards at a small table. Osman watched him go, then returned to the verandah.

"Any chance Tarek will join us?" Osman queried pleasantly.

Nura simply shook her head. She played another card, deep green eyes in total concentration. "He's working all the time now."

"Well," said Osman charmingly, "at least he had time to introduce me to the beautiful new cultural attaché at the American Embassy the other night. Have you met her?"

Nura shook her head.

"Oh, I saw her at the wedding. She was with the Ambassador's wife," said Sana, a Palestinian friend of many years, with a note of admiration. "Tall, slim, blonde and very beautiful. Osman will almost assuredly fall in love."

They all laughed, then stopped at the slam of the door within. Osman stiffened.

"Was that Abed?" Sana asked.

"Yes, Abed."

"He won't even have a drink with us?"

"No." Osman sat down next to Dina, his mistress. He stroked Dina's leg absently. "He's upset because they laid him off at the ministry. Cutbacks or something. Apparently," he glanced at Nura, "Musaid had something to do with it." Nura looked away uncomfortably.

"Was he also upset because he knew you brought me back

136

with you from Beirut again?" Dina asked.

"He didn't know you were here until just now. If he noticed at all."

"Somehow I think it's more than just Dina he disapproves of, Osman," Sana said archly. "Some of these young ones have become so conservative now with all of their fundamentalism." She ruffled the newspaper before her. "This new group they are writing about, 'The Generation of Arab Anger'..." She clicked her tongue, scanning the story of the young terrorists.

"They're not entirely without a point."

Osman, Sana and Dina turned in surprise at Nura's words.

"Nura," Sana was shocked, "you don't mean that you agree with them?"

"I didn't say that." Nura looked back to her cards; the brilliant light seemed to cut a line along her beveled cheek-bones. "I said they are not without a point. There is a certain amount of substance to the grievances they are pointing to—never mind the solution, that is a different thing." Nura's eyes looked at them as though the truth of her words was obvious. "Nothing political emerges that strongly without a certain point to it. Otherwise as a movement it would simply die, be something so peripheral that it would be unimportant."

"Yes, but Nura...," Sana started to interrupt.

Nura's even gaze stopped her, fixed upon her. "Surely, we have ills as a society. We could talk about them, couldn't we?" Her hand reached out to place a card on the table; her voice now seemed lost in thought. "We have such a history of silence when we should have spoken."

Sana stared at her. Osman's voice flashed in anger. "But what is so wrong for Abed, I ask you? I'm asking you this! Everything seems to bother Abed. Nothing pleases him. Anything I can give him, he doesn't want." The pain in Osman's

137

face was mingled with bafflement. "He wants nothing to do with business." He motioned his hand toward the vast expanse of the horse ranch, "None of this interests him. I don't know how to reach him." His eyes turned almost pleadingly to Nura for an answer. She only shook her head, then reached over and took his hand. Osman struggled to compose himself as the servant announced that lunch was ready to be served. "Should we wait for your husband?" Osman asked Sana.

"I think he must not be coming, Osman," Sana answered. "The bankers must be running late today. You know, chérie, I think they are all starting to worry about their money here in the Gulf. You think something's going to happen?"

"A lot of people are starting to move their money—if that answers your question," Osman said, directing the servant to begin serving lunch.

"You are flying to the U.S. to look at a new piece of property?"

"Just a quick trip. It's a few small islands off the North Carolina coast, for development into resorts. We buy them, build them, get an American agency to run them. With the dollar down, it's a relatively cheap purchase—anyhow, safe."

"Did the Ambassador arrange it?"

"The previous ambassador, the one you see at all the parties," Osman laughed. "He began cultivating me heavily after I made a large donation to the Metropolitan Museum in New York."

"For more charity?"

"For his own charity, shall we say. He is, it seems, quite interested in money. You remember the other ambassador? The one a few before this one? He practically viewed the Embassy as a personal base to stack up current and future business contracts. The President finally had to bring him home, call him on the carpet and tell him no more or he'd pull him out." Osman chuckled.

"You are disillusioned, chérie."

"Ah, my dear Sana, people are people. It is only natural. I never expected the Americans to be any more, any less."

"I saw Naila the other night," Sana said, changing the subject. "She has come back to be married, Nura?"

Nura nodded as she ate a pomegranate.

"Forgive me, I know a little about women," Osman interrupted, "and Naila does not look like a woman who is at all interested in the marriage Musaid has arranged for her."

Nura remained silent. Osman, comfortable in the years of their friendship, continued; he was genuinely disturbed by the turn of events for Naila. "Such a shame really. Why not let the girl stay in America and finish her studies?"

"Musaid, the brother, is a difficult sort, isn't he?" Sana mused, mindless of the position in which her comment placed Nura.

Osman glanced at Nura and gracefully moved past the point. "Well, Naila I've always liked—a lot of spirit, independent, and yet very warm. Ah well, I hope it works out for her. She won't have much choice really, will she?"

"No," said Sana as she looked at her watch. "Chérie, I must go. Nura you're driving back with me aren't you? Dina, darling, good-bye."

When they had gone, Dina caressed Osman's face. "You are leaving this evening?"

He bent over and put his hand through her long auburn curls, "Can you come with me? I'll fly you back to Beirut when it's finished."

She smiled. "I'd love that."

He gently touched her face. "I'll be back in a few minutes."

Osman walked into the house, down the hall, and then stepped quietly into a room where the shutters were closed against the midday sun. He walked softly, so as not to disturb the old man sitting in a chair, asleep. He patted the old man's shoulder. Outside he met a servant bringing a tray of coffee. "My father is sleeping," Osman told the servant. "Do not wake him."

He listened to the car door slam outside, saw the white Mercedes drive off. He watched the dark lean face behind the wheel, the unyielding intensity that seemed to burn within this second child. The intellect that had always flashed from the boy, the deep eyes always searching, seeming to look inward and outward at the same moment for a reality.

I have had it all, and it is Abed who is left with the fears, thought Osman, with a feeling of compassion for the turmoil of his younger son. *I have lived through the era of the great surge forward, the escalating successes. We have changed our world, and now it is Abed who is left with the earth rumbling beneath him. And what has it created? A mind, a soul straddling too many worlds. He looks in the mirror and sees not a single person, but an amalgam of pieces, East, West, a constantly changing middle. A being on the periphery, borrowing. Talking to his friends about pride, about his Islamic heritage, about the dignity of the past. Talking to me at night about how the Saud family should rule no longer because they have lost the way of Islam. I say they are men, no better, no worse than others. The intensity, the anger?* Perhaps, thought Osman closing the ledger, *it is just youth; it will pass.*

He walked on down the hall, to the master bedroom door. Dina was stretched across the bed, auburn tresses across the pillow, waiting for him.

140

Badr pushed open the door to Tarek's office, where he and Elaine were working through the afternoon on the reconnaissance photos of the Iraqi troops increasing along the border. Badr walked in.

"Hamid's report on the revolutionary training camps has just come in. You want me to go through it?"

Tarek nodded.

"Do you want me to go?" asked Elaine gathering up the reconnaissance on Iraqi troop movements they had just gone over.

"No, stay," said Tarek. Badr began to read Hamid's report.

"Volunteers, as they are called, are sent from over thirty countries. Students, between the ages of eighteen and twenty-five."

Elaine listened closely while Tarek made a note, and then nodded for him to go on.

"Usual training for guerrilla and sabotage work, indoctrination, physical endurance. Graduates are assigned to patrol guerrilla units throughout Iraq; others are sent to cells needed throughout the Middle East."

Badr looked down at the report, scanning. "Ah, here," he looked up at Tarek, "the specialty training categories and their locations in Iraq." His finger began to move along the map. "Here they specialize in military, para-military training, terrorist operations. This one specializes in training women from various Muslim countries. Here is the one for specialists in hijacking Boeing 727's and 707's and other civilian aircraft. This other one does training for Enteharis, the 'suicide attackers.' It says there is a current program under way, training pilots for suicide hits against major vessels in the Gulf."

Badr looked up from the paper. Elaine remained dead silent, her expression almost blank. Tarek glanced at her

141

curiously for a moment while Badr continued speaking.

"I'll leave the rest of this for you. There are some reports coming in from your bedu scouts about possible cell activity in the desert quarters." He held another spreadsheet from Hamid. "The compilation on Baghdad's publications and cassettes. Antar's operations," Badr began to read.

"Publication divisions…headquarters in Rome…copies of three-hundred different books, booklets created in French, English, Turkish, Arabic Italian…weekly newspapers printed in Netherlands, Britain, U.S., distributed to thirty countries. English monthly out of London, weekly in Lille, France, a biweekly in Toronto." He flipped the page. "Sound and video cassette division…operating in London. More than a million sound cassettes, approximately a hundred thousand video cassettes. Arabic, Urdu, English, Persian, Turkish…. Fronts: Islamic institutes and associations. Pakistanis heavily involved as cover for fronts in Europe, North America. Main office London, Paris, Bonn, Madrid, Brussels, Rome, controlled from Baghdad. Various safe houses with arms caches."

Badr dropped the sheets on Tarek's desk.

"Tarek, what do you figure on Abed? Is he delivering messages, information from here? Getting assassination orders? Delivering plans and diagrams from his old job at the oil installations? So Antar can mark targets from the inside, blow up the oil fields? All of the above, what?"

"Any of the above. What I do know is that as long as we leave him out there we're a lot closer to information than if we bring him in and they turn whatever he's doing over to someone far harder for us to trail."

Badr nodded, then turned when he reached the door. "What does Fahd say?"

"He says we have a deal with Iraq."

Badr shook his head slowly and started to close the door behind him. "Is Ray coming up with anything on the communication leaks?"

Tarek looked at Elaine, then back to Badr.

"No."

Exhausted, Elaine stood up, gathered together the material they had been working on, and walked slowly out the door.

❈ ❈ ❈

Badr got ready to leave for the night. On his way down the hall the delivery boy handed him a cassette. He read the label while Tarek reached out for it. "The cassette's from Rashid, the tap he put on Osman's. It's from earlier today. It says the voices are of Osman, Sana, Dina, your wife Nura."

Badr put on the cassette. They listened quietly to Osman's concerns about his son, to Sana's comments about the younger generation. And finally to Nura's voice speaking softly, "They are not without a point...we have such a history of silence when we should have spoken." Tarek's head turned slightly at the words. They finished listening to the cassette in silence. Badr walked down the hall and returned it to the file with the rest of the material Rashid was sending over.

14

Tarek sat into the night with the papers Elaine had left—the information from Hamid. Finally he put them down. The risk of the decision he had been wrestling with was enormous if he was wrong. He picked up the phone and placed the call. Ten minutes later the car with the Gulf Bank insignia pulled up. Said walked in the door.

Said stood for a moment at the entrance, the deep, even planes of his face reserved, unconsciously handsome, magnetic. Tarek reflected one last time on what he was about to do. For one last moment the risk if he was wrong stopped him, the eternal questions reeling through his mind. Could you ever truly know a man—know with certainty that there were no breaks in his persona, that he too couldn't be bought? And yet Said had proved himself trustworthy at every turn over the years. They had gone to school together in the U.S. and then Said had stayed on, first in the U.S. and then in Europe, negotiating major deals for the bank. Said, a man from a prominent merchant family, had risen over the years to finally head up the bank. A man of total integrity. A rarity, thought Tarek, in the banking world of the Middle East. And beneath his banking empire he had managed to move money for Tarek, unbeknownst to anybody else. Money for agents, for operations that were for no one else's eyes. Deeply trusted and, perhaps, Tarek's closest friend.

"Said, I want you to do something for me, immediately, quietly. I want you to run some checks on money moving from the Family. I need to know if you see anything unusual, any movement."

"What exactly are you looking for, when you say 'unusual'?"

"An agent," said Tarek, "an agent in the Family being run out of Iraq."

Said looked stunned. "In the Family?"

"Yes." He paused and looked at him intently. "This is without Fahd's knowledge or authorization. Do you understand?" He stopped and quietly put his hand on his friend's arm. "I want you to understand the risk, to you, to me..."

"I will begin tonight."

Said started to go. He glanced at the picture on Tarek's desk, Tarek standing with Nura and Naila. An odd shadow crossed his face.

"Tarek, Nura is well?"

Tarek glanced up, surprised, "Yes, she's fine. She asked about you the other day."

"Someone mentioned that Naila is back?"

"Yes, Naila came back. I'm afraid it was more Musaid's doing than hers, but she's here." Tarek watched curiously as Said seemed to linger on the photo. Then he left for the limousine waiting below with the Gulf Bank insignia on it.

145

The doorman looked up, surprised to see Said standing outside the large glass door at this hour. According to the huge onyx clock above the bank's majestic entrance, it was almost midnight. Bowing slightly, he admitted Said. Said moved to the elevator, unlocked it himself and disappeared without a word.

The elevator reached the top floor and then stopped. He hurried down the deserted corridor, its suede walls hung with modern art, the wool carpet swallowing the sound of his passage. He reached the tall oak door of his office and put his key into the small lock next to the scripted brass plaque that read SAID GHARASH, PRESIDENT GULF BANK. The door opened onto an unbroken expanse of glass and chrome that encircled his enormous desk at its center. He thought about what he had to do.

He opened a small panel inside the desk drawer. The tiny green lights blinked up as his fingers pressed the numbers. He thought of the faces behind the numbers—Abdullah, Sultan, Saud, Naif, as the printouts began to pour forth from the private computer in the paneled enclosure in a steady flow, multiple sheets of multiple accounts for each person, different names, thousands of wire transfers, stock purchases, nameless credits, debits, a history of staggering sums of money moving all over the world. Sheets that told the story of the financial monolith that Saudi Arabia had become.

And, thought Said, as he gathered them up, sheets that told nothing about where much of this money had really come from, before winding through channels and bank transfers all over the world, before departing from its stated point of origin, what any of these corporations really were even once you traced the transfer back that far, a process that could occupy an entire team of humans for months. Said put the sheets into large brown envelopes for Tarek.

He tapped a final set of numbers on the tiny blinking panel of lights. A faint click sounded and a drawer hidden in the paneling of his desk slid open. He opened it and looked down at the folder he would *not* be taking to Tarek.

He reassured himself of the repeated recent transfers of money from Riyadh into the New York bank, closed the folder, and looked at the tiny initials in his own handwriting at the top. The folder marked "N.S." slid silently back into the drawer, and a small lock automatically clicked shut.

He looked out of his window one last time at the panorama of Riyadh beneath him. He thought of the career he had built, the impeccable relations, and now what he was doing. The trust he was betraying—even Tarek's. He thought about the folder marked N.S. that would not be going to Tarek. Was there any love worth this much? He knew, as he closed the door, the answer was "yes."

☒ ☒ ☒

Elaine worked through the night on the new transmissions that had just come. Ray called to say there were even more and he would drop them off on his way home. Elaine reached for the satchel of the material that she had spread out on Tarek's desk earlier to double-check some of it. She opened the satchel and pulled out the mounds of paper. As she began to sort it into piles she saw a small leather-bound journal. She picked up the journal with the gold initials N.S. stamped on the hand-tooled leather and curiously opened it to the elegant pen script inside. She moved through a few pages and saw, after various entries, the signature Nura Saud.

She realized, as she put it down, that she had inadvertently pushed it with the rest of the papers from Tarek's desk into her satchel. She started to put it back in the satchel to return it to Tarek when she heard the knock on the door.

Ray stood there with a fresh mound of paper. "You look exhausted."

Elaine nodded wearily and appreciatively at the gruff older man's concern. She reached for the transmission printouts he handed her. He started to go.

"Ray, do you know Nura Saud?"

"Tarek's wife?" Ray turned to her surprised. Elaine nodded.

"Yes, I've known her for years." Ray shook his head in admiration. "One of the most fascinating women I've ever met. She was sent to school in Switzerland with King Faisal's daughters, then went on to study philosophy at the Sorbonne, where she was a brilliant student. Also one of the most beautiful, stunning. Deep politics, passions—never the expected answer, if you know what I mean. Truly, a mind to match Tarek's. That kind of intriguing ability to move between all of these worlds. Or," he laughed, "schizophrenia, which is what the situation here logically calls for. I'll introduce you sometime. Get some rest. See you tomorrow."

Elaine closed the door and started to turn the light out. Instead, she hesitated, then reached over and opened the small gold-embossed book with its elegant script inside. It seemed to be divided into segments. She opened to the first one, simply marked "Islam"—and was immediately intrigued by the words.

When Mohammad was in his forties, he retired to meditate in a cave on Mount Hira outside Mecca. There he heard a voice, the Angel Gabriel, which ordered him, commanded him 'Recite: In the name of the Lord.' Mohammad, frightened, pleaded his inability to do so three times. But each time the angel repeated the command. Slowly Mohammed began to speak, began to recite what would become the first five verses of the 96th chapter of the Koran. He realized then he was to be an instrument of divine will.

By the time he died, his followers numbered in the thousands, his Arab armies constituted the most powerful military machine the world had ever seen, an army that used the deserts where others perished much as maritime nations had used the sea. Soon the empire covered Syria, Egypt, Armenia, Persia, and North Africa. And by the beginning of the 11th century, they carried Islam west to Spain and east to China and Malay. Until they had created the greatest empire in the world, a world of might, of learning, of intellect, of art.

A world that held sway and dazzled and then slowly, slowly slipped back into a dark night of decline and chaos. Left with the word of the Koran, and searching, waiting for the Angel Gabriel to whisper once again. They stand, whispering their deeds out loud, whispering, waiting. The stillness of pillars of salt, the rumblings of columns of armies assembling. Whispering, waiting."

Elaine read on, fascinated now by the story.

I grew up in my father's tall house by the Red Sea in Jeddah with its wooden lattice screens, along with my sister Naila, my brother Musaid, and quite a number of aunts and uncles. I see it now in my mind as I believe it was, although memory and perception are illusive things. I close my eyes, and

149

I see again the tall house, five stories against the Jeddah sky. The wooden floors with the deep blue and sand colored rugs from Isphahan strewn across them, the burgundy of the dark weavings from the north, the shutters closed against the sun. I see the shadows from the latticework playing along the walls, the thick, pale green damask curtains pulled back at the doors and the gold samovar with its deep red coals and its smell of tea. I hear the soft gurgling sound of the pipe as the pale smoke rises from the tall stem.

And I hear voices and footsteps, like shadows of sound through the quiet afternoon. Footsteps of the servants, footsteps of the man carrying water to my aunts on the top floor, footsteps of the people in the streets that I watch from behind the shutters, peering down at the donkeys carrying peddlers' wares standing in front of the house, flicking their long tails at the flies in the afternoon heat. And voices murmuring in other rooms above me, calling out on the streets below, talking to someone as they walk past the door closed behind me. Ya Ahmed, Shokran Zainab, Maharba, Salaam Alekum, the words of the little songs, fragments of refrains of children's songs, footsteps disappearing down long halls and winding staircases, they weave together like some endlessly circling, spiraling tapestry of sound. A tapestry blowing softly in the stillness of the heat against the sound of the water, the sound of the dhows rocking and groaning on the torpid waters of the Red Sea port.

Perhaps it is from this stillness, this flow of sensibilities that I am formed. Tarek, I know, has often wondered at me, so "self-contained." I smile, I think that is interesting, for ultimately one is indeed self-contained. Reality seems more a movement, a crystal prism from which each draws his or her own reflection, chooses from the same small shaft any refraction, any color as it turns. For me the senses are not really separable.

It seems impossible to me to structure the senses, to define their roles, truncate the possibilities. I have watched women who enjoy other women lying at night on the deep silk cushions in the women's quarters. Stroking one another, petting each other until you can hear their soft moans, and then returning to their husbands whom they enjoy in a different way, a different form of sexuality.

Tarek has often said I live to my own rhythm more than most. Perhaps he is right. Many nights I have sat here feeling the night breeze along the silk of my robe, listening to the soft sounds of the palms brushing against the house, thinking of the voices, the faces of those around me, of the unreality we are living in now. The old ones who remember when their world was poor, closed to the outside. The young ones overwhelmed by so many possibilities, so much wealth. I see the old, the young, now facing one another across this chasm of reality, their world having lurched from dire poverty to enormous wealth on a whim of fate. I see them picking through the debris of this reality for an identity, all the while wondering if this world, this whim will lurch again beneath them. The fear that pervades, sifting through lies, grasping at formulas.

I feel that time is short now, closing in on us like a vise. Time is short now.

The question has become whether I or any of this will continue much longer in the same way. Or whether it should. But this other cannot end well. What they are submerging will surface. It will surface.

I am as I stand at this moment. I understand I am surrounded by great wealth. I understand it may disappear tomorrow, and then something else will happen. And like the smell of the samovar, the sound of the water in the tall pipe, this will be another moment disappearing in the past like smoke slowly wisping, disappearing in the haze. I will remain. Something else will happen.

Elaine marked the page and closed the book—fascinated. There was an intimacy to the woman's words that drew her back to the small book. A curious layering of thoughts beneath the thoughts. She put it down, wanting to meet the woman.

She looked out at the silent Riyadh night, thinking of the world that it had become. A world, a society so precariously balanced between the old and the new that the movement of a breeze could shatter it. The schizophrenia of trying to truly live in it, a world reeling, out of necessity, from the eighteenth century into the twenty-first. The soft Riyadh desert breeze gently moved through the room as she looked down again at the pages. The reference to Tarek. She sat there thinking of Tarek as a man. The elegant intellect, the physical, raw side to him that seemed always to linger just below the surface. There was something disquieting about him, something unsettling. Something she realized that struck hard at the walls she had erected around herself.

She looked back at the small journal and thought of this woman who slept with Tarek, wondering what she would be like. And then, as Elaine finally reached over to turn out the light, the face of the man she had slept with through the years until he had been killed came to her. The pain of the loss for a moment was incredible. She felt her body almost double over from the blow, from the emptiness of the room.

In the silence came the sound of the phone. She picked it up.

"I forgot to tell you," said Ray. "Tarek left a message. He wants you to meet his wife's sister tomorrow—to take you around for your cultural attaché thing. Her name is Naila."

15

The faint tone of the clock sounded in the stillness of the room. For a moment when Naila started to wake up she thought she was still back Washington. Then, her eyes moving over the white marble, the antique shutters of the bedroom, the Baccarat chandelier, she remembered that she was indeed back in Riyadh.

Since her return, time had felt almost a blur. Days turning into nights of endless small teas, visits with family members, with women friends. Seeing their children, hearing of their lives, their marriages. There was a sense of déjà vu as the old faces reappeared. There was a sense of the surreal as she was drawn soundlessly back into her past, back into the world that she had left. Slowly, silently being drawn, woven back into a world, a past, a seamless silken cocoon of a thousand threads.

The room was still, the shutters closed. The pale white marble, the draped silk of the room that had once seemed so graceful, so cooling against the desert heat, now seemed softly sepulchral. Her black abaya draped over a chair, a shroud, separating her finally from the life of the recent years. And as she had moved through the days and nights here she had felt endlessly, relentlessly, minute by minute torn. This was her world—and it was not.

✠　✠　✠

▲▲Dr. Naila, may I...?"

Naila looked up to see the little Pakistani housegirl watching her quietly, standing at the bedroom door. She entered with a tray of coffee, breakfast, and flowers.

"Dr. Naila, you asked me to wake you early since you begin at the hospital today." Naila suddenly smiled, remembering that was why she had woken up thinking of Washington—hospital. She sat up and thanked the girl who brought the tray over to the bed. The little housegirl started to walk out of the room and then turned hesitantly.

"Also, Dr. Naila, your brother Musaid is downstairs to see you."

The smile faded. Naila drank the coffee for a few minutes in silence. It suddenly occurred to her that he had come to try again to stop her from going to the hospital today. She dressed, apprehension and anger now warring with equal force to take over her. She walked down to see him. His thin face barely seemed to look at her. She braced herself.

"You had a nice evening last night, some women over to visit?"

"Yes." She heard her own voice, tentative, waiting for him.

"I just wanted to let you know I've announced the engagement and that the engagement party will be in a week. Your fiancé is returning from his business trip in a few days, so you'll be able to meet him then." The thin smile played over his face for a moment.

Nura walked into the room behind her and listened along with Naila.

"You'll be pleased to know," continued Musaid, "that since

the announcement many people have commented on what an advantageous match this will be." He waited for Naila to say something.

Silence, her voice, her eyes were silent. He stood staring at her. Finally he turned, irritated, and left.

Nura watched him walk out the door. She went over and touched Naila's arm. "Come darling, we will have a coffee," she said softly, "and then send you off to your first day at the hospital."

Naila shook her head, held Nura's hand for a moment, then put on her abaya and walked outside to the driver waiting in the car.

The car arrived at the entrance of National Guard Hospital about twenty minutes later. The director of the residency training program was waiting for Naila in her office.

"This is a little rushed, coming as you are at mid-term." She leafed through the papers. "Let's see, you finished medical school and did two years of ob-gyn and then pediatrics at Children's Hospital in Washington." She looked up curiously, "That's one of the world's best. You decided not to finish there?"

"Yes, I decided not to finish there."

The woman waited for Naila to continue.

"The family felt…"

"I understand, never mind. We are pleased to have you with us; your record in the States is excellent." She adjusted her black scarf around her head. "In general your work will be in the clinic." She stopped, took off her glasses.

"There will be some differences here from the States. The classes, of course, are strictly segregated; the men are in another building. If it is necessary to use a male instructor, it will be on video. The National Guard Hospital is a beautiful new facility with excellent equipment. But of course your patients will be only the families—the women and children. Many of the patients come from remote parts of the Kingdom, the villages where life hasn't changed as much as it has in Riyadh."

She stopped, then continued, concerned.

"Naila, you've been out of the country for some time; we are in very sensitive times. We've made tremendous progress over the past few years, by not trying to force everything at once. The strides have been enormous in a relatively short time. The girls are educated—high school, college, if they want, even medical school. But you are going to hear fundamentalist discussions about women's role being only in the home, to bear children and so on." She looked at Naila, embarrassed. "Try to do as the rest of us have—we work quietly in hopes that we won't lose ground."

She stood up. "You'll begin seeing patients at the clinic."

Naila entered the marble and brass lobby of the National Guard Hospital, adorned with huge portraits of Crown Prince Abdullah and King Fahd on the wall, and pushed open the door marked FAMILY CLINIC. She took the charts from inside the door pocket and told the nurse to send in the first patient.

❊ ❊ ❊

Across the city, Elaine moved side by side with the two techs on their makeshift team, searching the equipment. Ray buzzed her to come up at once.

"I got through to General Schwarzkopf," said Ray. "He's head of Central Command. He's about the only guy in the military who's been focused on the Middle East rather than the Soviet Union. He's been following the reconnaissance of Iraq's troops. He agrees with the analysis that you and the techs are coming up with here.

Four days ago there were Iraqi troops in tents near Basra, with armor, equipment, and supplies back at the rear. Today they're fanned out toward the southeast and southwest of Basra, pointing themselves toward the Kuwaiti border. Now if he can only get someone in either the State Department or the White House to wake up."

Elaine held out the latest reconnaissance and intercepts that they had compiled that morning.

"Ray, the armor has moved forward; the equipment is deployed by units that can use it—the helicopters by the special forces units, the pontoon bridging equipment next to the Marines." She gathered up the material and started to put it in a Defense satchel.

"You're going to Tarek's?"

Elaine nodded. She returned to Tarek's office, bringing him the information, and stayed with him while he moved through the material. She watched his expression growing stiller, deeper. When he finished he handed the portfolio back to her; she started to go. His next words caught her off guard.

"I've made arrangements for someone to take you around. You need to be more visible as cultural attaché, people are already starting to ask questions. There is a young woman doctor," Tarek continued matter-of-factly. "Her name is Naila." He wrote the address and concluded succinctly, " She is my wife's sister."

Elaine glanced at the paper. She looked back at him, amazed at the control of a man who knew what he had just read and still was able to keep every thread on track. She started to put the address in her pocket when the name struck her.

"Did she just come back here from Washington?"

Now it was Tarek's turn to be surprised. "Yes, but how did you know?"

Elaine smiled, feeling a sudden rush of warmth at the thought of seeing the young woman from the plane again. "We flew in together. She was lovely. Told me a bit about the history of the country, some about her medical studies."

Tarek, at first surprised, smiled as she spoke, then gazed quietly down at his hands. "I don't know if she told you anything about why she was returning. I don't know, Miss Landon," he looked up at her thoughtfully, "how much you know about the customs in our country. But here we have a tradition of arranged marriages. For some it works out well—there is a saying, 'Love follows in time.' For others it probably is a sentence in hell."

Elaine was touched by the sound of resignation in his quiet comments.

"Naila," he continued, "is one of the young women who has truly moved forward, her studies, her medical career. However, in the customs here, it is more than time for her to be married. She can refuse, but she is under tremendous social pressure to say yes. Since her father is dead, it is her brother whose place it is to arrange it."

"Is it that she doesn't care for the person she is to marry?" asked Elaine.

"She doesn't know him," said Tarek simply. "Some who marry do know one another from inside the family; they've met at social functions over the years. Others don't—the family picks the fiance and they meet shortly before the engagement party, which for Naila will happen in a few days. And for Naila," he finished softly, "it seems to be a sentence to hell..." He looked at Elaine, "When I got back last night, I went to ask her if she would be starting at the hospital soon. And I realized

159

she was inside her room crying.

"And so," his voice was quiet, "I have something of an ulterior motive here. I think you could be a good friend for her—just as she could for you. Shall I tell her you'll be by to see her at the hospital?"

She stood for a moment, studying the man in front of her, the sensitivity of his words, the grace of his approach, his perceptions.

"Yes, please tell her I look forward to it."

That afternoon Elaine's driver moved through the sprawling Riyadh traffic for half an hour, finally reaching the National Guard Hospital. The receptionist motioned her down the hall when she asked for Naila.

The door of Room 2304 was ajar. Elaine could see the back of a woman's head inclined toward a small figure, wrapped in bandages, sitting in the bed. The woman's hand held a playing card. "You top that one and you've beat me, but I don't think you can," she said teasingly.

The child instantly popped a card out from somewhere in the bed. "Dr. Naila, I win," the tiny voice crowed. Naila, stethoscope around her neck, recoiled in mock horror.

"Another riyal! Allah, I have lost another riyal to this fellow. I think he must be too smart. I am afraid to play him anymore." She cupped her hand under the child's chin.

"Dr. Naila, we play again tomorrow, OK?" said the small boy, deeply pleased with himself.

"All right, we play again tomorrow. But watch out, maybe my luck will be better then."

"Maybe not," replied the boy impishly. Naila burst out

laughing. She turned around, and Elaine felt a wonderful warmth upon seeing the face of the young woman who had sat next to her on the plane from Washington.

Naila's eyes filled with delighted as she recognized Elaine. "How wonderful! I never thought I would see you again!" She broke into a big smile.

Elaine, equally delighted, shook her hand. "The little boy looks like he's having a good time despite all the bandages."

Naila's face saddened. "Yes, you spend days and days working with them, trying to get over the fears." She smiled at Elaine. "Though I think you're right, this little fellow is starting to come out of it. Maybe if a I lose a few more riyals to him...." She took Elaine by the arm, smiling warmly. "But come, let's have a coffee and you tell me about you, and how you have been. Tarek tells me I am to be your guide."

Naila started to walk with her to the door. Suddenly the stat alert sounded. Naila's head turned quickly to the sound. "Elaine, can you wait just a few minutes, perhaps in the hall? That is an emergency alert, and they have called my code." Elaine nodded and stood back.

Naila moved rapidly toward the woman's unit. She pushed the door open—under the glare of the examination room lights, a young woman lay on a gurney clutching her protruding belly. She was heavily veiled; her hand marked with a tribal tattoo. Beside her, an old woman with leathered hands stood confused.

The Pakistani nurse thrust the chart at Naila. "They are from the provinces. The brother is waiting outside," she quickly ex- plained. "The mother says the girl has a stomach tumor and..."

The girl screamed. Fluid began to cover her skirt. "My God," Naila exclaimed, "she's..."

The director came in and rapidly cut her off.

"Scrub in," she said curtly, as she directed the old mother out to the waiting room.

The young girl's breathing now came in short gasps. The director looked at the girl's hands, as the anesthesiologist, a stocky Korean woman, bustled in. "Not married," the director said to Naila in a low voice. The terrified face of the girl contorted again. "Move fast. This baby's coming."

The nurses pulled off the girl's abaya and clothing. "They thought this was a tumor?" Naila was incredulous. The infant's foot began to emerge. "It's a breech. Check the baby's heartbeat."

The girl seized Naila's hand. She stared up at the lights. "The baby's in trouble," Naila said when the monitor began tracing the fetal heartbeat. "Pulse rate is around 70. We should do a Caesarean—now."

The anesthesiologist set to work. "They will put you to sleep," Naila said, bending close to the girl. "The baby is having problems. We must try to take the baby, quickly and safely." She held the girl's hand, "It won't be long now."

The nurse began prepping the abdomen with Betadine while the anesthesiologist applied the EKG electrodes to her back and the oxygen saturation monitor on the girl's finger. The anesthesiologist injected a sedative, followed rapidly by a medication to relax the girl's muscles during the procedure. A breathing tube was placed in the girl's trachea, and the girl's lower abdomen was isolated with sterile drapes.

"All right to start?" asked Naila. The anesthesiologist nodded, and Naila began the incision. "There, there," she whispered, "just a few more minutes, just a few more." She stood back. A nurse was ready with the retractors. "All right," she said quietly, "now…"

Naila moved her hand deftly inside the uterus. She felt the infant move as her hand closed around the slippery child. She checked the monitor, bent over the open abdomen, secured her grip for a final moment and then stood up straight, bringing the newborn infant into the light.

"A beautiful boy," Naila said, passing the infant to the nurse to suction the mucus from its mouth. The baby let out a healthy cry, its entire body turning bright red in an instant. "He sounds strong, too," Naila smiled as she removed the placenta.

The anesthesiologist tapered off the medication, and the girl began to regain consciousness. Naila whispered to the nurse. "The old woman must be worried. Tell her the girl is fine—the baby is fine too, a boy."

Naila held the baby for the mother to see. The girl's face turned to the side of the table and flooded with tears. Naila bent over, wiped the girl's face, and spoke gently to her. "You may hold him for a moment."

The girl reached up uncertainly and brought the infant down to her body. His tiny hands curled around her finger and his little head nestled in the crook of her arm. The girl looked at Naila bending over her with the infant and closed her eyes, sobbing. She held it, caressing its tiny head while she looked into its little wandering eyes.

Suddenly the nurse pushed through the door, a look of horror on her face, "The mother, the brother, I told them…," she stammered.

"Oh no," the director exclaimed, understanding the calamity in a flash. "You didn't…"

"I told them," gasped the nurse, trembling, "that we had just delivered the baby, both were well, and…" She stopped at the sight of the girl's face, now frozen in terror.

"Go on," snapped the director.

"And they want them killed," whispered the nurse. Naila stared. "They said she has shamed the family, the tribe…they say that we should kill them both, the baby, the girl." She stopped, then, finished, horrified. "This is barbaric. They can't mean to, no one could..."

The girl's face was ashen. She clutched at Naila.

"They can, and they will," the director said. "She is from one of the border villages up north. In the provinces the old ways still hold. The family, the tribe. They believe that she has shamed them, the baby has shamed them. They feel the honor of all demands they be brought to justice." She looked down at the small infant moving its tiny fingers. "That baby, the girl, they will be dead before the week is done. Unless we..."

She looked directly at Naila who stood, shaken and pale beneath the lights. "Are you willing to lie?"

"What do you want me to do?"

"I want you," she said in a measured voice, "to go through that door and tell the family the nurse is from Pakistan, she doesn't understand Arabic well. That she gave them the report from the wrong operating room." Naila stared at her. "Then you tell them that we have just finished operating on the girl for the tumor. Tell them she'll be fine now, that the tumor is gone, and she will be able to go home after a few days. We will cover the records," she looked to the anesthesiologist. "And take the baby to the ward until we find it a home."

She looked down at the girl holding the infant. "You will not have your baby, but he will live. And you will live."

She turned back to Naila. "You will do it?"

Naila turned toward the door. She looked back at the director for a moment. "You are sure? This is the only way?"

"Yes," she said wearily, "I am sure."

Naila found the young man standing beside the old woman, his body was stiff with anger. "Please sit down," Naila said, professional authority flowing into her words. "There has been a mistake..."

When they had gone she felt her legs go elastic. The reality of what had just happened shook her.

Elaine watched Naila emerge, stunned by the look on her face and the subsequent story she told her. Still shaking, Naila led her to the door. They got into the car.

"Take me to Tarek," Naila's voice was barely audible.

"It is barbaric," she whispered. She was silent, then finally looked at Elaine, agonized. "That girl, that baby—they are viewed as possessions to be done with, not as people. I grew up here—it is my country, my people, my customs. And yet being away you see it so clearly, the horror of some of the old ways. You see it finally through the eyes of the rest of the world, and you can't abide it any longer. I am back, I am here and I feel so torn—I don't belong anyplace anymore...not in your world, not in the world I'm returning to." Her eyes shot up to Elaine. "You must find this hideous."

Elaine started to say something, but Naila continued. "And," she said, seeming to look inward now, as her eyes caught Elaine, "do you know what I am? I am someone who has everything. And who has nothing. I have been brought back, like a possession, to be married to a man I've never even met. To stand up at an engagement party in a matter of days, to put aside whatever genuine feelings of love I might have had for a man," her voice suddenly choked, "and to walk lock-step as the possession of a stranger for the rest of my life. And to be asked to accept the kind of thing you've just seen at the hospital as right." Her voice broke, tears flooded her eyes.

Elaine picked up the hand of the lovely young woman and held it as Naila cried.

"I am so sorry," Naila whispered. "Tarek asked me to show you the culture, and this is what I've shown you. You came to be helped, and I've done nothing but inflict my own pain on you."

Elaine shook her head. "That's all right," she said softly. "I carry some of my own. Of a different sort. I am very glad to be here with you. I think you have more courage in dealing with yours than I do with mine."

Naila gazed at her questioningly but Elaine now seemed lost in own thoughts as the driver made his way toward Tarek's office.

Tarek stood in his office looking at the mass of paper that had just come in. Then he began to lay out the sheets that Said had given him—the secret numbered accounts held by Said's bank for Abdullah, Sultan, Saud, and Naif. The documents rolled out like a sea of paper in front of him, with endless numbered electronic wire transfers of money flowing all over the world. Nameless coded transfers moving in and out of nameless banks and accounts.

He tacked up the long furls of paper until they covered the wall. Then he began to write rapidly, scanning down the sheets. First the designator codes for the different Swiss banks followed by the individual code numbers of the accounts that electronic transfers were most frequently moving in and out of. He marked the code numbers that had been uncovered recently, the others that showed a longer history, erratic large sums of cash, and those with steady small streams. When he heard Badr's footsteps behind him, he ripped off the top page of his notes, covered with the markings, and gave it to Badr.

"Start with these. I want to know who all of these numbered accounts belong to. If it's an individual, I want an entire history on him. If it's a corporation, I want to know where they are chartered, nature and location of sales, who the account allegedly is—and then who it really is.

"The real identity of the holders or those numbered accounts won't be on the Swiss computers, only in writing, so you can't get the information by simply putting a tap on their computers. Use a tap to trace further transfers. To ascertain the initial identity you're going to have to apply to the Swiss government for access to closely held information."

Tarek handed Badr another sheet. "I don't want you to do it directly. No fingerprints, no possibly visible flags going up in those circles to alert anybody. Do it through Sam Nathanson in Swiss Intelligence. He'll know how to take care of it so it's never traced back to you."

"You trust him?"

"Enough. The import won't be lost on him. Besides, he owes us a few." Tarek turned back to the sheets and continued writing. "There are some numbered accounts here based in the Netherlands, Liechtenstein—Nathanson may be able to help you on those too. The ones I'm sketching now from Japan you can probably handle by simply working over the top brass there—a bribe, whatever."

Badr studied the sheets covering the wall. Tarek's hand moved rapidly along them, marking off large sums wired, and the small but steady transfers. "I'm looking for large sums for unidentified arms payments, beneath that a regular flow for operating cash for the cells inside." Tarek pulled out a piece of paper and quickly drew a zigzag of slashes across it between points. "If Antar were smart he'd move it something like this. Iraq to New York, New York to Montreal, Montreal to Saudi Arabia."

"If he were smart," muttered Badr wryly as he gathered the papers. "Yes, if only Antar were smart instead of fucking brilliant." Suddenly the door opened. Tarek was surprised to see Naila and Elaine standing there.

Tarek listened to the story without interrupting. Elaine watched his face as he leaned forward. "The baby, the girl were all right when you left them?"

"Yes, the baby has a touch of jaundice, nothing really. The girl is recovering from the surgery, routine. But I'm not sure the brother was convinced."

Tarek's tone startled her with its hardness when he replied, "You've done everything you can do. Leave it alone."

"But Tarek, what if..."

"Leave it alone."

Elaine was taken aback by the abrupt tone of his words to Naila.

He leaned closer to Naila and took her hand in a grip that made her wince. "Don't you understand? I hate this too. But you are dealing with some of the deepest beliefs, the deepest passions these people hold. You and I have moved out easily into the world, the twentieth century. But the others?" he asked harshly. "They are reeling from it, and they are clinging to the few shreds left of what they know, what they think is right, their understanding of order in the universe, honor. You have made the transition easily, but they are still struggling."

"Have I, Tarek? Do you truly think that my own life here is what I want it to be?" she asked quietly.

He leaned closer to her. "No. But the rest of us are going to have to make our peace with it on whatever terms we can. And we inch it forward whenever we can. That's all we can do. Anything else and we all explode."

Tarek looked at her compassionately, then spoke softly. His words surprised her.

"I want you to help me. I want you to return to the hospital this afternoon, go back to work." He nodded up to Elaine, who stood silently watching. "Then I want you to help Elaine. This is important, Naila. She is here to work with us. I want you to help her move around the society a bit. Take her with you to Osman's tonight." He reached over and took Naila's hand, his eyes on her gently, steadily, "I want you to help me."

Naila remained absolutely silent and then turned to Elaine. "Come, the driver will take you home."

They drove in silence for a while. Elaine struggled to find something to say, "Naila, the girl..."

Naila turned her head away. Elaine stopped. And then Naila finally spoke, quietly, as though listening to something inside herself at the same time. "It is the custom that the honor of the family rests on the women. A girl's virginity is the possession of her family. If she falls into disgrace, the entire family is disgraced, tainted. That is why girls have been so traditionally secluded behind veils, high walls, in women's quarters, seen only by the men in their own family, kept away from public sites, confined to segregated schools—to ensure that they will not lose their virginity. It has been the tradition that if a girl does so, the family shall kill her to restore their honor."

She stopped, then tried to smile. Elaine sensed that Naila's composure was deeply shaken. She struggled to begin a conversation, pointing to the old building they were now passing. "Naila, wasn't that the one in the book I was looking at on the plane?"

Naila looked up at the old Murraba Palace that King Abdul Aziz had lived in.

"Yes," she said softly. "Do you want to go in?"

Elaine nodded, hoping it would steady them both. "Will they let us in?"

Naila simply nodded.

The driver spoke briefly to the guard at the old carved front door, who then bowed to Naila and opened the door. Naila and Elaine stepped within the dark, unexpectedly cool clay walls. Elaine could hear the sounds of the water falling from the fountain as they approached the courtyard. Naila motioned up to the balconies overhead. "For the wives."

She sat down on the edge of the fountain deeply fatigued. Elaine sat by her in silence. Naila finally spoke.

"Elaine, you never married?"

"My husband is dead."

Naila looked stricken. "I'm so sorry, I didn't mean to...."

Suddenly Elaine felt her emotions rocked once too many times. Tears filled her eyes, as startling to her as they were to Naila, who reached out to her.

"Oh, Elaine I'm so sorry, I never should have...."

"No, that's all right. I need to learn to talk about it." Elaine now felt the words tumbling out. "I have been living in a shell." Her body shook. "I don't know why I am telling you this. I guess I feel very alone. I don't seem to be able to go on with life. I—my husband and I were assigned to Beirut. We had been married for three years. He was killed in the bombing...." She stopped, suddenly choking at Naila's touch on her arm.

"You have children?" asked Naila softly.

"No, no children. We had hoped later...."

Naila took Elaine's hand. "They say that your life will go on when you are ready for it. Come."

She continued to hold Elaine's hand as she led her back into the silent majlis of Abdul Aziz. She paused. "You see that telephone? The religious elders protested the idea of bringing a telephone into Saudi Arabia. The king thought it was a great invention. He had this one installed. As soon as it was working, he picked it up and recited the Koran through it, then hung it up and pronounced that anything that carried the word of God must be good. End of discussion." She released Elaine's hand.

"Now," said Naila, "let us go. I will pick you up tonight and we will go to Osman's party, right?"

"Yes," said Elaine.

Elaine said yes so quickly that it suddenly struck her how totally engaging she found Naila, and how lonesome for conversation with someone of her own ilk—which she realized is the way she perceived Naila—she had become. She sensed that Naila felt the same. They parted, to rejoin that evening.

She found the message to call Ray when she reached her house. He got on the line immediately.

"General Schwarzkopf called. He's finally pounded it into the assholes at the State Department—said Holt's right, it's a goddamned battle plan taking shape. So, I just got word from Washington, they have at least agreed to my pleas to send up two aircraft carriers." He laughed mirthlessly. "A small victory, of sorts, for one lone spook's voice in the wilderness."

"Ray, do you think they'll really have a party with all of this going on?"

"Sure. There are only about four people on the face of the earth it seems who actually believe anything is going to happen—you, me, Tarek, and Schwarzkopf. And a handful of others who aren't saying anything but simply moving their money quietly out. The rest are in total denial. Make it look good—the cultural attaché thing—it'll be useful in covering your tracks later."

16

Elaine put on an evening gown, as Naila had directed and waited for the car. Naila's driver came to get her. Naila sat in the back seat, black abaya covering a lovely designer evening dress and a sapphire necklace and earrings. Naila kissed her on both cheeks when she got in.

"The party is at Osman's house?" asked Elaine.

"Well, one of them," smiled Naila. "He has the ranch out in the desert, the large family home in Riyadh, another in London, and one in Geneva."

"He's a good friend? Tell me about him."

"Yes, he's been a friend of ours for years. He's really quite charming. Tarek calls him his favorite sybaritic philosopher. *The New York Times*, published an article recently about how, at the age of fifty-five, he has become one of the world's richest men. The young woman reporter was amazed when he said he did some of his best thinking while reading novels. He in turn found her delightful, called her when he was next in New York, and they've since become great friends," Naila laughed. "Actually, I think basically Osman did as others have, first made his money in Saudi Arabia and then invested worldwide. It is only that he did it better. Once I heard him explain that the instinct for financial placement is not unlike that for women. There is a flow, a movement, an uncomplicated sense of the natural order of finance, when to expand, to diversify, when to move on." She looked up when the car started to slow. "We're here."

The car pulled up to the great wall. A guard peered into the car at the two women sitting in the back seat, opened the high iron gate and motioned the driver up a wide circular driveway where a small army of house boys scurried about parking the stream of arriving Mercedes.

Elaine stared at the sprawling family compound, the massive house in the center surrounded by three villas, each with its own gardens and pool. The servant standing before the towering carved wooden door bowed when they walked up the polished marble stairs, and with a polite "Ahlan wa Sahlan" ushered them in, first to a room where the women deposited their abayas and then on to a general reception area.

Elaine found herself standing in a twenty-foot foyer hung with crystal chandeliers glittering above walls hung with French Impressionist paintings. Exquisite oriental rugs were strewn across gleaming marble floors, leading beyond to a vast room of modern furniture covered in pale silk. The room was filled with women in evening gowns and men in white thobes and suits. She looked for a moment at the European antiques lining the foyer. Then she and Naila stepped forward to meet a handsome man in a long white thobe who was smiling warmly, his hand outstretched.

"Osman," said Naila in delight, embracing him. "Osman, this is Elaine."

"Welcome," said Osman with a smile, "Why don't you come meet everybody—but first take a look at the lovely new print Nura found for me in Paris." A servant led the way down the long hall and Elaine followed Naila into a study lined with books and art. He pointed to the lovely Matisse sketch newly framed on the wall.

A man with a slightly graying goatee was standing across the room. His face was familiar.

"Naila, that's Yamani isn't it?"

Naila nodded. Elaine looked over to another man, a short, squat dark-featured man talking to Sultan. Something about him seemed vaguely familiar. "Who is that one?" She whispered.

"Khashoggi, the arms dealer."

Elaine looked surprised; she continued to steal a glance at the overly gregarious figure, of whose fabulous wealth she had read again and again.

"Tarek doesn't think too much of him, I know," said Naila, "but he has strong ties to certain members of the Royal Family." Elaine looked over to the two elaborately dressed women standing next to Khashoggi. "One of them is his daughter Nabila, and the other, who looks the same age as his daughter, is his wife Lamia," Naila explained. "Actually, I guess she is about the same age." Both women were draped with jewels.

"Once," said Naila smiling, "I heard that he told his last wife, on the way to an evening at Sultan's, to take off her makeup and her jewels so she wouldn't upstage Sultan's wife. I guess he got over that."

They were interrupted by Osman, who strode over to them. Next to him stood a small, almost frail looking young woman, impeccably dressed in western designer clothes, plain yet pretty with glasses, speaking to Osman in Arabic with a Kuwaiti accent.

"Elaine, I want you to meet Hussah al Sabah, the daughter of the former emir of Kuwait. She has a magnificent collection of Islamic art which the Embassy is planning to bring to the U.S. for an exhibition. It's a brilliant collection really. I tried to acquire a few of the pieces myself but she ultimately got them." He laughed, "Maybe that's because her husband owns the major share of Sotheby's." Hussah smiled, amused as Osman continued, "I've asked her to come to the house to see some of my latest acquisitions." Elaine spoke to Hussah about her collection and then gave her one of the cultural attaché cards Ray had printed up for her.

"Naila," Elaine said as they returned to the main reception room, "how does this all work? Osman and some of these other men are not members of your family, but you can come?"

She laughed softly. "Ah well, there are rules, and there are rules. As long as it's done quietly, at home, everybody knows which families mix, which husbands allow their wives to come, the sons, the daughters. Tarek said I could come even though my brother Musaid would never let me. Here, let me introduce you."

Naila handed her a glass of champagne from the servant's tray while Elaine looked at the people in the room, with its soft smell of incense. Arabic, French, English floated in the night breeze that drifted from the doors opening onto the swimming pool. The sounds of the oud and the nye curled above the glittering jewels, the beautifully coiffured hair, the long gowns of the women.

"You see, it's not like America. Here everybody knows everybody. It's actually a small country—there are only about six-million people, although I think they lie on the official figures and say eight-million or so." Naila laughed and took a small caviar hors d'oeuvre from a passing tray. "For instance over there, the Binzagers, they are very western, very liberal, traders from the old days, when the boats crossed the Gulf to India, or left from Jeddah and the Red Sea to the West. Even back then, when the country was still poor and isolated, they had enough money, enough contact with the outside world to send their sons out to be educated, to Egypt or Beirut."

She nodded her head toward a group of men on the other side of the room. "Some, like the Ali Rezas, even educated their daughters, although they had to do it quietly because a lot of people originally thought that was a shocking idea. Now some, like me, even get permission to finish their studies abroad. You see him?" She nodded her head toward a young man self-consciously adjusting the cuff links on the sleeve of his thobe. "His second wife has twice as many degrees as he does. And she's twice as smart."

Elaine burst out laughing. The young man looked over quizzically.

"What does he do?"

"Makes money."

"No," said Elaine laughing, "I mean really."

"I mean really," laughed Naila. "When the oil money started coming in the fifties and the country started buying cars and houses and buildings and roads, these families made incredible fortunes bringing it all in, and the sons all work in the business. He's fascinated by you, he's coming over so I'll introduce you.

"Karim, I'd like you to meet Elaine Landon from the American Embassy."

"It's a pleasure. You have just arrived?"

"Yes," said Elaine, "I'm the new cultural attaché."

Karim smiled. "You are bringing American culture to Saudi Arabia, or taking Saudi culture to the U.S.?"

Elaine laughed. "Some of both, I hope."

"You know," smiled the young man "when I first went to the U.S. to study, people were always asking me, how many oil wells do you have? Do you live in a tent? It was really embarrassing, the stereotypes, considering that I'd grown up in

Jeddah. But then," he laughed as he took a glass of champagne from the servant, "I guess the last laugh was on me. When I first arrived in New York, I was thirteen years old, and I got in a cab and asked the driver to take me around New York. We drove and drove and finally the guy could see I was so disappointed. 'What is it kid?' he asked in straight Brooklynese. 'I don't see them,' I replied. 'What, kid?' 'The cowboys and Indians.' The guy doubled over laughing, 'You looking for cowboys and Indians in New Yawk!'

"After all the years of seeing them on TV on our little channels here in the Kingdom and it was a myth, there weren't any! Oh, well," he shrugged, laughing again. "Please come visit us at home, we'll look forward to seeing you." He shook her hand and went back to join the others.

"He's charming," said Elaine to Naila.

"Yes," Naila smiled, "he really is."

"He has two wives?" Elaine whispered.

"I think he divorced the first one. It was a traditional marriage, you know, for the family, first cousins, didn't work out. The second one is another cousin, but I think they get on well." Osman walked up behind them, enjoying the conversation as it drifted back to him.

"What she really wants to know, Naila," he looked entertained, observing Elaine, "is what about the ones with four wives?"

Elaine flushed for a moment until she realized that Osman was teasing her.

"Those days are mostly gone," Osman said. "Only the old ones." He raised his eyes in feigned exhaustion. "Some like him," he tilted his head toward a gentleman in his seventies standing just beyond them, "still do." Osman nodded as the old gentleman looked over to him. "He has four identical houses in his compound—one for each wife. He told me once he keeps a calendar, which day to visit which wife. For me," he said amused, "it would be too much."

Osman turned as a manicured jeweled hand across the room shot up into the air like a nervous bird released. It gestured, punctuating the air, and then fell. An earthy laugh came from its owner, the woman on the white brocade sofa. She brought a cigarette to her mouth, exhaled and beckoned to them, her diamond earrings flashing in the light of the chandelier.

Osman walked over, looking curiously at the old man in a long white thobe sitting next to her. The old man seemed confused when the butler showed him a tray of drinks. Sana, the bejeweled woman, leaned over to Osman. "Darling, you know him?" She nodded her head sideways toward the wizened, white-bearded old bedu who sat like a crumpled artifact, his rusty dagger at his waist, peering around the room.

"Osman, I found him at the Dorchester Hotel when I was last in London. He heard me speaking Arabic and asked if I could help. He was checking in with several hugh trunks. He explained that he had brought his own food from the desert; one couldn't eat the stuff they cook in England. Trunks and trunks of food coming into the Dorchester, chérie. And the sons, the sons were with him, with those sour faces, chérie. I asked him where he was from, and the old man laughed and told me Saudi Arabia. He is sheikh of a tribe in the Nafud, fought with Abdul Aziz. The sons are waiting for him to die so they can take over, he thinks he is maybe ninety-eight. 'But I,' and here he laughs, chérie, 'I decided to come to London instead.' Now he says he is looking for a new wife. And then he looks at me, and I see what he thinks. 'Ah no,' I say, 'I am already married.' But he says, with a wink, a glint in his eye—

'maybe you will get tired of that one, no?' "

Sana's laugh pealed across the room. She looked at the old man kindly, lit a cigarette, and gave a shrug. "They are so lost, the old ones, you know?" She leaned forward. "I brought him over for a dinner party to our house in Grosvenor Square, just a little evening for some of the other Arab bankers. All night long the old man regaled these bankers, sipping their port, with his stories of fighting with Abdul Aziz as a young man, flashing his old silver dagger up to the chandeliers." Sana shrugged, "I sent him flowers every day for the rest of his stay in London. The old ones, they are so lost, no?"

Sana looked at the old man for a moment and then back at Naila and Elaine. "You know, when I told him I wanted him to visit me at our house in Riyadh, he asked me why I have so many houses, darling. I told him we have houses everywhere now, Egypt, Riyadh, London, Kuwait, because who knows where there will be left to go? When we will be asked to leave? We are guests, darling—we Palestinians are guests everywhere we go. Perhaps Palestine, chérie, is dead, is gone, so we are 'guests.' "

"But then," she leaned closer to him, "maybe we all are?"

She stopped for a moment. "You know, Osman, what I see? I see it all blowing in the breeze. These great houses along the Gulf standing empty one day, the breeze blowing through empty windows, empty halls, the foreign workers gone, the families gone, only the cicadas and the sand, and the desert wind. And then the rest will come, they will change it all, this way of life. And we will all be forgotten, Osman, all forgotten, only a curious moment in history."

She stopped suddenly and just looked at him, like an oracle, a voice borrowed by the gods for the moment, and now delivered of her message, emptied.

Elaine, Naila, and Osman stood silently, taken aback.

Osman laughed, "Sana, you should have been a Levantine fortune-teller."

"But I am, Osman, I am."

Osman uneasily motioned the butler to bring them drinks, glancing toward the small group of men watching the CNN report on the Iraqi troops by Kuwait.

Elaine struggled to make conversation in the strange silence that remained. "Naila, who is that?" Elaine nodded toward a young woman in a beautiful red satin gown and ruby earrings.

"Ghada bint Salman," Naila said. "I'm surprised she came tonight. Her husband has divorced her and is taking the children."

"Taking the children? She has no rights?"

"No," said Naila. "It is tradition, if they divorce, that she must give up the children to the husband when they reach the age of seven. Some of these women stay married when their husbands take a second wife so they can still have their children. But then their lives as women, as individuals are over. They can't remarry, they live in isolation, finished—some of them still in their early twenties.

"My brother, Musaid, I think he might do as much to his wife, Khadija. It is tragic really. He seems a tyrant in his own home. You see she's not here tonight. He doesn't allow her out. I'm not at all surprised he's not at Osman's tonight himself. With all his conservatism, this opulence would disgust him."

Naila looked back at Elaine, with a taut expression. "Elaine," she moved her hand toward the room of glittering gowns, "we are here tonight, and yet there are people living in the countryside in ways that haven't changed for a thousand years. I...," she paused, "am here tonight, and yet I must have written permission from the head of my family, Musaid, to study, to travel. And he has declined to give it to me any longer."

"I see," said Elaine quietly as she looked at Naila standing in her evening gown, gazing silently at her hands, "and so you live with your sister and Tarek, but it is Musaid who...?"

"Yes."

Elaine was relieved when the tension was broken by a voice behind her.

"Naila isn't Nura coming as well?" Sana, now stood behind them. "I'm really sorry Nura isn't here. She would have wanted to talk to him." She nodded toward a distinguished dark-haired man in his forties, wearing a suit, who was talking to the museum director.

"Him?"

"The archaeologist, Yusif Khalidi. You know the name. Nura speaks often of him. His work, really, it is quite impressive." Sana smiled, "Khalidi—a fellow Palestinian. He's working on a new book. It will be about ancient Sumer, the earliest civilizations that were created around the Tigris and the Euphrates Rivers in the fourth millennium B.C. He says it will move up through the era when the great caravans brought the frankincense and myrrh across Arabia Felix. Nura met with him the last time he came. A rather fascinating intellectual—I wonder if he brings the painter with him?"

She reached for a glass of champagne as the waiter passed. "You know, he lives mostly in Baghdad. He has had this affair, for a few years I think, with the Iraqi painter, Yasmina Tikriti. You remember her, when she brought her paintings here? Fascinating woman, no? They say she was married once to a man, ambitious in the Baath Party in Iraq. One night she and her husband were in the president's house, sitting with Saddam Hussein himself. It was in the early days when Saddam was solidifying his base as president, carrying out the purges. Saddam suddenly turns to one of his aides and demands, 'Are you loyal to me?' The man says, 'Yes, of course.' Saddam turns to a second aide and asks, 'Are you loyal to me?' 'Yes, I am.' Saddam then picks up a pistol and gives it to the first aide. 'Prove it to me,' he says. 'Yes, of course, what do you want?' 'I want you to kill him,' said Saddam pointing to his second aide. The first one is shaking. 'Saddam, I can't do this; you don't mean it.' Saddam picks up the pistol. 'I will show you,' he says, 'how it is done.'

"He fires; his second aide's head blows apart while they watch. They say Yasmina stood up, walked out the door, and never went back to her husband's house again." She murmured over the champagne, "Yallah, this world…"

She picked up another glass of champagne. "Darling, somebody was just telling me about these reports, Iraq by the Kuwait border?" Osman joined them as Sana continued. "Ah, but maybe the Kuwaitis deserve it?" she clucked. "They've been so arrogant, so rich, for so long…"

"Nobody deserves that." They turned around, startled at the intensity of Osman's voice. He started to say something else when the butler walked up and summoned him to a telephone call in the study. Osman walked in and shut the door behind him. He listened to his broker in London. The man's voice was tense. The reports about the movement along the border were increasingly alarming, he seriously felt Osman should move quickly, authorize him to transfer assets.

Osman considered the man's comments for a moment and then approved a significant transfer to move more of his money out of the Gulf. He concluded the conversation, returning to the room full of guests.

Sana waved him over. "Osman, let me introduce you to a

fellow Palestinian, another wanderer like myself. You've probably read his books. This is the world-famous archaeologist, Yusif Khalidi."

Yusif Khalidi extended his hand and smiled.

"I'm sure everybody here has read your works. You're quite famous, Mr. Khalidi. Are you here working on something now?" asked Naila standing next to Sana.

"Well, I'm actually making the arrangements to return shortly, to do some photography in the northern part of the Kingdom to complete a new work."

He stopped when he saw Osman's servants began to throw the doors open to the dining room, the tables, laden with food and candelabras, waiting for them.

Osman beckoned them toward the dining room, and Naila took Elaine's hand. "Come," she said. They followed the men in their long white thobes and the women in their gowns who began to move from the living room.

Elaine glanced at the beautiful works of art placed throughout the room and then saw Osman move quickly past them toward the door to greet the woman standing at the entrance.

"Naila," she whispered as her eye focused on the woman taking a cigarette from Osman's small silver case, "Who is that? She's exquisite."

The woman's hand brushed back the long dark hair from her high cheekbones, the beautiful green eyes, listening to Osman, while the emeralds at her neck glittered above the rich green satin of her evening gown.

Naila looked at Elaine in surprise for a moment. Then she replied quietly, "Yes, she is exquisite. That is Nura, my sister, Tarek's wife."

Elaine looked in fascination at the woman whose journal

she had read. The woman's soft full lips seemed to speak intently to Osman. His head bent toward her, listening closely.

Elaine was intrigued. "Does she stay at home...the conventional life, live by the rules?"

Naila gazed at her sister's beautiful face, the deep green eyes, and then looked thoughtfully at Elaine. "Nura," she said softly, "lives by all of the rules—and by none of them." She paused. "There are levels to Nura, so deep, I myself will never understand them. Beneath it all, I think, lies a lawlessness, a recklessness that you and I will never understand."

"Ray told me she is brilliant, took her degree in philosophy, wasn't it? At the Sorbonne." said Elaine. "But I don't remember him mentioning she was so beautiful."

Naila laughed, "Well he's known her since she was a child; I guess he's just gotten used to her. I thought you had met Nura. She and Osman are great friends." Nura had now walked over to Osman's son Abed and was speaking to him. Elaine stood fascinated watching the woman whose intimate, haunting words still moved through her mind.

"Would you like to meet Nura?" Naila asked Elaine, sensing her interest.

Naila started to walk toward Nura and then abruptly stopped as she saw the man standing across the room. She stood absolutely still, looking at him, his dark handsome face, the strong hands gesturing while the other men listened. She stood motionless until slowly he turned and saw her.

Elaine watched Naila's gaze flow over the man's face, his body, her breath catching, and she whispered a name. He stood there seeming to breathe Naila in with his eyes. And then, never taking his eyes from her, began to walk toward her as though the room were empty.

Naila seemed unable to move, watching the man's deep brown

eyes fixed upon her. Then silently, almost imperceptibly, she shook her head.

He stopped, watching her eyes close for a moment and then look again at him as though telling him to come no closer. Elaine felt Naila's fingers tighten around her hand as she stood transfixed, gazing at him.

"Please," she whispered finally to Elaine, "I must go. Please go with me now." Elaine watched while the man stared at Naila, oblivious to the people walking past him.

Naila turned quickly toward the foyer. "Please," she whispered to a servant passing by, "please could you call the car?"

She pulled her wrap from the library and then turned once more to see the man's eyes waiting for her. Then she walked out the door and stepped into the car. She breathed the night air in slowly, leaned her head back, the tears ran down her face.

"Are you all right?" whispered Elaine in confusion getting into the car next to her. "Is there anything I can do? Please, I want to help." Naila opened her eyes, looked at her sadly and shook her head.

"I am so sorry, it was a shock to see him standing there. You see, I didn't know he would be there, I…" She looked back at the man standing in the shadows and then toward Elaine as the tears came down her face. "No, there is nothing you can do. Nothing." She moved her hand across her eyes. "The rules bend," she whispered, "but they don't really change."

Elaine shook her head confused, "I'm sorry, I don't understand…"

Naila breathed deeply. "No, I have done this to myself. I have always known I would have to return, have to marry in the family." She looked at Elaine in anguish. "I never meant to, I have tried but…," she paused, "when he first came to see Tarek years ago, I was fascinated by him."

Elaine listened as the words began to pour from Naila.

"I always knew, but I couldn't help it. Each year I would say to myself, 'I must, I will forget'. And yet each year I only loved him more, there is only him. For years I've stayed away, where I could see him, be with him. And now..." she stopped. Her hand moved helplessly and then fell silent. "I love him."

She looked at Elaine. "Are you shocked?" she asked sadly.

"No," said Elaine quietly, "only very sad to see you so hurt. I wish I could do something."

"Can you understand that kind of pain?" asked Naila. "I feel like I am dead watching the living."

"Yes," said Elaine softly, "I can." Her voice sounded sad and faraway as she looked at the woman crying. "Yes, I can."

Naila touched her hand. "Please, stay. I'll be all right, I just need to be by myself for a while. Tarek will take you back."

Elaine walked slowly back to the house unnerved. The servant opened the door for her. She stood silently for a moment looking at the evening gowns, the crystal chandeliers, the jewels swimming in the soft music.

"Naila has left you?" She turned at the deep voice behind her and looked into Tarek's dark eyes. She stopped for a moment as she thought of how handsome the man was. The strength and the elegance of his body, the eyes that registered every sensitivity, every nuance in their silence. He watched her, bringing the glass to his mouth and drinking, his eyes never moving. She felt a surge when his hand reached to her arm. "Come," he said quietly, "meet the others inside. Naila must simply have been tired."

She stood for a moment looking at him, then followed him into the room past Osman, to the banquet table. He picked up a plate, put some of the hors d'oeuvres on it and handed it to her. "You have been working very hard. Are you all right?" he asked quietly. She looked back at him, aware of the effect that he had upon her.

"Yes," she said, "I'm just tired. Could one of the drivers take me back?"

"Of course." He turned to a houseboy with instructions to bring the car. Elaine, still unnerved, looked at her watch and directed the car to take her first to the house to change and then back to the office.

❉ ❉ ❉

Ray was peering at the monitor while Elaine sat sipping a cup of coffee before going back to join the team.

"Why does a girl like Naila come back?"

Ray looked up from the monitor. "What?"

"Why does a girl like Naila come back?" Elaine asked. She was too deep in the thoughts that had prompted the question to realize how startling it sounded to Ray who was working rapidly on the reconnaissance printouts. "How can she stand it after all of her western education, the freedom, to come back to these restrictions, the kind of confinement they have to live with here?"

"They all come back." Ray said, his attention now on Elaine.

Elaine pushed her chair back, waiting for him to continue.

"The ties are too strong. You see, you're asking the question from an intellectual point of view. That's not where you'll find the answer. There is a profound, deep cultural pull, a sense of identity, a sense of place that runs deep. Even when they have lived abroad for years, if you talk to them you sense they feel they belong to this place. They have a love of it, even when fighting the restrictions. It pulls them back. Beyond that, every minute of their lives has been inculcated with a sense of the family, of honor. It runs so deeply, it is so ingrained, it leaves them feeling that ultimately we, in the West, with our primary sense of 'I,' are rootless. All of it is too much to buck—their mixed feelings about our 'freedom,' their own internal censors, regarding leaving for good, and certainly the feelings from their own family that they have dishonored them, caused them disgrace. No, they all come back."

"Will people like Naila change it over time—the way the women live here?"

"Some of it. But you know, it will never become like the West. Don't ever expect them to turn into us. They won't. There are parts of all of this that you will never truly understand. I've been here for years, and even when you think you do, you realize you don't really."

He looked levelly at Elaine. "And there are also parts of a man like Tarek that you will never really know, parts of him you will never really understand."

Elaine was startled by his comment. "Why do you say that, about Tarek, to me?"

She watched an uncharacteristic softness play across the older man's face.

"I don't know. Nothing really." He turned back to his desk.

Suddenly he looked back to the movement on the monitor. "Jesus Christ," he whispered, "look at the new supply line the Iraqis are starting. In twenty-four hours they are going to invade Kuwait, sure as I'm standing here." Alarmed, he rapidly placed a call to Washington.

Hamid glanced at the dark streets of Baghdad as the car sped along. Antar sat in front of him checking his notes in the pre-dawn light. When they reach Hamid's apartment building, the car stopped and let him out. As the car drove off, Hamid went up to his flat and ripped the floor boards open. As rapidly as he could, he sent the urgent message.

17

The tanks began to roll at midnight.

Badr leaned closer to the radio. "Help us, help us…"

The voice grew faint and then disappeared. Kuwait Radio went dead.

Tarek's voice was tight. "Hamid went in with them?"

Badr nodded, "He's with Antar."

The Iraqi troops smashed across the border and roared toward Kuwait City. The explosion of artillery shells and machine gun fire ripped through the night. Kuwaitis, terrified, ran into the streets screaming. Iraqi jets and helicopter gun ships blasted the city. Rockets soared, setting ablaze the palace of the Kuwaiti emir and the Ministry of Defense.

Hamid moved quietly behind Antar as he methodically cut the lines to the outside world. He watched the main communications conduit to Saudi Arabia severed, the Kuwaiti guard standing by it shot in the head. Raising his hand, Antar gave the signal that the last lines to Saudi Arabia be cut, to start moving the tanks toward their border. He moved quickly to the next room.

Hamid saw the one line they had missed. The little red signal to Bahrain. One fax machine still connected. He ripped a sheet of paper, scrawled the message, and prayed the number he remembered for their agent was right. He jammed the paper into the machine, sweating, while the paper slowly slid through the last line out. Suddenly he saw Antar walking toward him. Hamid reached behind himself at the sound of the tiny beep indicating the transmission was complete. He pulled the sheet out, crumpled it into his back pocket, then pulled the plug on the machine. The guards rushed past him, ripping wires, while Antar called for him to come along. The last light on the control board went black.

❊ ❊ ❊

Elaine grabbed the copy of the fax from Hamid that Tarek had sent over. Ray, glued to the satellite surveillance of the troops pouring into Kuwait, barely heard Elaine's voice read of the additional troops being readied to go in after this initial assault.

❊ ❊ ❊

Naila at four A.M. struggled to hear the voice on the telephone through the screams of the ambulance sirens in the middle of the night. The director's voice, urgent on the line, repeated, "Dr. Naila, it's an emergency, come quickly. The Iraqis have invaded Kuwait. The people are trying to flee across the border. Women, children are pouring in right now; we can't handle…"

"I'll be right there." Naila grabbed her jacket and called for the car. She reached the hospital and rushed down the corridor.

Through the screams of the stat alert came the sobs, the cries of a human chain of misery. Stumbling, falling, leaning against the walls, they filled the halls. Children burned, carried by their parents, women raped, bleeding, a tiny girl whose leg had been blown off by a bomb.

The director looked up frantically when Naila appeared. "Come with me."

Naila hurried down the hospital hall to the women and children's emergency room. Naila stopped suddenly when she saw the child lying on the gurney. The small body was covered in burns.

"The child just came in from the bomb attack," said the director, "they keep coming. We're not really prepared for this…we don't have a burn center, but I know that the hospital you did your training with in Washington did. I hope you got some burn experience." The child moaned when the nurse tried to remove his clothes and start an IV. Every time she pulled away some of the charred cloth some of the child's skin came with it. The nurse looked up terrified.

Naila moved instantly toward the child, and saw that the child's left ankle was not burned. She quickly cut the pants leg open with bandage scissors, put a tourniquet around his calf and inserted an angiocath in the saphenous vein at the ankle. She aspirated 5 ccs of blood. "Send this for CBC, lytes and type and cross a unit of blood. You've got a good IV now, but you'll have to protect it. He doesn't have many IV sites left. Weigh him and calculate his fluid requirement from the Brooke formula. Don't sedate him until you're sure his blood pressure is stable and then just use small amounts of morphine intravenously. Start him on IV antibiotics, and once he's stable put him in a bath and try to soak the rest of his clothes off. Then we can get a more precise estimate of the extent of his burns.

Get him into a private room in the ICU and put him in reverse isolation. In seventy-two hours our big problem is going to be infection, provided we keep up with his fluids."

The director rapidly handed a second chart to Naila, moving toward the next room. "There's another burned child here. This one may be beyond..." She looked sadly at the child lying in front of them and shook her head.

Naila bent close to the child and spoke in a quiet voice. "Can you tell me your name?"

The child remained motionless. Naila sat down in the chair and quickly scanned the chart. No name, no age, about five years old. Naila's hand reached out and held the child's while she turned to the resident and reeled off orders for IV's, antibiotics and blood.

The director hurriedly motioned to Naila. "There's another one next door."

Naila gently touched the child's face. "You rest, I'll be back."

The director looked up wearily "Naila, I don't think the little one can hear you." She was surprised at Naila's crisp answer, "You really can't know that for certain." Naila touched a part of the child's hand that was free from burn and then moved on.

She hurriedly studied the chart of the next child, a five to ten percent burn case, then followed the director into the darkened room next door where a little boy lay in the bed. When the director closed the door behind them, the child started violently at the noise, a look of terror crossing his face. "The bombs, the bombs again..." Naila reached out quickly.

"There are no bombs," she said, "only a door."

The little boy whispered. "It's dark again; the bombs came in the night."

Naila watched the hysteria creeping over the child, his body covered in bandages and rigid with fear. "You know what?" She smiled down at him. "You haven't even told me your name yet. I'm Naila."

"My name is Suleiman." Suddenly he stiffened.

"What is it?" Naila said.

"The guns," he began sobbing uncontrollably again.

Naila cradled the child and soothed him. "The guns are very far away from here. Very, very far away. You are all right, darling."

Oh God, she thought, if only that were true. She felt the nurse tap her on the shoulder. "Dr. Naila," she whispered "I'll stay with him. Come quickly, they need your help down the hall."

The woman was covered in blood. Shaking, she moved back and forth as though mesmerized. The nurse whispered to Naila, "She was raped repeatedly by the Iraqi soldiers. They left her for dead. The people who carried her along with them to the border are here somewhere, but I can't find them..." she motioned her hand frantically toward the melee in the hospital.

Naila took the woman's hand and led her to a chair.

"Can you talk to me?" she asked quietly. The woman stared at her. Naila gave the nurse a sign to prepare a bed in the shock unit. She put her hand around the woman's again. "Can you tell me what happened?"

Suddenly the woman pulled her hand free and began clawing at the blood on her dress. Her mouth opened as though to speak but remained wordless.

"That's alright," said Naila softly, "the nurse is going to take you to a comfortable place. I'll be by shortly."

The woman, shaking, stood up to follow the nurse, then suddenly turned around to Naila.

"They raped me." Her strangled voice choked, then broke over the words. She stared at Naila, then struggled to speak again. "They raped me," she whispered. "I picked up a knife when they entered, but there were too many. Four of them held my arms and legs while the rest raped me. I begged them to stop but they kept on until I fainted. Again and again…" She stopped and looked wildly down at the blood on her dress. "The shame, I can never go back, my family, everyone will know, I can't…" the words broke off into terrified sobs.

Naila grabbed her arm quickly. "No, that's not true—your family will only be concerned about you."

The young woman shook her head slowly. "I am dead." She mumbled the words again while the nurse came to lead her away.

Naila took the chart they handed her for the next patient and watched the young woman move numbly after the nurse toward the room. It didn't seem long before Naila heard the nurse's scream. She ran to the room.

The nurse stood there with her hand over her mouth. "Dr. Naila, I only left her for a minute."

The young woman, dead, had hung herself with her bloodied skirt.

At 5:00 A.M. Tarek's helicopter landed on the stretch of sand along the Saudi-Kuwaiti border.

"Open up the borders. Let them in." Tarek walked up to the nervous border patrol officer who continued to hold out the normal forms.

"But our standing orders are to…"

Tarek took the papers out of the man's hand and threw them in the dirt. "I just gave you new standing orders. Let them all in." Tarek began to move through the throngs of desperate people trying to cross from Kuwait into Saudi Arabia. Women carrying babies failing from dehydration, old men lying in the sand unable to go on. He stepped across the border.

"Tarek," said Badr, "be careful." Tarek ignored him and kept on. He turned when a bedu boy from the desert came up behind him. The old man he was carrying murmured incoherently.

"Can you help me?" asked the boy, struggling to carry the man. Tarek quickly took the old man from the boy.

The exhausted boy spoke up. "There are others out there trying to come across. Some were able to bribe Iraqi guards to let them through, others slipped past them."

Tarek stopped him. "I'll go with you." Badr looked up, panicked. The bedu boy nodded and moved back toward the Kuwaiti desert, Tarek with him.

Streams of people struggled past them, carrying meager belongings in bundles while Tarek followed him deeper into the desert. A mile in, the doors to a car lay open. Inside the whole family lay dead. Further on, a lone woman sat in the sand trying to wrench water from an empty can for the glazed-eyed infant she carried. A man, shot in the head, sprawled behind her.

Tarek turned and walked silently back toward the border. He gave Badr the orders. "Bring as many across the border as you can. We'll have planes transport them to our hospitals."

Badr returned in minutes. "Minister of Defense Sultan says he can send a few, but the rest he has to keep at their stations. He mentions to you that our government has not decided to take any official action yet on this 'incursion,' I think he called it."

Tarek, enraged, walked over to the guard's phone. He pulled the phone out of the man's hand and dialed the number. The line clicked and Osman answered, the sound of CNN behind him reporting the invasion of Kuwait.

"Osman, I need your plane, Said's plane, and every other private plane you can get your hands on from friends. I want you to fly up here to the border, Badr will have you cleared in."

Within thirty minutes, Osman and Said had arrived. They stood, stunned, at the bodies, the human misery that lay before them.

"Oh, God, Tarek, this is ..."

"Don't talk now, just start getting them into the planes."

Osman nodded quietly and took the old woman Tarek was carrying, helping her gently into his plane. The border guards helped more into Said's and the other private planes they had been able to summon.

Tarek motioned Badr over.

"Get through to Bandar in Washington. As ambassador from Saudi Arabia, he'll be the first person that the White House tries to contact. Tell him I want him to do everything possible to keep the lines open for bringing U.S. troops in here." Tarek turned and picked up the phone. "Walid, I'll be returning shortly. I want to see the king."

❈ ❈ ❈

The guard opened the door. Tarek walked toward the king, sitting behind the desk, submerged in paper. Fahd looked up nervously.

Tarek pulled up a chair. "You've got to take a stand. My agent says they are laying new mines all over the Gulf, torch bombs ready to go in the oil fields. The refugees are streaming out. Across the desert here, to Jordan, wherever they can find to go. I've just talked to Ray Holt. He's coming to you with an official request from the U.S. to take a stand—to rally the other Arab states to stand up and condemn Iraq. They want you to join in on economic sanctions. If this doesn't work, they want the go-ahead from you for basing rights here so they can bring in U.S. troops. You have to reconsider, to work with them…"

The king sat back in his chair, his eyelids slowly lowering. "No."

"Iraq is escalating—we will be next."

"Iraq will not attack us."

Tarek stared at the man's immobile face. "But every indication is that they will. The U.S. is the only one who can effectively intervene—the Soviets are too weak now to do anything, and besides, you don't want them here."

"No."

"But what I see is…" Tarek's voice became desperate.

Fahd leaned across the desk with a flash of anger.

"What has Kuwait ever done for us? Their own greed led them into this. This is their fight. Why should I go up against Saddam for this—we are no match for him. As far as the U.S. goes, they'll promise a lot and do nothing, send a few planes and then run at the first gunshot like they always do. And then we'll be left here with the wreckage. And you know what I see then? Every conservative, every fundamentalist, watching while I do something else with the Americans, maybe the Israelis joining in a bit too, as they always do? No."

"Maybe you…"

"Maybe, Tarek," breathed the king, "I'm finished talking about this."

Tarek watched astonished as Fahd stood up and angrily left the room.

Cross the city, Elaine searched Ray's face as he held the phone. Turley's voice was tense on the line from CIA headquarters outside Washington.

"Ray, there's a plane waiting for you. Now. The Chief wants to see you in Washington. You'll be interested to know that Bush remembers you were the guy who warned them about Khomeini long before he took over. So I guess Bush figures that the poor dusty little mole they discounted last time maybe has something bright to say this time. Just get on the plane. And try to act civilized. It's an effort at your age, I know. You've been out there too long, but try," said Turley sarcastically. "I'll see you in Washington."

The line clicked off. Behind them the fax was already coming across confirming the meeting in fifteen hours with Bush, the Chairman of the Joint Chiefs of Staff, Colin Powell, General Norman Schwarzkopf, four-star head of Central Command, and Secretary of Defense, Richard Cheney.

"Ray," asked Elaine nervously, "what are you going to tell them?"

"What am I going to tell them?" Ray pushed his chair back. "The fucking truth, which they won't want to hear."

He looked at her. "What I'm going to tell them is, Mr. President, Kuwait is only the beginning for Saddam. He ultimately sees the whole Gulf as his target. Whether he tries to take it in a few weeks or a few months, he sees the whole Gulf as his goal."

Ray stared at her and continued. "That more than likely he's got a second invasion already planned for Saudi Arabia—hit the oil fields in the eastern province first, then take the rest if the Saudis don't fight back too hard, which they can't since they don't have the troops or the weapons. The rest of the countries below them collapse like dominoes. And we, along with them, are out of the Middle East.

"What am I going to tell them?" he pushed his chair back farther. "That Saddam's got the world's fourth largest army sitting north of the oil fields whose output is essential for the industrialized world, Our interests are too large—this man could be in control of the major oil reserves of the world. He could rock the world economy with a single flick of his finger. We know he's developing nuclear weapons, regularly threatens the Israelis with their possibilities. Demographics are on his side—Iraq has the population, the resources to emerge as the dominant power in the Arab world. We do nothing and the last major superpower standing—us, now that the Soviet Union has collapsed—is shown not to be credible, shown to be impotent even when our own interests are at stake."

He stopped. "And when they demur on all of that, I'm going to tell them a little story or two about their good friend Saddam. How he was trained as a boy in the Arab Baath Party, worked as an assassin. A party whose whole goal was to remove the old monarchies left in place from post-World War I colonial powers. A man whose movements are fast, instinctive. A man who through the years has emerged as a sociopath, a megalomaniac. Fascinated by his own self-created myth as the Salladin, the hero of the Arab world. A man capable of playing down to the wire and for final stakes."

"And then," Ray leaned forward, eyes nearly piercing her now, "I'm going to conclude my little speech."

He stood up and started to walk to the door. "Yes, I'm going to conclude it with one final comment, which is 'Respectfully sir, if we do nothing, it's all over for us in the Middle East. In fact, it's all over for the Middle East as we know it.'"

Elaine drove with him in silence to the plane. He left her with a final comment. "You're the contact now with Tarek,

Elaine. I'll be in touch, but plan on meeting with the Ambassador in about twenty-four hours."

"To...?"

"To tell him who you really are and why you're really here."

He got out of the car and boarded the plane waiting for him.

18

The U.S. Ambassador in Riyadh ripped the sheet from his computer printer the following afternoon and read it aloud.

"Secretary of Defense Cheney...Colin Powell, Joint Chiefs of Staff...General Schwarzkopf...Urgent...Urgent. Navy, Air Force, Marines, and Special Terrorist Commando Squads to coordinate plans. Further instructions to be sent from Washington shortly. Need better information." He dropped the paper on his desk, shaken. His gaze shot over to Elaine. "Ray called me from Washington, said it was urgent that I meet with you, that you had something to tell me."

Elaine spoke quietly. "The first information Washington sent us has already gotten out." The Ambassador looked stunned.

"Mr. Ambassador," Elaine continued quietly, "I've come to tell you why I was really sent here. The entire Embassy, our entire communications are being tapped into. I am a specialist in communications security..."

"Oh great God," the Ambassador was now totally speechless. Elaine continued. "Baghdad already has Schwarzkopf's communication about the fact our closest troops are down in Diego Garcia, 2,500 miles away. That even if we decide to do something, we're impotent for days. One of Tarek's men got information out to him that they are going to continue and move toward Saudi Arabia next. He also says that Iraq has tapped into our lines between here and Washington on the fact that…"

The Ambassador interrupted, pushing his hand through his hair in agitation, "on the fact that our goddamned troops are 2,500 miles away, down on the tip of Africa, heading the wrong way. We've lost all security to our communications." He brushed his hand across his forehead and then tried to regain his composure.

His expression was ashen as she continued. "Ray had some indication that your communications here might be compromised and wanted to see if we could trace it—without making the problem public—by flying me over here to try and check it with the small team he already had on board. We haven't been able to pin it down. Now, with the situation clearly at a crisis level, we've arranged to fly a larger team in here on an emergency basis. The first of the team has just been cleared to fly in tonight, and I have a report on what we've been able to determine so far—and what we're going to have to do."

He pressed the buzzer and called in his two top aides while Jack and the two lieutenants from the intel unit came up to join Elaine.

Elaine laid the papers out in front of her.

"Shall we go over it from the top? What we're going to have to do here?"

The Ambassador nodded shakily.

"All right," she said, "let's break it into two parts. First, how they could be tapping into our information here. Second, how they then could be delivering that information to Baghdad."

She laid out a chart with subheadings on it, and pointed to the top. "Jack's already been at work on telephones. Telephone lines can be tapped along the phone cable in the building, or the phones themselves can be bugged. Simply requires some access on location here by somebody to plant the original bug and to monitor the tap on the cables outside."

She moved her finger down. "We're bringing a specialist in tonight on typewriters. Typewriters and printers emit their own minute radio waves that can be received outside the embassy. A bug can be planted in them which will pick up and transmit the electronic signals given off by each key or even by the ball in a Selectric typewriter. The person receiving the transmission at a listening post outside the building can read the message almost as easily as if he were looking over the typist's shoulder. Obviously this is the first place you would look. Frequently, they will plant some fairly easy-to-find bugs so you think you've gotten them and stop looking for the other ones inside.

They'll also try to disguise or hide the radio frequencies of their transmissions. You do this by having the bugs send their data on frequencies that are very close to those used by standard radio or TV broadcasts, 'snuggling.' Or you can do frequency hopping—transmit for one millisecond at one frequency, then another, then another. Obviously the bugs hardest to detect are those that don't transmit through the air. They can be attached by wire to a listening post outside the building. The connecting 'wire' itself doesn't even have to be a wire. Almost anything that conducts electricity will work: metallic paint under the surface paint of a room, an air-conditioning vent, anything. These are a nightmare to find because they can't be detected by regular electronic sweeps—you have to literally X-ray every inch of the building."

She pushed the paper forward. "Jack's lieutenant here is going to take apart the encoding machines. All you need is one functioning bug in your encoding machine, and you won't have any secrets anymore. You might as well shout your secret communications through a microphone in perfectly straightforward English.

"Copy machines—they'll all be taken apart. Tiny cameras can be inserted into the machines to record pictures of the documents as they are produced. It requires someone with access to the machine so the cameras can regularly be downloaded and resupplied with film."

He looked down at the paper as she moved along.

"Computers. Another man's flying in tonight. When it comes to computers, you don't even need a bug. Computers give off radio waves that can be picked up by interception equipment outside the building—a van parked even a mile away. The only answer here is heavy vaulting in the computer room that can completely block the wave emissions."

She paused. "This is massive. Four other people will be arriving tomorrow to tackle it. This embassy, the whole embassy compound is new. The Saudi government buildings, Fahd's new palace, the homes of the Royal Family members, all new, right? Some of the building materials came from within the country, didn't they? All you need is someone with some access to the construction elements, say the concrete blocks as they were being manufactured. You can plant tiny bugs, mix electronic circuits into the concrete itself. Weave tiny filaments into the carpets, the drapes. They are weak transmitters to be sure, but all you need is someone close by with excellent equipment, and they'll get it. Computer signals, conversations, all of it."

She pushed the papers forward. "Obviously if you just want to listen to somebody's conversation, that's the easiest of all. Just put a little transmitter in the person's shoe when he's not looking. Or if you're only interested in the conversations he's having inside the building, even easier. Sound and words cause the windows in a room to vibrate. You can simply direct a laser beam at the window. The beam is reflected and picks up the vibrations of the window. A computer then reads the beams and converts it back into sound.

"In short, technically speaking, all you need is one competent person on the ground here with access of some sort and proximity to listening posts. If they have direct access, say they are somebody inside—someone who hears things in meetings or who can pick up the information, read it as it is typed or lies around—they don't even need to be technically competent."

She folded up the charts. "Now, getting the information to Baghdad is a different thing. Obviously you can't run it across any of the major communications lines or we'd get it as we search. You could do it on some little oddball back channel if it was cleverly encoded. Or you could send it via people. A person who moved back and forth, or could hand it off to subagents who moved back and forth. As you know from our inability to get great information from here by intercepting communications from Iraq's ships in the Gulf, it is highly unlikely they could be getting anything better on us from over there. The distance is simply too far. But somebody on the ground here? Somebody inside? Somebody with access to the buildings, the people? They stand a very, very good chance."

The Ambassador and his aides closed their notebooks. The possibilities, the gaping holes in their security seemed to overwhelm them. "Has Ray notified the White House about this break in security?" asked the Ambassador nervously.

"Sir," said Elaine, "I'm not sure he has. Perhaps you should discuss that with him."

"Oh Jesus." The Ambassador stood up as Elaine was about to leave. He looked at her once again, impressed by her acumen, and the tremendous distance, remoteness that seemed to emanate from her. He opened the door for her and said nothing, lost in his thoughts of the turmoil around him. His secretary called him and he walked down the hall through the chaos.

Elaine watched him go, then called for the driver to take her to Tarek's office.

Tarek was waiting for her when she arrived. She walked in and pulled a chair up to his desk. She took out the notes from the White House meeting that Ray had phoned in to her. Tarek leaned forward.

She started reading, "The President indicated his first choice was restraint, economic sanctions." She looked up at him quickly. "Ray told him to start with them but not be too surprised if they don't work, Iraq's got stockpiles, and somebody's always dealing underneath the table."

Tarek continued to take her in silently.

"Ray said he told him quite simply that we are at a crossroads. Iraq is coming at the rest of the Middle East. We are seeing all sorts of subversive cells seeded throughout Saudi Arabia, Bahrain, the entire Arab side of the Gulf, nurtured by Iraq—which is also busy terrorizing these countries with assassination attempts on their leaders, bombs planted in their oil refineries, and kamikaze runs on their shipping through the Gulf. That Iraq is dead-set on taking over the rest of the Gulf. And if they succeed it would be an unmitigated disaster for all of us."

Elaine looked up at Tarek, "Ray said General Schwarzkopf told him that what he was talking about could be the biggest military build-up we've taken on since Vietnam."

Elaine looked quietly at Tarek, put the notes down, and continued speaking.

"Ray said Schwarzkopf told him of the bodies he had buried in Vietnam. The futile blood, the legs blown off, the open staring eyes he had covered with sheets. Told Ray he had walked away vowing never to let it happen again. Ray said Schwarzkopf looked at the president and simply said 'If you choose to fight, you're going to lose if you do it like we did it in Vietnam. This time you're going to have to make a decision to fight—and to win.'"

Tarek listened to her silently.

"Ray said Bush then stood up and told them to draw up the military options."

Tarek remained absolutely still.

"Ray said the final point of the meeting was for him." She looked down at the notes.

"The President wanted to know if Ray was going to be able to get us the support we need from the Saudis for bases, docking, deployment, to work with us on this. Ray said Bush held out the overnight wires about Arab countries refusing to make statements condemning Saddam. About King Hussein of Jordan and the Palestinians actually backing him up."

Elaine looked at Tarek. "Ray said the President pointed out that they are going to convene an Arab summit and asked him if he could at least get them to speak out against this.

"Ray said there was dead silence when he said he didn't know whether he could or not. He explained that the countries are terrified. None of them has any military to speak of, King Fahd is terrified—realizes he'll probably be massacred, but he doesn't know which way to turn. There are those within the country who realize that this is a disaster, but they can't promise Fahd that after all of these fades we've done over the years that we will either step in, or stay in once we show up."

"And what did the President say?" asked Tarek.

"'Ray, we're dead in the water to really move if they don't. I can start economic sanctions, Secretary of State Baker is already talking to President Ozal of Turkey, but we need something firm from the Arabs themselves.'"

"Ray's reply?" asked Tarek quietly.

"Sir, I'll try. Christ, I'm going to try."

"And then," said Elaine folding up the paper, "he told me to come see you."

19

▲▲What did Tarek say?" Ray held the line from Washington as Elaine finished talking.

"He just listened."

Ray breathed deeply. "Elaine, I want you to personally take everything you're getting from surveillance—the AWACS, the KH-11, all of it, over to Tarek. I don't want to rely on Defense getting it to him. I want him to have everything we've got. He's our hope, the connection who can wire this for us. He's going to be sticking his neck way out there if he does. And there are already enough powerful interests that he's been bucking, perhaps galling would be a better word, that would like nothing better than to see him lead the king into a big misstep. A lot of old rivalries within the family."

He hung up the phone and returned to Schwarzkopf, who was dialing General Johnson, head of the U.S. Transport Command.

"General Johnson, we'd like you to prepare plans for some possibilities in the Persian Gulf." Schwarzkopf's voice clipped along before Johnson could even comment. "Here's what we are thinking about. The fastest, biggest, farthest military deployment in U.S. history." Schwarzkopf hung up.

Johnson simply sat holding the receiver in shock. He then shot the orders over to Military Sealift Command in Washington. Military Sealift Command looked at the incredible barrage of orders. The admiral in charge turned frantically to his file safe, fumbling for the secret MidEast Deployment Plan that had been mouldering there. He scanned the unbelievably out-of-date plan. It was for a world war between the U.S. and the Soviet Union, with a few ships going to the Gulf. "Oh my God," he groaned to his stunned aide, "how are we going to do this? We don't have a plan."

Schwarzkopf received the return advisory in icy silence. He motioned Ray to follow him.

S chwarzkopf tore into the computer room. The startled techs moved out of the way as the brusque general barreled past them.

"1 want the computer plans for deployment."

The tech looked up even more startled. "Which one, Sir?"

Schwarzkopf thrust the file folder at him. "1 ran this war game in June, a command exercise that had Iraq as the adversary. There should have been a deployment plan run for it in the computer—I told someone here that we should use this as the basis for beginning to update our old MidEast Deployment Plan. Get it out of the computer for me. Now." Schwarzkopf abruptly sat down in the chair, folded his arms, and stared at the terrified tech.

"I want all the data you should have in your computer, all the thousands of details we pay you Pentagon computer wizards here to draft up, with the millions of logistical details—on how we actually get our troops from the bases into the battle-field—that go along with this deployment plan. You know," his thick finger thumped the revised deployment outline, "how the

211

poor fuckers are actually supposed to fight this war." He took out a cigar and lit it. "Unless you all thought we'd just sort of wave them off with a big good-bye."

One of the techs in the back of the room laughed despite himself. He loved "Stormin'" Norman, "The Bear," as he was fondly known. What a piece of work the guy was. The tech standing in front of Schwarzkopf scrambled toward the machines.

"Sir," he said, fumbling with the controls for the right program, "I don't think you want to wait. This printout is probably going to be at least three feet high by the time it's all out."

"I've got all day," Schwarzkopf blew the cigar smoke toward the smoke detector. The tech in the back of the room suppressed a snicker.

"Yes sir." The tech began rapidly moving through the directories of all the computer programs on file in the Pentagon. Schwarzkopf watched as the back of the man's neck started to redden. He continued to search. Sweat beads appeared on his forehead. Finally he turned around. His voice, as he faced Schwarzkopf's stern gaze, was barely a whisper. "Sir, the file indicates that a new deployment plan was never drawn up. The old one was never updated."

Schwarzkopf appeared genuinely taken aback. "Get me the old one then."

The tech nodded and scrambled back toward the computer controls. He almost jammed the board as the minutes ticked on. This time he turned around, ashen.

"It's gone."

"What?" Schwarzkopf's voice roared, the cigar smashed into the coffee cup.

"You mean to say there isn't a single source document in that computer bank? The central piece of data that drives the whole thing isn't there? That plan to fight a fucking war has simply disappeared?"

The tech shook. "Sir, maybe somebody took it out to work on updating it and bypassed the rules about not removing it totally from the bank, sir, maybe…"

Schwarzkopf rose, a looming body of rage. He moved closer to the tech. The man in the back thought for a moment he would kill, simply break the tech into pieces. Schwarzkopf moved his face right up to the tech's. His voice startled everybody. It was perfectly, evenly modulated.

"In Vietnam, the Viet Cong had ways of torture that were heinous, beyond description. Would leave a man begging for the bullet." Schwarzkopf stepped toward the door. "Son, you're going to find that document for me in the next two hours. Or you're going to know exactly how that man felt."

When Ray returned that night to his hotel room, stunned by the disarray, he found the message from Elaine. He picked up the phone and quickly connected through to her in Riyadh. Her voice was quiet, the statement simple.

"Tarek has agreed to go to the meeting at the palace tomorrow morning."

The limousines pulled up to the palace door. Slowly Fahd made his way out of the car up the marble staircase through the phalanx of guards at attention. Abdullah, tall and erect, nodded a salute to his National Guardsmen, then pulled his black robe about his shoulders and went in. The ministry of defense car arrived, bringing Sultan. Finally the ministry of interior's car appeared. As Naif, the minister, approached the door, Tarek walked behind him and caught his arm. "You talked to the king?" Naif nodded. "He'll agree?" Naif shook his head as the servants with their gold swords filed past him into the conference room. Tarek scowled.

Naif shrugged. "He says we must be clever, take the long view."

"But, Naif…"

"If you can't convince him, you go along quietly." Naif drew him closer. "Because one thing we know for sure, Tarek. Divided we fall instantly. Completely, instantly, washed away like so much sand into the Gulf. Right? I don't have to add what will happen to your life, if you confront him."

Tarek simply stood staring at him, and then walked into the conference room and sat down.

Fahd sat, hands folded across his gold embroidered robe.

Tarek stood up, glancing at the men around him.

"Your Majesty, it might be useful to review our arrangements with Iraq."

Tarek watched Fahd's anger surface, the hooded eyes narrow. The others sat in hushed silence. Tarek continued.

"I have received a request from the U.S. for basing rights for their planes, their troops, and for additional platforms in the Gulf for surveillance, information intercepts. I understand the reluctance to appear to be tied to them, but we can't continue to rely on 'diplomacy' to deal with Iraq."

Abdullah flared up. "We are here to discuss an Arab solution."

Saud cut in. "The U.S. is totally unreliable."

Defense Minister Sultan looked up calculatingly. "Why don't we let Iraq have Kuwait or at least the islands?"

Suddenly, Tarek broke in. They turned, stunned at his words. "Cheney has been told to fly in."

Tarek watched as Fahd pushed himself from the chair, furious, and without a backward look walked out of the room.

Badr watched Tarek nervously as he returned to the office. "Tarek, be careful. The king might…"

They both turned as the aide rushed through the door. "A message from Hamid just came through." He pulled a chair up, catching his breath. "He says Iraq has just gotten in total official specs and information on the U.S. equipment, personnel, capabilities coming into the Gulf." Tarek's eyebrows shot up.

"They tapped into the U.S. Military Command head-quarters?"

"I don't know…Hamid doesn't clarify. He says Iraq's analysis is that the U.S. is woefully unprepared. So Iraq decided last night to move full speed ahead with terrorist activities. Plans to detonate mines beneath the ships. Artillery fire for the U.S. surveillance helicopters. Sabotage for any other surveillance units. To begin immediately to drive them out and frighten any of the countries in the Gulf that might be thinking of working with the U.S."

Badr interrupted, "I just called the rest of the Gulf leaders on a secret conference call. They're completely paralyzed. They won't make a move unless Fahd does. And finally," said Badr, "there's this from the tap on the cell."

Badr turned on the small cassette. The cell leader spoke quietly, the last lines of the ancient verse dropping softly from his mouth. "The blood of the lamb shall be shed at Ramadan. The blood of the lamb shall be shed. The feet of the West shall not walk the earth of Mecca. The blood of the lamb will be shed."

Tarek started for the door.

"There's one other thing from Hamid. They—Iraq, Antar— have been informed that you are the one trying to convince Fahd to cooperate with the U.S."

20

Ray got off the plane carrying a copy of the three-foot computer printout. "What's that?" asked Elaine.

"A little love note from General Schwarzkopf, with whom you are soon going to be working closely. In short, a plan for the fastest, biggest, farthest military deployment in U.S. history."

Ray wiped the sweat off his face as he got into the car. He handed her a sheet. "A summary. The plans are initially for a trip wire force of 2,300 men from the 82nd Airborne's lightly armed brigade. These will be protected by Navy carrier planes and Air Force F-15's. A 16,500-man Marine amphibious brigade with heavy armor will be prepared to go in next. This will be followed by 19,000 troops of the 101st Air Mobile Division who are good tank killers, and up to 12,000 troops of the 24th Heavy Armored Division, who are trained in desert warfare."

"As I was leaving, Powell and Schwarzkopf issued orders for fifty U.S. warships, including the aircraft carriers U.S.S. *Independence* and U.S.S. *Eisenhower*, which are already heading for the Gulf now to begin enforcing the economic sanctions. The rest—they're waiting on us to get cleared with Fahd. The basic plan is to draw a line in the sand. Send enough troops to let Saddam know that if he attacks Saudi Arabia, he attacks the U.S."

Elaine simply stared at him. Ray handed her the material.

"You're going to have to move this stuff back and forth to Tarek, personally. We can't communicate anything this critical until we find the leaks. This stuff gets out, and we've just lost the war."

Elaine took the bundle from him. "Schwarzkopf is terrified about the leak, but they've all agreed to hush it up in hopes that we can find it before they actually begin deploying. Cheney is flying over here to try to get Fahd to agree."

Ray wiped some more sweat off of his face. "Even the usual White House shit has quieted down for the moment, the normal pissing contests between White House staff and various Cabinet members trying to run the show. The usual battles for turf, prima donnas trying to outscream one another, brickbats flying through the air while the more insidious warfare goes on sub rosa. It's all quieted down—everybody's scared."

Ray winced. "After all these years of cutting and running, I'm supposed to be able to talk them into trusting us. Christ, can you believe we're running the country, the world like that?

"I'm going to have to go over these plans some more myself, and then take them to Tarek. We have to convince him that we have a plan that will work so he can convince Fahd. Tarek's our only hope."

The car stopped before Ray's office. "Part of this plan calls for Special Operations groups to infiltrate Kuwait. To help set them up, we need people to connect with in Kuwait. The Iraqis are apprehending Kuwaiti men trying to flee across the border. But I understand women and children are flooding into the hospitals. Go to the women's unit in the hospital and talk to the patients, to the doctors, debrief them. Places, names of those who stayed behind, anyone we can connect with inside." He got out and motioned for the driver to take Elaine on.

Elaine entered the chaos of the National Guard Hospital. Patients lying in the halls, nurses and doctors racing around frantically. The receptionist listened to Elaine's request, then abruptly turned to the pager. "Dr. Naila, Dr. Naila." The woman pointed down the hall. Elaine moved hesitantly past the women, the children crying on the gurneys.

"Where is Dr. Naila?" A nurse waved toward a room and hurried by. Naila stepped away from her patient and embraced Elaine, then listened as she explained her visit.

"Come with me." Naila moved down the hall and turned into a room. Elaine saw a middle-aged woman in bandages, an IV dripping into her arm. "Najwa, I want you to talk to this lady. Tell her what you saw." Naila pulled a chair up to the bed for Elaine.

"I saw the first bombs in the night. We heard the tanks, the firing in the streets," the woman spoke haltingly. "Our house was hit and we moved out to the street. The tanks were surrounding the Ministry buildings—Defense, Information, all the rest. We tried to bring my son to the hospital, but that was surrounded too. My husband said we should begin walking across the desert."

She broke down and started weeping. "I can still see all of those people, the ones who fell by the wayside in the desert trying to cross to Saudi Arabia. Others tried to go by boats in the night to Bahrain. If the Iraqis found us, they would let the women and children sometimes pass, but they held back the men. We heard gunshots, and then would see their bodies across the desert as we went." She drew a breath and then tried to go on. "We made it to the border, and then they flew us to hospital." She broke down completely. Naila put her arm around her. The woman looked up finally. "But there are those who stayed on to fight..."

Elaine interrupted her, "That's what I want. Help us please, to know who they are; we want to work with them."

The woman nodded and Elaine took out a pad of paper. Naila leaned over. "Do you want me to write them for you? The Arabic names might be hard for you if you're not used to them."

"I actually know Arabic a bit," Elaine smiled back at the surprise on Naila's face. She began to write.

When she was finished, she carried the information back by hand, afraid to communicate by any other means because of the leaks.

※ ※ ※

Said had gotten Tarek's call to meet him at the house that night. Said walked in past the houseboy and stopped at the sight of the open door to the living room. Nura was standing there, totally rapt up in the report coming over the television. Musaid, standing behind her, watched the television for a minute, then sat down. "Where is Naila?"

Nura looked at Musaid in surprise. "She's just come back from the hospital for a rest; she's due back there in an hour and I don't want to bother her. Surely you've heard the reports? All of the doctors are on emergency call there."

He pushed the small footstool in front of him away. "I think the time has come to end this."

She remained silent, watching the anger, the ugly temper.

"Musaid, she can hardly decline to work at a time like this."

He cut her off abruptly. "She can hardly decline to do what I tell her." His hand gestured dismissively toward the television screen. "There is always another reason. The hospital can find somebody else to help them. You can tell her I don't intend to delay the plans we've set."

Musaid got up and walked out of the door as abruptly as he had come, brushing past Said standing silently in the hall. As he passed, Nura caught sight of Said standing there. Their eyes locked for a moment. Said, staring at her, seemed unable to move. Then he turned quickly and walked into the study where Tarek waited for him with a drink in his hand. He entered, his face drawn, and handed the sheets to Tarek.

"Tarek, on the money, I'm not finding anything."

"Nothing unusual?"

"Nothing."

"Keep tracing it for me."

"Yes, of course, Tarek." Said spoke in a low voice. "Everybody in the Arab coalition is afraid. They want the U.S. protection, but they are terrified that Saddam will retaliate. They won't make a move until Fahd does."

Tarek slowly shook his head. "Said, the dangerous, dangerous games," he whispered as though to himself.

"The insidious games, Said. The ones inside. We have done this to ourselves." He turned the drink in his hand, the ice rolling like dice. "The whole time the Gulf countries poured money into Iraq to keep fighting the Iran-Iraq War, the southern Gulf countries were hedging their bets. The dhows going right over from the U.A.E., from Dubai to Iran, loaded with food, refrigerators, electronics from Taiwan, Japanese air conditioners, tea from India, washing machines, you name it. And so," Tarek looked at Said, "Iran just kept going." His eyes narrowed as he looked at his hands. "Saddam knew it the whole time and hated them for using him, hated us for double crossing him. He decided that Khomeini was right, our governments ought to be overthrown, we were weak, indecisive, greedy, duplicitous, someone ought to sweep us under one major power in the Gulf. And he concluded it ought to be him, Saddam, heading it up. And so now he uses all of the cells, the terrorist networks Iran set up. Uses all of the discontent—the poor, the Palestinians. He puts on the robes and makes the hajj to appeal to the fundamentalists, he'll put on his bedu kaffiyeh and talk about reinstating the pure Arab world. Wears his western business suit to give dinner parties for people in from Washington and buy arms and technology from the West. And finally, he has somebody on the inside who is helping him. Somebody who isn't leaving any tracks."

Said spoke quietly. "I'll keep tracing it."

Tarek looked at him. The web of doubt that snared everyone in his life, laying its tiny, suffocating filaments, now included this man, the friend who had always been beyond question. Tarek's insides gnawed at him as his eyes searched Said's face for the crack, the camouflage. But all he saw was the inherent decency, the honor that seemed to flow in Said's blood, the steadfast, trustworthy eyes of a man whose allegiances had always been profound.

aid returned to his office and sat in the darkened room. He glanced down at the messages on his desk, from the head of the BCCI importuning him to assist on their latest scam. Begging him, just this once, to come in on their deals. He pushed the messages into the trash basket. He hated the sleaze of it, of them. The corruptness that seemed to engulf the Arab world, the venal self-interest that smarmed every aspect of their lives. Tarek's words came back to him: "The insidious games. We have done this to ourselves." Tarek was right. Utterly, tragically right. They had dishonored themselves before the world. When would it end?

Said stood up and caught his reflection in the glass window. The straight back, strong shoulders, the tall torso beneath the handsomely etched face with dark serious eyes, eyes that seemed to gaze steadily back into himself—finding a man of honor, of integrity—a man who did what he truly believed was the right thing at a time when the compass had been lost in the Middle East.

He sat down, his feelings suddenly wrenching him. The whole time he had been talking to Tarek, a man he loved as a brother, he could hear the footsteps from the other room. At each step he wondered if it was her, at each step consumed by feelings that overwhelmed him. Even as he looked at Tarek, tormented by the betrayal of his actions, he knew that what they had done was right. He thought of the clandestine meetings over the years. He had hated the hiding, the duplicity that she and he had had to engage in, the deceit. And yet, he looked down at his hands, he knew they were right.

The voices in his head telling him he was courting disaster—he had long since pushed away. The old system that strangled them, corrupted them should be swept away. There was no dishonor, rather only honor in what they wanted. His life for a moment to unrolled before him—the prestige, the position that he had spent years achieving and now had totally jeopardized. It no longer meant anything compared to the other. What they were doing was right.

21

Badr rushed into Tarek's office the next morning, where Elaine and Ray were going over Schwarzkopf's plans with him. Badr thrust the new communiqué from Hamid at Tarek. Elaine and Ray scanned the sheet with him.

"The Iraqis are moving some more Scuds, tanks, and chemical gasses toward our border. The satellite analysts are still at work on this imaging that came in yesterday, but they say there is a possibility that these two points," he put the map down on Tarek's desk, "are locations, plants where they are manufacturing more chemicals. On this one, the imaging of the chemical plant in Samarra is much clearer."

He waited while Tarek brought the enlargement glass over the printout.

"This other one," Badr moved another satellite scan onto his desk, "is a better version of the one they were trying for three days ago. The analysts say those are new missile launch sites Iraq has put into place. The target range is obviously more than adequate to reach Kuwait. The target is Saudi Arabia."

He pushed the chair back and handed Elaine the next sheet.

"The final one is the overnight satellite. These are the night movements of the speedboats from Iraq in the Gulf. It's impossible to tell from the satellite which ones are laying more mines. We're going to need sonar for that."

He stopped and stared at Ray and Elaine.

"But it is clear that one of the basic movements of the speedboats is up and down the shipping lanes the U.S. carriers are going to come up."

Ray's head shot up nervously; he reached for the printout that Elaine grimly passed to him. Badr handed Tarek the final sheet.

"Hamid has it arranged." Badr pointed to the communiqués. "You will cross the border into Kuwait with a group of bedu. The Iraqi patrol has become accustomed to some of them located in the desert by the border. Inside a man named Nasser will meet you. You leave now."

"Tarek," Elaine's voice, full of apprehension, cut through the air as he stood up to go. Tarek turned around and looked at her curiously. "Tarek, what if they find you?"

Tarek stopped, he seemed to consider her rather than her question in the moment of silence that followed.

"They won't." He walked out the door.

❈ ❈ ❈

Tarek moved with the bedu band toward the border. The waves of heat hung in layers in the air. The Iraqi guard lethargically perused the dusty bedu and goats that had passed to the watering hole in the morning. Bored, he motioned them along. Tarek pulled his dirty kaffiyeh tighter around his face and began to walk past. Suddenly the guard moved toward him. His machine gun pointed to the dust-smeared pocket of Tarek's bedu thobe. The old bedu alongside Tarek moved nervously closer to him. Tarek's hand nonchalantly reached toward the pocket.

"Mindfadlak." He pulled out the package of cigarettes and gave it to the Iraqi guard, who smiled a broad, almost toothless smile.

"Shokran," said the guard with a wave of his machine gun to the kaffiyeh-covered face. The old bedu closed his eyes in relief. Tarek simply nodded and continued behind the straggling band of goats. They moved on across the desert past abandoned cars, dead bodies, some shot, others dead of thirst and the heat. At nightfall they reached an oasis where Nasser waited for them.

Nasser reached into his goatskin bag and handed the Iraqi army clothes to Tarek, who put them on wordlessly. Nasser then pulled out the Iraqi-issue guns and they strapped them on. Tarek and Nasser moved on toward the city, the sounds of gunfire now within hearing.

The blackened streets were interrupted by a few lights still on, glaring over the tanks rolling by. Nasser saluted one of the contingents of Iraqi guards and moved on past the bombed-out houses. They walked past a woman wailing over the bodies of two dead men, one with his head bashed open, the other with his testicles cut off and eyes gouged out. The woman's wail disappeared behind them as they turned down a side street toward the back entrance of a basement.

Making sure no one saw them, they entered. Men and women huddled silently inside. Tarek glanced around the room of Kuwaiti shopkeepers, some of the younger members of the Sabah family, foreign workers. After Nasser introduced Tarek to them, one young man spoke up.

"We have gotten people across the desert, led by the bedu. But we need to get many more out."

"The westerners, who were trapped inside the city, we are hiding in our homes," interrupted another. "The Iraqis are talking of moving them to Baghdad and around the strategic parts of Iraq to use as a human shield if the U.S. decides to move against Iraq. The Iraqis are issuing orders about running the city, and we have engineered a few mass refusals, but whenever they trace the rebellion to the instigaters, they torture and kill those involved."

A young woman in the back of the room nervously spoke up. "We have no arms, no way to communicate, no way to really carry out a resistance."

Tarek looked at the people in the room, and understandably, was overwhlemed by doubt that these people before him had the ability to carry out a resistance—these Kuwaitis, who had led a totally cossetted life of money, servants, ease. They had become the spoiled children of the Gulf, in fact of the world. Now they pulled their chairs closer, begging him for survival.

Tarek began. He drew it all out for them, praying they could undertand—the essential elements of information he needed— Iraqi troop identifications and dispositions, command and control measures. How to communicate via satellite with intelligence authorities in Saudi Arabia. Ways intelligence could move through back channels to him. The tiny mobile lasers he would get to them via the bedu so they could mark Iraqi targets within Kuwait to be seen from satellite reconnaissance—Iraqi headquarters, arsenals. How to structure sniper fire to harass the military, car bombs, molotov cocktails, how to steal arms, blow up cars. How to manufacture Iraqi ID's, use harmless looking hotel clerks to listen at the Iraqi watering holes and then pass the information out. How to bribe the Iraqi soldiers at checkpoints—stereos, cassette players, cigarettes. How he would feed them the black-market money to buy supplies and food and how to move the arms through the bedu. Then, Nasser indicated that it was an hour before dawn when they must go. Tarek finished his instructions. As dawn approached, Nasser listened, then opened the door from the cellar to go. Tarek followed him.

Tarek got back to his office and Badr handed him the phone. Ray was on the other end. "I tried to get you last night. Tarek," Ray's voice was taut. "Iraq is escalating. The U.S.S. *Independence* is approaching, and its advance helicopters are sighting Iraqi speedboats all over, laying mines.

"Tarek, it's only a matter of time before this blows up. You, us, all of us. You've got to convince Fahd to step forward. Now. Tarek, I'm lobbying the President and Congress to do this, the largest U.S. commitment of ships and personnel since Vietnam, but I'm doing this unable to report to them that any of the Arab Gulf countries will back us up, even let our ships dock." Ray's voice began to sound desperate. "Cheney is flying in in forty-eight hours. Powell and Schwarzkopf want to begin sending troops. Tarek, you've got to get Fahd to…" Ray heard the click on the other end—Tarek had hung up. Elaine watched Ray grimly put the receiver down.

She returned to the board and listened to the feed from the control room of the U.S.S. *Independence*, starting to move up the Gulf. The U.S. captain's voice methodically checked off the newly located mines, the ship's navigation points, the second in command confirming.

She listened, stunned, at the communications coming back from the advance helicopters. She sat down at the control board and put the headphones on. She adjusted the channel and heard the crackle of static, then the slow rolling sound of the Gulf waters below a helicopter circling overhead. The helicopter circled three times and then moved on, leaving only the low sounds of the water lapping. She adjusted the channels toward a deeper frequency and began to hear the deep rumbling sound of a large ship's engine. The static flared again, and then a voice speaking English with an Indian accent came across the intercom of the ship immediately in front of the U.S.S. *Independence.*

"*Star of India,* commercial cargo, reporting clearance for channel north. Please confirm." The voice from the control tower came back. "That is correct *Star of India.* Proceed north. Dhahran has confirmed your berth." The tower intercom clicked off. Static again, then the sound of the waters of the Gulf and the low churning of the ship's engine moving north. Elaine glanced over at the pile of communiqués Ray had left on the desk for her. She put the headphones down on the desk and began to skim the overnight communiqué from the National Security Council.

Suddenly the sound of an explosion ripped through the earphones lying in front of her. She grabbed the headset as the sound of screams reverberated through the earpiece, followed by the captain's voice. "Urgent, *Star of India, Star of India.* This is the captain of *The Star of India.* I think a mine has exploded to our starboard. We have been hit. Urgent, we are on fire."

Wildly, she jammed the panel board, switching to the U.S.S. *Independence.* She heard the crackle of charts, then the low voice of the second aboard the *Independence,* only feet away from the burning ship. The edged, hoarse words, watching the ship in front of them aflame. "Captain, I'm scared. I'm just goddamned, fucking scared."

ithin the hour a call went out from Fahd for an emergency meeting of the small council. By the early afternoon, those summoned had arrived. Fahd walked into the meeting room in the palace and closed the door. Walid watched him go, and then sat alone in the anteroom, his back to the door, feet on the desk, papers in his lap, staring out the window as the clock ticked through thirty minutes, then an hour.

"Walid?" He whirled around with a start.

"Oh God, Musaid," he said with relief, as he saw the thin dark figure. He motioned him toward a chair. "Musaid, I'm sorry, I should have called to tell you the meeting was canceled." He pushed his kaffiyeh back in exhaustion.

"At least tell me what's going on," demanded Musaid.

"Shit, I'm nervous. Nobody knows what the hell's going on." Walid tilted his hand toward the closed doors of Fahd's chamber. "He's called an emergency meeting of the small council. Abdullah just flew in from meetings with the Syrians, Saud got here from his session with the Soviets, Ray Holt sent over his latest information, Sultan's in there with defense layouts in the rest of the Gulf."

Walid shuffled the financial papers on the desk. "God, you should see the money flowing out of this place. I haven't seen so much cash transferred out of a country since the Kuwaitis had their Souk al Manakh stock crash in 1983. About the only thing staying is the real estate, and that's because the fucking businessmen can't pull it off the map and wire it out to Switzerland."

A red light lit up on Walid's phone. "So they're going to break in five minutes."

"Good, I'll wait," said Musaid.

Walid looked at Musaid, "I'm going to have to ask you to

go, it's only the small council, OK? I'll reschedule you as soon as I can, old pal," He dismissed him with a pat on the back.

As Tarek hurriedly emerged from the chambers, Musaid brushed by him in the hall as he angrily walked out.

Tarek went from the chambers directly to his car, picked up the carphone and called Ray Holt. "Meet me in ten minutes at the souk."

Elaine and Ray walked up as Tarek, waiting in the souk, inhaled from a cigarette and then threw it on the ground. "Fahd won't agree to work with you until he gets two things. First, his own arms he's been trying to buy from you so he can defend himself if Iraq retaliates, and second, a deal on the Palestinians. You have leverage with the Israelis –use it. Now. Can you do it quietly?"

"Quietly?" Ray looked quizzically at Tarek, "What do you mean, quietly?"

"Move the arms, the artillery through Bahrain, through Egypt, whatever. Make it look like back orders, someone else's orders." Tarek handed a riyal to the tobaccaner and reached for a small pack of cigarettes, and turned back to Ray. "However you can do it. But quietly, back channels. No political debates in your Congress. Fahd's right, you've left him in an untenable position. We come to you with a request for arms, you allow the Israeli lobby to block the sale in Congress. The same arms you're selling to Israel. That leaves Fahd embarrassed in front of his own people. He looks totally ineffectual, he can't even get arms from his supposed ally. He's left standing there with no way to protect the country in the face of this kind of threat."

Ray looked down at the old men hunched over their back-gammon table, puffing slowly on the long stem of the wood-and-glass hubble-bubble. "Move the arms and no leaks from your intelligence network." Ray stopped in front of the glass window with its rows of hanging gold, the gleam of the intricately wrought necklaces and bracelets. "Tarek, for Christ's sake, it's not intentional, we have our systems."

"It's irrelevant whether it's intentional or not," said Tarek tautly. "It creates a situation that is impossible for me to work with. They are afraid to deal with you. You have a National Security Council meeting, and within the hour the Israelis have the entire transcript. You plan a coup against Khadaffi and before it can take place your news media prints the plans."

He glanced down at the old bedu with his ancient silver kunjars laid out on a rug, the silver dagger blades shining on the colors of the woven camel's hair. "We move money around for you, all the dirty deals you can't do for yourselves, millions to the anti-government rebels in Angola, and every other god-forsaken place you're nervous about. Money, arms," he breathed angrily, "in the asshole deals you arrange with Iran. Deals that blow up in everybody's face while your intelligence units fight among themselves, doctor assessments to support somebody's current policies, leak information to jockey for position. And you walk away."

Tarek stopped before a bookstall where the vendor feathered the desert dust off of the volumes. He shook his head. "The carnage. The whole time your intelligence, your State Department, is lying to assure the administration that their policies are brilliant. They leak information your press prints about arranging coups with Egypt and Sudan. And so Egypt and Sudan are left exposed, with blood on their hands and Khadaffi alive. Fahd moves money, arms, and he's exposed. Ridiculed in your press for being your lackey. The man is on a tightrope and the Americans write in astonishment that he gave $86 million to the PLO in one year, $700 million to Syria, money to Khaddafi," Tarek moved closer to Ray. "Yes, we give money to them. Millions. We are in the middle of these people, they must be dealt with. Yes," his eyes locked on Ray's, "we buy them. We buy them because there is no way else we can have any leverage over them. And," his words moved slowly, "we buy yours."

Elaine watched the anger rise in Tarek's eyes while Ray remained silent. "We buy your way out of every dirty little problem you can't resolve," Tarek concluded.

"Ray, you will do what I ask, won't you? Because I'm all you have. And the equation is utterly simple. If the Arab side of the Gulf goes under to Iraq, one-half of the free world's oil supply is held hostage. Every analyst you have knows you can't compensate for that loss; it would throw the free world into chaos."

He picked up a worn, dusty copy of the Koran from the stall, leafed through it, then put it down. "And you know the rest, don't you? The rest of the Middle East would start to collapse after us, Jordan, Egypt, on down the line across North Africa."

He glanced at the scribe on the rug with the coins in front of him. "I want a deal on the Palestinians, and on arms, and assurances, proof that we'll be protected in this."

Ray said, "I'll try. I just don't know if I can succeed."

Tarek's silence to that reply was deafening.

Ray and Elaine walked silently back to the office. She opened the door and was handed the alert that had just come across. Another explosion in the Gulf, this one a small mine-detecting boat that had preceded the U.S. ship by only a few yards. The fire, stated the communiqué, had killed two; the third was badly burned. Suddenly she started shaking. Ray's eyes shot up to her, startled. "What is it?" His voice was alarmed.

"I can't do this," she whispered. Her body shook as though from its very center. "Ray," she whispered again, "I need to go. Now."

Ray looked at her, absolutely silent.

"Ray, I can see it all happening again, I can feel it…the bodies, the death. Ray," her voice dropped to a bare decibel, "I can't be part of it again."

Ray watched the nerves that he had seen go in the very best of them, raw before him. The instincts, the nerves of those who hadn't died emotionally beneath the covers, beneath the professional patina they employed, but truly saw and felt what was in front of them. They were the best, ultimately the best, and the price they paid was the one that Elaine was now paying. The shakes in the night, the fears. He walked over and said the only thing there was to say. The truth.

"But you are part of it. The only question is whether you are going to walk away from it." He was quiet for a moment, his eyes fixed on her. "And the result," he continued softly, "if you do, would only buy more bodies, more blood, more death."

Minutes passed, Elaine said nothing. Finally she looked up at Ray and nodded. Her eyes saw images from inside, recurring now like blows, living again like ghosts moving through her body, sounds, explosions echoing and echoing again.

She took the cup that Ray offered her and went back to work.

Tarek returned to his office, picked up the phone and dialed one last time to petition Fahd.

"Walid, I need to see Fahd. Now." Silence. "Walid, are you there? I need to see Fahd."

"Yes, yes I'm here." Walid paused. "You want to come now?"

"Yes."

"He's going to leave in a half an hour with Naif. Going to inspect part of the new oil installation. I just finished calling the U.S. Embassy to notify them that his meeting with the Ambassador is canceled."

Tarek listened, startled.

"He canceled his meeting and he's going with Naif?"

"Yes," Walid's voice wandered in bored nonchalance. "He does what he wants, you know. I only keep the schedule, or what there is of one. He decided an hour ago he wants to go with Naif, so he will."

"You're going with him?"

"No, no," murmured Walid in his blasé tone of voice. "But I suppose you could drive with them and have your conversation along the way. You don't mind Naif being along, do you?"

Tarek paused. "I'll be there."

"Good." Walid hung up and looked at the clock, then picked up the phone again and called the king's driver.

Tarek walked down the long hall to the Royal Protocol Office. Walid was sitting alone, his back to the door, feet on the desk, talking to a contractor on the phone about the small fee for himself that would have to be paid for his help. Walid hung up just as Tarek got to the door. He took a book from his desk. "Here, I have something for you. The archaeologist, Yusif Khalidi, left me a copy of his last book when he came to schedule his return visit." He handed it to Tarek. "Can you imagine? Everybody knows I don't read. The car's in front."

The king's car waited at the entrance of the palace. The young driver, busy dusting the hood, adjusted the flag and bent down to check the tires. He glanced at his watch. He nodded a hello to Tarek, smiled, then looked up at the doorman scuttling down the steps, motioning to him to move the car.

The driver's smile disappeared. He shook his head. The doorman insisted. Extreme agitation covered the driver's face. Finally, seeing soldiers approach, the young man scowled and got into the car, glancing agitatedly back at Tarek.

He turned on the ignition. The car moved down the driveway for fifty yards. Then suddenly it exploded into an enormous swirling ball of fire.

The king and Naif, now by the door of the palace, drew back stunned before the shattering glass, metal, and flames. Suddenly from one of the loudspeakers above the mosques came an ear-splitting sound of static. After the static came the sounds of Radio Riyadh broadcasting. A young woman's voice broke into the broadcast. Her words—short, brief and steady—flowed across the city.

"At this moment the king has been killed. A martyr for Allah has given his life to destroy Fahd the corrupt. It is the will of Allah."

The static flared again and then the voice called its final words. "This is only the beginning. The downtrodden will rise. The least will be first. His will be served."

The guards quickly ushered the shaken king back into the palace and rapidly put out the fire.

Tarek walked over to the car, the charred body inside. He waited for the heat to subside enough for him to reach under what was left of the hood. He moved his fingers down below the cylinders until he found what he was looking for. He took the small exploded plastic bomb device out, turned and walked away.

Badr was waiting for him when he got back to the office. Tarek opened the drawer and pulled out a packet of photos. Badr watched while he brought the light down over one picture. "This one. That was him—the driver."

Badr looked at the photo—it was the young man who had walked into the Riyadh cell meeting behind Osman's son, Abed.

"It was an unscheduled trip. Who knew Fahd was leaving with Naif?"

"Abdullah, Sultan, and Saud. The information had gone over also to the American Embassy. Walid placed the calls." He put the photo back in the drawer.

"And you were to be in the car, too," mused Badr. "You, Naif, and Fahd. The king and the head of intelligence, along with Naif who oversees internal security. Not a bad hit—efficient. Sounds like Antar. What do you think?"

"That they missed the first time—and will try again."

An aide walked in the door with the satellite scan Tarek had called for. Tarek traced it under the light and handed Badr the tracking. "There's no break in the satellite scan."

Badr looked at him, uncomprehending.

"The break into the Radio Riyadh broadcast didn't come from outside. It wasn't beamed from Iraq," said Tarek. "It was from inside the country. The voice was from somewhere inside the Kingdom."

When Tarek returned home that night, he found Nura writing in her journal. She looked up at him. "Tarek, what happened?" Her voice was quiet. He told her the sequence of events with the car bomb attempt.

Tarek felt Nura's eyes. He watched her hand move slowly through her hair while he finished his sentence.

"Abdullah, Sultan, Saud. The American Embassy got the information. Walid placed the calls."

Suddenly she leaned up and pulled him down toward her. Her hand moved over his face, bringing his mouth down to hers.

"I was so terrified." she whispered. "When I talked to Badr, he told me you were on your way to see Fahd. And then I heard the radio broadcast..." She moved her body closer, slowly drawing her hand down Tarek's leg.

Tarek looked curiously at her for a moment. "You knew I was going to go to see the king, then?"

"Yes, Naila and I called to see when you would be back."

She brought her mouth onto his as the sound of the muezzin rang softly across the city.

22

Elaine moved alongside Naila in the hospital, interviewing the refugees while Naila worked to treat the rest streaming in. Those who could talk and had some information to offer she turned over to Elaine once they were stabilized. Elaine filled pad after pad until she felt her hands begin to cramp. She heard Naila call for her to see another and then saw Naila's knees suddenly begin to buckle from exhaustion. Elaine reached out quickly to steady her.

"Dr. Naila," said the nurse next to her softly, "it's late, go home. One of the other doctors can spell you for a while."

Naila started to shake her head, and then felt Elaine's hand on her arm, "Come, Naila, I'll drive home with you."

Naila nodded numbly. Elaine watched with concern as Naila leaned her head back in the car and then seemed to fight against a flash of nausea. Elaine walked with her into the house, past the houseboy, and helped her up the steps to her room. Naila lay down across her bed and slowly the color started to come back into her face. She appeared not to hear Elaine's question about the nausea. Elaine stood up to go and then heard a knock on the door.

"Dr. Naila," whispered the housegirl. "He's here. They are waiting for you downstairs." Naila looked up—uncomprehending.

239

"Dr. Naila, your brother Musaid called you at the hospital to remind you this was the day they are formalizing the engagement contract." Naila stared at her dumbfounded. Elaine stopped, felt helpless, not knowing what to do.

Naila, trembling, stood up, then, bowed down toward Mecca and began to pray. "Oh please, God, let me accept..." Her body started shaking. "Please, please let me accept what I must."

Naila struggled to pray. The thought of giving herself to a stranger, making love to some faceless person, filled her with revulsion. The passion, the love she had for the man she had to give up, choked the prayer she struggled to whisper. She looked up at Elaine but could only see his face, his eyes, feel his body. He had been everything to her—encouraging her with her work, taking care of her when he could, loving her for herself, as a person, as a woman. She loved him; she admired him—a man of utter trust, of depth and of true respectability. They had seen the best in one another—and loved each other for it. And now she was to walk away with someone else for the rest of her life. The irony of it, the sadness of it, the reality of it choked her. Elaine reached down to try and hold her and heard the small voice that was a whisper. "Please, God, let me accept what I must."

The knock on the door sounded again, and the little housegirl drew back, shocked to see Naila crying, humbled on the floor.

"Dr. Naila," she whispered, "he is waiting."

Naila walked down the stairs while the little housegirl motioned for Elaine to follow her. Elaine paused as they started to pass the parlor that Naila had entered. The scene before her seemed unreal, from another world.

Musaid stood there. Next to him was a young man, dressed in a white thobe, who extended his hand to Naila. "I am deeply honored that your family has accepted my proposal," he said. Silence hung in the room. He waited, confused, for her response.

Naila struggled for words. "My work in the hospital…you are very patient to wait until I have finished." It was all she could manage to say. Had it been this way for all the others, generations of others?

Musaid interrupted tersely. "I've drawn up the marriage contract with his father, so there is no reason to delay the arrangements I've made for the engagement party this evening."

"Yes," Elaine heard Naila's voice, barely a whisper, as the servant girl motioned Elaine to move on.

Elaine drove back to the office, the almost surreal scene of Naila being given to the stranger haunting her mind. When she entered the office, Ray looked up sadly.

"You just missed a call. It was Naila. She sounds pretty broken up. She said it would mean a lot to her if you could come this evening for the engagement party."

"It's like something out of another world," said Elaine softly. Ray just nodded. "It used to be they never even met until the actual marriage."

"Ray, what is the thing this evening?"

"They've formalized the contract, the family is gathered right now probably, for an official announcement. Tonight the women have a party; it'll be pretty glittery and big. And in a few weeks the actual marriage takes place. The end."

"And they won't wait, given all that is going on?" asked Elaine somewhat amazed.

"Apparently, Musaid feels they've waited long enough. I think it would mean quite a lot to Naila if you were there. Forget about us for a while here," he said softly, "and go. It won't start until midnight anyhow."

At midnight the car drove up to the house. Elaine got out and followed a servant girl who said to a not-quite-comprehending Elaine, "She has just gone in." Elaine nervously, looked on as the servant girl opened the door to a large room and ushered her inside. The room was filled with women in evening gowns and jewels who were clapping while Naila, drawn and pale, was led into the women's party. The musician struck a note for a dancer in the center of the room to begin. The soft flesh of the woman's belly moved once slowly as she arched her neck. A servant woman passed through the room with a tray of sweets while the women in their evening gowns stretched out on large satin pillows strewn across the marble floor. Elaine moved quickly to the back while Naila began to walk through the room of the women she had known growing up. Elaine saw Nura, Naila's sister, the beautiful face, the intriguing eyes she had seen at Osman's, move with Naila through the crowd. Nura saw Elaine and came over to introduce her to some of the women around her, settle her amongst them.

One of them, Farah, brushed a crumb from the beaded strapless dress. With a bored drop of her hand, she picked up the cards she had absently left off playing when the dancer arrived, and began a new game of solitaire. Nura lay back on the pillows, eyes half closed. While another, Jahara, leaned against the open shutter staring off into the darkness.

The music of the oud rose like a dark gold snake winding its way into the night. The flute, like a haunted sirocco, called back. The dancer stood motionless, as though in a trance, and let one arm slowly wind its way toward the sky. Then the drum struck, and she whirled around, driven by the rhythms, swaying, undulating. She swung her hair like a dark whip until it circled around her. From her throat came an undulating melancholy sound. The music engaged her body and left it driven by the frantic rhythms. When the music stopped, she stood motionless, in another world.

Naila looked at the women around the room—at these women she had known all her life. She had gone to school with them, little girls who had learned art and mathematics and talked of the match their families would make for them. Girls who had put on the veil at thirteen and stayed in the women's quarters when men outside the family came to visit. Girls who stared in disbelief, consumed with both horror and envy at the women from the West running loose in the streets, dating. Girls who then went to college there, met men they fell in love with, all the while knowing nothing could ever come of it, knowing that to defy tradition would cast them out from their families, their society, so that they returned ultimately to the boring rituals of tradition, the women's quarters, the veil, a marriage arranged by the family to someone in the family. They had their babies and they spent their nights dressing up for one another to kill the boredom, to kill the time. They slept until noon only to begin it all again the next day.

She watched Samia began to massage Nura's back, and at the woman breathing in the incense, silent now, at Jahara sadly, slowly circling her wedding band around her finger, at Sara across the room showing her new emerald barrette to another woman in the low light of the candles.

"Yallah, Nura," Naila said softly, "I need to be somewhere else, away." She looked at Nura. "But then there is no place else to go, is there? I really have no way to go, do I?"

The woman reclining next to Nura listened to Naila sadly and then turned her face away. A small boy opened the large door and looked in. "Umi, umi," his eyes searched the incensed filled room for his mother. "Umi, umi." A woman from the other side of the room rushed over to him and picked him up. "Ay, he has nightmares. My little one, how did you get here?" She kissed him and then stretched the half-sleeping child on a pillow and softly began to stroke his penis while she hummed. Slowly the child fell back asleep. She rose and opened the large door and called for the nanny to come get him. The nanny picked up the sleeping boy and gently carried him off.

The woman came and sat by Naila, inhaling the incense from the burner beside them. "Ay, but Naila you could be me. I know he will take the boy you see." She drew again on the incense and sipped some of the cardamom tea. "If I refuse the other woman, he will take the boy. When he becomes seven the child will be lost to me. He will go to his father's house. So," she leaned back wearily, "I don't ask for the divorce. He will have the second wife. It was never good between us really."

She stretched her arm back, adjusting the ruby bracelet. "I mean, really, what is to be gained by divorcing? Most of Faisal's daughters are divorced and you see the life they live. Like little nuns, shuttling between a gold cage here to their apartments in Paris. For all their education they can do nothing other than visit the other women, read another book, unable to marry outside the family and with no one there they want. And me? What am I exactly to do? Lose my children when they become seven? Take my money and go to Paris for good? The money that's supposedly my own that my brothers have been controlling for years. Even if they would sign the official permission for me to go, I would always be in some strange country, away from home, taking foreign lovers I could never marry. Or I stay here and live like a nun in my parents' home while my husband takes our children. Or I try to go back to school and learn something and get a job where I am a teacher teaching only women, a doctor treating only women and children, and talking only to women.

"So?" She took some sweets from the tray, "I stay. For sex I pretend he's another man and get some pleasure. I put my mouth on his penis and I suck him and stroke the shaft until it feels good, and in my mind I pretend he is someone else. He likes to come from behind," she started to laugh. "You know, like the old ones in the desert? So it makes it easier, I don't see his face. He has his lovers, I have my fantasies. A little pleasure." She lay back laughing.

Farah looked up from her cards toward Jahara on the other side of the room. "At least there is some pleasure. That one has nothing." They looked at Jahara leaning against the window as a palm frond slowly blew back and forth. "There are no children, now still after five years no children. She is disgraced. She says she tries everything, doctors in the West, medicines. Still nothing. She says she sees her husband begins to avoid her. All day long she is waiting. Her maid dresses her hair, her face, she puts on beautiful dresses, jewels, and waits. And he doesn't come to her anymore. She is lost, he will get another. I say to her as I sit with her one day, how sad, to try this and this to give him pleasure to bring him back. I tell her what the other women say works, and she listens. And then I say something about her pleasure, and she says, 'I don't feel the pleasure. When I was a child they made me cleansed.'"

Farah put the cards down. "She looks at me and says, 'When I was a child, we left Mecca and lived in Egypt for many years for my father's business. My nanny, she is from the village. She believes in the old ways. She tells me these women she sees in Cairo are wanton. I must be pure or no man will want me. I hear from my mother that a family must kill the daughter if she becomes pregnant, or loses her virginity, to maintain the honor of the family. This is very frightening to me. And so,' says Jahara, 'one night my nanny comes to me and says we have something we do in the village to save the girls from this, from their desire. And she takes my clothes off and tells me lie down on the bed. Then she spreads my legs apart. And she bends over and opens the lips and begins stroking inside so it swells, and I don't know what she is doing as I become wet. And then she smiles and says, now I will make you pure as the snow, and takes a razor in her hand, and I see her coming between my legs and I start to scream, and she puts her hand over my mouth, and says sh, sh, this is all part of being a woman. And she brings the razor against the ridge of flesh and cuts. And I am screaming in pain, and she says sh, sh, just a little more. She cuts round and round as I am screaming in agony, in terror. The blood starts to pour. And finally she stands back holding this small finger of flesh. And says, 'There we have it all. You will be free of desires, pure as the snow. This is the way for the women, the good girls have it done.'

"Yes," said Farah sarcastically, "this is the way for the women, 'the good girls'— Jahara is free. We are all free." She dropped the cards to the floor and looked at Elaine, sitting absolutely silent, behind her. "You are from the Embassy, no? Come, I go right past there, I will give you a ride home."

Elaine walked over and quietly embraced Naila, then followed the woman down to the car waiting below.

It was not until nearly dawn that the rest of the women left. Naila stood in the room alone listening to the last guest depart. She closed the door behind her and walked up the stairs to her room, where she stood in front of the mirror, looking at the long dark hair cascading over her shoulders. She felt the fear rivet through her as she thought of the truth the calendar now revealed, and that her body would soon evidence. She closed her eyes summoning the image of the face she loved and felt his hand as she moved her fingers across her cheekbone down to her lips. She felt his mouth on hers, his body. She could hear his words whispering to her as he made love to her. She moved her hand across her faintly rounded stomach, the seed, the child within, while the tears flowed down her face. She knew she must terminate the pregnancy but could not bring herself to do so. She lay down on the bed crying, depression engulfing her. And then she walked back down the stairs to the Pakistani houseboy sitting by the door.

"Will you drive me someplace?" she asked quietly. His surprised look, first up the stairs where the rest of the household slept, then to Naila, gave way to acquiescence. Twenty minutes later Elaine heard the knock on her door. Naila stood there, face streaked with tears.

"My god, Naila," she whispered, "come in."

The young woman walked in and sat down. "I want you to help me," she whispered up to Elaine. "I have decided something and I want you to help me."

Elaine sat down across from her, reaching out to her hand.

"Yesterday," said Naila, "the director at the hospital called us into the conference room. She said that they need someone immediately to send to a medical outpost they're setting up on our border with Kuwait. She explained that they've had a primitive, small one there for years mainly to handle the needs of the bedu who would come in. Now hundreds of refugees are flooding in and many need emergency treatment. Those that need more intensive treatment can be sent in the helicopter to more sophisticated facilities. She said they needed a doctor there quickly to oversee it; they want a volunteer to go on the plane leaving here at 7:00 A.M. I've decided to go."

Elaine looked apprehensive. Naila started to say something, then her voice broke, "Oh god, please help me Elaine. I don't think I can go on, I..."

Elaine held her hand. "What is it you want me to do?"

"I wrote these two notes, could you give them to Nura and Musaid for me, after I've left?" She handed the notes to Elaine.

Dearest Nura,
They have requested somebody to go to the border on an emergency assignment. I have decided to go. I have become increasingly depressed with my work at the hospital, my life, the terror always now in the Gulf. I feel I need to be away for a while to think, perhaps to come to grips with it all. I feel I don't know where my life is heading anymore, why...I know you will understand.
My love always,

Naila

Elaine opened the second note.

Dear Musaid:
There's been an emergency at the hospital and I've been assigned to one of the border clinics for a brief period. I'll be in touch just as soon as I return.

Sincerely,
Naila

Naila handed Elaine one final note. "I wrote this just in case I couldn't see you."

Dear Elaine,
I am sorry I won't be able to help you any more at the

hospital. I've decided to take a posting at a small clinic up on the border. The refugees are coming there for medical aid and I hope, I can truly be of some help there. I will miss seeing you very much. Perhaps our paths will cross again.

Sincerely,

Naila

Elaine held the brief note. She felt her heart wrench looking at the soft lovely face of the young woman who had written it, all of the words and heartbreak that lay unwritten between the lines of the simple note. The realities of Naila's life filled her with compassion, and something she could not name left her very frightened for the young woman.

"Naila, I'll do anything you ask me. But Musaid, what if he becomes angry about this, if..."

"I just need some time," Naila said desperately, "just some time to come to grips with it all. Please, help me." She looked at her watch. "I must leave for the hospital now; the plane is leaving there with supplies to go up to the front, and I want to be on it." With that she stood up and kissed Elaine on both cheeks, and left.

When Elaine got to the office she called Nura and left a message that she needed to see her. Nura returned the call at the end of the day. She sounded surprised but told Elaine to stop by. Elaine drove over and gave her the two notes. She watched as Nura read them, struck again by the enigmatic beauty of the woman.

"She has gone?" Nura looked up quietly at Elaine. Elaine

nodded, then saw Musaid come through the door. Nura turned around, surprised to see him, and then simply handed over the note marked for him. His face clouded as he read it. Then a red flushed crept over his face. He dropped the paper on the table. "This is unthinkable!" his voice started to rise. "Naila should never..."

Nura's hand reached out and interrupted him. "It's only for a little while, Musaid. It doesn't have to change any of your plans. She called me to say she was trying to reach you to get your permission."

Elaine's eyes shot up to Nura as she heard her lie to protect Naila.

"Naila said she was unable to get through to you, Musaid, and the hospital administrator said that Naila was the only one that she could spare and would have to go."

Elaine remained completely still while Nura's eyes engaged Musaid, while her words moved out to manipulate him. Musaid paused, then suddenly seemed to remember that Elaine was standing there. His eyes shot over to Elaine with a questioning look. Nura once again spoke up quickly.

"Elaine was just leaving, she had forgotten her wrap at the party last night."

Elaine took the cue and departed quickly. For a moment as the car sped off she thought of Nura, the fascinating, clever mind behind the beautiful face.

And then her mind turned back to Naila. The utter sadness of her life. And the deepening, growing fear for her that Elaine now felt welling up.

23

Throughout the following day, the minesweepers flew over the Gulf while the ships continued heading up the channel. Elaine and the crew worked frantically, culling whatever intercepts they could. The team now arriving from Langley spread out under her instructions and literally took over the Embassy, pulling the equipment apart.

Said arrived at Tarek's office late in the evening. He simply stood in the doorway and shook his head. "Nothing." He watched Tarek's exhausted face as he took the sheets from him. He paused. "Tarek, maybe it is somebody without a reason—at least a reason that would be apparent."

"What do you mean?"

"I mean that when I think of King Faisal lying dead, I think of the pathetic deranged nephew with his confused grievances who shot the man over nothing—some anger over Faisal's modernization, feelings that he had somehow been slighted. Maybe the Israelis used him, as many believe, to assassinate the king—but it was he in the end who pulled the trigger."

Said stopped, seeing the look on Tarek's face.

"Tarek, I'm sorry. My God, Faisal was like a father to you and I'm standing here talking about this like it was…"

Tarek shook his head and put his hand on Said's arm. "Keep

tracing the money for me. Anything you see I want to know about, all right?"

Said nodded. "I will."

Tarek watched him go, then sat down and closed his eyes.

In the dark the image of Faisal's face moved slowly across his mind. The look in Faisal's eyes at the end still haunted him. The sad, deep eyes that seemed to see beyond somewhere. The hooded darkness, the startling clarity of those eyes that had watched Tarek as a boy.

He could see his hands, moving liquidly, elegantly, pulling the gold of his thobe around him when he stood to go back to his work. He could see his head bent late into the night over the boxes of papers he worked on. And finally, again and again in exquisite slow motion he could see the gun come from the folds of the young man's clothes. Faisal had looked at the young man with the gun as though he had been expecting him. He waited. And when the sound of the gun shattered the afternoon, Faisal simply closed his eyes. He sank, slowly, slowly, slowly to the ground while Tarek watched.

"Will you take me home?" Tarek opened his eyes. He saw Elaine standing before him, in her hand surveillance reports that she had been going over with Badr. He looked at Badr standing behind her.

"Badr, anything yet on the taps I asked you to personally monitor for me?

"Nothing. Absolutely nothing so far that indicates anything."

"Intensify the surveillance."

Badr's weary voice confirmed.

Tarek stood up. "Yes, I will take you home."

She moved closer to Tarek when he opened the car door for her. Tarek glanced down at her hand lingering on his arm when he helped her into the car. Her clear blue eyes seemed lost in thought. He started the car and began to drive through the streets. Elaine looked at him, her eyes full of fear. "Tarek, the car bomb for Fahd, the leaks, Cheney flying in tonight, the possibility of bringing all our troops in while we're wide open like this..." Her voice trailed off, then softly came back, "Tarek, I'm terrified."

She looked away from him as the car moved down the desert road, then she faced him, her voice barely a whisper, "Tarek, I never told anyone what happened to my husband. How he died."

Her voice choked. "It was horrible. My God," she whispered, "it was horrible. The sound," she whispered, "the sound." Her hands moved involuntarily to her ears. She tried to steady herself.

Tarek pulled the car over to the side of the road and sat back listening.

"And the horror of the fact that we knew it was going to happen and could have prevented it," she said. "I knew." She looked at him.

"We had intercepted and decoded cables the week before from Iran to the Iranian Ambassador in Damascus telling him they wanted a major attack on the Americans. We had other intercepts from the Revolutionary Guard in Baalbeck to Iran's Embassy in Damascus saying they wanted to do the job. And then," her voice dropped, "on that Sunday morning one of our contacts in Beirut, a Lebanese intelligence officer, reported to us that the Iranian Embassy had just been evacuated."

She looked up at Tarek, anger in her eyes. "They followed up on none of it." She stopped.

Then whispered, "I can't talk anymore about this now."

He drove to her house in the embassy compound, fascinated, finally glimpsing what isolated and compelled her at the same time. She started to open the car door and then looked at him, "Forgive me, I don't want to be alone. Would it be possible for you to come in for a while? Sometimes I can't get past the nightmare."

He followed her and turned on the light in the small house. There was a silver framed picture of a handsome man on the table. She nodded when she saw him look at her dead husband's face.

She opened the small cabinet and pulled out some brandy. "Sometimes when I feel like this, it helps, at least to go to sleep. Will you have one?"

Tarek gently took the bottle from her, opened it and poured out two. He sat down in a chair and watched while she sipped the cognac slowly. Her voice sounded soft and faraway when she began to speak again.

"My husband was an intelligence officer with the embassy. We had met there when I first was assigned, and we got married. It would have been four years that year if he had lived. After our first assignments were over, we asked to stay on—we loved Beirut, our work was fascinating. I suppose it seemed as though none of it would ever really touch us.

"He was at a meeting that morning with some of the Marines in the Battalion Landing Team, briefing them. I was to pick him up to go up the coast by the shore to join some friends for lunch.

"While I was driving towards the entrance, this yellow Mercedes truck sped past me. I saw the driver's face for a moment, dark hair, a mustache. He turned and smiled at me. He drove right through the five-foot-high roll of concertina wire. I could only watch. He picked up speed and drove through an open gate in the chain-link fence, and before anybody could move to stop him, he speeded up again and aimed directly at the headquarters. I saw this man inside suddenly comprehend what was coming and start screaming.

"And then it hit."

Her voice broke off and her hands went to her face. Tarek heard the words choking from her mouth through her hand.

"That horrible orange flash," she breathed deeply, "and the sound, the sound. The explosion. I looked and saw the center of the entire building lift, blow up. And then in seconds, three, four seconds I watched the concrete, the whole building collapse.

"Then there was nothing but this fog, debris—this dust, falling down out of the sky. This horrible smell of explosives, cement powder, and for a moment there was silence, and then screams."

She stopped and looked at Tarek. "I only remember hearing my own scream—it sounded like it came from outside, from somebody else's body when I realized what had happened. I got out of the car and started running toward the building, shouting my husband's name. I began running toward these huge blown up slabs of concrete."

Tarek watched the tears roll down her face.

"There were crushed Jeeps lying there, bodies strewn across the ground in horrible, broken positions, one dead man hung across the trees. I stumbled across the legs of one man and then looked down at the body and realized it was decapitated. There were unattached arms, legs, strewn over the ground. Without thinking, I tried pulling at the concrete slabs, not even feeling the heat, looking for my husband. The smells of charred flesh—most couldn't be recognized, Oh God."

Tarek reached over and held her hand as she stifled a moan.

"I woke up in the hospital; I don't know how much longer, how much later. They found my husband, dead with the others, two days later—241 dead men."

She closed her eyes and leaned her head back on the sofa.

"Later the CIA reconnaissance photos found the mock-up of the concrete obstacles in front of the headquarters. At Baalbeck there were tire tracks where the suicide driver had been practicing."

"You stayed on?" Tarek asked quietly.

She turned her head toward him.

"Does it seem odd?" she asked softly. "I didn't feel I had any place else to go; I felt like everything I had, everything I had lost was there. The loss was more than I could..." She stopped and gazed out the window. "The only thing I knew to do at the time was to work. To bury it all in my work."

She turned back to Tarek, and picked up the cognac.

"They sent Buckley, William Buckley in as new chief of the CIA. Everyone else was gone, dead. I stayed on to work with him. He was to be the new point man in terrorism."

She looked up at Tarek. "When he was kidnapped, I knew who had done it."

Tarek eyes widened. She nodded.

"A young Shia, from a middle class family in Southern Lebanon who joined the Hizbollah, where I began tapping him. His brother was one of the terrorists being held in jail in Kuwait. He vowed to get him out. He saw his work of taking hostages as a tool.

"He was a very clever young man, far more urbane and articulate than most. A tremendously useful operative. When I tapped into him, I realized that he was taking direction from the leaders of the Hizbollah, who were, of course, taking their direction from Tehran.

"Before I came here, while I was working on intercepting the trigger parts for Iraq's nuclear weapons, he showed up again on our intercepts. This time in communication with somebody else. Somebody deep inside the command structure in Baghdad who had accurately identified the potential in this fellow. The intercepts were difficult, the communications with this person cleverly done, but I finally broke through to who was running him out of Baghdad. At that point they apparently realized they were being intercepted and decoded and they lost me. But I had some initial instructions. I had the identity of who was handling him from Baghdad."

Tarek looked at her for a moment. "Antar," he said quietly.

She nodded. "Antar." She stopped and looked up at him, her voice choking. "It's like some hopeless, endless circle, isn't it? And I wake up at night, knowing the hideous possibilities. That if we come here—troops, planes, ships and we still haven't tracked the leak—it will be a massacre. Thousands dead. I am devoured by guilt; now I'm terrified I may fail again. Can you understand that—how it eats at me?"

Tarek sat as she put her head in her hands, and then looked silently back at the picture in silver frame.

"I am a man," he said quietly, "who watched the man who was like a father, King Faisal, shot in front of me."

Elaine looked up surprised as Tarek spoke Faisal's name and continued.

"Shot in front of me while I stood by helplessly, watching. Could I have stopped it? Even today I do not know the answer to that question. Protocol, niceties, tradition took precedence even though we had some warning. And so he died. I carried his body to the grave. The body of a king, wrapped in a simple white cloth, carried through the streets, surrounded by people. I can still hear them crying, 'We come from the dust and we return to the dust,' as we carried his body through the streets, toward his final rest, to an unmarked grave, for kings as for all men. I could only whisper the verses from the Koran, the eternal questions and answers of the angels Naaker and Nakeer to ensure his passage to Paradise.

'Who is thy God?'

'Allah.'

'What is thy religion?'

'Islam.'

'Who is its Prophet?'

'Mohammad.' "

Elaine listened transfixed. She saw before her a man who lived with his irretrievable loss, his face at that moment haunted still. A sadness so profound that he hardly breathed, barely moved.

"And now," he finished quietly, "I look at the possibility of another king dying, a whole country finished."

She was so stunned by the man's emotion that she could think of nothing to say. He stood up to go.

"You are all right now?" he asked gently, putting the brandy down.

"Yes," she whispered.

He looked at her hand, still clenched. He reached over and took it, opening it.

"Let it go, and then go on." He said softly. "What was is no longer. And the tragedy would be to waste the life that remains. Yours."

24

Secretary of Defense Richard Cheney, landed at midnight, General Schwarzkopf with him. Elaine and Ray monitored the contingent sent for them, waiting for them in the office. When they arrived. Elaine opened the door. For a moment she studied Cheney, the quiet face of an associate professor of political science, decisive, straight. Schwarzkopf, a massive man with eyes that took everything in quickly, candidly, a man who seemed confined by whatever space he was in no matter how large. Schwarzkopf gazed back at her. She brought them into the room and for the next hour she and Ray briefed them on all of the information and background they had prepared. Then the car then sped them to the palace, where Fahd, shaken, waited with Tarek to meet them.

Through the night, Cheney and Schwarzkopf drew out the plans, the assurances of what the U.S. would do. Abdullah, Sultan, Saud, Naif listened as they tracked through, item by item, what they could bring. Arms, men, weapons. Toward morning they suggested that Fahd might want to be left alone to consider his decision. Fahd stared at them and then shook his head. He had come to his decision.

The light on Ray's secure phone from Langley lit up shortly after dawn. "Ray, old boy!" Turley's voice lilted. "Ray, turn on the monitor from the CNN feed."

"Christ, Turley, what am I supposed to see?" He fumbled for the controls while Elaine looked on curiously.

"You won, old boy. Ray's Last Stand!" chirped Turley, as Ray tuned in to what was obviously President Bush's last phrase of a statement.

"Fahd just agreed to let Cheney bring the troops in."

Elaine stood absolutely still while Ray held the phone and appeared alternately horrified and pleased, but unequivocally stunned.

"It appears that you and your team did it, old pal," Turley stopped for a moment and then continued. "Tarek tried to get you and then called here an hour ago so we could pass the information along to the president and the Senate."

Elaine turned at the footsteps behind her. Tarek stood, silently watching the monitor as President Bush's broadcast finished. He watched for a moment longer and then handed a small sheet of paper to Ray. "Just across from Hamid."

Ray looked at the code transcription. "Iraq immediately beginning to lay more mines to sabotage U.S. ships planning to enter the Gulf. Fahd and Saudi Arabia to be target of escalated terrorist attacks to send a message to other Gulf rulers."

"Oh sweet Jesus," breathed Ray, handing the sheet to Elaine.

Tarek looked at him, the long, slow calculation of a man who has just put everything on the line.

"You know Fahd is counting on you to protect us, don't you? We don't have the arms, the means. They are counting on you."

"Oh, God, I know," breathed Ray. "Not to mention all the

U.S. boys I'm bringing in too. Over a hundred mines, and a thousand terrorists. 'Ray's Last Stand.'"

* * *

S chwarzkopf and Cheney emerged from their briefing meetings with Fahd.

"Should I start the forces moving?" asked Schwarzkopf.

Cheney simply nodded to the new Commander in Chief. He started to leave, then turned as he reached the door.

"Good luck, Norm."

Schwarzkopf stared at him, watched him go. He looked down at the sheet of preliminary plans. Then he simply closed the door behind him. He shut his eyes and quietly prayed. Prayed to God that they would succeed this time.

He walked almost numbly into the temporary office that Ray and Elaine, now waiting for him, had set up in their headquarters. He looked at the two of them, and almost on automatic pilot picked up the phone, firing off the first orders. He then boarded the plane waiting to take him back to the U.S. and began barreling through the material trying to scrap together a defense plan with an initial call to Navy Ops.

"Schwarzkopf here. The U.S.S. *Wisconsin*—what targets in Iraq can it hit with its Tomahawk Cruise missiles?"

The Navy Ops guy came back in a minute. "None, sir."

Schwarzkopf was incredulous. "None?"

"No sir. You have to program the Tomahawks with electronic terrain maps so they can find their targets. We don't have any for Iraq. The satellites were all programmed to monitor the Soviet Union's departure from Eastern Europe. None of them were left to make maps for Iraq."

He heard Schwarzkopf breathe deeply on the other end of the phone. "It says here on the specs that you got ninety-six moth balled Victory ships from World War II we can use to get military cargo to the Gulf. Get them ready."

The Navy Ops guy turned around horrified as Schwarzkopf hung up on him. He turned to his colleague behind him, "Schwarzkopf wants us to use those hulks? You got to be kidding. You want someone to ride across the Atlantic in that piece of junk?" He shook his head in disbelief. "God, we're going to have go dig out some of the old guys from the Navy union halls who still remember how you work the old boilers that run these tubs."

Schwarzkopf's next call was to the experts in anti-terrorism. "I want a demo of what you can do—and how it's really gone before. I land at ten, I'll be there by eleven."

The commander took Schwarzkopf out to a cordoned-off area for the demonstration. He gave the code words. Suddenly the sound of automatic weapons cut the air, and then the blast of an explosion. The small group of commandos rushed forward toward the building in front of them. Within minutes they emerged—escorting the rescued hostage, the terrorists inside "dead."

The Commander nodded, dismissed the squad, and turned to Schwarzkopf. "The helicopter unit of our anti-terrorist squad can conduct nighttime raids on the Iraqi warships and the boats planting the mines at night. The men are well trained. Our underwater squad as well. They are fast and efficient—on a par in their training and abilities with, say, the British, the West Germans. Maybe just a fraction behind the Israelis. That's the good news." He waved Schwarzkopf back to a hut.

"The bad news?" asked Schwarzkopf, watching the tired face of the commander.

"The bad news is that logistical, bureaucratic, and political obstacles have frequently destroyed our ability to function." Schwarzkopf looked startled. The Commander continued, "I think you should be advised—warned—that our boys, when we've tried these operations elsewhere before, keep being thwarted by breakdowns in the aircraft that are meant to carry them. Beyond that, we have to rely on intelligence from other units.

"All of these operations require lightning-fast movement to be successful, and yet we have to get endless OK's from myriad desk men in various bureaucracies back in the U.S. and the White House. At key times, in emergencies, we couldn't get any response whatsoever from the White House—no orders, nothing. It's like they are all dead or permanently paralyzed, out to lunch there."

He pulled out a pack of cigarettes. "I mean, a number of these boys here were stationed in Beirut in '83 when we had the bomb attack on our Marine barracks. Our commando team almost instantly tracked down the ones who had ordered the attack. They immediately devised a plan for a retaliatory strike at the terrorists. They were ready to go, at alert. You know what happened? Nothing. They never could get a response from the White House. No orders, nothing. It was unbelievable."

Schwarzkopf listened, dead silent.

"In '85, during the TWA hijacking, we had our boys set and ready to go. They stood on full alert in Italy ready to go to Algiers where the terrorists were holding the plane. You know what happened? They kept standing there. For days. No orders whatsoever from the White House, no response. We didn't get a red light, we didn't get a green light, not even a yellow light.

Nothing. It's as though the whole communication gets lost in some circular vacuum in the White House, rolling around some endless circle between the CIA, State, the Joint Chiefs of Staff, the Secretary of Defense, the Secretary of State, and last, but not least, the President—none of whom seem to talk to one another."

He took the coffee the aide brought them and shrugged. "And even if they do? Well...," he stirred the coffee for a moment. "In '85 we were ready with an assault attack on the Palestinian terrorists who had hijacked the *Achille Lauro*, the cruise ship loaded with passengers. You know what happened? Our commandos were delayed by eighteen hours just trying to leave the U.S. because the fucking transport plane broke down and there was no replacement available. When they finally got to Egypt, the only helicopter waiting for them had a range of less than 275 miles. We have fewer available aircraft than we had back in 1980, if you can believe that, for a force whose entire success is dependent upon being able to arrive at a site quickly."

"Commander," Schwarzkopf stood up abruptly, "that's not going to happen again." He looked at the man and shook his head sadly. "That will not, I repeat, happen again."

Schwarzkopf walked back into his office. He put his head in his hands and closed his eyes. Not enough planes, not enough ships, a command structure that was chaos, Iraq with a terrorist operation surrounding him headed by Antar, and he, Schwarzkopf, with an anti-terrorist squad that couldn't move. After a minute, he pulled out a bottle of scotch. He looked up at the surprised aide who walked in.

"I hate what Vietnam has done to this country," Schwarzkopf said quietly. "I hate it."

✠ ✠ ✠

Ray, Elaine and Tarek stared intently at the TV monitor. Fahd slowly rose before the camera and began to explain to his country that he was bringing in the U.S. troops. Nervously he told of the need to defend the Kingdom. Badr walked in the door looking grim.

"Hamid just got through with this." He began to read.

"Iraq has just gotten in all the specs on the U.S. ships, and the anti-terrorist squad from their agent within the Royal Family." Tarek's head pulled up abruptly. "It gives them info on how to infiltrate commands, communications, limits of the abilities of the U.S. operations."

"They have finalized plans for an assassination. He can get no specifics, other than that the agent seems in place and ready. The agent has just received orders in Riyadh—they are totally aware of the king's schedule for the next week. All he can advise is extra guards around him, tight security, changing the schedule repeatedly. Whoever the agent is is still a highly guarded secret, and Antar is talking to the person, communicating through totally outside channels that Hamid can't trace."

Badr folded the paper, then took another one out. "And this," he said quietly, "is from Riyadh. The tap on the cell meeting last night. First some vague comments on the assassination to come soon. Then this. The cell leader announced that he was reading from the journal of the designated assassin."

"The journal?"

"The journal," said Badr. He mused for a moment, looking at Tarek "Have you ever thought how interesting it is, how often in history assassins have kept journals, Oswald, Booth…?" He looked back at the paper. "Shall I read?"

Tarek nodded.

"I am an instrument of Divine Will. I have been viewed as less than I am, insignificant. The past makes little difference. I have sinned, but I have seen, I have understood. The basis of power of those who rule is fear. I fear no longer. Deceit, trickery, they are means. I will be called an assassin. But I am an instrument of Divine Will. It is through the blood that I will shed that the brilliance of Mohammad's empire will rise again."

The room was absolutely quiet as Badr finished. Ray was startled by a tap on his shoulder. Ray took the small piece of paper from the aide who rushed in with it. He read, then looked up incredulously. "Fahd is taking Cheney to Taif to see a ceremony before he leaves. Says he thinks a real bedu desert ceremony would be a good way to introduce the idea, make the idea of an American presence in the kingdom more palatable to the surrounding Arab nations and the conservative elements of the country. To show that the ways of the kingdom, tradition, the Arab world, remain as always."

Ray turned pale.

25

The road to Taif stretched out through the burning desert. Cheney's car followed that of King Fahd; the emir of Kuwait rode behind him.

The sound of drums reverberating from the foothills of Taif seemed to well up from the desert floor as the caravan of limousines crawled like a long black snake through the sand. The sirens of the National Guard cars screamed while the guardsmen surrounding the king's limousine darted in and out on their motorcycles, machine guns strapped to their bodies. Equipped with walkie-talkies, the bedu boys of the Guard circled the flapping green flags on the front of the gleaming cars. Ray finished the instructions to his office from his car phone, checked the extra guards around Fahd, and then picked up his binoculars. He wiped the sweat from his forehead, handed the glasses to Elaine, seated beside him, and walked off toward the mobile security units equipped with the monitors they had brought.

Elaine picked up the binoculars, feeling the perspiration along her neck, and focused on the bottom of the foothills. The tribesmen were slung with bullet bandoleers across their chests, daggers at their waists, long black hair wildly streaming and matted below their red kaffiyehs.

Slowly one old man among them picked up a sword, his body swaying, and began keening to the drums. He held the sword like an arc into the hot blue sky, a flash of liquid silver toward the sun, and then slashed it down toward the pale desert floor. The old bedu's war cry ululated from his tongue, and the others began to chant behind him, their voices rising into an eerie, then deafening sound of ancient tribal calls as the king's entourage approached.

The old man raised his sword again, and the drums beat faster. The bedu around him pulled their daggers from the leather at their waists and held them up, echoing the cry with him, swaying and bending behind the sweeping arcs of the old man's sword cutting the sky. Fahd's car kept coming.

Then came a single, piercing cry from the hollows of the foothills. And suddenly a surge of horses ridden by barefoot bedu careened wildly over the blue-veined mountain, circling down toward the old man's silver sword. He swayed and called Allah's name into the sky. The dark bedu on a glistening white Arabian horse who led them screamed a war cry while he motioned them toward the caravan of dark limousines. He raised his arm with the rifle and the sound of the shot pierced the sky, shattering the deep pounding of the drums.

With a wild laugh he pulled at the red-and-black braided rope bridling the horse's foam-flecked mouth, dug his heels into its sweating, heaving sides, and waved his rifle toward the others to follow. The old man's sword moved in a trance below the burning sun. The drums pounded, the horses surged forward, and rifles fired into the sky, charging toward the king's car.

Elaine's breath caught in her throat. The moment stopped in time while her eyes froze on the king. And then, suddenly inches away, the horses, as though on a trip wire, stopped with a scream and reared up into the sky.

The bedu on the white Arabian uttered a wild laugh into the hot Taif sky. He pulled the bloody red-and-black rope through the horse's mouth, and slowly, elegantly, the white beast bowed before the king and his caravan.

Clusters of black tents fanned out beyond the elegant white air-conditioned ones cordoned off for the members of the Royal Family. The tents were filled with the tribes coming in from the mountains and desert. Women in black hunched over, cooking on open fires. The camels, with their bright colored rugs for saddles, were led by small boys who looked up in awe when the king, Cheney, and his entourage passed by, then cheered wildly as Crown Prince Abdullah's car followed. The official viewing stands were starting to fill up. Elaine caught a glimpse of Nura and Musaid in the Family box, then put the binoculars down and got out of the car. She walked toward the mobile station unit, looking back at the stretch of desert marked out for the races as the patrol choppers spun above in the sky.

Beneath the din of the helicopter blades the first crack of the gun sounded. The small boys, most of them no more than eight or nine, weighing about fifty pounds a piece and tough as sticks, scurried to ready their mounts for the start.

Tarek, standing in the official viewing stand, jumped at the hand on his back. He turned as one of the visiting princes of the kingdom walked onto the stand and kissed him in greeting. Arms clasping from beneath long flowing thobes, the officials filed onto the flower-laden platform. The Sabahs from Kuwait, the al Thanis from Qatar, Sheikh Zayed from Abu Dhabi, Rashid from Dubai, mingling with the Saudis, Crown Prince Abdullah, Defense Minister Sultan, Foreign Minister Saud, Interior Minister Naif. The lesser princes moved to the back.

The bedu boys lined up as the bedu raised his pistol and fired. The camels started to lumbered upright from the sand as the small boys scrambled up on the humped, ragged backs. Yelling, and kicking at them with bare feet, they goaded them toward the starting line. The king sat on the platform, next to Cheney, surrounded by dignitaries and a bevy of television monitors.

The gun sounded again. Now, with wild screaming the camels, whipped on by the small boys, surged forward. The television cameras, mounted on trucks, rode in front of them. Tarek watched as Abdullah's aide slipped in the back of the tent and moved up behind the king. He whispered something to Walid. Walid listened and nodded. The screams from the crowd rose.

A gun cracked again. Tarek watched in horror as Fahd's head fell forward while the screams of the spectators rose up beneath the burning sun.

Tarek felt his breath stop. The king's face blurred in his mind with Faisal's. Faisal falling, falling before the gun. Fahd's eyes closed, his head slumped forward.

Tarek lunged toward him while Walid rushed to his side. Fahd, face flushed, momentarily overcome by the heat, raised his head and smiled weakly while the servant rushed forward with cold water.

Tarek looked at the king for a moment. Then began to walk down the steps of the viewing stand. Exhaustion poured over him. He stood for a moment looking back up toward the foothills, silently watching the bedu boys in the distance, in the quiet of the desert away from the tents, holding their falcons. His head swimming from fatigue, he began to walk toward them.

One boy held a falcon on his arm, a thick wrap over his wrist beneath the claws, while the small hood rested on the falcon's head. As Tarek approached the boys, he saw an old man smiling at them, showing them another hood. He gently placed the hood on the beady-eyed falcon and then turned and smiled at Tarek. Tarek recognized with a start the face of his grandfather. Suddenly he felt a flood of relief as he looked at the old man's familiar face. For a moment he felt the peace of the long nights in the desert sitting and talking to the old man. He walked over to embrace him.

"Salaam Alekum," said Tarek softly, "you have come down with the tribe?"

The old man nodded. "Alekum Salaam," he said, and offered him the falcon.

Carefully the old man wrapped the leather around Tarek's arm. Gently he placed the hood over the falcon's eyes while he put the claws to the leather wrist, then raised his hand for the boy to release the prey bird. He reached swiftly for the hood, pulling it from the falcon's eyes.

The falcon, with a scream, hit the bird midair.

As the scream rang through the air, Tarek heard the crack of the gun. In an instant he knew.

Like crystal shattering, Tarek watched the light of the afternoon fracture into thousands of small pieces. The blood flowed from his face as he fell to the black ground.

❋ ❋ ❋

Ray stood in one of the mobile security units fixed on the monitors. He reached for his cup of coffee, feeling the nerves along the back of his neck. "Christ, I'm tight as a tick," he muttered to Elaine. His eye kept returning to the monitor. Every second the U.S. ship moved deeper into the

Gulf he held his breath. "No helicopters, no mine sweepers, shit, we don't know what we're doing." He turned to go out.

At the moment his hand touched the door knob, the explosion sounded behind him, the sound of metal exploding into fire. He swung around. Elaine stood frozen. From the monitor came the screams of the sirens colliding with the echo of the explosion. The mine had ripped the side of the ship open. Elaine watched the pieces of metal erupting into the sky as the vessel next to the U.S.S. *Independence* slowly keeled over.

The alert sounded in the mobile unit as the aide rushed in.

"Tarek has been shot!"

"You mean it wasn't the king...?"

"It was Tarek."

❈ ❈ ❈

The three people in the tiny cell room looked at the message the courier brought from Antar. One man opened it and read: "Plans proceeding. The next stage has been set."

He read further, then handed it to the man next to him. "Yusif Khalidi arr: Baghdad from Riyadh 8:30 P.M. Wednesday, Flight #364." He scanned the explanation below.

"The Palestinian? He will not know? It is brilliant. It will work." He paused and looked at the paper again.

"What a fascinating choice. And the bedu? You will use the bedu?"

The third person, still silent, simply nodded.

26

Elaine watched while they put Tarek into the ambulance. Ray walked back to her where she stood, her face ashen.

"He's breathing," he said while giving orders where to take him. Her hand trembled violently. Ray finished the orders to his security unit. "No one in the family is to be allowed in or given any information where he is. We don't know who is involved in this."

"Ray," she whispered, voice choked "I have to go to him."

Behind them the monitors screamed with the sounds of the siren after the mine had exploded beneath the ship accompanying the U.S.S. *Independence*. His eyes rested on her for a moment. He motioned one of his security unit over while listening to his medics report on Tarek. He gave instructions for a circuitous route to take Elaine to Tarek after he had been stabilized.

Elaine sat silently in the back of the car as it approached the house hours later. Tarek's face kept swimming in front of her. His eyes, the movement of his hands, words, phrases. He seemed to come alive in her mind while the car moved closer to the house which had been cordoned off. She felt something twisting inside her. The car stopped. The orderly was waiting for her at the door and motioned for her to follow him.

She walked behind him, down the hallway of the old house. He opened the door to a room and pointed. Tarek lay, absolutely still on the bed, blood soaking through the bandages wrapped across his face. She walked over to the bed and bent over him.

Elaine looked at Tarek's closed eyes. She could hear his slow, methodical breathing in the shadows of closed shutters while the sound of the call from the muezzin began to fill the room. She shut her eyes and began to whisper the words. "I praise the perfection of God, the Forever Existing…the perfection of God. The Desired, the Existing, the Single, the Supreme: the perfection of God, the One, the perfection of Him who taketh unto himself no male or female partner, nor any like Him. His perfection be extolled."

The sound hung in the air, an echo, then silence. The man breathed slowly, methodically.

Elaine watched the stillness of Tarek's dark face. The fine bone structure, the intensity even in repose, the taut body now still. She leaned over him, feeling his closeness like a heat.

Tarek's hand moved hesitantly toward his head, the blood covered bandages. His fingers felt along the cloth for a moment and then his eyes opened. "Ray said I could come, Tarek," she whispered, leaning closer to him.

"Tarek, he said to tell you that you are going to be all right. You took a bad blow when you fell; the wound across your face is deep, but you are going to be OK."

Tarek's eyes took her and the words in silently.

"You are in Faisal's old home. Ray brought you here until we find out what's going on. At the same time you were shot, they exploded a mine beneath the ship accompanying the U.S.S. *Independence* into the Gulf. It was clearly meant for the *Independence*, and Ray says they also clearly meant to kill you. He says you were about an inch away from being dead. The scar that's going to be along the side of your face was meant to be a straight line through your brain."

Tarek moved his hand along the bandages.

"Ray brought you here instead of the hospital because of security. He's put it out that it was an accident in the desert, nothing more. He's got the house and the garden cordoned off with guards so you can move around when you feel like it." She touched the bandages while he looked at her. Unconsciously, like a man searching for some release from his pain, he held her hand.

For a moment she couldn't move, her feelings swimming in chaos while his deeply handsome face, the dark eyes riveted her. She felt herself move toward him, closer in the silence of the room, then drew back stunned, confused by her feelings. His eyes only watched her, understanding her. Her words were a whisper.

"I am afraid for you, I'm afraid for me." Her voice caught on the last word.

"Do you want to leave?" His voice, the question, came quietly in the stillness.

Suddenly she felt her profound respect for him wash over her as she watched the need, the isolation in his eyes.

"No," she whispered finally. "No."

She stood up to leave, then hesitantly took out a small piece of paper. "Ray said I should bring this to you—an intercept we picked up. " 'The Palestinian,' 'the bedu.' What does it mean to you?"

Tarek didn't answer. She stood back, her hand offering him

the small piece of paper. Slowly he took the note. She watched for a moment as he gazed at the words on the paper, "the Palestinian," "the bedu." His eyes were still staring at the words while her footsteps echoed down the hall.

✠ ✠ ✠

Ray watched the monitor as the first plane loads of American soldiers were touching down at the military air base outside of Dhahran. He saw the red light on his phone and picked it up. The faint hiss of the line from Washington, then Turley's voice.

"Ray, old boy, I've been going over the figures Schwarzkopf left us. In sum it's going to be a bluff. All these 'Pentagon sources' telling the journalists how our forces are going to be 'impregnable' in the first week—it's all a bluff."

"What the hell do you mean by that?"

The line hissed, then Turley's voice filtered through. "Schwarzkopf has calculated what we have for troops, what we can get over there quickly, and it's shockingly little. He's terrified about our vulnerability. He says that if Saddam figures out how little we can deliver rapidly it's all over for us. He says that if in fact Saddam decides to push on now into Saudi Arabia, or anytime in the next three weeks, he'll be able to take the place."

Ray sat absolutely still.

"Ray, are you there?"

Ray hung up on Turley and looked at Schwarzkopf sitting in front of him. Schwarzkopf nodded. "If he breaks through and takes the ports that we need to bring troops in—Dhahran,

Jubail— we're dead. If he decides to go for an offensive now, he could take Saudi Arabia's main oil fields, the desalination plants. The small air power we have here couldn't stop it. Every fucking thing that can go wrong has. I keep calling my staff, waving these charts we drew up for the president—all the goddamned stuff we said we could deliver—and haven't. I scream at them, 'Where the hell is it?' Transport Command says we send the planes down to Fort Bragg and they keep loading on the wrong stuff. Fort Bragg says bullshit, we've got an empty airfield—troops lined up and waiting and the assholes at Command don't send an airplane." He kicked over Ray's wastebasket, "It's fucking chaos. And we're vulnerable as hell. The paratroopers in the 82nd Airborne Division," he nodded toward the monitor showing shots of them arriving, "they know they're nothing against this—one paratrooper grimly, but accurately, referred to himself as little more than a 'human Iraqi speed bump.' " Then he moved his face inches from Ray's. "That's one problem…

"Now the second. They are going to try to kill Tarek again. And they are going to succeed in killing not only him but every man and woman I bring in here if you don't find the leak who's feeding everything to Iraq. Tarek's attempted assassin and the leak—they are one in the same you know." The voice was controlled, Schwarzkopf's facts were right. His terror was real.

Baghdad, Iraq

The plane from Riyadh landed in Baghdad and the Palestinian archaeologist Yusif Khalidi disembarked. He glanced at the TV news in the airport: U.S. troops were arriving in Saudi Arabia and moved through customs, past the armed guards. He gave the taxi driver an address in the old section of the city along the Tigris River. As they drove deep into the old city, Yusif perused the familiar architecture of carved stone arabesques, turrets, balcony windows, and balustrades that had seen Baghdad under British colonialism, kings, generals, and now the massive looming billboards of President Saddam Hussein. He glanced down at the old dealers in the gold souk sitting in their empty shops beneath the signs: SADDAM—THE NEW SALLADIN, THE NEW IRAQI MAN. They gazed dully across the cheap Japanese cars, the few dented dust-covered Mercedes left in the streets of the old labyrinth, the half-completed buildings begun during the oil boom while the women in their worn, resewn dresses now walked past their open doors, without money, no longer stopping.

Yusif could smell the river as the cab driver pulled to the end of the street. He pulled out dollar bills; nobody wanted Iraqi dinars anymore. He took his suitcase and book and walked up the old stone stairs feeling a rat scurry by his foot. By the door at the top he saw the light. He knocked, listened to the faint sounds of the balalaika music, and then knocked again. Yasmina opened the door, music and the faint smell of incense trailing behind her. "Yusif, come in!" Yusif pulled her to him, smelling the perfume with the tinge of incense, the sensuous-ess that emanated from her body like heat.

She picked up his hand and brought it to her mouth, lightly

moving her tongue across his fingertips. She smiled languidly. "Come Yusif, have some wine. Tell me about the rest later." She brought them wine and stretched out on the sofa.

She sat without a word, as she often did, sipping the wine, listening to the sounds of the balalaika, the unfinished painting on the easel behind her, and then lay back smiling at him, waiting, her dark eyes and lips full with a sense of abandon. He wondered how the nervous energy of her paintings and this languid, passive sensuality had ever come together in the same person. She smiled at him lazily, the slow pleasure in the air like incense, waiting now to become totally lost in him when he began to stroke her, when he moved his hand first down her throat, then slowly across her full breasts. He moved his mouth over hers, slowly, then forcefully.

She pulled him toward her, arching her back. He traced his tongue along the fine down at the center of her belly, moving his hand up slowly between her legs. She began to whisper up to him, "Yusif, now." He traced the line at the middle of her stomach with his tongue. Then he parted her legs and came into her. She gasped with pleasure. Her sensuality struck a violence in him. He thrust again and again, watching her exquisite face beneath him contorted in pain and pleasure. He felt himself drowning in her like a deep river to which there was no end, and then his senses finally exploded. He opened his eyes and saw her gazing at him lazily with her smoky eyes and knew what she would do now. She lit him a cigarette and put it in his mouth, she poured some wine, and then, never speaking a word, like the courtesan of some ancient king, she slowly put her mouth over him until he became hard again, begging him to do anything to her, to dominate her, until he would come again, take her again. Then she lay back purring while he drifted off to sleep.

When Yusif woke the next morning, he saw Yasmina painting, brush in one hand, coffee in the other.

"The trips to Riyadh, Jerusalem went well? The lectures?"

She turned toward him when she spoke, silhouetted by the easel. He thought of the first time he had seen her three years ago, standing by one of her brilliantly-colored abstracts at an exhibit of her work. The painting had been striking with its deep slashing strokes set in vibrant tones, but it was she who had fascinated him. Regal, voluptuous, dark horizontal eyes, full lips with a sense of timelessness smiling faintly below the strong, high cheekbones. She seemed a reincarnation of the classic stone etchings along the walls of the ancient palace at Babylon. The women of the kings at the lion games, her black hair a thick dark mane in its own right.

She had looked directly at him, assessed him. He commented on her paintings, her work as director of the Museum of Modern Art. When he finished, she simply took his cigarette from his hand, and brought it to her mouth, drawing on it deeply. They had begun an affair that had lasted for these three years. He came and went from his work in the archaeological tells, always more intrigued by her. She had been married once, but never talked about it. The more intimate they had grown, the more elusive and intriguing she had become to him, sensuous and yet somehow unpossessable.

She bent over now, looking at the photographs he laid in front of her.

"Yusif, they are beautiful." Her fingers traced the lines of the etchings along the walls of the ancient palace, the regal women holding urns, the figures of young athletes wrestling with lions, the chariots. "Is it from Babylon?"

Yusif nodded and pointed above the long wall in the photograph. "These are the hanging gardens of Babylon the king built for his wife." He pointed to the long processional walk into the center of the palace enclave. "Hammurabi received his visitors here, the processions, the feasts. And here," he pointed toward the rooms at the back of the deep clay palace walls, "here is where we found the clay tablets with Hammurabi's famous legal code, others detailing the household expenses of the palace, some early books. He smiled. "But the most stunning thing is what we are finding now."

She looked at him curiously. "Yes?"

"There is an entire city buried below this one. Totally preserved below the water line."

She was fascinated. "How amazing. Will you be able to dig for it?"

"I don't know. It depends really on whether the government thinks it has the money." He turned at the sound of radio report on Iraqi troops in Kuwait.

She gazed at him quietly for a moment. "You're still going down to Basra now?"

"Just for a while. I'll be back."

She walked over to him and put her mouth on his. He watched the concern in her eyes. "Yusif, be careful," she stroked his face. "Don't stay too long," she whispered, "I'm waiting for you."

Yusif drove through the crowded Baghdad traffic and parked behind the old museum building. The guard dozing at his post by the front door jerked awake as Yusif walked up. He mumbled, "Professore," and motioned him into the dark cavernous building.

Yusif stood in the stillness of the room's shadows. The half light filtering through the window gave an eerie semblance of life to the remarkable creations left behind by those who had lived here thousands of years ago. The faces of the looming sixteen-foot statues from Hatra seemed to be breathing in their classical Roman repose, waiting for their time to begin again. Jewels worn by the priestess of the Moon God, the urns of Babylon, seemed carried off by mistake from Cyrus of Persia's court to which they belonged, lying like booty, a mistake in time, in the dusty Baghdad rooms with the traffic blaring outside. Lying, thought Yusif, in this land that has been trampled, burned, built, and buried by every madman who surged to conquest and then collapsed before the forces of the next. Sumerians, Persians, Romans, Greeks, Arabs, they all had triumphed for a small portion of infinity, built monuments to their eternity, and then become a layer beneath the next in an end they never expected. An artifact left in the dust of the Baghdad museum halls.

Yusif started when the assistant tapped him on the shoulder. "Your meeting, Professore, with the director." Yusif followed him through the winding labyrinth of the ancient building and smiled at the old man sitting in his study.

"Yusif," the director looked up over his glasses, "I'm reading the reprint of your lectures from Jerusalem, Riyadh. Nice, very nice." The old man smiled, "If you weren't such a good archae-ologist, I would say you should have been a poet. I practically see ancient Sumer rise, the caravans of frankincense cross the desert when you talk. So you come to see me for a few minutes before you go again?"

Yusif smiled and handed the old man a piece of paper. "This is the agenda for the next few weeks. Some final photography for the book. First some work down in Basra, then back to Saudi Arabia, Madain Saleh, then to Jordan, for Petra..."

"You go to Basra now?" The director sounded concerned as

he took his glasses off and tried to wipe the heat from the bridge of his nose. Yusif nodded. The old man stirred his coffee.

"Yusif, I don't know who you see, how you get around in the marshes off Basra. That's your business. But Basra is near the border with Kuwait. If this gets worse," he shrugged wearily. "They say it has become a real no-man's-land down there now. Iraqi troops, deserters hiding with families in the marshes, refugees, all mixed up." He stopped. "Do you really think you should go there now?"

"It's all right," shrugged Yusif, "I know my way around."

The director put up his hand. "Take care, call when you're back."

Yusif shook the old man's hand, walked back down the hall, gazing at the smiling dead faces of Ninevah, and then got into his car and began to drive south.

The peeling layers of Baghdad's sophistication receded as the car descended into time itself, into the bowels of the country. The western-dressed women of Baghdad disappeared and women in long black chadors began to emerge from the small clay houses of the little towns. He reached Najef, the ancient Shia city where Khomeini had fled and gathered his followers when the Shah exiled him from Iran, and pulled the car over to the side of the road.

He watched the long line of Shia making the pilgrimage from Najef to Kerbala according to the ancient rites, women in black chadors with baskets on their heads, children tugging at their hands. Old men walking barefoot, silently like a long black unbroken string of humanity from Najef to Kerbala, to seek a blessing.

I have no religion, thought Yusif. I understand this intellectually, but emotionally, no. Behind them streamed refugees from Kuwait, Pakistanis, Egyptians, Jordanians, fleeing with bundles tied on their heads. The sounds of artillery carried through the air.

He continued south until finally the outline of Basra began to appear. The old port city rose up in front of him through the torn fringe of palm trees surrounding it, ushering one in like an old decrepit doorman. Yusif looked at the bomb scars, shell pockmarks, sagging lattices, and worn terraces. The once stately colonial British Consulate mansion, now closed, stood sentinel behind the palm trees, locked in a remembrance of the time when the British held Iraq as a protectorate and ruled the Gulf. The British had packed up and gone long ago.

And now the ancient winding streets of Basra, with its high wooden lattice fronts peeling from the sun and the humidity above the dusty streets, held those who didn't go: the thieves, the merchants, the deserters, the sailors that the waters of the Gulf lapped onto its shores. The Indian sailors gambled and drank in the old waterfront casino while a babble of Arabic, Farsi, and Urdu called through the labyrinth of streets and canals, selling chickens on a spit for a quarter, cheap cigarettes, and magazines from Bombay with pictures of Indian actresses. Deserted tankers lay like dull whales along the dock, while soldiers absently carrying guns talked to the vendors and bought women for the night.

They are all there, thought Yusif. Those for whom the end of the line is the beginning. Those who know you can always find a cigarette stub, sell a chicken, move a cargo for somebody going somewhere, find a whore at night with a cot and a dim light bulb and some gin to help them forget.

He wandered into the Blue Moon of Paradise for some curry. He listened to the Indian waiters yelling and screaming at one another in a garble while bringing him a bottle of beer. The day-old newspaper lay on the table with its picture of President

Bush calling for sanctions, King Hussein of Jordan supporting Saddam, a meeting in Riyadh of King Fahd, Crown Prince Abdullah. He read a few paragraphs, then dropped the newspaper and glanced about the dingy room. The voices of the two men sitting in the corner drifted above the din. Their phrases, "Palestine," "coalitions," caught Yusif's ear.

He turned back to his beer. Let them talk on into the night, he thought, bemused by their earnestness. He leaned back and looked up at the dirty light bulb hanging overhead and waved for the check. God, he was so sick of it all. Arafat, Habash, the little kings set up in their own fractious courts, their endless dialogues going nowhere. Talks always breaking down exactly where they had ended the last time, while the rest of the Arab world alternated between helping them and playing games with them like pawns on a chessboard.

What they were searching for was as dead and gone as the bones he unearthed from the tells. "Palestinian" politics, he thought, checking into the hotel, walking up to his room, was a morass he would not descend into. The place itself seemed elusive, a blurred photograph. The images that came back to him sometimes in the night—the scenes of Haifa and his home in that city that had once been the jewel of old Palestine before being subsumed by Israel—were they even real, or imagined?

He lay on the bed thinking of the nights when he would sit out at the tells, when the images would come back to him, of the early years. He would sit in the dark and feel sometimes that he could see it again, the old port city of Haifa on the Mediterranean lying like a beautiful, serene jewel even as chaos seemed to surround it. Looking up from the water, the harbor, upward into the hills, he could see the beautiful rows of houses created by the old artisans that circled toward the rich blue sky with its soft white sea clouds. The five-story houses with the beautiful Arabesques of the Arab masonry and latticework, the cool, dark high-ceilinged halls of the entrance foyers where the families visited one another. The old men in the souk, the little girls all dressed up going to school. The oxen pulling carts with the villagers in traditional robes and veils coming in from Nablus to buy, to sell. The smell of the full, soft grapes, the bitter delicious olives, the goat cheese, the fragrant, rich coffee, tobacco. It had all seemed timeless. Until it stopped.

Until the chaos descended, the partition, the exodus began. Until the men came in the night and told them to take whatever they could in a small suitcase and leave the rest of their belongings behind. They left in the night.

His family had given up, taken out what they could, left most of what they had owned, and tried to find a place to live. Their wanderings had led them first to Jerusalem, then to Beirut, and finally, exhausted, to the U.S.

This had all been a blur to him, flashes of violence, desperation, a child terrified to see his parents terrified. He had no desire to look back.

Tomorrow he would begin his work in the marshes.

✖ ✖ ✖

Elaine returned to the old house the next evening and walked quietly down the hall. The orderly nodded at her as she started to enter the room. "The doctor just left, said he can begin to get up, try to walk around. He'll be unsteady but should be alright now."

Elaine walked into the room and pulled the chair up close to Tarek. She handed him the day's surveillance reports. His eye immediately went back to the sheet "the Palestinian," "the bedu."

She shook her head. "I checked off the last name on my list this afternoon." She looked exhausted. "Tarek, I'm very close to the Palestinians—from my earlier work. The PLO, the young leaders of the Intifada. All of the disaffected factions, I know them, how to get through to them. But now," she pushed her hand through her hair, "with the situation in the Gulf, no one will talk. I can't get anything." She looked at Tarek in absolute frustration and then saw the driver waiting by the door for her to go.

She bent over him once more. "I'll be back tomorrow." And then followed the driver down the hall.

Tarek looked once more at the papers Elaine had left him. He leaned up in bed, felt a flash of pain, dizziness. Slowly he sat up, breathing deeply. Beneath the bandages came alternate sensations of pain and numbness. He moved his legs over the edge of the bed and stood up. For a moment the dizziness, weakness, swam over him while he held onto the bedpost. Then he walked over to the old chest and stood in front of the mirror. He gazed at the right side of his head, covered in bandages, the dried blood showing along the line of his cheek. He pulled at the edge, loosened it and then peeled the bandages off.

He turned abruptly, unsteadily to the door. Outside was the old foyer where he had waited so many afternoons for Faisal to return. The dark, long, melancholy face seemed to breathe in the shadows, to appear for a moment in the old marble and gold circular foyer now covered with dust, on his way to the long rectangular room with its rows of blood-red velvet chairs for the afternoon majlis.

As Tarek stood there, a small cat nosed one of the chairs and then on silent feet, sprang up past the frayed gold tassels and settled into the burgundy cushions, looking curiously back at Tarek while it licked the desert dust off its paws.

Tarek pushed through the wooden door and walked out to the garden, where Faisal's palms swayed and groaned quietly in the wind and brushed against the house. He stood for a moment, and then looked down at the note in his hand, the intercept—"the Palestinian," "the bedu," "the plan." He walked back in the house and dialed the number.

27

Tarek took the forged passport from Badr, smoothed his linen suit and passed through the checkpoint leading from Amman into Jerusalem. He checked into the hotel and made a phone call.

"Excellent," said Ibrahim, "I'll meet you." Tarek hung up and stood by the arched windows of the old Jerusalem hotel, the late afternoon light flooding onto the whitewashed walls and the high ceilings. He looked at his watch, listening to the muffled sounds of the surrounding city, the echo of distant tones—a bell, a hammer, the sound of an old clock striking, then silence. He pushed open the window and gazed at the city stretching below him. Walls upon ancient walls, domes, cupolas, the crumbling houses of the old city, the stones of the streets, the gold and blue gleaming arches left behind by the Muslims, the monks, the Crusaders, the traders, the thieves, the saints, the shopkeepers. Layers of stone, layers of shed blood, bathed in this ethereal light. A city where the tongues of different Gods conflicted in confusion with the greed of human desires— power, land, money.

He thought of all the lies and treachery that had disappeared into this place, truth and fiction all drowning, hopelessly confused and intertwined, in a nightly sea of rose-gold light that turned to black. And in the soft black echoes, the bell from somewhere, a voice, the chime of the clock, another lie would hover and disappear, wisping as cigarette smoke into nothingness.

He waited five more minutes and then walked down to the street. The rose light of sundown began to engulf the entire city. He walked three blocks and then waited until a graying man in rimless glasses and a rumpled shirt walked up behind him. He spoke with an elegant Oxford accent.

"It is almost nightfall," said the man softly. "Would you come with me; my car is over there."

Ibrahim Husseini drove the old car out of Jerusalem toward the hills of Ramallah, glancing curiously at his passenger. He drove in a distracted manner, braking and gunning the car until they reached their destination, an old rundown house with multiple entrances, peeling paint on the doors, and various doorbells with names taped to them, the ink blurred by the rain.

"Please, this way. We share this with my uncle and some others. Good, we have made it before dark," he said, now relaxing inside the door. "Sometimes my work in the archives leaves me unmindful of the time. I realize almost too late it is about to be dark," he muttered.

He closed the door behind them. The phone began to ring. Tarek watched the man's body stiffen. Small beads of sweat appeared at his temples as though the ability to control himself, the look of hatred moving across his face, required such exertion, such tension that it threatened to explode the man's very being. The phone rang one more time.

"They call at night, you know," he mumbled. He picked up the phone. "Yes, yes, no, no, there is no problem." He hung up. "They call at night, at nightfall," he mumbled apologetically again.

Tarek looked around the room. The old blue tablecloth with

the cheap yellow tassels, the worn sofa, old armchairs soiled from years of use, the threadbare doilies covering them, the cheap new lamp—so different from the magnificence of the Husseini home of old, when they were a family of wealth, intellectuals and merchants. He watched Husseini's wife, a thin shadow of a woman, graciously offer a tray of sweets, a ghost of the young beauty Tarek remembered betrothed to one of the merchant princes of their world.

Husseini sighed when she left them. "It is hardest on them—my wife, my two children—the isolation. I can at least go into the city during daylight and work a bit at the archives."

"This has made it a bit difficult to get the information you need, being under arrest again," he said. "I may go out at day between certain hours, within a certain circumference within Ramallah Jerusalem, but I am watched constantly. I may never congregate with groups. I may not act politically. Every night the Israelis call to see that I am home by dark. It is always the same. There is never a specific crime. I am simply a Palestinian, 'a security risk.' " He stopped when he heard the sound of a car. "That will be Abu Jihad."

The heavyset man with the dark lined face, the voice that whispered from Arafat's many phones in the night from PLO enclaves strewn around the Middle East, entered. Abu Jihad nodded to Husseini and eased into a chair.

Bitter lines crossed his skin, his mouth as he talked, coldness, sarcasm illuminating the dead eyes. "We have not always been so candid with one another through the years have we?" Abu Jihad's voice slid slowly through his lips as he leaned toward Tarek. "We have been playing games with one another for a while, have we not, my dear friend?"

He reached for the cup of tea and sighed. "These games, so unfortunate really. But it is, you see, so many years now that the

Palestinians have been rotting in the camps. Certainly there were some easy answers along the way, but they were never reached, were they?" He opened his palms briefly, then dropped them to the table. "Of course, there was the obvious thing to do—we are Arabs, you are Arabs, you take us into your countries and give us a home. But no. And so this goes on for years and we are now, shall we say, unpleasant?" He opened his palms in mock despair.

"The once cultured Palestinians smell, they are poor and dirty. And they have ultimately developed bad manners." He pursed his lips. "This terrorism as it is called. Ah well, the options are so few really, aren't they? Everybody pretending we aren't human. So unpleasant the problem, no elegant solution." He sighed. "Perhaps the sand will simply cover us over. It is not nice, is it? So many years go by. Israel herding us around in a police state, the West doing absolutely nothing, and the Arabs doing as little while they talk on. King Faisal cared, you cared. But nothing happened, did it?"

"So we plant bombs, hijack planes in lieu of the 'normal routes of conversation.' Whether you like it or not, we say to the world 'we exist, we have not been wiped from the face of the earth yet.' " He shrugged, luxuriating in his quarry, Tarek waiting for the one answer he had come for.

"And now," he leaned forward, "suddenly there is a new player—a new power. They want something, we want something. They detest Israel, we detest Israel. And finally, to put this delicately, they have lost respect for the other Arab governments? We have lost respect for the other Arab governments." Tarek watched the man's hate slide slowly behind his eyes. "We find we have, yes, a great deal in common. Iraq could be the new power in the Middle East.

"And we?" Suddenly his voice changed. "We are a dangerous loose cannon rolling around the Middle East waiting to be used by whomever can play to our exhausted, bitter hope."

Abu Jihad put the cup down, his next words abrupt. "Perhaps, Tarek, I have not always been totally honest with you, perhaps you haven't been totally honest with me. After all, we beg, don't we? We steal. We suck up to anyone who can help, don't we? We crawl down back alleys, we plant bombs." He stopped, then focused directly on Tarek. "But as desperate as we are, we make a mistake siding with Saddam. He will do the same to us as Khomeini did. Use us and then discard us. Arafat and I have been arguing—I tell him all that has been gained by the Intifada will be lost if we go with Saddam. For the first time we disagree."

Abu Jihad got up abruptly to leave. "My disaffection for aligning with Saddam, Antar, is known. Therefore Antar's plans, the particular Palestinian he refers to, and how he is going to use him to carry these plans out will have been kept from me. However, for my own reasons, I too think it is critical to stop them. I have made arrangements for you. Do not connect me with any person you might speak to, any information you might get. In four days a man will meet you in Gaza." He stood up and walked out the door.

Ibrahim Husseini drove Tarek back. "In four days, Gaza," he whispered, then left. Tarek walked back into the hotel room, the rose light fading over the walls. He looked down again at the small piece of paper. The words stared back at him. "The Palestinian," "the bedu."

28

The little wooden house was a few feet from one of the two dusty roads that led into the small bedu town. A small clapboard house painted in a faded green, comprising three rooms, with a handful of orange trees planted behind it. Inside, an old wooden table, dime-store lamps, a few worn chairs, a bed, some candles in case of electricity failures.

When Naila had arrived the day before, she was given the keys, told this was where the clinic doctor was supposed to live, and sent a helper for the day to bring in food and clean bedding.

At the end of the day, she thanked the helper and then saw the small note in the girl's hand. "It came on the helicopter to the clinic for you," she said offering it up to her.

Naila opened the letter. It was from Nura.

Dearest Naila,
After you left, Musaid stormed over. He was irate about your departure. There truly is an insidious side to him I do not understand. And yet it is there, and I am worried about it. I am worried about you. He is fairly easily manipulated in some ways and his anger seemed somewhat assuaged when I told

*him you would only be there for a brief time. I will do what
I can here for you.*

> *As always,*
> *Nura*

The girl watched Naila read the note a second time and then crumple it and drop it on the table. The evening light was beginning to fade and the helper moved to go.

"Dr. Naila, the clinic opens at seven in the morning. Shall I tell them you will begin then?"

"Yes."

The following morning Naila walked across the square of the small bedu town. The clinic was a one-story cinder-block building.

"I imagine," said the nurse, watching Naila's expression from the doorway, "it's quite a bit different from what you were used to in Washington and Riyadh." The nurse motioned Naila into the small dusty, waiting room. Naila put her own instrument bag down and gazed at the tiny examination room and the pharmacy with its old glass case of medicines.

"Is there more?" asked Naila.

The nurse shook her head, embarrassed. "In the past, when we had something we couldn't handle, we'd ask for a helicopter to Riyadh."

Naila silently picked up an old stethoscope, the small box of instruments. "The women in the desert," continued the nurse nervously, "usually give birth at home; we help if there is a problem. The children, they have mostly…"

Naila stopped her with a warm smile. "Please, don't apologize." She walked over and clasped her hands in hers. "I find this very exciting."

The nurse was surprised.

"You see," smiled Naila, "I have been in training so long, with so much equipment, that the idea of doing something simply sounds wonderful."

The nurse breathed in relief. "My name is Benazir."

"You are from Pakistan?"

"Yes. I think they like to send the Pakistani nurses into the rural area because we are Muslims, too, and it is very conservative here. We understand it a bit better." Her face brightened as she talked on. "We are used to life in the villages, the ways, so…"

Naila followed her down the rows of refugees lying on cots, sitting along the floor.

"They just keep flooding in."

Naila checked patients as she went. After a few hours, exhausted, she sat down. Benazir looked up at the clock.

"That will be all the new ones for today. They close the borders at noon each day. I will go rest for a bit and then be back." Benazir closed the medicine cabinet and set off across the small village. Suddenly a knock on the door sounded. Naila reached for the latch and there stood a boy, a sweating horse behind him. His lean dark face looked intently at Naila, "I have come for the women's doctor."

Naila motioned him in. "I am the women's doctor. What is it?"

The boy walked hesitantly into the clinic room.

"I am from the Bani Sa tribe in the desert. One of the women is giving birth, but the others are afraid for her; they say something is wrong. Please, can you come?"

Naila nodded quickly, "Yes, but…"

He stopped her. "The men in the town will help us. They have a car that can get into the desert; I will bring them and go with you." He swung back astride the horse and rode off. Naila pulled out her instrument bag, wrote a note for Benazir, and draped her abaya over her head.

The boy returned with a car driven by a village man. Naila locked the clinic door and went over to them. But when she approached the car the man behind the wheel became suddenly agitated, and he motioned for her to stop. He called the boy over to him. The boy listened, and then walked back to Naila.

"He says the Pakistani woman doctor is to come, not you."

Naila answered surprised. "Tell him the other woman doctor is not here. I am replacing her; I will go." The boy returned to the man and spoke to him. The man began to shake his head.

The boy walked back to Naila nervously. "He says he can't take you."

Startled, Naila looked back at the driver then at the boy, "Tell him I am trained; I am able to do this."

The boy flushed, embarrassed. "It is not that," he said quietly. "It is that you are a Saudi woman, not a foreigner. You are not to go without a man from your family. It would be a dishonor to…"

Naila felt the anger rising in her. "You tell him that the dishonor would be to leave a patient without care. I am the doctor, and I will go."

The boy walked back to the car. Naila saw the man continue to shake his head. She stood for a moment and then picked up her bag. She strode toward the car, reached out and opened the back door. She hesitated for a moment, then got in the back seat. The man stared, stunned.

"Drive."

The man's face clouded with indignation.

"Drive the car," breathed Naila. "The woman may be dying out there while you go on with this nonsense."

His face contorted in rage. He stared at her, his eyes narrowed in fury. Then slowly he got out of the car and spit on the ground.

The boy silently watched the man go. Then his dark troubled eyes fixed on Naila. "I know how to drive, will you go with me?"

Her anger nearly choked the words. "Yes." The boy quickly got behind the wheel, put the car in gear, and sped onto the winding road to the desert.

Rapidly the palms and the clay houses of the village began to disappear. The long rolling sand dunes of the Nafud stretched ahead as the car moved steadily into its deepening silence. The edges of the sand on the horizon seemed to curl up, blur into small rivulets of heat while the car wound its way through the rolling cascades of sand.

The boy looked up at the sun. "We will have light until we are there."

"Is it far?" asked Naila.

"Far?" he said as though the question seemed curious. "Yes, it is far."

Naila closed her eyes. The straight slash of road cut through flowing rivers of sand. Silence and heat swam up from the desert floor. She struggled to keep her eyes open beneath the heat while the motion lulled her to sleep, the brilliant yellow of the sun turning inside her closed eyes to a burning red, then blue.

"We must walk now."

She pulled awake at the boy's soft voice. "The road ends

here," he said. "You will walk with me?" She saw nothing but the low rolling sand.

He pointed to her feet. "Take off your shoes. Your feet must hold the sand." She slipped off her shoes and felt her feet sinking into the warm sand.

"I will carry your bag," he said quietly. "Follow me."

Naila walked behind the straight back of the boy. She saw him glance toward the sun and then move, as though to a compass, across the desert. Naila struggled against exhaustion as they wove their way up the dunes beneath the burning sun.

"I have to rest for a moment," she whispered. The boy nodded and sat down. Naila eased down and leaned her head on her knees.

"You must take some water," the boy held out the skin flask.

Naila reached for it and drank deeply. She handed it back to the boy. She turned as she saw a thin line moving at the edge of the desert.

"What is that?"

The boy turned and peered. Through the heart of the desert the long line of trucks began to appear, rolling quietly in a row. Grinding slowly through the sand in a convoy, the massive trucks gleamed in the blistering sun, their hulls carrying enormous cylinder-shaped objects covered with canvas. The winding convoy filled with U.S. troops snaked silently across the desert. "Where are they going?"

The boy remained silent.

"Why don't you answer?" Naila looked at him curiously.

"We have been told not to say anything," the boy said. Then he stood up and waited for Naila to continue. Naila got to her feet, watching the convoy and the armed bedu guards surrounding it disappear deeper into the desert. The boy said nothing. He looked back at her when they started up the low dune, then stopped. He gazed at a mark in the sand, then dropped down and touched it.

"They have come to look for us, this camel has only just passed." He reached his hand back to her. "You are all right?"

"Yes," said Naila.

"We are not far now."

Finally, the boy turned and pointed. "There, you hear?"

Naila shook her head listening to the quiet. The boy laughed softly, "If you were from the desert, you would hear."

He motioned her to follow, walking quickly now.

Naila watched the figures begin to emerge before her eyes. Hundreds of camels stood silently against the red sun slipping into the desert. Behind them low black tents stretched across the desert. Their blackness, slashed with colors from the bedu rugs lying beside them, was brilliant against the sand.

She focused her eyes and began to see the long black skirts of the bedu women, the leather burkas covering their faces. Stark black figures bending over pots above small fires on the desert floor. A woman turned to the small girl in the colored cotton dress as she caught sight of Naila. The girl ran toward a tent while the woman moved hurriedly toward Naila.

She reached for Naila's hand, staring at her in fascination. "The girl giving birth is over here," she said, pointing to a tent. Naila moved quickly as the boy handed her the bag.

When she entered the large dark tent, she saw a girl lying on a bedu rug on the soft sand, eyes closed, breathing rapidly. Naila bent over. The girl's face was bathed in sweat; a grimace of pain contorted her dried mouth. Naila spoke abruptly to the women crowded beside her stroking her hands.

"How long has she been like this?" asked Naila deftly opening her bag.

"The baby," said one in an agitated voice, "began to come

before the sun rose, but it does not come, she is not strong now."

Naila listened with the stethoscope, looking at the young girl's face, "She has had others?"

"No, this is the first."

Naila reached for the small monitor and affixed it to the girl's belly while the women watched. "How old is she?"

"She was born," said one woman, "the year the white camel was born."

Naila realized the woman could neither read nor write and had no understanding of a calendar.

"I see," she said quietly. "Maybe she is fourteen?"

"Maybe," nodded the woman, "she is as you say."

Naila moved her hands across the girl's belly, apprehensively feeling the baby. She watched the fetal heart monitor.

"It is alive still?" whispered the woman next to her.

"Yes, where is some boiling water?"

The woman pointed to the pots bubbling outside the tent. Naila got up quickly, pulled her instruments from the bag, and plunged them into the water. The boys outside the tent stared, intrigued. She glanced up at the older men with their long beards, watching her as she washed her hands.

Back in the tent the women looked expectantly, while she pulled on a pair of sterile gloves, soaked some sterile gauze in Betadine solution, and swabbed the girl off. The girl looked up at her with blurred, frightened eyes when she reached down with her hand to check the dilation.

"The baby is twisted inside. It's heart is beating, but the girl is quite weak. I am going to try to reach in and turn the baby. The cord though is dangerous—it could strangle the baby before we can get it out. You will help me, you are not afraid?"

The woman shook her head, chagrined. "We always bring

the babies, the women, we know how, but this." She stopped and looked at Naila. "Some like this have died, the babies, the girls. The last woman's doctor came to us and said they could help these ones, to ask."

"You have done the right things," Naila said. "I hope to have as much wisdom as you. You are a good friend to the girl."

"I am her sister," said the woman simply. "The boy who brought you, he is her brother. Her husband," she pointed to a bedu boy of about sixteen closing Naila's case for her as he watched nervously, "cares for her a great deal. He is afraid for her."

"Come," said Naila, "we will try."

The women stared intently while Naila began. She placed her left hand in the vagina and her right hand on the girl's lower abdomen. Feeling for the child's head, she moved her hand slowly, then struggled to turn the child within the uterus. The girl started, then screamed. The women held the girl's hands when the pain spasms overwhelmed her.

"I need a little more time," said Naila, the sweat trickling down her brow, "her feet, hold her feet...now, now it's moving."

Suddenly the girl gasped, choked in pain. Naila slowly edged the head down. "Almost, almost..."

The girl's head rolled slowly to the side. Her breath caught. The woman looked terrified.

"She is dead," one of the women whispered in fright.

"No," said Naila, "she's just exhausted, she's breathing."

Naila worked for several more minutes, then leaned back. The women's faces flickered before her in the dim light from the fire.

"The baby is turned, its head is down," she said. "But it is still fairly far up. She's very weak...I think..." The woman waited. Naila saw the girl's eyes focus again.

Suddenly the girl's face contorted. Naila bent over her.

"Now, now," she said, "push. Push as hard as you can." The girl clutched the edge of the blanket, sand covering her hands as she pushed. "Push, more, more. Breathe deeply, then push again," said Naila urgently to her. "Breathe again, once more..."

Suddenly the girl's scream ripped through the night. Naila quickly put out her hand to hold the infant head starting to emerge.

"Once more, now, the child is coming."

The girl shook violently. Naila gently edged the baby's shoulders out, then its arms. Finally she was able to lift it toward the light, its first small cry filled the tent as she clamped and divided the cord. She looked down at the infant as she held it in the light, rapidly checking its heart, its limbs. Finally, as they waited nervously, she bent down to the girl.

"You have a beautiful girl," she said softly. Naila wiped the child clean then held her for the girl to see. Tears ran across the girl's face as she touched her baby for the first time.

"Your name?" the girl whispered up with grateful eyes.

"My name," she said softly, "is Naila."

"Her name," said the girl cradling the infant, "then, will be Naila. May her beauty be as great." Naila held her hand and the girl whispered, "Please, show her to her father, so he will know."

Naila picked up the infant while one of the women helped deliver the placenta, and placed the baby in the arms of the waiting man. He reached for her hand.

"We are so grateful to you, I cannot say," he said, holding the child. "I have no way to repay you."

"There is none needed," said Naila.

She watched him hold the child, then walked toward the small fire and looked up at the brilliant stars in the desert sky. She turned as she sensed the woman standing behind her. The woman held out a cloth and began gently to wipe Naila's face.

She smiled when she saw Naila feel for the abaya that had been draped about her shoulders while she worked.

"It has fallen to the sand," she said. "I will bring you a burka, then you must eat."

The woman called back to a small girl staring in wonder at Naila. The child darted into a tent and came back carrying the leather mask of the bedu women. The woman reached out shyly and fastened the leather band across Naila's brow, moving it so her eyes shone through the opening above the leather that covered her cheeks and nose. Then she draped a scarf over Naila's hair. "Now, come."

She led her to a rug spread before one of the tents, picked up a bowl and walked to one of the camels tethered close by. She reached for the camel's udder. The fresh milk flowed into the bowl while the woman worked. She took a date, scooped it through the froth at the top of the warm milk, gave the bowl and dates to Naila, then watched with satisfaction while Naila ate.

The small girl ran over to them, bent down and whispered in the woman's ear, then hurried back toward the fire burning at the other end of the encampment.

"It is time," said the woman to the others. Naila looked up questioningly.

"Tonight," said the woman, they are to circumcise the boys. It is time, come." Naila surprised, stood up and began to walk with her across the desert floor, cool now that the sun had set. They approached a circle of men gathered around a large fire. Women and children sat behind them. At the center stood an old white-bearded sheikh.

Nine boys began to walk toward the fire. The old sheikh stood silently holding the knife.

As they came toward the light, she could see them, boys of

about twelve or thirteen years old, backs straight, heads held high, their loins wrapped with only a cloth. When they reached the fire, they stopped. Slowly, one by one, members of their family came forward to remove the cloth and rub their bodies with butter and saffron until they glistened.

The sheikh told them to sit on a rock and approached the youngest first. He tied the boy's foreskin tightly with a string and moved on to do the same to the other eight boys, one of whom was almost into manhood with a beard.

"This one," whispered the woman to Naila, "has waited until the night before his marriage."

The boys kept absolutely still as the old Sheikh approached them. He held the blunt knife above the first boy, then bent over. The knife flashed as he hacked the dead tied skin until it fell to the desert floor. The boy's face remained immobile. The sheikh went on to the next boy while blood trickled down the first boy's legs.

"The blood," whispered the woman again, "usually stops in a few hours, although some bleed through the night."

The sheikh stood back from the fourth boy. Suddenly the boy keened and fell over.

"Ah," said the woman clucking her tongue, "his family will be disappointed, but..." she shrugged, "but it happens sometimes." The sound of the desert drums began.

"Now watch," said the woman, "the dancing."

The boys picked up the daggers in the sand in front of them, blood still flowing down their legs. Raising their daggers, the other men joined them. Weaving back and forth beneath the light of the fire and the moon, they moved in a hypnotic rhythm, chanting. Long white thobes flowing, raising their daggers up into the night sky and down to the cold desert floor, their chant, the sound of the drums woven with the ancient desert flute, throbbed wildly, eerily into the night.

A woman touched Naila's arm. "Your eyes are closing, you are exhausted. You should sleep now," she said gently.

Naila followed her into a tent. She stretched out upon the rugs scattered on the deep sand and felt the warmth of the bedu rugs they laid over her as she drifted off into sleep. The women in their burkas sat silently outside her closed tent in the stillness of the desert.

Naila's eyes opened when she felt the light tap on her shoulder. The eyes behind the black leather face mask smiled. The woman handed her the steaming cardamom coffee, and Naila saw the streaks of dawn light across the sky.

"The girl, the baby, they are all right?"

The woman nodded, "They are resting, inshallah they are well."

Naila drank the coffee, watching the camels shift slowly about the sand, lowing quietly beneath the man's voice calling out the morning prayer. A second woman came in, bringing some hot cornmeal and fresh camel's milk.

"The boy will take me back?" asked Naila. The woman smiled and pointed to him waiting outside the tent.

Naila washed her face in the bowl of water. She looked about for her abaya and another woman came in carrying it neatly folded.

"We washed it for you last night, the sand..."

Naila thanked her. "Will you come to the clinic to see me, for any help?" she asked. They nodded while they helped her.

She looked into the tent with the mother and the child sleeping, the women surrounding them. The boy stood waiting.

"Before it is hot," he said quietly.

When she began to walk, the woman held out her hand. She opened a cloth and Naila looked at the hammered silver and carnelian of the bedu necklace.

"The sheikh asked us to give this to you." She held up the broad silver collar with silver links from which bells of carnelian dangled gently against Naila's throat. "You will look very beautiful I think. The sheikh says that when he fought alongside Abdul Aziz, leading the Bani Sa as a young man, that Abdul Azziz gave this to him. He says you should have it now."

She stepped back shyly while Naila held the necklace and thanked the woman. "Shokran, shokran jazeelan."

Naila held her rough hand for a moment, then she turned and followed the boy across the sand for the long trek back across the desert.

❈   ❈   ❈

As Naila and the boy approached the dusty clinic, Benazir rushed out the door. "Dr. Naila," she cried, "where have you been, your note said you went into the desert?" Benazir's voice stopped suddenly. She stared toward the small town square. Naila turned, hearing only the sound of Benazir's, whispered "Oh, no."

Naila looked beyond her to the square filling with people under the hot midday sun. Dusty trucks and horses were streaming down from the foothills. Bedu—outlined against the deep veins of rose and blue that streaked the gold of the rolling low mountains—rode bareback, toward the square below. Below, the shopkeepers in the souk lowered the doors of their stalls.

The old man with the spices stood up, adjusted the old worn silver dagger at his waist, and then walked solemnly to join the others. Slowly, silently the women in their black veils guided their small children to stand with the others in the hot midday sun until the square was completely full.

The people stood, and waited.

Naila touched Benazir's shoulder. "What is it?"

Benazir said, "They will want us to go, we are to go and watch."

Naila caught her hand, "Watch what?"

There was a loud knock on the door. Hesitantly, Benazir opened it. A bedu guard with a gun slung over his shoulder motioned them out toward the square. Benazir nodded and then turned to Naila. "You must come, too." Naila followed Benazir to the edge of the crowd in the square.

Then she saw the boy in white. He stood in the center as though transfixed, apart from the others. His wrists were tied behind him. He wore a freshly washed white thobe. His palms were stained with henna like those of desert brides. His eyes, lined with kohl, stared straight ahead. His voice, in a strange and faraway tone, began to repeat, "There is no God but God, and Mohammad is the Prophet of God. There is no God but God, and Mohammad is the Prophet of God..."

An old man, followed by two others, walked to the center of the crowd and stopped a few feet from the chanting boy. The old man raised his hand for silence, and his voice thundered out, echoing against the foothills.

"We have found Abdullah guilty." A whisper ran through the crowd.

"That is his uncle, the old one," said Benazir under her breath to Naila. "The mother and father are standing behind the boy."

The old man turned toward the parents. The crowd waited.

"He asks no mercy from you. He is prepared."

Abruptly he turned back toward the boy and motioned him

over. The boy walked step by step, chanting softly, toward the man.

"Kneel."

Slowly the boy knelt down and touched his head to the dirt.

The old man motioned to the other two men.

They walked toward the outstretched figure. One stood on either side. The boy's chanting quickened, his voice trembling in the heat of the sun.

Suddenly, the large black man drew a sword.

Naila gasped in horror. The second man pulled a thin sword from his belt and jabbed it into the boy's side. The boy lurched upward with a scream.

The black man stiffened. He drew his arm back and then slashed the sword forward. Brilliant, violent in the burning sun, it flashed through the stillness toward the boy. The sound of the blade hit. Naila's scream caught in her throat as the boy's head tumbled into the silent crowd, blood spurting from the truncated body.

Benazir looked numbly back toward Naila. "The head, they will leave it there," she murmured. "They will leave it there on the ground until sunset for the people to see."

Naila was shaking as Benazir took her by the hand.

"It is over now," Benazir whispered. "It is all right for us to go now."

Benazir walked Naila back to the clinic and closed the door behind them. Naila sat down, still shaking. "What is it?" she whispered. "What happened?"

Benazir sat next to her. The crowd outside the window started to move away, the bedu slowly disappearing back up into the foothills.

"The boy was from the Bani Sa tribe. The trial was yesterday. I don't know what happened really, but they say he killed his brother. They say his brother found him bringing a cache of arms in from Iraq. He knew the brother would report him, so he killed him."

She stopped, and looked back out the window at the parents standing by the dead boy's body.

"He admitted it. There was no question."

She looked at Naila for a moment. "Dr. Naila," she said quietly, "they haven't really told me anything about you. I know you are from Riyadh, that you trained in the States. Perhaps you don't know…" She paused, choosing her words carefully. "…the ways, the traditions of the people here." She paused. "Riyadh and all of the modern things you know are very far away. These people have lived in this desert for hundreds of years. Maybe you would be stunned if you knew the conditions they have been able to survive." She pause, then resumed. "When I first came, I saw people living in the desert, up in the mountains, in ways you can't imagine a human being surviving for days, much less hundreds of years. But they do it."

Benazir sighed. "And you begin to understand why they formed the laws they have among themselves. The family, the tribe is everything. Order, allegiance. If a crime is committed, the rules are known. Punishment is dealt quickly and used to show the others to stop more."

She gazed at the empty square and then back at Naila. "There are cars, big homes, hotels, airplanes in Riyadh, roads that lead from there to here. The government sends money, water, supplies to the bedu tribes in the desert to put up a school, a clinic. Some of this the bedu take, some of it they don't. In the end, they return to what they know. They give hospitality to a stranger in need. They take care of their own, the old ones, the sick ones, and," she stopped, "they will kill their own if they have transgressed."

"The old ones carry it on," murmured Naila.

Benazir shook her head. "Not just the old ones. Some of the younger men, some who have gone out and seen the new," she said. "They come back feeling more strongly than ever." She shrugged, "They come back and spit with disdain on the country's new ways. Now these western troops starting to move into the desert..."

Her voice was hesitant, "These are difficult times here now, a lot of unrest, talk. The people are very split. Some help the government now; others talk of insurrection. I don't know what your politics are..."

Naila stopped her. "I am not a political person. I am here as a doctor."

"Good," said Benazir. "Do not get involved, try not to see too much."

The small clock on the wall chimed again. "I must go now; I have one house call before it is evening." She stood up and walked out of the clinic, across the square, and disappeared among the ramshackle houses.

Naila sat in the empty room, still trembling. Absently she reached over and turned on the small radio on the desk, feeling strangely disconnected, exhausted, stunned. The static crackled for a moment and then the voice "...the fighting raged in Kuwait as Iraqi planes..." A helicopter sounded overhead. She turned the radio off and gazed wearily at the clinic, the stethoscope on the desk, the small bedu town. Then she looked at the calendar and down at her soft, round belly, and the fear lingering for days gripped her again. His dear face flowed across her mind—the emptiness of the room seemed to reverberate.

29

Badr pushed the door to Tarek's office open. "Hamid got a communication through. Saddam is hesitating. He's confused by the infusion of U.S. troops—he never thought the U.S. would really come through. He doesn't have good aerial or ground reconnaissance, doesn't know how big the build-up here really is. He held a big meeting last night with his generals. They were set to roll into Saudi Arabia in two days—and decided by the meeting's end to delay in hopes of getting better information on just how much Schwarzkopf has here, where it's stationed."

Tarek suddenly smiled. "So we help them a little, eh Badr?"

Badr grinned, nodded, and picked up the phone.

Elaine and Ray moved through the reconnaissance material at their headquarters with General Schwarzkopf. She turned as the messenger came in and gave her the small sheet with Badr's message. She handed it to Ray and General Schwarzkopf. Just then, the chilling sounds of Radio Baghdad carried through the room.

Saddam Hussein's voice called out. "You, the President of the United States...you are going to be defeated. Thousands of Americans, whom you have pushed into this dark tunnel, will go home shrouded in sad coffins." Elaine turned the sound down and finished her briefing.

"As Ray will tell you, General Schwarzkopf, I've been able to set this up without divulging our 'particular' fears about leaks. I simply stated that the available U.S. military communications systems were so poor we were going to have build a secure satellite-communications from scratch. So far Ray says everybody has bought the story—in large part because it also happens to be true."

Ray grunted humorlessly.

"Ready to go take a look?" Ray and Schwarzkopf followed her to the car which sped toward the Saudi Ministry of Defense.

"Tarek found the location for me. He said it was half-completed and then forgotten. The entire intel crew has been arriving over the past few days, and they've already set up quite a bit." She looked at Schwarzkopf amused. "One of them dubbed it 'the Black Hole' for reasons that will shortly become apparent."

The car pulled up to the Ministry of Defense, and they followed her inside, down two elevators, through a heavily guarded hallway, down another flight of stairs, through more heavy doors until they reached a sub-basement five stories below the ground. She opened the door. There a huge room, two stories high was already jammed with desks and cubicles, people and equipment.

"Sweet Jesus," murmured Schwarzkopf.

Elaine motioned him to follow her into the cavernous room where a maze of military intelligence and a CIA team, just flown over, awaited them. She introduced them to the members of the first team working to set up better systems of intercepts within Iraq and to sift through the reams and scraps of intelligence that main CIA and military intelligence were now feeding them.

"One of the fellows said we ought to call this Antar's suite," she smiled amused again, motioning them along. She walked briskly through the next unit, explaining that they were working laptop computers on a special system that could not be tapped into by anybody, no matter what their rank in the Allied Central Command. They functioned under an oath of secrecy in three different cubicles. The first working on determining locations and means to eradicate Saddam's arsenal—nuclear weapons, chemical and biological plants, and missile-pro duction factories. The second, focusing on the Republican Guard, their artillery and tanks along the Kuwaiti border. The third studied infiltration possibilities within Kuwait. A beehive of additional units were being constructed around them.

She looked over her shoulder at Schwarzkopf. "Tarek says they found some sort of palatial headquarters for you, but you prefer to just sleep in a room upstairs in the Ministry?"

Schwarzkopf muttered something as she pointed to a large glass conference cubicle. "Well, here's your War Room, General."

Schwarzkopf entered the glass cubicle, momentarily floored by the extraordinary intel feat, which she seemed to have erected in this structure, almost overnight. A technician was working furiously to connect a complicated looking fax machine with an even more complicated telephone set-up. Elaine reached down, examined one of the wires, then nodded to Schwarzkopf.

"You're going to have to communicate on a daily basis with General Powell in Washington. We're concerned with the possibility of leaks on both ends. We want the loop as small as possible. This phone should be secure and goes directly to him. We have set up a fax on the same secure line since you may have to send him documents or diagrams. You hand it only to Colonel Bell here," she pointed to the man who had come up to join them, "he will notify General Powell's one designated aide by phone that it will be coming, and that aide will stand by the fax to pick it up by hand and personally carry it to General Powell as Colonel Bell will do on this end for you." She saw Ray motioning to them from one of the cubicles outside.

He pointed to the flow of information being beamed down from the reconnaissance satellites overflying Iraq. "Hell, you don't have to be a rocket scientist to interpret that one," cackled the lieutenant in front of the infrared scanner, picking up the temperature change in the Iraqi bunker. "The guy's running a motor down there, they're manufacturing."

Ray pointed to the other monitor. "Saddam's built bunkers for himself and his family in case it gets a little rough. Look here," he pointed to the images. "Probably moved quite a bit of money for himself out of the country, too," added Ray acerbically. The lieutenant motioned to the other screen where they were monitoring Saddam's nuclear plant. Ray looked on, worried. "I'm telling, you from what I can interpret, this guy has all the ingredients necessary for a nuclear bomb. He only needs time."

Tarek and Badr walked up behind them, silently watching the monitor. Schwarzkopf finally turned around. "You come over for the bad news?"

Tarek was momentarily amused by Schwarzkopf. "No. In pursuit of more news." Schwarzkopf gave him a puzzled look. "Perhaps," said Tarek, motioning Ray, Elaine and Schwarzkopf toward the War Room, while he glanced around the Black

Hole, "you have been too efficient in plugging up 'leaks.' "

Schwarzkopf sat in the glass room with Ray and Elaine listening to Tarek outline the plan. "Sounds perfect." The big man, still scintillating at the wonderful perversity of the idea, lumbered up from the chair. Before Ray and Elaine had cleared the door, Schwarzkopf was already placing a call to Washington. Ray went outside quickly and pulled up a chair alongside the tech in the first cubicle.

"Gentlemen, we have a little something new in mind for today. A little reverse. Or should I say, perverse." He smiled as they looked at him expectantly. "You know how Iraq is spending a lot of time trying to tap into our communications to find out what we've got and what we're doing? Well today we're going to send some 'secure' communications back and forth within our military that even the crudest system of intercepts could get."

"Meaning Iraq's?" The analyst practically fondled the equipment in front of him.

"Meaning Iraq's. Meaning, I think we should feed them some crap, fantasy that it is, about our troops and capabilities that will stand their hair on end."

The young analyst began to hum at his words, smiling, sketching notes on his pad, before Ray had time to even continue with the details. The tech rubbed his short goatee and gave a euphoric grin toward Elaine. "It's sick I know, but I just adore feeding them this shit."

He hummed along while they drafted out the "appropriate" communiqués.

General Schwarzkopf hung up the phone and rejoined them. The military attaché, who had been on the other end, held the phone for a minute. He repeated Schwarzkopf's orders, blatantly confused, to the aide sitting next to him.

"They want the press in? They never want the press in." The attaché mumbled something about the inconsistencies of the world, and with a sigh began to weed through the stacks of hitherto denied requests from network correspondents all over the world. The screams and shouts of the irate, locked-out press all over the world still ringing in his ears, haranguing his very dreams at night, he began calling them one by one. "The Pentagon has reconsidered and you'll be able to…"

▲▲Yes sir, that's right, as many cameras as you want." Schwarzkopf beamed at the correspondents. He waved the boys on the camera crew over while the military attaché looked on in disbelief. Schwarzkopf, looking more like a middle linebacker than a general, slapped the correspondent affectionately on the shoulder.

"That's right son, we got a massive amount of material, troops, and weaponry here. Massive. More coming in every day. Desert Shield is a goddamned formidable array of manpower and high tech." He motioned them closer to the dock where troops were streaming off of the ships. The dock loaders struggled under the barrage of cargo in front of them, unloading as quickly as possible. Schwarzkopf chatted amiably with the correspondents while the camera crews recorded the dock scene.

At the end of an hour, Schwarzkopf groaned to the camera crew, "God, I'm bushed let's go for a bite of lunch, take a rest." The crew nodded and followed along behind the burly general.

A couple of hours later he had them out in the desert for more shots.

He waved them toward a display of planes and pilots. "We got the 101st Airborne Division, the 82nd Airborne Division..." Minutes later he directed them over to the row of troops standing in the desert by their tanks and tents. "This here is the 24th Mechanized Infantry Division, over here we got the 3rd Armored Cavalry."

"But those are the same troops you had them record coming in, the ones on the boat," whispered an aide.

"Shut up son," breathed Schwarzkopf back, "they're maybe going to see these same troops even a few more times." The aide watched in amazement as Schwarzkopf instructed the troops, out of earshot from the cameras, to run in circles so it would look like there were four times as many as there really were. "Jesus, god," whispered the aide, "the man is a stitch."

Schwarzkopf pointed over to the squadron of Arab troops arrayed along with them. "These here are the forces from the Kingdom, from Egypt..." he continued on down the line. "Now this over here..."

"General," a voice from the camera crew interrupted. "We just went past the main hospital unit. Can we stop and take a look, get some shots?"

"Aw, son, it's just the usual bunch of docs and hospital equipment, come with me over here, I've got some far more interesting stuff for you..." The camera man nodded obediently and followed along. Schwarzkopf turned to his aide. "If the bastards find out I cancelled half of the hospital unit to get more troops in here, if they notice we only have eighty docs and five-hundred beds for all these guy, it'll be a disaster. Jesus we could hardly find transport ships to get them here."

"General Schwarzkopf," the aide whispered, amazed. "I

thought the computer specs called for the first transports to bring the hospital stuff."

"Son, I did a little editing." The aide's shock was palpable.

"Took the computer specs and tore them up," smiled Schwarzkopf. With a wave, he departed in his jeep. The aide just stood there and stared.

Ray turned, as Elaine found a chair behind him, "Where's Tarek?"

"Out in the desert taking his 'deliveries.'"

Mr. Moselli handed Tarek the order sheet. The Italian manufacturer wiped his brow in the desert heat and chimed along while Tarek ticked them off one by one. "American fighter-bombers, F-4's, F-15's, and F-16's." He gazed upon them as they rolled off the trucks into the desert. "This one is a beauty, no? We copy them from specialized magazines. The real trick is to keep the weight down. You need to equip them with your own tapes so they hear radio communications coming from them."

Tarek looked up from the sheet to the Italian and pointed over at the tapes all ready to go. The Italian waited until Tarek got down to the end of the sheets. "It's not so bad is it," asked the manufacturer, "$35,000 for each plane, just $30,000 for the tanks?" The manufacturer took the check and headed for the airport.

Within hours, Tarek and his troops had the decoy weapons set throughout the desert terrain. Glistening, the hundreds and hundreds of fake weapons, beeped and beamed up their little fake communications breezily toward whatever radar reconnaissance Saddam and his generals might have looking for them. Tarek gazed at the array. Walid walked up behind him. Silently, he sat down on the desert sand beside Tarek. He looked at the U.S. soldiers encamped across the desert floor.

"I don't come out here too often. It's nice." Walid interrupted himself to take a small swig from the flask of scotch he'd brought along with him. His eyes wandered over the U.S. soldiers again as they began turning into their tents for the night.

"You wonder what impact it's going to have, whether the Kingdom will ever really be the same again," mused Walid. Tarek turned, surprised at the thoughtful tone in Walid's voice. "That's what you were thinking, isn't it Tarek?"

Tarek shook his head. "Actually I was looking at the black soldiers, the brown soldiers, the white soldiers. You know it's interesting, you never spent much time in the States, but I did. They discriminate against these guys—the black ones, the brown ones. It's a very color conscious society. Surprising isn't it, for a country that prides itself so on equality and freedom?"

Walid shrugged. "Here we just have oppressive monarchies. But nobody cares what color you are." He looked back at Tarek again. "It's never going to be the same, is it Tarek?"

"No."

Walid sat silently for a moment. "Then why did we do it?"

"Because we had to."

Walid stood up to leave. Tarek glanced up at the slight figure, now somehow smaller, shadowed by the campfires outside the military tents.

"Walid," he said softly, "it wasn't going to stay the same much longer anyhow."

❂   ❂   ❂

Elaine finished working with the techs setting up the multiple small units stationed around the troops and the city of tents they had raised across the desert floor. The last tech finally looked up at her, exhausted, "I think that's all we can do tonight." She nodded, and told him to get some sleep. Elaine checked two more installations and then pushed her tent's flap-door open. She watched the troops, some still shouldering their heavy packs and weapons, clutching their water bottles as transport dumped them onto the sand. Watched the young faces of the men, their eyes, wondering what was going to happen to them. She quickly shut her mind off from the thoughts that welled up. She walked to the edge of the desert and sat, looking up at the incredible stars above her in the night sky, feeling the profound silence that seemed to emanate from the desert.

A voice yelled out the final call for the night, and two captains walked past behind her. Then she felt herself go rigid with fear as one of the captain's voices floated back "...the terrorist thing worries me. I mean all these tents out here together, kind of makes it easy like the Marine barracks in Beirut." She tried to breathe deeply as she felt the sweat break out on her hands, the images start again in her mind.

Then she felt him sit down next to her. Tarek said absolutely nothing as he came beside her. His presence, the

321

warmth from his body, the strength from it was like a comforting balm beside her. She felt herself steadying as she watched the night sky, the small shooting star that edged over the side of the desert and vanished. They sat in the silence of the night for a long time and then finally she spoke.

"Do you know what I was thinking, Tarek?"

He shook his head, watching the last trail of the small star.

"It's odd, in the middle of all of this I was thinking about my life. Where it's been, where it's going." She stopped, wondering what it was she wanted from him. Why she was telling him this?

He seemed not at all surprised. His eyes took her in, the question was one he long ago must have answered for himself. "You are here, now. This is what we have."

She looked at him quizzically "What do you mean?"

He gazed at the desert stretching in front of them, his voice seemed gentle. "It is an irony, really. Man's fate is to only truly have the moment we live in, the rest is conjecture, you may never have the chance to know it. Our life in the end is the moment we live in and what we did with it." He looked thoughtfully at her. "That is what we leave behind—what we did with it." He paused, his gaze seemed to look at something buried inside of her. "To not understand that is to watch your life disappear in front of you."

Elaine watched his eyes turn back to the desert silence—the strong, even bone structure of his face, delineated against the sand; he was now lost in his own thoughts.

30

▲▲ Crown Prince Abdullah says he must see you now. It is to
be a confidential visit," the messenger declared, standing
before Said's massive desk in the bank. Said looked at the
messenger for a moment, then rose and pressed a button to
order his car.

When he reached Abdullah's palace, the doorman delayed
him. "They're all still there?" asked Said.

"The dinner has gone late sir," the doorman said. "There
were over a hundred bedu in from the Shammar tribe that His
Royal Highness didn't expect, so the cooks had to add them to
the usual seventy or so that show up for dinner on weeknights.
Please..." The doorman hurried to open the dining room door.

Said looked into the huge room. Down the center of the
floor lay steaming platters of whole lamb carcasses, rimmed
with mounds of dates, rice, and oranges. Upon cushions sat
more than two-hundred men of every age. At the end of the
room was Abdullah.

Tall, with an arrow-straight back, pitch-black hair, and
black triangular beard, Abdullah presided over the room,
listening intently to the chief of the Shammar tribe, who had
brought his men down from the north.

The chief of the tribe whispered in his ear. Abdullah nodded,
then the sheikh gave the signal. The men in the room, young

boys, old men with long beards, stood up instantly. One by one they approached Abdullah, embraced him, kissed him on both cheeks, then filed out of the room past the guards. The old sheikh whispered once more to Abdullah, then followed the others.

Abdullah stood in the huge empty room as the tribe returned to the desert. Abdullah would follow them if he could, thought Said, who Abdullah now seemed to remember was standing there. He turned his brilliant smile toward Said and motioned him toward his study.

Abdullah entered the wood-paneled room, picked up first a cigarette, then one of the pool cues from a case on the wall. He chalked up the end of the cue. "Same stakes as last time?" He squared the balls on the billiard table and took aim. Said watched the keen black eyes of the old sportsman and noticed for the first time the small blue rim around the brown-black iris.

He's getting old, thought Said sadly. The man's vitality, the flashing black eyes and the startling candor, the ramrod straight back, the long-strided brisk walk, all of it made one forget that the man was getting old now. In his sixties, thought Said. Abdullah neatly dropped the orange ball into the left pocket. His eyes cut to Said with a wry expression.

"Ah, Said, my friend. The whispering that is going on, the whispering. No one, of course believes that Fahd's car blowing up was an accident. No one. And now Tarek's 'accident.'"

Abdullah lined up another shot. "And you know, my friend, what they are beginning to say? They are beginning to ask, who? Someone from outside, or inside? What are the possibilities? We have a crown prince who now sees he may never rule, who may die before Fahd, may spend his days as number two to a man with whom he disagrees at almost every level. They know I fought against Tarek in the meeting with Cheney.

That I didn't want the U.S. to come in, pushed for an Arab solution. And so, perhaps, they whisper, 'It is him.' "

Abdullah turned and fixed his eyes intently on Said.

"What I am telling you, Said," Abdullah's eyes glinted fiercely, "is that you must be very, very careful about how you move my money over the next few weeks. Nothing must be seen as unusual."

"Should I continue the transactions that we had discussed, your Royal Highness?" Said asked. "Continue the operations into the camps?"

Abdullah stood for a moment, a man lost in his thoughts as he softly chalked the cue stick. His next comment came unexpectedly. The voice of a man searching for his ballast, his bearings.

"Nura continues to send money?"

"Yes."

Abdullah's eyes seemed opaque, to mirror some distant image, remorse that had moved many times, for many years, through his mind. He turned back to Said. "Continue."

�҉ �҉ ✻

Tarek held the piece of paper—the intercept Badr had just brought in from Abdullah's meeting with Said—and stared at it. He had waited for two days for Said to tell him about the meeting with Abdullah. Said did not. Said made no mention of the meeting whatsoever. The face of the tall bedu prince, born in a tent to a mother from the Shammar tribe, circled through his mind with the words from the intercepts—"the Palestinian," "the bedu."

And finally again and again, his eyes riveted to the words about Nura. Badr walked into the office and found him staring at the piece of paper. Without a word, Tarek got up and walked out the door. For an hour he walked through the streets of Riyadh, his mind choking at the thoughts that welled up. Finally he returned to his office and ordered the driver to take him home.

He walked into the house and up to their bedroom. He looked at his wife stretched across the bed writing in her journal. Nura gazed up, the deep, unfathomable green eyes focused on him.

"Hussein of Jordan and the Palestinians are working closely with Saddam," he said sitting on the edge of the bed in exhaustion.

"Of course."

He was surprised by the evenness of her voice.

"Hussein in Jordan is shipping arms through to Saddam against the sanctions," he continued watching her more closely.

For a moment she said nothing, then slowly turned to him, saying, "No one here had a conscience. We held on to our money, our self-interest while the rest were buried alive under poverty, martial law. The Gulf country rulers closed their eyes to the have-nots surrounding them, the poor, the women, the Palestinians. There had to be a revolution."

He listened, absolutely silent. Then his voice was low, hoarse. "Nura, did you ever send money to any groups I ought to be concerned about?"

Her expression was enigmatic—a mixture of both question, surprise.

"No, never."

"Never?"

"Never." She drew back ever so slightly as he stared at her.

He looked down at Nura's pen, then back at the depth of her eyes. A woman who had studied philosophy—brilliantly, passionately—at the Sorbonne in Paris. Studied there through the very years that Antar and the Baath Party had assembled their followers there: men, women, rich, poor—idealists, all. Committed to overthrowing the old order. The eyes, the enigmatic eyes continued to stare at him.

Standing there, the possibilities, the questions, now wracked his very being. Tarek turned slowly and walked out of the room.

The door that closed between them echoed down the long corridor as he left for Gaza.

❋ ❋ ❋

The car wound slowly toward the South. They passed the ancient olive trees, citrus groves, then open fields of green. A donkey cart, another car, an Israeli patrol car, then quiet, while the heat of the day began to rise. Now the terrain became more arid, the citrus gone, the olive trees turning into cactus, into dry desert. The old driver drove on toward Gaza.

Tarek looked in front of him at the dusty crumbling town they were entering. The main street of Gaza was tawdry blue, dirty pink cinder block, with old bazaar sellers hawking cheap utensils for sale, men working in the streets, and peeling paint, old signs, Coca-Cola bottles lying in the road. And the dust, the desert dust that rose up from the land to cover everything, already buried in poverty, heat and flies.

The driver found the trailer, an old army surplus unit dropped on cinder blocks years ago. An ancient air conditioning unit labored hopelessly against the desert heat in one window. The Israeli guard looked at Tarek curiously then signed the pass and flagged him on.

They drove through the dust of Gaza toward the water. Along the edge of the sand and water stood the corrugated tin roofs of a shanty town. A labyrinth of sticks and aluminum, sewage strewn on the ground, burning beneath the heat of the Gaza sun. Women with black abayas pulled across their mouths with their teeth, others with ragged white scarves tied around their heads, carried naked babies. Old men sat on the ground smoking, staring at nothing.

They arrived at a wood shanty, where Tarek was to meet Zahi and Tarek knocked. In a moment the door opened onto a dark room. As Tarek's eyes adjusted, he saw before him the figure of a compact, sinewy young man with dark eyes, dark hair, unsmiling. He did not extend his hand, he did not move, but stood there staring at Tarek.

"Ahlan wa sahlan," Zahi said coldly. There was a radio on the floor, some dirty pillows, a table, two chairs, a mattress along the wall. He motioned Tarek to the chair and sat down on one of the dirty pillows, knocking over a pile of books. Finally he said, "You are alone?"

"Yes."

"Then we walk." His hand motioned to the walls, "They listen. I have nothing for you, yet. I am not," he said, walking past the shacks, "turning up an actual operative. There are certainly many of Arafat's men, the PLO working with Iraq. Then, also the fundamentalists. They are all working with Iraq. But I have not come up with information on the specifics you are looking for. Although," his voice was sarcastic, "you certainly have enough enemies here who wouldn't mind seeing you collapse. Enough saying Saudi Arabia, Kuwait, all very nice, very rich, use the Palestinians, then get rid of them. The Arabs don't seem to do a lot more for us than the Jews, do they? Or maybe they do the same thing really. All of these nice little capitalistic, comfortable countries, little puppet governments tied to the West."

Tarek watched the coldness, the sarcasm, the hooded eyes. "Yes, they say it is time for a new order, something that will sweep all of this away." He shrugged, then stopped and pointed to the one-room shacks, and beyond to a lean-to, a canvas thrown over poles above an old man and a young woman with a baby. "Unfortunately I have just lost one of my best operatives working in Israel. He was an interesting man, a Palestinian from the camps here who trained as a dentist in Egypt. After the training he came back but couldn't get a job, so he took work as a maintenance man in Haifa, for I don't know what—$1.50 an hour or something. His employer locked him in the building so he could stay overnight. There was an electrical shortage, the building caught on fire, and he burned to death. His younger brother made some radical statements. Yesterday the Israeli patrol car pulled up to their shanty and ordered the whole family out. Had them stand there and watch while they blew up the house. They are not allowed to rebuild for three years. They don't have any money anyhow to rebuild."

Tarek watched the naked baby urinate in the dirt, while a young woman stirred a pot on a tripod above some burning sticks.

"Hard to imagine, isn't it, that entire families live in there, in one room. The children hear their parents making love at night, see the babies born, hear the fights, watch the old ones die. Many give up. Some try to leave. But they have no money, no passports. They have papers with citizenship marked as 'undefined' so that countries turn them away when they try to enter."

He stopped for a moment and looked at the squalid camp. "In the end, we have become slaves, servants of Israel. You see that?" He pointed past the shacks burning beneath the heat toward new apartments on the waterfront. "The Israelis keep those for themselves, they like to call it a 'little Riviera.' They leave the Palestinians back here, 600,000 of them herded together in this strip of squalor."

He pointed to the Israeli guard standing by a shack with a machine gun and lowered his voice while they walked past. "The fundamentalists groups are centered around this man."

Tarek followed the man's eyes. Through the glare of the sun he could see an old man in a chair by one of the lean-tos talking to some young men as another Israeli guard strolled past smoking a cigarette.

"He is paralyzed from the neck down," whispered Zahi, "since the age of fifteen. Sheikh Ahmad Yasin. Along with Sheikh Abdul al-Aziz Odeh he has been preaching Islamic Fundamentalism for years, but now the people—the young ones—they are coming to him."

Tarek watched the old man talking to his followers.

"They have created an organization, Islamic Jihad. They are behind some of the recent violence." He looked at Tarek. "I am looking for your man here."

"But?"

"But so far nothing."

"Nothing? What will it take—money?"

Zahi shrugged. "Certainly they will take your money, just as they take whatever the Jordanians, the PLO, the Israelis, the Iranians, the Kuwaitis want to dole out. And then," he looked at Tarek, "they will spit on you and do whatever they were going to do anyhow. The real problem is determining their allegiance, who they are really working with, and what is sham. There are walls surrounding walls hiding what they do, they are tough to see through. I may come up with something, and I may come up with nothing. Only one thing is for sure—if I move too fast, I'll just be one more agent discovered, dead. "I am checking up in Beirut now," Zahi said. "Of course you know Iran still works a lot of their cells out of there. Their man, Hussein Mussauvi, heads up their operation there from his headquarters in Baalbeck. Trains the secret cells, the militias." He turned curiously to Tarek. "Have you ever met Mussauvi?"

Tarek shook his head.

The young man smiled wryly. "No, that would be a bit difficult, wouldn't it? A curious man, actually. In his forties, a former chemistry teacher. Speaks pleasantly about his suicide force, the Enteharis, about how his two-man unit drove right in and blew up the U.S. Embassy in Beirut. How his other boys went on to kill over two-hundred U.S. Marines and fifty-eight French paratroopers.

"He looks at you and recites the numbers, 'sixty-nine dead in the U.S. Embassy, two-hundred anf forty-one Marines dead, fifty-eight French,' and then leans forward and says, 'those numbers mean nothing—what we really blew away was the U.S., France, Britain, Italy, all their troops when they turned tail and pulled out of Lebanon.' "

Zahi shrugged. "Of course he's right." He laughed humorlessly. He turned down another dusty road in the camp. "I'm checking on the connections into Beirut. But it's going to take time, it's gotten tangled, very tangled. It may take time."

"There isn't time," said Tarek.

Zahi suddenly flashed in anger. "You understand what I'm doing, what Abu Jihad is doing for you is dangerous—going against the PLO as we are, helping you. We have to move very carefully."

"Any traces of members of the Royal Family connected to it—Saud, Sultan, Naif?" Zahi shook his head. Tarek came back quickly. "Abdullah? Crown Prince Abdullah is secretly sending money here, isn't he?"

Zahi looked at Tarek surprised. "Yes."

"I want to know what this money is connected to."

Zahi shook his head. "Abdullah's money has been coming here for years, to the Palestinian refugees in the camps here. It has no connection whatsoever to anything else."

"Why covertly; why does this money come secretly if it's for the Palestinians, if there is nothing else to it?"

Zahi shook his head again. "He wants no thanks. We have promised all these years to say nothing. He feeds them, clothes them, sends many on to school. He never wanted it to appear to be a 'statement' that King Fahd hadn't done enough for the people here." He paused. "Your wife Nura does the same thing."

Zahi watched the odd expression that crossed Tarek's face. "No, Abdullah is not your man. Abdullah is simply a profoundly loyal, decent bedu. A rare man."

He turned and walked off in the dust, and Tarek knew what he'd always known deep in his heart. Abdullah was not his man. Within the Royal Family, Abdullah was not the traitor he was searching for. The Palestinian he was searching for was not here. He sat down for a moment, exhausted, a man for whom every lead came to a dead end. He looked down once more at the crumpled sheet of paper. The nerves at the back of his neck tightened, the words seemed to leer at him "the Palestinian," "the bedu."

When 'Tarek returned to Riyadh the next day, Elaine was waiting for him, grim.

"An hour ago, Abu Jihad was gunned down by his bodyguard."

A half-hour later the next report came in. Elaine handed it to him.

Zahi in Gaza. Dead.

31

Naila sat with a patient in the clinic, holding her while another refugee, just across from them, told the woman what had happened to her family.

"The Iraqi soldiers held the little one by his ankles and carried him over to the window. Your husband begged them to let the child go. The soldiers opened the window and held him outside. They told your husband to tell what he knew of the Resistance or they would drop the child and kill it. Your husband finally told what he knew. When he was finished, they brought him to the window and made him watch." The refugee stopped and then went on "They flung the child down shattering him on the pavement. And then they shot your husband."

The woman's screams ripped through the small clinic as Naila tried to hold her. Then she saw Benazir at the door, trembling, motioning to her.

"Dr. Naila, a messenger came from the governor's office," she pointed to the old green building across the square. "He has just returned and says you are to come now. The man with the car was outraged; he went to the authorities; he says you must be sent back to Riyadh; the people will not tolerate you treating the bedu without proper escort."

Naila turned to her, furious. "Tell him that how I take care of patients is none of his business." Then she saw one of the guards by the door of the office start to walk toward her.

"I will go with you," said Benazir.

"No. Stay here and take care of the patients. I will go."

The bedu boy who had taken her into the desert to help his sister's labor, had returned for medications. He walked silently to her side. "Aziz, the boy, will go with me."

Naila felt the silent stares of the people in the square, the hush when she walked past with the boy. The man in the souk with the spices, the old one with the silver daggers spread on the rug before him, all stopped to follow her with their eyes. Slowly she and the boy crossed the square and stood before the two guards at the door.

"Please tell the governor I am here."

The men, waiting in the corridor outside, fell silent and stared when she passed the two guards with the boy. The door to the office opened.

"Dr. Naila," the governor stood up, "please sit down. The boy will wait outside."

Naila nodded; Aziz remained fixed to her side, but she indicated he should leave.

"I am very sorry about this," he said. She waited, feeling the governor's eyes upon her. "I understand what happened, and I want you to know that I think it was very generous of you to help in the way you did."

Naila looked at his tired face in surprise. His gaze wandered to the rows of old overstuffed chairs lining both sides of the dusty green room. He looked back to her with a weary expression.

"I also want you to know that my impression is not

representative of the people here." He distractedly flicked at a fly hovering over the stuffed in-box, then stood up and walked over to the armchair beside her. "Dr. Naila, you and I are both educated, sophisticated people. The rest," he nodded toward the door to the corridor, "for the most part are not. They don't understand the new ways. They…"

He handed her a small cup of sweet tea from the tray beside him. "May I speak honestly?"

Naila nodded, taking the tea.

"I am here to govern. I have no right to force people from their ways, their traditions, despite my own beliefs. In fact, I couldn't if I wanted to."

He took off his glasses and tiredly rubbed his eyes. "The problem at the moment is compounded by the political climate around us. The fundamentalism coming from the other side of the Gulf touches a nerve here. There are those who come back from the city who talk of the Royal Family, how they have lost the true Islam, they are corrupt, they should go, the country should return to the old ways. Now, with the U.S. troops coming, these sensitivities are heightened." He raised his hand in exasperation, then his eyes narrowed. "We watch the borders for arms. I think you know that the vast majority of arms smuggled in for the takeover attempt of Mecca by the zealots from Iran a couple of years ago came through here."

Naila remained silent.

"Now," he shrugged, "the same sentiments exist, even though this time the rifles come from Iraq. I think you can understand the sensitivities here. In deference to these feelings the medical service has always sent a foreign doctor. Until now."

He stopped. "I will not ask you to do anything you feel you cannot. I do, however, want to tell you that if these people's sensibilities are offended, they will not allow their women and children to come to you for treatment, and that if you could send your Pakistani assistant on such calls as last night..."

"She is not trained for that," interrupted Naila.

"Yes," said the governor, "but what was it someone once said, 'The choices before us are between bad and worse?' Could you..."

He stopped, looking nervously at the red light blinking on his telephone. Then sounds of shouting erupted in the corridor. "Forgive me, I..."

He crossed quickly to the desk and picked up the receiver. As he did so, the door to the office burst open. A young man, kaffiyeh wrapped about his face, pulled free from the guard holding him. He thrashed toward the governor behind his desk. Behind him a young woman clutching an infant beneath her abaya, cowered, surrounded by guards.

The man screamed, pointing to the guards around the woman. "They have no right!" His face was twisted with violence, his voice choked in rage.

"They all lied to us. But now that we wish to do what we must do," the man's voice rose in fury, "you send these guards to further 'consider' the matter?" He slammed his fist down on the governor's desk. The guards rushed forward as the governor pulled back.

In that instant the woman jerked herself free, turned with the baby, and tried to run. Her abaya fell from her face.

Naila's breath caught in her throat as she recognized the terrified face of the unmarried girl whose baby she had delivered in Riyadh—the girl from the border village up north.

As Naila looked back to the man, his voice raged. "The Indian doctor that was here lied to us when she told me to take my sister to Riyadh. Then," he leaned across the desk seething, "in Riyadh they lied to us and tried to hide the baby. But" he breathed in his rage, "we have a member of the family who works in the hospital. We found out."

He stood back in fury. "We went to the authorities; we demanded to take her back to justice in her village. And now, you try to stop us?"

The governor started to walk around the desk toward the young man, reaching out to him. "We only want to…"

The man swung around and faced the girl. "You see this whore. Our honor will not…"

The governor raised his hand. In that instant the young man pulled the dagger from his belt and lunged toward the girl. The dagger held for a moment in the air. The young man made a violent blood curdling noise from deep in his throat and then plunged the dagger into the girl's heart. Naila watched frozen in horror as the girl fell to the ground covered in blood. The guards rushed toward the man as he ripped the baby from her dead arms and raised his dagger again.

Naila's voice rang out. "Wait, you are right."

The governor turned, startled.

The young man spun around. Naila quickly reached for his arm, the bloody knife hovering above the baby.

"You are right," she said in a hushed tone.

The young man stood still, looking at her in confusion.

"Yes," she continued, "the baby must die too. The honor of your family must be restored. Come, I work in the clinic, we will dispatch it mercifully."

The man hesitated.

"Surely," she looked at him evenly, "you are a decent man. You agree before God that it need not be sent to its end in pain?"

The governor watched her in silence.

"Come, you carry the baby if you wish." Naila motioned the

guard to unlock the door. The man bent over, dagger in hand, and picked up the crying, bundled infant. He stepped over the girl's body.

Aziz, the bedu boy, was waiting in the corridor as Naila, the man and the infant walked out. She nodded for the boy to follow as well and then walked slowly out of the building across the square to the clinic followed by the staring eyes of the people. She entered the clinic and motioned for the man with the infant to follow her. Benazir looked on in shocked silence.

Naila took the infant from the man and lay it on the examining table. Its small hand began to move and then suck in hunger on its tiny fist. Naila walked over to the medicine cabinet and pulled out a hypodermic needle while the bedu boy watched from the corner of the room in silence. She reached back in the cabinet for a vial and filled the hypodermic needle with a clear fluid. Then she walked back over to the baby and held the needle aloft.

"Do you wish to commend its soul to God?" asked Naila while the man watched. "I know you are a religious man."

He mumbled a few words from the Koran, then nodded at Naila.

"Hold its hands down," she said crisply to the man. He walked over and held the tiny arms down while the baby cried.

"Good," said Naila, and she lowered the needle, emptying its contents into a small vein in the infant's arm.

Benazir gasped as the infant stiffened and its muscles went into spasms. Then the eyes shut, the head rolled over, and the tiny infant lay still.

Naila looked evenly at the man. "It is done."

He nodded, his eyes upon the motionless infant in front of him. "It is done," he repeated slowly. He turned and walked out.

Naila watched the crowd outside circle around him. She

walked over to her desk while Benazir and the boy stared in shock. She picked up the cloth with the necklace the bedu sheikh had given her. The infant's body lay behind her. Carefully she opened the cloth and picked up the necklace holding it toward the light of the shutters, listening to the tiny noise of the carnelian and silver bells. Then she placed it back in the cloth and handed it to the bedu boy standing silently in the corner.

"I want you to tell the women, to tell the sheikh, that this necklace is very beautiful. I want you to tell them that originally it came from Abdul Aziz. It means a great deal to me, perhaps more than he might know."

"But," she stopped. The bedu boy stood absolutely still. "I want you to give it back to him."

Aziz looked at her in silence as she continued. "I want you to tell him that the law of the desert is a life for a life. Now, I have saved two lives for him."

She walked over to the still infant and put its lifeless arms back inside the blankets. She looked at the boy. "Tell him I want one back."

The boy stared at her uncomprehending.

"Your horse," she said, glancing at the animal drinking from the well, "is ready? You can go back now?"

The boy nodded.

"Good, I will put the medications you came for in a saddle bag." She reached in the tack room and pulled out a large bedu saddle bag. She reached into the medicine cabinet for some tablets and glanced at the boy. "These are for your sister. Now, hold the bag open."

Aziz stood up and held the bag, then watched in shock as Naila picked up the baby's body, brought it over to the portable oxygen unit and started ventilating the infant. She readied the medication to reverse the scopalomine she had given the baby earlier to paralyze it. She gave him a few more breaths of oxygen with the ventilator and then injected medication intravenously.

Benazir and the boy watched in amazement as the infant began to move and breathe. Naila stood for a moment quietly looking at Aziz.

"Your sister asked me my name. I told her only Naila. Please tell her it is Naila bint Ahmed bint Abdul Aziz al Saud." The boy stared in fascination at Abdul Aziz's granddaughter. She lay the baby in the saddle bag and closed the leather flap.

"Tell her I have given her two lives, her's and her baby, and now I want one." She handed the boy the saddle bag. "Ride quickly; the child will sleep for an hour more."

The boy looked up stunned, first at the saddle bag and then in awe at Naila.

"Tell no one, no one, where he has come from. And let him disappear into the desert to grow up a Bani Sa."

He moved toward the door and then turned back to her. "I am honored to know you," he said quietly, and then gently placed the saddle bag across the horse. Naila put her hand in her pocket and pulled out a crumpled sheet of paper she had been given by one of the refugees.

"And when you have done that, I want you to return. This time," Naila continued "I want you to bring others with you whom you trust."

She read him the scrawled words of the doctor in charge of the disabled children's hospital in Kuwait. He had written in haste as the Iraqi soldiers took over the hospital. "I have fled with the children to a house. We have been hiding here since but I have no way to care for the patients."

Naila finished reading him the plea to help them escape

across the border, followed by the instructions on where they were. "Can you do this?" she asked quietly. "Can you bring them here?"

The boy nodded silently.

Naila watched him go off into the desert and then sat in the empty room. She looked at the dusty souk, the last light from the fading sun. She stood and locked the clinic and walked slowly toward the orange groves, toward the small house. She opened the door and looked at the dim little room, then walked toward the bedroom. She flicked on the lamp and unbuttoned her dress.

She looked at herself reflected in the dusty mirror, the light falling across the shadows of her body in the silence of the room. She felt the quiet terror growing as she gazed at her full breasts, the soft roundness of her stomach. While the light played across her body, tears began to fall down her face. The calendar seemed to scream at her in terror. She knew another night would go by, and she would be unable to do what she must do. She steadied herself and picked up the phone. She heard Badr's voice.

"Tarek. I must speak to Tarek."

"He'll be back tomorrow."

Hours later, Naila heard the knock on the door. Aziz stood there with the others behind him. They took Naila's directions and left silently in the night.

By dawn they were returning on horses, on camels, by foot, carrying their tiny charges with them swathed in bedu garb. The crippled tied gently but firmly on the horses, those that could walk led behind the camels, the frightened one's cries covered by the bleating noise of the goats Some were sedated to hush them, carried on shoulders, the smallest ones were carried in the camel bags. Into the small dusty desert clinic they came, where Naila and Benazir waited for them.

⁂ ⁂ ⁂

▲▲ Saud," said Tarek.

The Foreign Minister Saud bin Faisal sitting in his Riyadh office looked up, startled. Before the foreign minister's desk stood the banker Said with a folder he had been about to hand Saud.

"Come in, please." The urbane, sophisticated Saud seemed momentarily caught off guard, jarred by the intrusion. Tarek walked up to the foreign minister, embraced him, his eyes still on the bank papers Said held in his hand. The unasked question, the suspicion, the wariness widened in front of them. Said placed the papers on Saud's desk and embraced Tarek. Tarek's every sense, now knew that there was something Said was not telling him, something he was holding back.

Saud pulled up a chair for Tarek. He walked back to his desk, and put the papers into a folder marked FOREIGN MINIS-TER/CONFIDENTIAL. "Said is doing some stock transfers for me. He was kind enough to come by this late."

"Stock transfers?" asked Tarek pleasantly, watching each movement of Saud's elegant features.

"Yes, I'm moving a bit of my money out of the country."

Tarek sat utterly still. Saud brushed his hand across his forehead. His normally unflappable composure seemed distract-ed, ruffled.

Tarek spoke softly. "But why don't you just telephone over to the bank to carry out these stock transfers?"

The words slid into the silence between them and hung in

343

the air. Saud glanced up, skimming over the bank papers Said had placed in front of him.

"I prefer that this remain confidential."

The silence was now deafening. Saud moved uncomfortably, feeling Tarek's eye trained dead on him, then leaned across his desk and said in a low tone, "I don't want to add to the hysteria already going on around here. You can hear the whispers, can't you, in the market? 'The foreign minister is getting his cash out.' A few moves like that and the country's stock market would take a nose dive and crash within hours."

Tarek absorbed the cool logic of Saud's words. Saud was a man who had always been a brilliant gambler and statesman. He had always known when and how to follow an ingenious thread of logic, to scatter decoys politically when he was diplomatically cornered, how to match wits with the canniest, Assad of Syria, Saddam in Iraq. When each thought he had the upper hand, Saud had won, often—without their ever knowing the game had been played. Elegantly, succinctly, brilliantly, he could weave fact and fiction into a tapestry, the threads so finely and cleverly woven that one became indistinguishable from the other. Carrying out overlapping conflicting negotiations as he had been ordered. Secret treaties to undermine public ones, conflicting stances to the West and to the East, juggling them with different hands. The perfect foreign minister. A brilliant, impatient man who would go no further and knew it.

The purist philosopher, he looked with disdain on the corruption, the vices of Fahd's protocol court, the venality of Walid and his minions. Fahd, in turn, hated Saud for his intellectualism, his moral arrogance. Even as used him he hated him, and had long ago let Saud know he would go no further.

Saud's long, elegant, tapered fingers signed the papers and handed them to Said, who departed. Then Saud began writing a note to himself in his broad scripted hand. Tarek watched, stunned as Saud penned the name Abed bin Osman, and dropped the paper on his desk. Glancing up, Saud, caught Tarek's eye riveted to the sheet of paper.

"You know him don't you, Osman's son?" Saud's voice was casual, nonchalant. "He's coming to work for me. I must remember to call him tomorrow." Tarek said nothing, waiting for Saud to offer some reason why he would be taking on Abed in particular. Saud seemed to have lost interest in the conversation. And Tarek knew better than to speak until either the lamb led him to the lion or it was clear that Saud was not his man. Saud stood up and walked over to the chest by the side wall.

"Come Tarek, let's play some backgammon like the old days."

Tarek watched Saud's handsome head bend over the backgammon board. The man's face was older now, lined a bit. He was in his early forties, but looked, at the moment, astonishingly as he had years ago when they sat up night after night at Princeton playing backgammon—Saud, Antar, and Tarek—into the night. Saud laid out the board, shook the dice, then made a move. He waited for Tarek.

Tarek rolled the dice, moved his white hajar on the board, and then sat back. By the table was a picture of Saud's father, King Faisal.

"I think of him often." Saud said, appearing to know what Tarek was looking at without ever having taken his eyes from the backgammon board. "I think often of what might have been if he hadn't been assassinated."

"What might have been?" Tarek moved his piece slowly.

"Yes, what might have been for the country." Saud looked up abruptly. "What might have been as well, I suppose, for me, for you." He moved the next hajar forward. "We, Faisal's sons, will always be shunted aside while Fahd and his Sudeiry brothers consolidate control. Have you ever thought about that, Tarek, as you go on working night and day? For whom? For what?"

Saud fixed his dark eyes on Tarek. Bitterness coated his words. "For whom do we work? For Fahd, a man, shall we say, of modest intellect and talent and even less morality and vision. And the future? If Fahd dies? It goes to Crown Prince Abdullah. A rough bedu—a man I like, with his own brand of integrity, but a man singularly unsuited to govern in an international world. If Abdullah dies, then what? It goes to Sultan. Sultan is even more corrupt than Fahd and his coterie."

Tarek saw the resentment in Saud's eyes. Saud bent forward. He was a man who said what he wanted, did what he wanted when he believed he was right, no matter what the cost. Saud's voice was low.

"The era when a family can rule the country is past—we are an anachronism that ultimately will be swept away, a piece of history." Saud stood up abruptly. "You know what I'm saying is true, don't you?" His eyes were as dark the next startling words he uttered.

"You know Antar was right, wasn't he? Years ago when he said ours was a house built upon sand, and that ultimately the sands of time would run out."

"And what will replace it?" Tarek spoke the words cautiously.

"I don't know. I really don't know." Saud sat back and slowly moved another piece on the board.

"You see Antar still?" Tarek struggled for nonchalance.

"Ah," Saud shrugged, "it is a small world. Once in Damascus, another time in Beirut. You know how these things are..." He smiled, a cool, undecipherable gaze, and then nodded toward the board. "You know, Tarek, with another move, I may win. You must watch it. With another move, I may in fact win."

He moved the hajar that secured his victory, then smiled wryly. "You see, Tarek, you weren't looking for it there, were you? You weren't looking in the right place."

Tarek stood up to go. Saud picked up a note and handed it to him, "You are going to see Said tonight, aren't you? Give this to him. He left it on my desk when he picked up the other papers."

Tarek looked at Said's notes. At the bottom was written "transfers for N.S., notebook." Next to it was written Tarek's address.

Tarek walked quickly out into the dark night air. The sound of a small bug moving before him seemed to scream, circling around him, trailing behind it the faces of Said, Nura, Saud. His mind froze at the possibility of "N.S." Suddenly his head began to swim.

Tarek closed his eyes as the sounds of muezzin poured over the city, through the walls of his office. He pulled out a sheet of paper and began to write furiously, translating automatically into the code that Hamid would understand from the Radio Riyadh broadcast.

"Intensify your checks re Saud. Alternative: could it be someone with access to or aligned with the members of the Royal Family? Said? Abed bin Osman? Urgent—who is N.S.?"

Tarek ripped the paper from the pad, strode quickly down the hall, and dropped it on Badr's desk. Badr scrutinized it silently, got up and took the small piece of paper to broadcasting.

He watched Badr go. Nura's deep enigmatic eyes drifted in front of him. The face of his friend, Said, a man he had utterly trusted. The swarm of questions, the questions that now careened sickeningly through his mind, walling off finally the people closest to him. Nura, Said. He ordered a tap on Said. And one on Nura.

Then he stood up, a man now empty inside. His feelings for them paralyzed, dying, slowly slipping away, leaving a void inside him.

32

Elaine was waiting for Ray when he walked into headquarters. "Saddam was infuriated by what he saw; the
buildup, the troops. He's already moved his top Republican
Guards to southern Iraq, and we're picking up commands to
reinforce them with another 150,000 troops. He's bringing in
mechanized and armored units to station behind them, and
moving the rest of the heavy armored divisions to the coast of
Kuwait—and along the neutral zone between Iraq and Saudi
Arabia."

Ray started toward the intercept cubicle of the Black Hole.
Elaine stopped him. "Here's something else, a transmission from
Tarek's man Hamid, inside Baghdad. Orders from Saddam to
escalate production at their chemical factories, Scud plant, and
nuclear facilities. And to deploy Iraqi planes to Libya—a whole
squadron has already gone. Khadaffi agreed, they flew in during
the night. Another is going right now by ship to the Sudan."

Schwarzkopf's grim face appeared behind Ray. "A nice little
present in retaliation for Egypt's sending troops to work with us
here. From Sudan they could easily fly north and bomb the
Aswan Dam—the flood could wipe out most of Egypt, kill
everything in its path. They could also head east across the Red
Sea and bomb the coast of Saudi Arabia."

Elaine nodded and continued, "There also appears to be

some communication with Iran about planes, which they haven't responded to." Ray wiped the sweat off of his forehead, "Beyond that every terrorist in the world, Abu Nidal and the rest, are streaming into Baghdad. Tarek's man sent on information from a meeting last night there, plans for explosions in the international airports around the world, torch bombs set up in the oil fields, plans to flood the Gulf with oil to kill everything."

"Here are the overnights from the U.S. press," interrupted one of aides. " 'Growing AntiWar Movement...' goes on to say groups are lobbying Congress not to send more troops. 'Shades of Vietnam...'" Ray threw the sheet down.

Elaine took the next piece of paper coming through from the radar unit and started to hand it to Schwarzkopf, but Schwarzkopf was going out the door. Elaine watched the man walk out of the building and then stop at the edge of the desert. He sat down in the sand and stared at the array of troops and their tents. Motionless, wordless, he stared.

Elaine followed and walked up quietly to sit down alongside him. Finally Schwarzkopf's bulldog face turned to her. She thought of the curious complex man she had grown to know over the past weeks. The emotional conscience-ridden man beneath the frequently bluff, outrageous exterior. His eyes had a strange, hollow stare. His voice choked, "I see all the dead ones, Elaine." He looked at her, understanding the terrors that she wrestled with herself, then back at the troops, his voice very low. "I wake up at night, I see Saddam Hussein leering at me across all of this wide-open border. We're completely vulnerable to attack, have no real strategy, and my troops are hopelessly outnumbered." He paused, then went on more forcefully. "I don't want to live the rest of my life as 'Norm Schwarzkopf, the Butcher of Baghdad,' the commander who got a hundred-thousand Americans killed with chemical weapons because of stupid planning."

Elaine looked up as Ray came and sat silently with them. Finally Schwarzkopf's voice continued, his eyes now staring fiercely at Ray. "Ray, I'm a man of conscience. After Vietnam, I went to the woods for a longtime and thought about what had happened. And I said to myself that if it ever again came to a choice between compromising my moral principles and performing my duties, I would hang up my uniform." Schwarzkopf's eyes stared. "We're right up to the line, Ray. Unless we get more troops and weaponry in here so these boys have a real chance, so this isn't an instant massacre of these men counting on me, I'm resigning." Schwarzkopf's body lumbered upward out of the sand.

"Norm, where are you going?"

"To call Bush, Cheney, and Powell."

"Norm, be careful about making it sound like an ultimatum."

The eyes flashed. "Ray, I don't give a rat's ass if it does."

Ray walked back into headquarters unnerved. He picked up the phone and dialed Tarek's number.

"Tarek isn't there?" Ray heard Badr's voice on the other end of the line.

"He left for Tehran. After he got Hamid's communication."

"What in the name of God is he doing with Iran?" whispered Schwarzkopf, stunned. Ray, who had watched Tarek gamble brilliantly before and knew he'd do it again, simply stared.

Tarek walked past Beheshte Zahra cemetery in Tehran and entered the suffocatingly hot little room with blood smeared on the walls, where voices rose up around him—"There is only one God." The chant reverberated against the heat of the cinder block walls while flies swarmed listlessly beneath a bare bulb.

He watched the old mullah, who was head of the local komiteh, speak to the family of the dead man while he gave them extra ration tickets for meat and sugar. Tarek then stepped out into the scorching sun of the Beheshte Zahra cemetery. Its grounds were covered with women in black chadors, huddled over the graves of the dead from Iran's war with Iraq, the headstones tacked with cheap colored photos of the dead. Tarek began walking toward the center of town. The black smoke of the traffic congestion billowed up through the screech of brakes and horns and lay like a coating on the walls of the seedy buildings.

He passed an Iranian Pasdaran guard leaning on the butt of his rifle in front of an appliance store, TVs playing in the window, the slow undertones of the mullah reading the Koran. He walked past the writing on the walls, the posters peeling, like some excrement of zeal, from the store fronts. He continued past the bazaaris sitting on bales of rugs, smoking listlessly in their empty shops, and then turned quietly into a side door.

He breathed in the musky smell of the rolled carpets and watched for a moment. In the dim light, he saw a man bent over an old rug, slowly sewing a worn spot at the center.

"Mansour."

The man straightened. He turned his head, holding the needle aloft midair. He looked at Tarek, then motioned him toward the back room. He closed the door of the tiny office behind them and showed him to a seat by an old desk strewn with papers. He reached over to the small teapot on the burner and handed Tarek a cup.

"I am grateful for the shipment," Mansour said quietly. "It passed the ports, and the rugs should be received in Europe in a week. These times are difficult for us," he shrugged. "The new export laws, no one buying here..." his voice trailed off. Tarek nodded slightly. "But it must be so, I suppose." Tarek waited.

Mansour leaned closer to Tarek. "The young ones, they have pictures of Saddam. They speak with pride of the cells he has set up around the Middle East, the world, to bring the revolution, drive the West from the Middle East, topple the old corrupt monarchies, take care of the Palestinians. "But," his eyes narrowed as he looked at Tarek with a half smile, "Rafsanjani is a sly man is he not?" He shook his head respectfully. "He moves this way, that way." He nodded thoughtfully. "And he motions to all at once. For the money, to the West," he shrugged, looking at the seedy shop walls, "for how long can we last like this, with so little money coming in? He tells the West perhaps a deal, perhaps no more terrorism." He chuckled. "A sly man, Rafsanjani."

"He will deal?"

"Yes," said the man, "he will deal."

The rug merchant watched from his door as Tarek glanced toward the Shah's old palace, standing like a relic above the traffic of Tehran, and disappear down the street.

Tarek listened to the sound of the Speaker of the Iranian Parliament. Rafsanjani's voice rang out from the Parliament chambers. Tarek walked down the hall and opened the door to the chambers, slipped into a back seat as Rafsanjani's voice continued to echo through the room, his fist pounding on the podium, his sly, alert eyes fixing his audience. The applause and the yells rose up through the room while the Speaker stood momentarily silent, his rounded face rimmed with brown hair, the black rolled head cloth of the mullah bathed in sweat, beads glistening on the wispy mustache above his pursed mouth.

Tarek watched the old mullahs shifting warily in their chairs. Rafsanjani wiped the sweat from his face and began to speak again. A moderate, some had whispered, a man who deals with the West, a man who has lost the vision, the will to export the revolution. Ah, thought Tarek, but Rafsanjani was indeed a wily man, capable of a clever, clever game. A man who could, who would, shift with the winds slowly, skillfully. Rafsanjani brandished a rifle at prayer meetings and screamed to the crowds. Cried for action against the West, the corrupt Arab Gulf, while thousands of young war veterans beat the stumps of their arms upon their chests and screamed, "Set the Gulf on fire!" "March to Jerusalem!"

Rafsanjani stood before them, and then quietly walked back to the moderates and told them he was with them, to bide their time. And ultimately? Ultimately, thought Tarek, Rafsanjani will use them all. Ultimately Rafsanjani will move with the winds as they blow again.

The gavel slammed as Rafsanjani finished. Rafsanjani left the council of mullahs debating amongst themselves. Tarek was waiting for him.

Rafsanjani listened for the next hour to the plan that Tarek laid out for him. A way to regain Iran's position in the Middle East and at the same time with the West. A way to repay his hatred of Saddam. Tarek went through the plans—the Shia, with whom Iran had strong ties in the southern part of Iraq, the planes. At the end, Rafsanjani's small venal eyes shifted once more. He agreed.

Tarek left the chambers as Rafsanjani placed the call to his "friend" Saddam.

Tarek boarded the plane that was waiting for him. "To Hafiz al Assad in Damascus."

The plane flew over the Gates of St. Paul. Coming into the airport, Tarek took a helicopter, landing at Assad's palace door. The Syrian President, the man with probably the closest links to the world-wide terrorists networks, listened while Tarek outlined the plan.

A small sly smile crossed Assad's face at the thought of the ironic role, that he, the legendary "king" of the terrorist world, was about to play. Tarek detailed how he, Assad, would sabotage the terrorist activities Saddam had begun to initiate. He agreed.

Tarek's plane made one last stop. President Ozal of Turkey cleared Tarek's aircraft in while Hamid moved cautiously across the border from northern Iraq into Turkey to meet him. The Kurdish rebel leader, Barzani, followed minutes later. Tarek outlined the weapons, the ammunition he would move to them to work the insurrection.

The Kurdish leader went over the supplies with Tarek and then filtered back across the border into northern Iraq. Hamid followed him shortly thereafter. President Ozal of Turkey began moving Tarek's supplies down across the border to the Kurds within hours.

Elaine listened to Badr giving her the final details as Tarek's plane headed back. She drew up the lists of further arms he wanted for this incredible maneuver and shot the request off to the National Security Council while Ray tried to contact Powell directly. When she was finished, she sat back letting sink in what Tarek had accomplished. Complex, seemingly impossible—a dangerous gambling ploy, which if it worked could help keep the Middle East from collapsing.

33

Schwarzkopf listened the next morning, intrigued by the plans Tarek had set in motion. Tarek outlined to him how he had gotten Rafsanjani in Iran to agree to pose as an ally to Saddam while in fact siphoning off materiel and plans. How he had gotten Hafiz al Assad in Syria to pose as part of Saddam's terrorist network as an ally while in fact selling him out. And finally, how he had begun to move weapons and materiel across the border from Turkey to the Kurds to arm them for an uprising from within Iraq against Saddam.

Schwarzkopf leaned forward, fascinated by the detail, the ingenuity of the plan. "A net," said Schwarzkopf softly, "a net we pull in at the right moment."

Schwarzkopf's face was a study in admiration. He looked at Ray, and Elaine. Then the six-foot, three-inch 240-pound frame of the balding fifty-six-year-old man, dressed in fatigues, leaned toward them.

"I talked to Powell last night, and I did some thinking. I sat out in the desert and did some thinking. We have one answer really." He leaned forward even more while they waited. "We have nothing out there to speak of. Saddam can advance in any direction he chooses—into Saudi Arabia, down the Gulf coast to the United Arab Emirates, across Jordan to Israel. We'd have no way to stop him." Schwarzkopf paused for a moment. "I am pleading with the President to send in ground troops quickly. Powell concurs. But as of now we have only a contingent of Air Force, some carriers in the Gulf. If Saddam figures out how truly little we have, he might roll right in, take over the ports to stop us from bringing more troops in, take over the oil fields. Hell, he wouldn't even have to take them over; with a small incursion of successful saboteurs, he could just blow them up. There's no way to stop him."

Schwarzkopf's chunky hand reached for the cigar and unwrapped the cellophane cover. "If he figures it out." He struck a match to the tip of the cigar. "I need to buy some time, to bluff, until I can get more troops here."

He blew the cigar smoke out. "Then we're still not OK. With all of the troops I could muster coming in, he's still going to outnumber us two to one on the ground. We're going to have to win from the air, early on, quick. The only way we can do that is if we have his troops, his supply lines, the plants where he's manufacturing Scuds and chemicals precisely pinpointed. We can do some of that from the air—satellites, AWACS, is that right?"

Elaine nodded and started to say something, but Schwarzkopf interrupted. "What you're about to say is that we can only do some of it from the air, not all. Right?"

Elaine nodded again.

"So what I'm proposing" Schwarzkopf leaned forward again, "is that the key to winning this war is to team the Special Operations Forces with your people, Tarek, people out in the desert you trust, people who can help us infiltrate."

Schwarzkopf tapped his finger on the map in front of him, along the Saudi-Iraqi-Kuwaiti border. "We need Special Operations teams that can infiltrate into the desert and up across the borders into Iraq and Kuwait. Disguised, moving around with whoever the hell moves around out there in the desert innocuously, from outposts that are already there and cause no suspicion. We can equip these guys with infrared emitting markers that can be seen only by aircraft with infrared sensors looking for these targets in Iraq, paint what can be seen with our radar to pinpoint targets. They can observe the Iraqi buildup, let us know what Saddam is moving where, when."

Elaine spoke up quickly. "They could set up intercepts on Iraqi communications that we can monitor back here. Even some 'snatch' operations, maybe, to get some of the Iraqi electronic equipment we can bring back for analysis."

Schwarzkopf blew the cigar smoke out, his eyes intense as Elaine continued. "Getting intelligence back from the Special Ops teams is going to require some makeshift channels to pass it along back to us. Once again, absolutely secure. Any leak and their cover is blown and they and everybody working with them are dead."

Schwarzkopf leaned back, "Not to mention that we then also lose this war. The key is to team them with people you completely trust."

Tarek pushed the buzzer for Badr. He spoke abruptly in Arabic as Badr walked in the door.

Schwarzkopf looked up, uncomprehending. Tarek turned to him, "My grandfather heads up one of the bedu tribes along the border. I've infiltrated a few times with his people to help set up the Kuwaiti Resistance."

"You've personally been in and out with them already?" Schwarzkopf sounded amazed. Elaine and Ray watched Schwarzkopf suddenly smile, a man who had just found an equal.

He moved closer to Tarek. "Are there others, other tribes maybe in other outposts up there, he will know?"

"He will know others," said Tarek evenly. "Abdullah, the

crown prince, is from the Shammar tribe up north. He's always stayed very close to the bedu, he will know more."

"Tarek, are you sure you can trust Abdullah, it's a critical call," interrupted Ray nervously.

"You can trust him."

"Anybody else in any other locations?" Schwarzkopf pressed closer. "We need more. This is the key to it—people in the desert we can trust."

"Naila." Everybody turned around surprised at Badr's voice. "Naila," repeated Badr. Badr briefly explained to Schwarzkopf who Naila was and her post at the clinic along the border. "She called a couple of days ago while you were away and then again this morning while you were out. She's had some problem with the Governor there and is afraid he's going to try and have her removed from the post."

"Sweet Jesus," Schwarzkopf sat back flabbergasted, then beamed. "You mean this lady has already been working with the bedu? An inconspicuous doctor, in a hospital..." Schwarzkopf's mind was racing, "a hospital where supplies are always being transported in and out—the perfect makeshift channel for information transfers? Sweet Jesus..."

Schwarzkopf began to hum a few bars from his favorite Pavarotti recording. "Tarek, get the goddamned authorities to lay off this lady and then let's get a Special Ops team up there right away to rig her up."

Tarek nodded to Badr to set it in motion. Elaine looked on nervously, then suddenly broke in. "Tarek, this could be danger-ous. To put Naila in such a position, do you really think...?"

Tarek cut her off abruptly. "I'm as concerned about her as you are. But what we're talking about here is a whole country. Potentially thousands dead that the U.S. has brought over. Whoever can do whatever, will."

He stopped and looked at Elaine. "The helicopter to the clinic flies up this evening. Go to her and tell her what we need her to do."

34

Naila bedded the last patient and began drawing up the list of medications needed. She said good night to Benazir who was leaving for the day, and watched her walk off through the fading light of the little bedu town. Naila sat back down at her desk and worked through the final orders for the supplies. She leaned her head back for a moment, feeling the deep fatigue of the long day and then heard the distant sound of helicopter blades. She quickly finished off the list, signed her name and walked out to meet the helicopter arriving from Riyadh. Elaine got off.

Naila stared in surprise and then rushed over to embrace her. "Elaine, you're here?"

Elaine held her and then looked at the little bedu town, the dusty souk silhouetted in the dusk light, the tiny cinder block clinic. She looked back at Naila's face, the fatigue, the dark circles under her eyes.

"Naila," she asked softly, "are you alright?"

"Yes," said Naila gently, touched by her concern. Her hand motioned to the clinic behind her. "We have many to take care of, many to help." She reached for Elaine's hand with a soft smile, "Here, come see," she said quietly.

She led Elaine into the tiny clinic and showed her the admitting room they had set up. "The rest is in here." She opened the door to the small ward and began to walk quietly through the room, bending over one small patient who was whimpering, smoothing the covers over another, whispering to one of the mothers nursing an infant, adjusting the IV of a baby, touching the forehead of a feverish child. Elaine followed her silently as she whispered some words to a young mother and then quietly closed the door behind her.

"You see," Naila said softly, "we have many to care for." She saw Elaine gaze again at the tiny clinic. "It isn't very big, is it?" said Naila reading her thoughts. "But truly, we can do a lot with what little we have. Come with me, I live in a little house just over there."

They walked into the poor, small house and Naila closed the door. She reached over to put some water on for tea and looked at Elaine. "Elaine, why did you come?" Then Elaine watched, startled, as tears started to flow down Naila's face.

"Elaine, I'm so glad you're here." She stopped, unable to say anymore, exhausted and frightened by the events of the past week.

Elaine reached out to her. "Naila, what is it?"

Naila told her the story of the governor. "Elaine," she whispered, "I'm afraid he will do something, send me back. Did Tarek get my message? Did he send you to...?"

"Tarek will take care of the Governor. You won't have to go back."

Naila's head shot up. "Do you think so, really? Elaine, is that why you came?"

Something in Elaine made her want to look away as she spoke the words to Naila. "Naila, there is something we need you to do."

Naila stood still, watching the expression on Elaine's face, and then silently sat down at the table. She listened while

Elaine outlined the plan. Her mind struggled against the fear that gripped her at each word Elaine spoke.

"General Schwarzkopf is preparing the Special Operations team now. They and the details of the operation should be finalized by tomorrow. Then we will return with the equipment and the Special Ops team under cover on the next helicopter in. We can give you the detailed instructions on how you are to carry out the plan. In general, it is an infiltration operation with the clinic being used as the central transmission station."

Naila's hand shook as she listened to Elaine telling her what they wanted her to do. She took notes as Elaine told her about the members of the team and how they would work, trembling as she wrote.

When Elaine was finished, she looked at the young woman's frightened face, her final words barely audible. "I fought against involving you, but they all agreed the plan was vital, and you were too perfectly placed."

Naila nodded mutely. She stood up and, while Elaine watched, held onto the back of the chair struck by what seemed to be a wave of nausea. Elaine reached over to help her. "Naila, what is it?"

"It's nothing really, " said Naila quickly. Elaine stared at her as a second wave of nausea seemed to hit. "Naila is there anything I can do to help? Anything I could…"

Naila shook her head "It will pass in a minute."

Elaine stood up and held the young woman. She looked directly into her eyes and spoke softly. "Naila, this is not 'nothing.' I want you to tell me what it is."

Naila looked up at her, touched, and then in a voice that seemed resigned, lost, finally spoke. "I am pregnant, Elaine."

"Oh my God," whispered Elaine. The stunning ramifications of the announcement seemed almost more than she could absorb.

Naila's tears flowed down as she held onto Elaine. "Elaine, please don't tell anybody. I'm so glad you're here, I've been so alone. Oh God, I've been so all alone."

"Naila," whispered Elaine, "what are going to do? Is there anything I can do.?

"I don't know what I'm going to do." the tears streaked down her face. "I want to have the baby." She breathed deeply, trying to talk. "When I came back, I vowed I wouldn't see him, I would end it, I would do what I had to do, the marriage that Musaid had arranged. I told him when I left Washington, when we were together last, that I would have to do this, and when he tried to call when I got back to Riyadh, I didn't answer the calls. I've struggled so hard, when he was there the night we went to Osman's, I just..." she broke down, unable to go on for a moment, and then continued.

"And then I realized I was pregnant. I realized that I would have to have an abortion. And I tried to make myself do it, and I can't, I just can't. I want the baby. I want him. I want my life. Oh God," she whispered leaning her head into her arm, "I don't know what I am going to do."

"Naila, whatever you decide, whatever you want to do, I want you to let me know how I can help."

Naila nodded mutely. "For now, the only help you can be is to tell no one. I want you to promise me that. Tell no one."

Elaine nodded, and then turned startled by the knock on the door. The helicopter pilot stood outside. "It's time for the flight to return."

"Naila, I'll be back within the next day or so. You'll be alright?" asked Elaine softly.

"I'll be alright."

Elaine held her hand and then boarded the helicopter back to Riyadh, profoundly shaken.

⊠　　⊠　　⊠

The following afternoon Elaine walked up to the front door of the old mansion where Schwarzkopf and Ray were due. The young houseboy at first looked confused when she mentioned Tarek, but then smiled and led her to a large door to the right of the massive foyer.

Elaine stopped, startled as the eyes of the women sitting there all turned to her. They sat with small porcelain teacups and sweets before them on the massive inlaid mother-of-pearl table, their chattering suspended mid-sentence when she entered. She stared back at the old woman with the kohl-lined eyes, antique jewelry along her arms and throat over the long, flowing layers of silk. The young, tense looking woman with the long conservative gray Islamic dress, the others young and old in the traditional dress of the Gulf, some in silk western dresses. From the back of the room, a woman in a long, pale-green silk caftan, crafted with gold and pearls, stood up. Elaine looked at Nura's green eyes, above the exquisite cheekbones, gazing at her.

Nura's eyes flickered only the slightest question mark as she moved forward to take Elaine's hand. "Welcome, please. Come in."

Elaine flushed. "I'm so sorry, I didn't mean to intrude."

Nura motioned her into the room. "Don't be sorry. I am pleased. Naila has told me so much about you since we first met. Now that you are here, you must stay, it would be a great pleasure for us."

"Oh no," said Elaine, even more embarrassed. "I am here to meet..."

Nura shook her head, smiling, "This is the Gulf, we would be hurt if you didn't accept our hospitality. I'll have the houseboy take you to Tarek to drop off your materials, and then you can join us." She pressed Elaine's hand. "Say you'll stay."

Nura motioned for the houseboy. Elaine followed him to the other side of the house. The houseboy knocked on the large wooden door and then opened it. Tarek's head was bent talking in low tones. The old man sat beside him listening, a leathered, lined face, swathed in the long bedu thobe and the black robe with the gilt edge of the sheikhs. His spotless white kaffiyeh fell like a frame around his white-bearded face. Elaine was struck by the magnificence of his face, the dignity, the intensity, the calm of a Rembrandt portrait. He turned to meet her gaze.

"Elaine, I want you to meet my grandfather," Tarek said coming toward her.

The old sheikh stood up and took her hand. "Ahlan wa sahlan." He turned to Tarek and continued in Arabic. Tarek smiled. "He says you are very lovely, with eyes like the sky."

General Schwarzkopf and Ray arrived within minutes. They closed the door in the study and for the next half hour outlined the plan. How they were to integrate the Special Ops people with the bedu, the equipment they would rig at their outposts, how the information would be transferred back and forth. They brought in the two team leaders to introduce them.

Captain David Frazee and Captain Mark Long shook the old bedu's hand and spoke to him in Arabic. Captain Long continued to talk to the old sheikh, and Elaine was fascinated by the equanimity with which he absorbed the details of the operation. When they finished, Captain Long and Captain Frazee followed Ray and General Schwarzkopf to the car.

Elaine started to go. Tarek's grandfather stopped her.

"My grandfather says that you must join us for dinner," said Tarek, "that an old man of the desert would never understand if you declined his hospitality."

Elaine hesitated, then followed them to the large dining room. All stood up instantly as the old man entered. The children moved forward to kiss his hand, the adults to kiss his cheek. They settled in around the large table while the servants brought on the food. Tarek turned briefly at the sound of the front door opening and then continued the conversation.

Musaid entered the dining room, then stopped at the door, staring at Elaine. He bent down and kissed the grandfather's cheek. When he stood up, his voice was icy, "I didn't realize that there were other guests. I've brought my friend Ali from the ministry." Ali took a seat at the table. He turned to Musaid and spoke in a half-whisper.

"And so, now we even have the Americans in our homes eating dinner with us." A hush filled the room. Musaid looked at Elaine. Ali continued now more loudly. "The Americans who are so useful when it is convenient for them to interfere in our politics. When their oil supplies are threatened, they rush to the side of 'poor attacked Kuwait.' And yet are quite preoccupied for the forty years the Palestinians have been displaced."

The silence in the room now was stunning.

Ali's tone hurled the insult beneath the words. "This is our part of the world—the Americans have no place here. The Americans who send Christian soldiers with their little Bibles on to the ground of Islam, the country of Mecca. The Americans who come with a display of brute force like some colonial power of old. The poor Arabs, they believe so condescendingly, are unable to take care of their own. The American's who now so thoughtfully send us women along with their other troops to confuse our women here."

Suddenly the sound of a fist smashed the end of the table.

"Silence!" The grandfather rose. His straight figure loomed before the table, his eyes piercing first Ali, then Musaid. "This is a guest in our house. You are an Arab. Who has raised such a person to disgrace us so?"

The old bedu stopped. In fury he waited. The authority of the voice paralyzed Musaid. He stood up, apologized for Ali, and took him out of the room.

The old man folded his robe and sat down as Musaid left. Elaine looked searchingly at Tarek, who motioned for her to stay. Nura simply looked on. The tension was palpable as all struggled to restore the hospitality of the meal.

At the end of the dinner, Nura came forward when Elaine bade them all goodbye.

"I know you've been working very hard. Come with us— Osman will be taking his boat out in the Red Sea this week. I will send you a note, what day, what time. Come."

❈   ❈   ❈

Nura spoke softly when Tarek returned that night and put the papers he was carrying down by the side of the bed. "You are gone always now. Tired, distracted." The deep green eyes fixed on him. "The woman, the American, Elaine," she continued softly. "She is good?"

Tarek nodded, "Her work is very good."

"Do you know any more about who in the Family?"

Tarek shook his head. She brought her hand toward him, the silk of her robe falling across his arm, her eyes holding him. "You are gone always now," she whispered. "You have so much in your life."

"And you?" he asked.

"I have only you," she whispered. "Only you."

And then she placed the small book on the table, its tiny gold pen lying at the center of a page, and reached up to draw his body down to her's. He stood back, unable to look at her, took the papers, and left the room.

35

Naila listened in the darkened clinic to the sound of the helicopter approaching. The bedu boy, Aziz, and her grandfather waited with her as the thump, thump, thump, of the chopper blades came to a stop.

Naila took the key and unlocked the back door. She glanced at the American woman pilot and then at the Special Ops men that emerged silently from the plane; Elaine was with them. Captain Long and Captain Frazee motioned to the teams behind them. Each with ten enlisted men: a master sergeant, a communications specialist, a radio operator, a demolitions expert, an operations NCO, an assistant operations NCO, a supply man, a medic, an SF tech, and a backup—all armed with M-16's and Beretta 92-F's.

Captain David Frazee went up to Naila and shook her hand. "It's a pleasure to be working with you, m'am."

"They've brought the clothes with them?" Elaine asked softly, looking at Naila's grandfather and Aziz.

Naila nodded. The bedu boy and her grandfather opened the saddlebags and took out the thobes, daggers and bedu kaffiyehs. Wordlessly the men of the Specials Ops team put them on. Elaine attached the electronic and radio equipment to the radio operators and communications specialist, and tested the equipment one last time against the small receiver. Then they reviewed the codes with Naila. Finally the men adjusted the equipment beneath their thobes. Elaine indicated that all was ready, and watched while the men filed silently out door, one team behind the bedu boy to the west, the other team behind Tarek's grandfather to the north.

Elaine followed Naila toward the small makeshift lab where the blood analysis equipment was kept. She moved the microscopes aside and pulled the blood separator machine toward her, feeling behind it, she placed the small receiver in the space and tested its transmission. Then explained to Naila, "Just look for the little red light here; that will indicate it's functioning. Don't touch it, but if at any time, when you do the daily check, you see that it's off, we'll probably already know, but try to get word to us as soon as possible anyway."

Naila took the pouches that Elaine handed her. The markings were the same as those on the medicine pouches going back and forth between the clinic and the hospital lab, but with one small additional letter on them.

"Anything they give you as they move back and forth with the bedu, you place in here. Then just send it with the helicopters going on their usual runs to the hospital in Riyadh. The pilot will know it is for us."

Elaine stopped and looked at Naila's soft brown eyes in the darkened clinic, the sounds of the patients in the refugee ward behind them. "Are you going to be OK?" she asked.

"Yes."

Elaine reached over and held her hand, frightened for her.

"If you need help, call us instantly."

The helicopter pilot opened the door for Elaine, threw the switch heading back toward Riyadh. Naila stood in the tiny clinic door watching it go, surrounded now by only the sounds of the desert night.

36

Tarek listened from his office to the first report coming in from the Special Operations team in the bedu town. The systems in place, operating. He looked up as Badr came through the door. Badr handed him the piece of paper, the transmission just across from Hamid.

"OPERATIONS TO BEGIN...ANTAR IN THE SOUTH. ASSASSINATION TARGETS CONFIRMED, IMMINENT. ABED BIN OSMAN CONFIRMED. PLANS FOR MINES TO DETONATE BELOW U.S. SHIPS CONFIRMED. ASSASSINATIONS WITHIN KINGDOM CONFIRMED."

Tarek stood up.

"Where are you going?" asked Badr.

"To Osman's," Tarek closed the door behind him.

Sana floated in Osman's pool beneath the night lights like a drifting sea anenome. "Yamani has gone to Hong Kong for acupuncture." She sighed and continued to float while Osman played cards and sipped absinthe. "It is hard to imagine exactly what he hopes to cure, isn't it?"

Osman walked over to the cabana and stretched out on the massage board. The Pakistani masseuse opened the bottles of oil and began kneading the muscles in his back. He had thought to call the boy for his visitors last night. But he had let it go as the evening wore on and the girl seemed to suffice.

He smiled as he thought of the dancer. She had been perfection really, a girl who delighted in becoming every man's fantasy. A sense for the moment, for the instant when the exotic becomes the erotic. Her timing had been exquisite. The smallest trickle of sweat slowly edging down through the cleavage of her breasts encased in gold, down the rounded belly girdled in twine and silks. Whirling in a staccato frenzy as the musicians played the hypnotic rhythms, her body undulating, punctuated by soft moans, as though possessed. And then suddenly she stopped perfectly still, throwing her long black hair over her shoulders and looked, eyes inflamed with desire, at the man he had indicated for her.

He will see my gift, Osman had told her, and go with you. You will be his pleasure in the midst of all this business, before he returns to his endless offices and meetings in the West.

Osman smiled again as he thought of her leading the man away to another room. Art, artifice, so fine a line really. In the end the human being was a simple creature, with simple needs, simply met. Osman tipped the masseuse as she finished. Yes, art, artifice, device, desire. The human being was a simple creature really.

He left the cabana and walked back into the house, across the marble foyer, down the steps into the living room. He looked at the box the houseboy had placed on the oriental rug and picked up the tools the boy had left for him. He pried the lid of the crate open. Gently he reached in and felt the painting.

He lifted it out, glancing at the Persian miniatures encased in gold along the walls, the fine intricate lines of the ancient artists, interspersed with the modern, brilliant strokes of the Cézanne, the dreamlike Chagall, the languid Gauguin, and thought of the beauty of this Matisse along with them. He unwrapped it and looked at the jewel-like tones, moving the light closer to see the brushwork that so fascinated him when he first saw it in Paris.

"It's beautiful, Osman."

Osman turned in surprise at the sound of Tarek's voice behind him. "Tarek, what an unexpected pleasure." He rang for the servant to bring drinks. "Come close, look, this Matisse is quite beautiful."

Tarek smiled as he bent over the painting. "Yes, it really is a masterpiece, Osman." He sat down on the sofa and waited for a moment until the servant left the room. "Osman, I have to talk to you."

"Yes, of course, what is it?"

"Abed."

Osman put his drink down and looked at Tarek. "Abed?"

"How much do you know about where Abed goes? Who he sees?"

Osman shook his head slowly. "He is a man now. I don't ask; he has his own life." He looked carefully at Tarek. "Why do you ask?"

"You know he goes out of the country from time to time?"

"Yes, of course. He has friends in the West, down the Gulf as well," Osman replied hesitantly, "throughout the Middle East."

"You know where he is when he's gone?"

"No, not really, I..."

"You know about his activities here?"

Osman's voice caught, "His activities here?"

"He's under surveillance." Tarek felt the words like a dead weight in his throat when he spoke them. He watched the man slowly close his eyes in pain, his hand tighten around the drink.

"He's under surveillance?" Osman's voice was hoarse.

"There is a network of cells being run out of Iraq," Tarek continued. "Abed meets with them."

"Oh God," whispered Osman, leaning against the back of the chair.

"I'm not sure yet how far it goes, how deeply he's involved."

"You are coming to tell me...?"

"I am coming," said Tarek sadly, "to tell you that I can't protect him."

Osman nodded silently.

Tarek leaned toward Osman and spoke quietly. "I can only give you this. Warn him in hopes that he will listen to you, that they will, not try to use him as an active agent in something that will require..." Tarek stopped.

Osman looked at him.

"This is the most I can do, Osman."

The voice came in a hoarse whisper again. "Thank you, I understand."

Tarek stood up to leave and turned once again sadly to him. "Osman, you should be prepared. He may not care. They may not care."

Osman tried to steady himself as Tarek departed. He went back to his study, looking at his papers, struggling for some degree of normalcy. He switched on the radio and listened to the reports of the carnage in Kuwait. He picked up the phone and ordered some more transfers of stocks and currency to Switzerland. He hung up the phone and heard Abed enter the house. He sat in silence, thinking of the distance between him and his son, like a chasm, though Abed's room was only a short way down the corridor. The silence between them seemed to thunder. He felt the ache of the love he carried for this disaffected son, how it circled back on itself and lay with no way to connect to the boy. Osman stood up. He would try again.

When he heard his father open the door, Abed twisted from his desk.

"Abed, I had hoped we could talk."

Osman's hesitated in confusion. His eye caught a movement that broke his train of thought. Abed's face was tense. But it was his hand that arrested Osman's words, a hand moving furtively behind him. Moving, thrusting something toward the open drawer, away from Osman's eye. There was a momentary glint and a thump of something heavy before the drawer snapped shut.

"Abed, what is that?" Osman's voice caught in his throat.

Abed looked up, agitated, then flushed red, angry.

"I could have some privacy, couldn't I?" Abed's voice sputtered. He clicked the lock on the drawer and stood up, shoving the chair behind him, his eyes furious upon Osman.

"What if I walked into your room unannounced?" he demanded. "Into your room while you're counting your money, your endless money from endless deals. Into your room with your whores stretched across the bed."

Osman's hand shot out and hit Abed across the face. Abed reeled back. Osman's voice choked with pain. "How dare you talk to your father like that?"

Abed flashed defiance. "How dare I? You—this paragon of 'virtue'...money, paintings, palaces, and whores, a lifetime of them. The real question is, 'how dare my father?'" He brushed past Osman and stopped at the door. Tears of rage filled his eyes. He spoke with a rising voice. "Yes, father, the question is, how dare my father?"

Osman stood in the middle of the empty room, the sound

of his son's footsteps fading down the hall. He looked at his palm, still red from the unrestrained blow, and thought of the incomprehensible depths of the boy's alienation, and the deeply wounding effect of it on Osman himself. Then he remembered the drawer. The lock was a simple mechanism; it yielded almost at once. In the drawer lay a short-barreled but large-caliber revolver. Beneath it was a small notebook.

He pushed the gun aside and picked up the notebook. It was bound in green cloth, and the pages were covered with Abed's scrawl. Names, telephone numbers, addresses in all parts of the Gulf, small scratches of some sort of code next to them. One section was marked "U.S." There were more names, codes, and then a page of women's names, phone numbers, addresses, more codes. One of the names was familiar, but he couldn't place it. After each name were more codes, future dates, and finally the tiny scrawl, Allahu Akbar. Some of the dates in the book were past and some to come in the next few weeks. He put the book back and started to close the drawer.

Suddenly the name, why he knew it, hit him. He was engulfed in horror. Picking up the book, he hurried to his car. Turning on the ignition, he suddenly buried his head in his hands knowing what he had to do.

Later that night, Tarek's houseboy bundled up the mail, and the stray envelope for Tarek he had found in the drawing room. He sent it all over to the office where Tarek was working late. Tarek leafed through the pile, then suddenly stopped.

"What is it?" asked Badr.

Tarek looked curiously at the green notebook and shrugged. He began to look at the scrawl of names with the codes beside them. He turned the pages and paused when he got to the one marked U.S. with the dates. He stopped suddenly at the name of one of the women. He looked at the date beside it.

"The name of the American girl whose still unidentified Arab boyfriend put her on the Pan Am flight with the cassette that blew up the plane. The one that killed 220 people."

"My God, what else is in there?"

"A lot more names, a lot of codes with a lot of dates, some of which are about to come up."

Badr picked up the green notebook and quickly headed for decoding.

"Where did it come from?"

"Osman."

"I lock up Abed now?"

"No. We keep a guard patrol on him so he can't carry out anything and we follow him." Tarek paused. "The rest? I think the time has come. You can be ready in an hour?"

Badr nodded.

❉   ❉   ❉

▲▲All right Badr, now." Tarek watched the last of the cell members enter, the door of the cell meeting close.

Badr phoned and gave the signal to the men in the cars while Tarek adjusted the monitor.

The first car started to move down from Al Imam Ibn Turki Street. The blue van headed in from Khazzan Street, and two sedans started up from Thumairi Street. The last people from the souk filtered off into the evening while the cars made their way toward a single door.

Tarek and Badr watched the four vehicles approach and the sixteen special agents file out and surround the building. Within seconds they had moved, silencers on their guns: six into adjacent buildings emerging moments later on the roofs, ten surrounding the building from the street, blockading the doors and windows. Poised, they awaited the signal. Tarek looked up at Badr and nodded.

Badr pressed a button.

Tarek's men poured into the building. The stunned members of the cell stopped their prayers midword. He watched his men shoot one trying to flee through the back door. When the prisoners emerged, Tarek looked at the face of the leader, whose voice he had listened to so frequently. The tight arrogance, the narrow eyes. Tarek gazed at the others— soft, confused Arab boys. Boys who had had the world handed to them, when they wanted to fight for it.

He turned off the monitor and waited for the call that would come next. When the phone rang, he got up and left his office.

※ ※ ※

Tarek opened the door to the interrogation room. The agent who had been working the cell leader over with the back of his hand, turned when Tarek came in. Tarek motioned for him to leave.

The cell leader stared at Tarek with frozen eyes, blood dripping from the side of his head.

Tarek untied the man's hands, took out a pack of cigarettes, and handed him one. "We have papers on you, the forgery from

Baghdad on your 'Saudi' citizenship. A dossier tracing your work back to the U.S., your travels back and forth between here and Baghdad. We have all of this."

The man remained silent while Tarek continued to scrutinize him. "I think we should talk, don't you? I think we should talk a little about all of this. Now, I know," Tarek motioned toward the door, "that my colleague has asked you a lot of questions. We don't need to go over those again. No."

He leaned back in the chair. The man watched him warily.

"No. I know you have many plans. I don't want to talk about all of that. You and my colleague I am sure will be going over that. No, I'm really interested in discussing one thing. I want to know who Abed is reporting to in the Royal Family."

The man looked at him, startled, but still silent.

"Talk," breathed Tarek.

The man said nothing.

Tarek flashed open his lighter and held it to the side of the man's face.

"Now."

Finally, the man rasped out. "Abed is nothing. A foolish, lost playboy. Fodder. Abed knows nothing."

He looked at Tarek curiously and said, "You let Abed go, didn't you? Follow Abed and you will find nothing, because now there are only two people who matter. Antar is one and the other is a member of the Family. And you will not find them."

He took a deep breath, gazing arrogantly at Tarek. "You won't be able to crack Antar's plans, they are at work right now. Your country won't be yours much longer."

Tarek stood absolutely still. He turned to go; then the man felt the crash, the blackness as Tarek's fist smashed into his face. Falling to the floor, he heard Tarek's words to the agent, who now stood beside him.

"Finish him."

Badr watched the body carried out. He looked at the small piece of paper they had confiscated from the man before interrogating him. Lists of cassettes going out through the country into the mosques. Schedules of the U.S. ships coming in. And finally a quote from the journal of the member of the Royal Family identified as "the blessed arm of Antar," to be read to the group.

In the Name of Allah, the Compassionate, the Merciful...
They ask you what is lawful to them. Say: "All good things
are lawful to you, as well as that which you have taught the
birds and beasts of prey to catch, training them as Allah has
taught you. Eat of what they catch for you, pronouncing
upon it the name of Allah. And have fear of Allah: swift is
Allah's reckoning."

'The Table,' Holy Koran

37

The groaning hulk of the U.S. ship rolled slightly to its side as it docked in Dhahran. Elaine, nerves taut, watched the monitor from Dhahran as an Iraqi speedboat buzzed the frigate protecting one of the tankers and then darted off.

"We need to get some barges out there with some intercept equipment," said Elaine abruptly.

Ray nodded in agreement. "If they decided to send in one of these little suicide speedboats to crash into the side of a tanker with a load of explosives, I suppose it doesn't make any difference what communications stuff we have. But Christ, we could try to cover our ass a little more than just flying it up a flagpole like a target waiting to get stiffed. Fuck, our intelligence in Iraq is almost zero."

He looked at his watch, then back to Elaine. "There's a transport plane leaving for Dhahran in an hour. I'll take it and get work going on some intercept equipment to place on the oil rig out there and make arrangements for a barge we equip to move on out a bit past it. You take the helicopter out to join me when you're finished here."

Elaine took the pouch coming into headquarters from Naila. She began sorting through the material while the helicopter readied itself for the short trip to Dhahran. She boarded bringing the material and the intercepts on the Riyadh cell along. As the helicopter ascended, her hand stopped midair holding a paper from the cell tap. The transcript read simply: "The blood of the lamb shall be shed. At Ramadan the blood of the lamb shall be shed. Those who defile the ground, the ways of Islam shall die." The transcript indicated that the voice paused and then spoke a list of four names. She quickly flipped the sheet over and froze as she read Tarek's name, Schwarz-kopf's, Ray's. And finally, her own.

She held the paper, staring, unable to move. The helicopter began its descent. She got out, shaken and started to walk over to Tarek who was watching from on shore while their two men placed the intercept equipment to monitor communications from Iraq.

Suddenly, two speedboats circled around the oil rig off the Dhahran shore, darting back and forth, the men in them shouting up in broken English, "Have nice day, have nice day."

The young laborer on the platform looked down while the men in the speedboat laughed and headed back toward Iraq. "It's starting to get to me," he said to the man working beside him, then sat down and reached over for a thermos of water. Squinting up at the sun burning overhead, in his last act, he watched the speedboats moving farther away across the water. The explosion ripped apart the oil rig beneath him.

Elaine's scream was lost in the roar of the funeral pyre that consumed the two men. She stared at the flames of the oil rig and the secretly installed intercept equipment—lost. Tarek stood behind her silently watching the dead being dragged out of the water.

Elaine looked at Tarek, then sank down to the sand. Her voice choked. "Within hours, they knew. They get everything, within minutes, our information, our locations. We are hopeless targets." Paralyzed, she stared at the dead bodies from the explosion. She reached out to him unconsciously as he bent over to her. "Tarek," she buried her face in her hands and then looked up and saw the exhaustion on his face. He led her to his car and drove without a word down the Gulf road. She stared out of the window unable to speak.

"You knew Antar, didn't you?" Elaine said finally.

"I knew Antar."

Elaine waited for him to continue. Tarek drove around the low sloping roads covered with sand along the coast. Elaine turned her face toward the window and the humid breeze from the Gulf waters.

"You haven't seen him for many years?"

"Not for many, many years."

"What was he like? A man who could become so truly evil."

Tarek was completely still now, watching her, the smallest flicker of a question moving across his eyes. "No one ever sees themselves as evil." His voice was quiet. "Only as someone who must carry out the one next step that circumstances have forced upon him."

She asked, her voice still choked, "What was he like?"

Tarek frowned. "A student of architecture when I first met him. From a middle-class Iraqi family that had made their way up under Saddam's Baath Party reforms when they ousted the old king and British colonialism. His family sent him to be educated with the Jesuits in Iraq."

"The Jesuits?" interrupted Elaine in surprise.

"Yes," Tarek nodded. "Iraq, you know, was the one Gulf country that truly had a religious mix for a long time— Christians, Muslims, Jews. When the British and the French were around, the Jesuits came. They established some of the best schools. Antar's family wanted the best; the religion was secondary to them—they told him to just disregard that part of it and play along. Tarek Azziz, their foreign minister, is a Christian, for instance."

"And Antar?" asked Elaine.

"An idealist," said Tarek. "We became friends in the way that foreign students from the same part of the world become friends. He was extremely careful to hide his Baath Party activities from me and everybody else. We had long talks about how the Gulf must move forward, how it had become at once buried in the past and yet unhinged by the onslaught of the West with its modernization. Long intense discussions about how to change the world we were returning to."

He spoke slowly as the image of Antar moved across his mind. "He was an idealist, clever, canny, who mixed easily with everyone else, in the Gulf and in the West, to advance his ideals. He'd been trained well by the Jesuits; he had self-discipline, and a vision past the immediate to reach the long-term goals. When Saddam became increasingly ruthless, he had the ability to look the other way and call it a short-term necessity—the executions, the purges, gassing the dissident Kurdish villages in the north, the Shia in the South. After a while, you become used to it. The beatings, the tortures, the interrogations. The blood, the dead. And then after that," he gazed at the Gulf, "you must continue to believe, because if not, then everything you have done before would devour your soul. You are too far down the road to turn around."

Tarek looked back at her. "He was always brilliant—a fascinating command of philosophy, history. Saddam has never been out of the Middle East, barely past the Gulf. He didn't understand how to deal with the people he needed to use. But Antar did. He masterminded getting aid and materials out of the

West, and then re-establishing ties with old terrorist networks when the war with Iran ended, pulling on the old Iranian Revolution dream of ousting the corrupt monarchies and throwing the West out of the Gulf as well."

Elaine leaned back against the window, regarding Tarek's dark intense face studying the road ahead. "And you?" she said quietly.

"And I?" He pulled the car over to the side of road where a small, ancient abandoned adobe mosque stood. He stopped the car, his voice pensive, hushed.

"I see the Arab world in one of the saddest periods of history. Unable to take a stand, giving lip service to everything, sinking into corruption, stagnation. Bitterly, painfully confused about who it is, what it is. Struggling backwards, forwards from the past, which is dead, to the future which is unknown. Convulsing the rest of the world until its own throes are over."

He got out of the car.

She walked behind him into the tiny dark deserted mosque. At the low entrance, he bent down and left his sandals in the sand. As her eyes adjusted to the dim light, she watched him move toward the center of the room and then bow down on the mud brick floor. He extended his arms in front of him and whispered the words of the prayer. She was riveted by the intensity of the man as he repeated the verses. At last he rose and stood before her.

She followed him as he left the mosque and walked into the abandoned adobe hut next to it. The coolness of the dim room with its handmade mud walls seemed totally insulated from the world outside.

She was transfixed by the pain, the need that moved across his face as he stood alone with her. A man haunted by the fears, the suspicions about everyone around him, the loss of all he trusted. The stunning isolation, the terror that must reside in a man who had pushed his country to a course, which, if it failed, could mean its destruction. She reached out to touch him.

"And you?" he said, stepping forward. She stood absolutely still as his mouth came down upon hers. He touched the back of her hair and she felt herself moving deeper into his kiss.

"And you?" he repeated as he stood back listening to the small catch in her breath. She felt her mind, her body fill excruciatingly, wildly with images of her dead husband. His face, his touch, his voice seemed alive, ripped her with pain, with the loss.

She pulled back abruptly, her face flooding with tears. "I understand," he said.

Suddenly her voice sounded, as though it had a will of its own, spiraling upward from need, desire.

"Tarek."

His name hung in the air as though a call for life itself. Elaine stood waiting in the dim light of the abandoned hut. He walked back to her and brought his mouth down to hers.

"Do you want me?" The sound of his voice, harsh, low, hung in the silence.

"Yes," she whispered "yes."

With a raw electricity his mouth closed on hers and his hand moved softly through her long blonde hair and then down her neck. He drew back, listening to her soft moan. Her eyes filled with tears at the pain, the pleasure of being alive. He touched her with extraordinary gentleness, and she stood motionless while he reached out and pulled the dress from her shoulders. He brought his mouth onto her breast, moving his tongue slowly, exquisitely over the nipple as her breath caught. She felt his hands bringing her down to the adobe floor, his mouth kissing gently down her neck, over her breasts, down the soft line of her stomach.

"You've waited a very long time, haven't you?" he whispered. He watched her eyes close in pain. The soft inaudible "yes" formed on her lips.

He took her hands and slowly raised them above her head, as one hand stroked her outstretched fingers, down along the inside of her arm, her breast, her belly while her body arched up to meet him. She felt his hand as he spread her legs further, the strong hand above holding her as his mouth tasted and probed her body until she moaned, begging him to come inside her.

He leaned toward her while she whispered and then slowly, exquisitely entered her. He began to turn her, to move inside her with a power that consumed her—to stroke her until he could feel her pleasure building. Her eyes looking up to him; he thrust deep inside, her long moan shuddering beneath him as she cried out and her body finally dissolved into the waves of pleasure he gave her.

꽃 꽃 꽃

Elaine lay awake through the night in Dhahran, in one of the small houses set aside for the Intel unit. It was as though Tarek were still with her. His face, his voice, the heat from his body. She thought of him, of making love to him, feeling him, breathing him. She wanted him. Her mind would go no farther. She wanted him. Something in him struck the chord of need so deep within her that she was stunned by its power.

It was three in the morning when she heard the knock on the door. She opened it and Tarek stood before her. "You are alright?" he asked softly. She reached out her hand and brought him in. She put her arms around him and held him as he kissed her face, her eyes, her hair. "Tarek," she whispered, "I want you to tell me something. Whatever your answer is will be alright. But I want you to answer."

He looked at her and spoke softly. "I know what your question is. There aren't others. There haven't been others. I have loved Nura, I have been faithful to Nura. Until now."

Her hand moved up to his face when she felt his words stop, falter at what she knew he couldn't say.

She looked into his eyes and seemed to see the need in her own looking back at her. The caring, the understanding she felt for him mirrored. He brought her fingers to his mouth and kissed them. "You have come to stay with me?" she asked gently, his mouth now moving to hers.

"I have come to stay with you."

❋ ❋ ❋

Ray watched quietly from the guest house across the quadrant when Tarek left shortly before dawn. He went to the dock and waited for her to join him. Ray watched her turn pensively back to the ships in the Gulf. He watched her eyes roam absently over the gray tankers moving through the water. He spoke softly. "Whoever it is, Elaine, they'll try and kill Tarek again. From inside, from outside, whoever. They're going to try and kill Tarek along with the king. You know that, don't you?" She nodded.

"I understand how you feel; he is an extraordinary man. Just don't get in too far. Be careful," he said. She looked at him while he continued, amazed at his intuition. "Whatever happens, Tarek will ultimately go back to his own world—and you to yours. You know that, don't you?"

Elaine smiled at his concern. "Yes, I know that. I just want this for now. It's enough to feel again." Ray turned silently back toward the Gulf.

"Ray, Nura…?" Her voice trailed off, her eyes searching his.

"I think you know Nura's under survelleince," he replied quietly.

She stared at a small boat moving across the Gulf. Finally she turned back to him. "Ray, you remember Nura's invitation to go out on Osman's boat with them? Osman's going to take Nura and some friends out on the Red Sea. Nura invited me to go; I said I would. What should I do?"

He shrugged, "If you told her you were going to go, you should go."

When she returned to Riyadh that night, she tried to sleep and then finally turned on the light. She picked up the small book she had left by the bedside weeks ago and hadn't returned to Tarek. Nura's journal, the words spilling across the page. She began to read.

I have known Tarek since I was a child and in many ways, he has always been my lover—in my imagination as a child, in reality as a woman. I have always known Tarek would be my husband. He is what I have always wanted.

As a girl I was fascinated by his intensity, his dark handsome face. I can see his eyes look up from a book, look at me in his even, deep way. I would sit by him as our parents talked and feel his body respond and wish the time would pass so I could have him, so he could show me, so I could move into those dark fascinating eyes. That I met no other men as women do in the West is inconsequential to me. It is Tarek I have always wanted. When I was at school in Switzerland, in France I watched others who came with me fall in love with European boys, released as they were from the family confines, dreading to return to arranged marriages with men they cared nothing for. To me, the Europeans were interesting, but somehow brittle. Pale, overt, a simplistic set of sensibilities. And so I refrained. Not for any sense of morality—I am no more moral nor immoral than the others who took their European lovers to bed, and then had themselves sewn back up by the weary French doctors who have been reconstructing the vaginas of Arab women for the marriage bed for years. No it was Tarek that I wanted. And so through those years I read philosophy and French literature.

It became quite interesting to me, reading philosophy, the fundamental distinctions. The Western idea that somehow politics and religion, are, should be separable, as opposed to a continuum of a central philosophy, seems to me unrealistic. Beliefs and motives, actions and reactions, avarice and altruism all tumble over one another incessantly. Like the senses they are not separated out, stacked in different corners like various drawers of clothes. Wars in the Middle East arise from a cauldron of greed, geography, sexual frustration, vision, religion, despots and crusaders. Or the idea that all are equal, an ideal that has never been seen borne out by history. And so I read philosophy for my degree. Today I listen to those who yearn for something unattainable—a return to the past in the present. A return to something they hope has answers for them, definitions, certainty, when of course none exists. There will be a new order. But it will not be what they think.

Elaine put the book down and looked at herself in the mirror. The woman's profound love for Tarek haunted her. The depths of her passion, the intriguing turns and sensibilities of her mind. Elaine finally turned off the light with a glance at the message she had found waiting for her when she returned. The time and place, the driver who would pick up Elaine for the cruise on Osman's boat, written in the elegant script of Nura's hand.

38

Osman sent his plane for Elaine to bring her to Jeddah to join them on the boat. When the plane landed, a driver was waiting. They arrived at the dock and as she stepped out of the car, he pointed out a massive white GulfStar cruising vessel. Osman stood on the gleaming white and teakwood starboard deck rocking gently beneath the brilliant Jeddah sun on the diamond blue water's reflection. She could make out Nura and Sana behind him. Nura smiled, stunning in a green sarong wrapped loosely over her bathing suit while Osman called out a buoyant hello.

He sent the boat boy to fetch her and bring her on board. When she came alongside the boat, Sana waved, smoking a cigarette and laying out a deck of cards while the boat boy helped Elaine aboard. The crew immediately began to loosen the enormous ropes mooring the boat to the harbor.

Osman escorted Elaine to a deck chair. One of the servants came over with a cool drink, and a plate of caviar surrounded by small canapes.

"Give culture a rest for the day," smiled Osman, "you work too hard Elaine. You need to enjoy some of the natural beauty of the area."

"Osman has failed to say that he is also enjoying your's," quipped Sana.

"I would never fail to say such a thing," laughed Osman. "But women as beautiful as Elaine, I think, tire of hearing this same thing all the time." He shrugged charmingly, "I try to be more original. Her beauty is a given. She would perhaps like to hear about her accomplishments, her talents. She is the cultural attaché and perhaps we will discuss art. Whatever. She graces us with her presence, as you do with yours Sana." Sana amused by his usual graciousness, waved him off with a laugh, diamonds glittering on her fingers.

The 120-foot yacht began to move out into the water of the Red Sea. Sana smiled at Elaine. "Come, chérie and play some cards with me. I promise not to cheat unless you say it's alright."

Elaine pulled her deck chair up toward Sana's while Sana dealt out a hand. "We skip playing for money, chérie? Purely the thrill of pitting our talents against one another's?" She glanced up at Osman affectionately, "That's his favorite, you know. He has so much money now, he has no idea what to do with it anymore, isn't that true chérie?"

Osman laughed. "Counting money, warfare, that's for the others. I prefer the simple pleasures of life." Elaine, enjoying him and entertained by Sana, picked up the cards and began to play. The servants lingered behind them offering seafood hors d'oeuvres and refreshing their drinks.

Osman picked up his binoculars and focused on a massive white yacht moving across the water. "Perhaps Khasshoggi takes a day off. Perhaps Khashsoggi concludes another arms deal."

Osman put the binoculars down while Sana studied the cards in front of her. "It all depends on who he's got on board with him, darling." She looked back at Osman. "Abed's not coming?"

"No," replied Osman, "he decided at the last minute he had other things to do."

Osman walked across the deck of the boat and placed a card from her hand onto the others. Sana's throaty laughter rang out. "Osman, if I need your help, I'll call."

Osman smiled and sat down with his gin and tonic and picked up the novel he was reading. "The author's premise is that all men are unfaithful. I don't know that I agree with that."

Nura gazed down at the spiraling coral reefs below the water's surface. "All men are unfaithful." Nura's voice floated quietly in the still, humid air. She walked over from the edge of the boat and stretched out on the deck chair. "Perhaps it is that they don't care. Or perhaps," Elaine watched as Nura's deep green eyes held her for a moment, "or perhaps it is that they care too much."

Nura stretched her arms above her head. Osman seemed intrigued.

"And the women?" asked Elaine.

Nura turned to her. "The women? There is a belief in the Arab world that whenever a man and a woman are left in a room alone there is a third person standing with them, the devil tempting them to follow their desires. Perhaps an unsophisticated thought. There is a belief that it is the woman who in fact has the stronger desires, the woman who is weak and will fall to them and will ultimately tempt the man. It is a belief so strong in this part of the world that it has led to the women being secluded, veiled, protected. Not against the men, but against themselves and their desires, really. The men follow. Perhaps another unsophisticated idea. Perhaps true."

"But is it the same thing that they want?" Osman asked thoughtfully.

"Not at all. A woman wants a man's body. But beyond that what she truly wants is his soul. It is not a thing that is done quickly."

She stood and walked to the edge of the boat.

Osman watched her with appreciation. "Sometimes, Nura, I feel you are two, three different minds, different people."

"Perhaps I am, Osman." She brushed her hair back. "Or perhaps it is simply like the truth—you will never really know it."

She bent over and picked up the diving equipment. "Osman, this looks like a good spot here. Tell them to stop the boat." She turned to Elaine. "Won't you come with me?"

Osman glanced up from his book. "Nura is a mermaid in the water, Elaine, she swims like the fish through the coral reef. You've scuba dived before?"

Elaine stood up unsteadily on the boat rocking on the swell. "Yes, but it's been a while. I am not too good, really."

"Don't worry, the equipment is fine. I checked it myself," said Nura.

Nura helped Elaine strap on the tank. She smiled slowly, then put her hands on the ladder, elegantly stepped down and slipped into the water. Beneath the surface she turned and dove deeper and deeper into the blue-green sea. Elaine climbed slowly down the ladder, turn and swam hard, trying to follow.

Nura slid effortlessly through the hollows of the brilliant reefs, spinning past the fabulous fish that swam around them. They moved farther and farther away from the boat. Elaine dove deeper, fascinated by the reefs, the fish.

She looked up and saw Nura far ahead of her. Nura motioned her forward. She followed Nura who waited for her to catch up. Then Nura pointed at the brilliant fish and plant life deeper down. Elaine shook her head, but Nura motioned her to follow. She dove deeper following Nura's green suit and long legs. Deeper they went, Nura pointing to the fish, the coral, swimming ever downward.

Suddenly Elaine felt her breath begin to catch. She moved her hands quickly to the oxygen controls, struggling to adjust them for more air. The tiny lever broke off in her hand. Terrified, she looked around frantically for Nura. Nura watched her for a moment, the jerking wave of Elaine's arm pointing to the tank. Stunned, Elaine watched Nura suddenly turn and swim off in the distance.

Osman, for an extra precaution, had sent one of the yatch's small boats out to keep an eye on the two swimmers. It was the boat boy who saw her. He dove quickly for Elaine who was thrashing toward the top of the water. Sana looked over the deck railing, horrified, while he put his arm around Elaine and swam with her to the ladder, bringing her onto the ship. He stretched her out and pulled the gear off while the others came running. Osman looked down, shocked, while she gasped for air.

Elaine opened her eyes to see Nura's green eyes looking down at her.

🗵 🗵 🗵

Elaine, profoundly shaken, returned to the little house in the embassy compound later that night. She turned on the light. She was startled by the abrupt knock on the door.

"Delivery m'am." The hurried errand boy thrust the box of flowers at her. She closed the door and opened the box. The explosion catapulted the box from her hand. Her scream ripped through the compound.

Terrified, her hand trembling, she called first Ray, then Tarek. Ray arrived within minutes and sat with her for an hour.

He glanced up at the clock.

"Tarek said he was coming over?"

"He said he'd put a trace on all vehicles entering the compound and then be over."

"Will you be OK if I leave to take the shreds of the box over to the lab? The analysis might be useful." Elaine nodded yes but was in fact frightened. She watched Ray leave to rush the materials to the lab. She looked at the clock praying Tarek would come.

Across the city, Tarek listened to the report on the efforts to trace a vehicle. The trace on the delivery proved fruitless. He got up, walked out of the office and drove home.

Like a man going mad, he pushed open the door of the bedroom and tore open the drawer holding Nura's journals. Violently, he began searching through the pages for something, anything. The pages spewed up at him, empires, history, religion, philosophy. The complexities of an unfathomable mind. Passions that were deep, brilliant, dark. Sensibilities that flowed one into another, a continuum that all wove together like some ceaseless, ingenious tapestry.

He looked up as Nura walked in. Her stunned face saw the notebooks strewn wildly across the floor. She stood absolutely still, staring at him.

Her eyes held him as she leaned forward to touch him. She saw him recoil. He stood up and walked out of the door.

"Where are you going?" Her voice was a whisper, remote.

The door shut and he was gone.

He stood before her when she opened the door to his voice.

"Tarek," whispered Elaine. She stopped, unable to go on. He walked inside and closed the door behind him. Without a word he drew her to him. His hand traced the side of her face, the tears coming from her eyes. He drew her body ever closer, as though to absorb it into his. His mouth touched her eyes, her cheek.

"Do you want to go?" His eyes held her. "I will understand if you want to go." A sob racked her body. "Tarek, they are going to kill us all. oh God…"

He held her and brought his mouth onto her's. "You can go, tell me…" She moved blindly toward his mouth, took his hand and moved it to her face.

"Tarek…" In answer her hand careened across his face, stroking it, scratching it. She drew back, horrified at the blood on her fingernail. He held onto her. "You can go," he whispered. She felt like she was going to break apart then she felt him lay her softly across the bed, never leaving her until the morning came.

39

Naila opened the pouch that would go back with the others to the hospital. In the darkened clinic's backroom, she stuffed in the materials for Elaine and fastened the clasp. She heard the sound of footsteps; turning around, she was startled to see Musaid standing there.

Quickly she dumped the pouch on the floor with the others. Musaid continued to stare as she called out, "Musaid?"

"Why are you still here? Your fiancé and his family are starting to ask questions." His voice was abrupt, the tense face enraged.

"They needed a doctor," she began softly, "to oversee the clinic here. I thought that..."

"What kind of a place is this for you?" His spat out the words harshly. "I didn't give you permission to do this."

"Musaid, I'm very happy here. I informed Tarek and Nura that it would be a bit longer and they..."

Musaid's hand shot out and slapped her across the face. "You don't *inform*."

Suddenly behind them came the soft sound of sandals. Aziz, the bedu boy, stood behind them. The boy's deep eyes held Musaid, while his hand moved down to the dagger at his waist. Musaid wheeled around and stared at him.

"Who is this?"

"He's just a boy from the tribes who is helping us bring some of the Kuwaiti refugees into the clinic." She reached out to stop Musaid, fearful that he would harm the boy. The boy never moved. Musaid stood absolutely still, staring first at her, then at the boy.

"You help the refugees across the border into the clinic?" Musaid's question now seemed genuinely curious. The boy nodded. Musaid listened while the boy explained how they came across the border in search of aid, and he and others helped them reach the clinic. The boy, saying nothing about the movements of the Special Operations team which he guided going the other way, fell silent as Musaid continued to stare at him.

Finally Musaid looked past the boy and back to Naila. "Another week, Naila, that's all. I want you to tell them you have been called back home. I want this to end." He departed as abruptly as he had come.

⊠　⊠　⊠

Back at headquarters, Elaine picked up the phone when the colonel indicated it was Naila on the other end. She listened to Naila's concerns about Musaid, his threat to bring her back to Riyadh.

"Tarek will take care of it," said Elaine. "Naila, you are alright otherwise?" She asked softly, then listened to her affirmtive response. "Good," she said and hung up the phone.

Elaine turned back to Ray. "There is another message—about 'the bedu,' 'the Palestinian.' About 'transferring the material for Saudi Arabia.' Something about 'the marshes.' I keep picking up 'Mecca.' " She shook her head as the frustration grew. "But I don't get enough to make sense out of it all. After the 'materials' comes something about the subsequent ability to shut the entire country down." She handed him the sheet of paper. "The small amount of info that passed through the embassy yesterday—it showed up in Iraq almost immediately." She paused. "So did the entire conversation from Fahd's cabinet meeting yesterday."

"This is lethal," breathed Schwarzkopf heavily. "We're going to be massacred unless you find out who's doing this, and how it's done. The rest of what we do won't make any difference, unless…"

The colonel from intercepts interrupted them to pass Ray and Schwarzkopf the latest sheet. "The Dutch firm just shipped Iraq, via Jordan, night vision devices to equip their tanks." Ray wadded up the paper and threw it on the ground. "So much for sanctions, the U.N. embargo."

Elaine held out the material from the Special Ops pouch that had just arrived from Naila. "They've infiltrated up to Samarra. The chemical plant is working round the clock. The manufacture of Scuds is more than we thought they had the capability for."

Tarek's car pulled up outside. Ray reached for the Terrorist Unit report he had ready for him and walked out to meet him.

Suddenly a car swerved forward toward Ray. It accelerated. Elaine screamed as the car headed directly for Ray. He stood as though frozen. Tarek swung around. With a lunge he pushed Ray back into his car, and his driver fired his machine gun at the car heading for them. The blast shattered the car window. The car spun wildly into a tree. The bodyguard rushed forward with his gun and opened the door. The young man was slumped dead over the wheel. The small paper the man had brought to pin on Ray's dead body lay beside him on the seat. It had two lines.

"God is Great. Death to those who would stand in His Way."

❊　❊　❊

From the clinic window, Naila saw Tarek's grandfather carrying the body. The old man walked slowly across the desert, Aziz, the bedu boy in his arms. The boy's eyes were closed, his body lifeless. Her heart froze in her chest as she felt her legs buckle beneath her. The red and white kaffiyeh lying over his throat was covered in blood. The old man's grief-stricken eyes held her as he gently laid the body down on the clinic floor. Naila fell to her knees, sobbing as she held the dead boy. She looked at the blood-stained kaffiyeh and then up beseechingly at the old man. Gently he reached down and pulled the cloth away. The child's throat had been slit.

"He was lying in the desert when I found him." He shook his head in grief. "No one saw anything. They used the boy's own dagger to kill him." The boy's dagger, covered with blood, had been placed back in its leather sling.

Naila, crying, stood up and reached for her abaya. She took the cloth and began to wash the boy, whispering softly to him. When she had finished, she wrapped the still body in a white cloth. Silently the old man carried the body to the desert to be buried with the bedu.

By the end of the day, bodies from one of the Special Ops team, who had worked with the boy, were also laid upon the clinic floor.

Schwarzkopf smashed his fist down on the table as he read the report. The pain on his face silenced the room, anguish echoed in his voice when he finally spoke.

"We can't stop the operation. It's our only hope. Pray to God, the boy and his team didn't have any indications with them of the rest."

They heard Ray's voice, strained. "Turn on the monitor."

He leaned across Schwarzkopf and switched the channel. Everyone in the Black Hole was suddenly quiet when the picture of the congressional vote came on. They watched the tense, concerned faces of the members casting their votes.

"They've given Bush the OK to wage war if Saddam doesn't pull out by January 16th." The room was strangely silent. Ray thrust them the newspapers from the overnight State Department pouch.

"They can't believe that Saddam would go up against all of this. They all talk about how crazy he would be, he'll certainly back down, how only a megalomaniac would threaten his own country with such destruction." Schwarzkopf's voice came up behind them.

"A megalomaniac would do that—so would someone who knows that their mole inside could sabotage the entire U.S. effort." Schwarzkopf held out another newspaper headlining the disappearance of a laptop computer one of the British officers from Allied Command had accidentally left in a taxi. The article talked of the terror this incident could unleash—that it could undermine all the plans.

"They are terrified by this," mused Schwarzkopf, "Christ, if they only knew the real truth." He stopped unable to go on.

Tarek looked at him, then walked outside as the street lights turned on. The steaming heat of the pavement rose up as he walked in silence, a man for whom time was running out. Lost in thought, he was startled by a tap on his shoulder—Badr stood there.

"Hamid got a communication through. He just heard Antar talking to what was clearly the agent within the Royal Family."

Tarek's head shot up.

"He says it was the end of the conversation, he didn't get any information, but he is sure he can obtain the secure phone line on which they communicate."

Tarek felt an almost incredible surge of hope. He closed his eyes like a man just thrown a lifeline.

Badr nodded, out of breath. "Tarek, he thinks if he monitors the phone line closely enough he can get it."

❊　❊　❊

Hamid put the papers down on Antar's desk. He glanced at the note Antar had left him saying when he would return. The old janitor was shuffling down the empty halls, sweeping up the debris of the day. Hamid nodded to him and started to close the door behind him. It was midnight.

The phone began to ring. He hesitated, then picked up the receiver of Antar's secure phone. He heard the satellite beep the code for Saudi Arabia. Quickly he moved his hand to the controls under the desk to activate a tracer, speaking quietly into the phone.

"Yes?" His hand fumbled, then pushed the button.

At first, the muffled hollow of the satellite phone connection filled the silence. And then he heard the quiet breathing on the other end.

"Yes?" He repeated watching the clock for the time needed to record the trace. "Would you like to speak to Antar?" He dragged the words out, counting the seconds. "Shall I put Antar on the phone? Can you hear me?"

The quiet breath on the other end held for a moment more. And then the small click of a receiver hanging up.

Hamid stood up quickly and went to the communications control room. He unlocked the door, pressed the buttons on the trace machine, and waited for the sheet to appear.

Slowly the paper fed out of the laser printer. "INSUFFI- CIENT TIME TO TRACE. INSUFFICIENT TIME TO TRACE"

Exhausted, he crumpled the paper and dropped it into the waste basket. He walked back to the office and began to close the door when he saw the transmissions begin to come across.

Hamid watched the last of the transmissions move. The plan for shutting down Saudi Arabia, sabotaging the U.S. military. Then suddenly—the name. He rapidly committed the text to memory as the sounds of the Baghdad traffic faded into the dawn.

❈ ❈ ❈

Badr ushered in Minister of the Interior Naif for his meeting with Tarek. An hour later Badr pushed open the door to Tarek's office. "Tarek, Hamid has just contacted us. He says it is urgent—he has to meet with you tonight. He has information on Antar's plans."

Badr stopped abruptly when he saw Naif still sitting in the

chair before Tarek's desk. "Forgive me, I'm sorry, I didn't realize you were…"

Tarek swung around in his chair. His eyes bored into Badr who continued. "The helicopter is set to leave in thirty minutes."

Naif stood up to go and looked at Tarek curiously, "You have an agent attached to Antar you are meeting with tonight?"

Tarek nodded. "He says he has information on Antar's plans."

Hamid walked along the streets of Baghdad and turned into the small house on the side street. He didn't notice the man outside the house cutting the telephone wires or the car parked farther down.

He walked up the stairs to his room. He was reaching into the refrigerator when he heard the sound of the door open behind him, saw the two men with hoods over their heads.

The silencer pistols made barely a sound as their bullets spewed, twenty in all, into Hamid's body. The men checked the body swimming in blood on the floor, then walked out the door.

Tarek stood by the cliff entrance, waiting for the sound of pebbles falling which would signal Hamid's approach. There was only silence. His throat tightened. Another hour passed. Apprehension now deepened into a feeling of dread. Hamid was never late. Hamid must have sensed the suspicion, and yet he never once asked to be pulled out. Tarek watched the lights on the U.S.S. *Independence* as it moved north up the channel. He looked at his watch again, and now filled with forboding, made his way back to the helicopter.

✠ ✠ ✠

Badr saw the message coming in from Tarek. He picked up the phone. "Rashid, quick. All channels immediately. Hamid."

Rashid hung up and drew the code pad from his desk drawer and then began to scratch. When he was satisfied, he picked up the telephone and leaned back nonchalantly in his chair as the broadcaster answered on the other end.

"Talal, how is the family? Ah, wonderful. Look, we'd like to do an interview tonight with the head of the Sharia Court. Yes, yes, Sheikh Mohda. Yes, I think it would be both TV and Radio Riyadh. I'll make the arrangements."

The soundman adjusted the microphone on his robes while the old Sharia Court judge sat quietly in the high-domed room surrounded by books, intricately scrolled Korans, judicial interpretations. Rashid nodded approvingly. Then he handed the broadcaster a short list of typed questions.

"Talal, I would be most appreciative if you could use this intro and these three questions. You know, just as an opener. Perhaps you could be certain to read them exactly as is."

Talal glanced down at the perfunctory questions about the role of Sharia law in the society and nodded, bored. The technician gave the cue. Talal smiled for the camera and read

409

the intro welcome that Rashid had written, followed by the questions. The judge warmed to his subject and talked on for the next hour before the cameras about Mohammad's law.

Badr waited for Hamid's answer. The old judge droned on. Nothing moved on the board. "Rashid, rebroadcast."

The judge gathered his robes around him and prepared to leave. Talal, more bored than when he had started, was taking off his microphone.

"Your excellency, Talal, that was fascinating. I think we will replay the broadcast again, for those who might have missed it earlier."

Talal, amazed that anyone would find the stupefying interview interesting, went home.

❊ ❊ ❊

Badr sat for the rest of the night hunched over the communications board. When Tarek came in, he simply shook his head.

Tarek walked back into his office and closed the door behind him. The sorrow, the despair that welled up inside him seemed beyond description. Hamid was dead. A friend, a loyal agent, gone. Murdered. His only hope, his only tie to the information, severed.

He sat there, a man who had forced Fahd to agree to cooperate with the U.S., engineered the thousands of U.S. troops coming in. And who now wondered if he had in fact led them all to their deaths.

Elaine came in and quietly sat beside him. She reached over to touch his hand. She watched the grief on his face. There were no words to say. Her hand moved softly up the side of is face. Her other hand took his.

"Come with me," she said gently. She took him back to her small house and closed the door. And through the night she made love to him. Through the night she tried to comfort him with a gentleness burned out of her own pain. Like water searching the path of a stream, her hands, her mouth, her body moved over him as she tried to soothe a pain that she alone could understand.

40

In the night Antar's aide received the call. Antar's voice simply said, "It is time to proceed. Commence the final plan." The aide checked quickly on Yusif Khalidi's progression. And placed the call. Down into the bowels of Basra.

⬥ ⬥ ⬥

The old man ferrying the Palestinian archaeologist poled the boat through the water lilies. They moved slowly north, away from Basra and the sounds of gunfire. Yusif glanced down at the equipment he was bringing and then back up at the strange nether world they were entering.

The tiny islands of the marsh dwellers began to appear, floating in the stillness of the deep marshes of the Tigris and Euphrates. The extraordinary shapes of pale-yellow reed huts standing on these tiny islands, some no larger than twenty feet by twenty feet, rose up in front of them. Standing in the mist like primitive straw cathedrals, the oval domes with flying buttresses of woven reeds floated in this insular world, built as they had been built since the time of ancient Sumer.

Yusif pointed from the far end of the canoe toward a hut.
The old man tied a rope from the bow to a branch on the the
island, and Yusif stepped onto the edge of the reeds. A woman,
wrapped in her black scarves, was sitting in front of the hut
milking a water buffalo. The animal eased past Yusif, silently,
back into the water, and the woman motioned Yusif toward the
door. He bent down and entered the single oval room of the
reed hut, where they were waiting for him.

His eyes accustomed themselves to the dark. He saw the old
father and his three sons, sitting cross-legged on the rug
stretched across the reeds of the floor. Behind them, a young
girl in bright skirts tended two babies playing on the floor and
chewing pieces of flat bread. The men handed Yusif the hookah
to smoke.

Yusif inhaled and passed the pipe back to the father,
listening to the faint sounds of the mortar fire in the distance.

He considered the old man and the sons. They were oblivious, he thought, to the fighting that raged over the marshes
between Iraq and Kuwait. They sat, as always, simply waiting
for the smoke to settle, turning a blind eye to the deserters
hiding in the reeds. Going on about their business, hoping to be
forgotten.

The women brought food while the men listened to Yusif's
account of how Baghdad fared. Picking up the rice from the
platter in front of them, working it in their fingers, they listened
until he was finished. Then the old man nodded to the eldest
son.

The son went to the corner of the hut, dug in the straw
beneath the rug, and brought out a small reed basket. He
carried it over to Yusif and laid it in front of him. In the
basket were small shapes wrapped in pieces of dirty cloth.

Yusif gently picked up the first shape and unwrapped it. He

413

brought the object toward the light of the brazier. And then he drew his breath.

It was a small, perfectly smooth black quartz statue of a man. His eyes gazed contentedly ahead, cloth over one shoulder of his erect figure, his hands clasped in front of him. A small smile crossed the lips beneath the straight nose. Yusif gazed at the symmetrical serenity of the pose, the clear detail, and gently, awed, laid the piece from ancient Sumer, the earliest civilization known to man, on the straw in front of him.

He reached for the next piece while the men watched. Slowly he unwrapped the cloth and examined the green clay and bronze figure. The benign smile of the woman above the rounded bronze belly of her fertility caught the light. Yusif turned the figure slowly in his hand and marveled at the work, the tiny precise etchings of the face, the feet, the magnificent movement from within that these artists from four-thousand years before Christ had been able to capture.

"This one," said the son, producing another, "came from the North."

Yusif took it from him. As the cloth unwound he saw the raised right hand, the carved jewels and tall headdress above the detailed flowing gown. He held the miniature deity from Hatra perfectly still before the light.

"These are magnificent," he said finally.

The son nodded. "There is one more you will like especially." He handed Yusif a small plaque wrapped in cloth. Yusif pulled the cloth away and gazed at the tiny, exquisitely carved piece of ivory. An ivory plaque inset with a deep bed of coral carved in the design of a flower above a flawless rendering of a lion and a young boy. A priceless piece from Nimrod. The eldest son smiled.

"When the Europeans came to dig in the old places, we saw

them take away many of the beautiful things. These we keep." He took the money Yusif offered him with a nod. Yusif continued to turn the small ivory plaque in the light of the brazier. He glanced back at his photography equipment. "I have my equipment with me, but if I could take them back with me where the light is better…"

The son nodded, "Take them, photograph them, and bring them back to us, but tell no one. We help you, our friend. The rest we don't trust."

The young wife poured some more tea as the night began to set in. Finally Yusif stood up and motioned to the old boatman waiting outside that it was time to leave. He carried the basket and settled it into the canoe in the dark.

"I will photograph them and return them tomorrow by nightfall," he said.

The boatman pushed off into the dark waters and began to weave the boat slowly back toward Basra. Yusif closed his eyes and thought of the treasure he had in front of him. The Europeans had plundered the tells in the early 1900s, but many of the Iraqi diggers had seen from their European employers how valuable these artifacts were and had become ingenious at hiding pieces for themselves despite the strip searches and beatings to weed out the thieves. Yusif gazed at the exquisite, previously unseen treasures lying in front of him as the old boatman poled on. He closed his eyes and thought of the beautiful face from Hatra beneath the headdress, while the sounds of mortar echoed faintly in the stillness of the marshes as they drifted silently back toward Basra.

Suddenly he felt a bump. He opened his eyes and saw a man with a lantern in his hand, a kaffiyeh wrapped below his eyes, pull alongside their canoe. The man spoke to the old boatman quietly, while Yusif strained to hear. The old man answered what seemed to be two questions, moving his hands as he talked, then turned to Yusif. "He says he has something for you. You must go with him."

The man with the lantern moved toward Yusif and a second man from the back of their canoe stood up from the darkness. "Professore, we know of your work. We have something for you."

Yusif hesitated, thinking of the risks, following an unknown through the marshes. He looked at the old boatman who had carried him through the earlier trips. The old man nodded to him. "I have arranged it. Go quietly. You will be safe." Yusif stood up and stepped across into their boat.

The man with the lantern motioned him down into the hull of the canoe. They picked up the reed basket and his equipment. One man murmured to the other and then placed a heavy cloth over Yusif, blocking out any light. Next, layers of reeds. They spoke once more, and then the only sound that Yusif heard while he struggled to breathe was the soft slide of the reeds, the lapping of the water as the canoe moved through the marshes.

Yusif could hear the lowing of a water buffalo, then felt its bulk swimming, moving, then nothing. Sounds of voices, radio calls, drifted from the Basra harbor. The sound became fainter until only the soft slide of the reeds against the canoe remained.

Yusif felt the mud thicken beneath the bottom of the boat, then a thud as the boat slid to a halt along land. One of the men leaned over and pushed the reeds off him, and then pulled him up. The man holding the lantern motioned him to follow.

He began to walk unsteadily on the land, through the soft mud. Ahead of him he could make out a dim light. The men said nothing as they walked on toward the light. He heard a door open and then one of the men motioned him to a halt.

The other went forward through the door. In a moment, he motioned Yusif inside.

Yusif's eyes blurred for a moment. He dimly made out the radio equipment lying around the shack. Guns, rifles, and pistols were strewn on the ground; charts and papers covered the old chairs. Finally he saw a man behind an old wooden desk looking at him. He turned as one of the men came in and placed the reed basket and the camera equipment beside him, then left. Yusif looked back to the man sitting quietly in front of him, at his black hair, his black shirt sleeves rolled up, and his eyes, dark and penetrating.

The man got up from behind the desk and walked toward Yusif. He stopped in front of him, glancing at him curiously, then bent down, picked up the basket, and carried it back to his desk. Slowly, gently, he picked the objects out of the basket and unwrapped them, examining them one by one.

When he had placed the last one on the desk in front of him, he turned back to Yusif. Then, in accented but perfect English, he said, "Professor, I am an admirer of your works."

He turned the small black quartz statue in his hand, gazing at it under the light as he continued. "Your volume on ancient Sumer I thought particularly excellent. I am surprised though, that you deal in contraband. I would have thought..." He let the sentence trail off. "A man of your stature?" He shrugged. "Ah, but there is a lot of money to be made, and then, one must live."

Yusif didn't move. The man leaned forward.

"Please forgive me, you would like a cigarette? Some tea? Please," he motioned him to a chair, "sit."

A man from outside came in and brought him a small cup of tea, lit a cigarette and handed it to him. Yusif watched the man behind the desk with the elegant English, the fine features, the eyes looking seriously, thoughtfully at him.

"Why have you brought me here?" Yusif asked.

The man put his hand forward, silencing him, the dark eyes never leaving Yusif.

"It is not this contraband, Professor, I have brought you here to talk about. I think," he said leaning back in his chair, "we have far more important matters to discuss. Far more important. I have something of significance to give you."

He stopped at the sound of footsteps outside the door. He stood up and walked to a man standing there, waiting. The courier drew him outside into the dark and then handed him some papers. "The reports from Saudi Arabia are in."

The man nodded, took the papers, put them in his pocket and walked back into the room where Yusif waited. He sat down again and picked up his cigarette then continued as though uninterrupted.

"Yes, I have something to give you."

A barrage of mortar fire echoed over Basra from Kuwait. Then quieted. Antar looked at Yusif in front of him. Everything had gone as planned. This one could be extremely useful if he chose. He could be useful even if he didn't choose.

Antar looked back to Yusif.

"I do hope you will forgive the events of this evening, the intrusion. However, I have something to discuss with you that I think will be of great interest to you, to your work."

Antar listened for a moment to the radio transmitter behind him. He turned back to Yusif. "I would like you to go with me for a short while to another place. I have some artifacts that I think you will find quite intriguing, perhaps important. That, of course, will be for you to decide. Another cigarette?"

Yusif accepted one from the proffered box, and Antar walked around the desk and flashed a lighter to its tip.

"Allow me."

He looked at Yusif bending forward to the light, the classic Palestinian features, the black hair flecked with gray, the trimmed moustache, the dark-lined eyes. A certain aesthetic precision to his look. Perhaps a sybaritic element to the hands. He closed the lighter.

"I do not wish to make a mystery of this really. I am greatly embarrassed by the crude measures of the early evening. It is hardly the welcome for a man of your stature. But," he waved impatiently, "the times are such." He sipped his tea. "It is a small place here in the marshes. Frankly, I find it a refuge of quiet in these times. We can talk here. I can, I assure you, guarantee your safety. You will be free to leave at any time you wish."

Yusif hesitated for a moment, then silently nodded.

"Excellent. It is only a short distance through the marshes." Yusif leaned over to pick up his equipment when Antar moved toward the door.

"You won't need that now. Leave it, it will be safe here."

The small boat poled silently past the water buffalo, through the reeds. Antar smiled while the old man guided the boat through the dark.

"It is the tranquillity really in the marshes, the stillness. But perhaps you experience that at the digs, also. For me, it is only here." He lay back in the hull of the boat. "You once photographed a beautiful harp that came from the tomb of Ur, an exquisite thing inlaid with gold and pearl beneath an arc of an animal's head. And I have often thought how fascinating it would be to know the music that was played upon it. Perhaps we would be stunned by a different tonal system, a different movement, a different ethos of sound altogether."

The boat bumped gently against a tiny marsh island.

"Please," Antar smiled, "we are here."

The smell of kerosene was pungent for an instant when he lit the lantern and then faded into the cool night air. He offered Yusif a hand, as he put his foot upon the island, and then motioned Yusif to follow him. The lantern lit up the beautiful ancient designs of red, yellow, blue, within the cocoon of the painted reed house. The lines and geometry and tones swam up from the patterns of the carpets laid upon the woven reeds of the floor, all of it rocking ever so gently on the night waters. Antar lit the brazier in the middle of the room, and Yusif waas startled to see two of his books in the corner. Alongside them was a small cardboard reproduction of one of Yasmina's paintings. The light flickered.

Antar smiled without looking up from his brazier, "I have been a longtime admirer of your work, as you see." He dropped the match into the fire and stood up, warming his hands. Then he stretched out alongside the fire, closing his eyes for a moment.

"Forgive me, it has been a long, somewhat difficult day. It would give me great pleasure if you too could relax."

"Your lecture series was successful, I hope. And now I believe you go on to Madain Saleh and other points for the photography? Really, a remarkable work, this book. I am greatly looking forward to it. So little is known in the West about our ancient civilization."

Yusif said, "You seem to know a great deal about my plans."

"Oh well, the Gulf is a small place. And you are quite well known. Welcomed by all." Antar turned and leaned on his elbow toward the brazier.

"I, in fact, first saw your work back in the States, learned that you were a Palestinian." He moved one of the coals with a stick. "I can't tell you what solace it was to see your work on

Middle Eastern civilization. One felt so tremendously deracinated at times, studying abroad, surrounded by people who knew nothing of the magnificence of our past, our culture, who despised us as ignorant foreigners."

Yusif watched him. Antar touched the coals again with the stick.

Yusif spoke quietly, "You are Iraqi? You are involved in the government, politics?"

"Yes, I am Iraqi. The government, politics, well, it is difficult these days not to be involved at some level. But then, that really is irrelevant to our discussion. You are Palestinian, are you not? But your involvement seems minimal; you have little interest?"

"I leave that to others. I have no interest."

"No interest, none. I see. Well, it is unimportant really."

Antar sat up closer to the fire, "I want to help you. Perhaps it is the intellectual yearnings of an intellectual gone astray. We are, you know, caught up in difficult times. My life has not taken the academic direction I once as a student thought it might," he smiled at Yusif. "However, as I say, I am a great admirer of your work. I have spent much of the time in the past few years here in the marshes and so I knew of your coming. I know that you are looking for the artifacts that the people have held away from the museums. There are two that you have not seen yet that I think you will find exquisite. I came upon them myself when a part of the old city in Basra was hit by mortar during the war with Iran."

Antar handed Yusif a piece of flat bread lying beside the brazier. "I am, you see, in a rather awkward position. The very cradle of civilization lay here in ancient Sumer, in the heart of Iraq. Our brilliant military leaders were able to rule all of the Middle East within a single empire, our art and music permeated the entire Middle East and down into the subcontinent." Yusif watched the man's dark eyes as he continued.

"So you see, I feel strongly about this. These earlier magnificent periods of history need to be known, understood by the world. They have created us and our perception of the world. I may be in need of money later, therefore, I keep them. But I wish them to be seen, understood. I hope you now understand my need for such secrecy and that I can trust you in this matter."

Yusif remained still, studying the man's complex face. "You have them here with you? I'd like to see them."

Antar shook his head and glanced at his watch. Only a little more time was necessary now.

"I have one here; the other I will bring. I wanted to meet with you first to determine your interest. You will be going to Madain Saleh from here? You can return to Basra when you are finished there, and they will be here. Call the hotel for a room in Basra when you are leaving Madain Saleh, and I will know you are here and contact you."

Antar reached for a tin of water and put it on the fire, smiling. "Ah, you see I stayed in the United States so long I have forgotten my manners. I have not offered you tea."

He stood up and went to the side of the room for the small cups while Yusif watched him. He had so far not asked him to take any contraband out of the country, to sell any items on the black market. Perhaps that came next. He hardly, however, seemed like the bedu from the digs coming to him with artifacts rolled in cloth stuffed in their thobes asking for a price only to photograph the material. He thought of his materials back in the man's headquarters. He'd done more than that already by trying to carry the marsh artifacts back to his hotel room to photograph them in better light. The man seemed to have no interest in that, no innuendoes of compromise, apprehension.

"You stay in Baghdad mostly?" Antar asked pleasantly, walking back with the cups of tea.

"May I see the one you have here?"

"Certainly," Antar put the cups down. He went to the far corner of the room and put his hand where the reeds of the sloping wall met the floor. Slowly he pulled out a small bundle. He walked back and handed it to Yusif. "I think you will find it fascinating."

Yusif unwrapped the cloth and looked at the tiny exquisite bronze figure. Antar spoke pleasantly. "Please, examine it. I will be outside."

Antar walked out into the wet night air. He pulled the small signal machine from his pocket. The tiny green light was on. They were done. The materials had gone into Yusif's equipment satisfactorily.

He listened to the stillness of the night, the small sound of the thrushes burrowing in the dark reeds. It was still stunning how effective they had been, how rapid. He mustn't let his fears derail him now. The Palestinians had been desperate, therefore useful, extremely useful. Now, one who had "no political interest" was perhaps to be the most useful of all. The symmetry of it pleased him. The archaeologist seeking the past would unknowingly leave the marshes a walking time bomb for the future. There was a grace to the silent sweep of the pendulum. Dealing funds out of the back of carpet shops to seed bands of dissidents throughout the Gulf. Slowly, methodically peeling off the bills to release them all into motion like hot encapsulated atoms ready to explode the old order of the Arab side of the Gulf and blow it to pieces. Yes, the coalitions had been building as they should. The small bands they had funded had grown, reaching well beyond themselves into the middle class, the technocrats.

Kuwait had been ripe. Arrogant, overly secure. Antar thought of his key people now in the oil fields, the ministries. Beautifully entrenched. The Sabah family who ruled Kuwait, a rich small country of a million and a half people, should have known they merely tottered on the edge of a morass. A population of whom only forty percent were citizens, living in a sea of disaffected foreign workers that outnumbered them.

Antar thought of his agent who had carried out the failed assassination attempt on the Kuwaiti emir in 1985. The emir lived on, but the terror grew. The explosions in the oil fields in June of 1986 had been the next key escalation.

Antar could see, as he breathed in the wet marsh air, those six men standing in the courtroom. Sentenced to death for trying to blow up the oil installations and overthrow the state. They had raised their hands as they stood locked in a steel cage and heard the verdict and shouted, "God is great!" while hundreds of people outside the courthouse had raised their fists when the verdict was read and screamed, "Death to America."

He thought for a moment of the explosion they had planned should the U.S. attack. The Kuwaiti oil fields would go up like a huge propane torch in the night, a funeral pyre of oil for the Sabah family. Yes, should it come to that, they would collapse this tiny artificial entity called Kuwait, spilling the Sabahs and their frightened little ruling group into the sea.

A sea, thought Antar, that would now belong to Iraq.

And so now it was time to turn his attention to Saudi Arabia. Antar turned back to Yusif in the reed hut who was still examining the tiny bronze figure. Saudi Arabia, the final linchpin of the Gulf.

"It is exquisite, is it not?"

Yusif looked up from the light of the brazier. "It is," he said quietly, "a very important find. It is one of the very few pieces that still exist from this era."

Antar nodded silently while Yusif wrapped the tiny figure back in the cloth. "I will bring the other so that you can photograph them when you return from Madain Saleh. Come, I have kept you long enough."

The old boatman poled them back to the small head-quarters shack. Yusif picked up his equipment. "I will call from Madain Saleh."

Antar watched the boatman take Yusif across the waters toward Basra until the boat faded from sight. "Tell the helicopter pilot I'm ready to go back to Baghdad," he motioned to his aide. "And contact Saudi Arabia. Tell them it is on its way."

The tiny squares of black plastic were now embedded in Yusif's equipment, fastened securely by Antar's technicians while he and Yusif had talked. Fastened in equipment that would move through borders without being examined by customs. Carried by a man who could tell the authorities nothing in the inconceivable event they ever found the material on him—because he would know nothing. Yusif, the perfect vehicle, carrying the final element of the plan. The technological element, the device, that in the sequence of events Antar had planned would ultimately bring the rest of the Gulf to its knees.

"Yes," he breathed to himself, "it is on its way."

He turned once more. "And the bedu?"

"It is being arranged."

Elaine stared silently at the two small pieces of paper the colonel from decoding had brought her. She looked back up at him.

"We think they are saying 'archaeology.' To run with the rest of the code it's got to be something like that. The transmissions moved between Baghdad and Basra." He stopped and saw she was waiting for him to continue. He brushed his hand across the paper in frustration, "The rest is the same as we've been getting 'bedu,' 'Palestinian.'"

Ray walked in and looked over her shoulder. "Saddam's stockpiling his material by the ancient archaeological sites around Iraq. The nuclear elements are already located there in the north. He knows the international community would hesitate before bombing them." Ray nodded his head toward the paper. "That's probably what it's about."

Elaine shook her head, "There's something about the flow of the transmissions. I don't know, something about the flow... 'archaeology,' 'bedu,' 'Palestinian.'"

"Yes? What?" Ray and the colonel now waited for her to continue.

She looked back up at them, the fatigue in her eyes matching that of her voice. "I don't know."

She stared back down at the paper. "Archaeology," "the Palestinian," "the bedu."

41

A faint knock sounded on the door of the house. Naila glanced at the clock and put down the medications sheet. A bedu, kaffiyeh wrapped around his face, stood at the door. He entered without speaking and Naila pulled back in fright. He unwrapped the kaffiyeh from his face, and Naila, relieved, recognized Captain Long of the Special Operations team. "Dr. Naila," his voice was low, "we have something we must ask you to do."

He paused, concerned by the exhausted shadows on Naila's face. Then he handed her the small piece of paper. "One of our men got this. It is about a cell located here. A meeting tonight. We have communicated the information to Tarek. He wants you to go."

The old house creaked in the night breeze. Naila looked around the empty room alarmed.

"You're sure *I* am to go?"

"I'm sure. The directions to the house are there." Captain Long silently turned, closing the door behind him. Naila looked once more at the empty house. She glanced down at the address and then walked out into night air.

She walked past the souk, the foothills silhouetted by the moon, toward the small cinder block and wooden houses at the outer rim of the village where the foreign workers lived. She peered at the numbers on the shanties, some painted on the sides of the houses, others missing, stepping back and forth along the dusty side street until finally she arrived at the unmarked house that she calculated must be the one. She saw a dim light through curtains on the window and knocked on the door. She stood outside, covered in her black abaya until the door opened.

"I am here…"

The woman raised her hand to silence her, then ushered her into the back of a dark room filled with women of all ages.

"Sit," whispered the woman. "It has begun already."

Naila struggled in the dim light to see through the dark cloth of her abaya as she sat on the floor behind the others. Their eyes remained fixed on a screen in front of them.

The small room held young women, poor women, Pakistani and other foreign workers, a few bedu women from the tribes around the foothills. At the front of the room stood a screen. A young woman's face appeared on the screen. The narrator's voice on the cassette began to speak.

"Zahra Rahnavard is a graduate of several guerrilla training centers in Lebanon." The voice stopped while the cassette flickered for a moment. The young woman on the screen began to talk, eyes burning.

"Compared to our veil, America's atom bombs are nothing. The veil must be seen as the greatest achievement of Muslim women in the past hundred years. The veil protects us from the ills of invading cultures; we feel safe behind it. As long as Muslim women retain their veils, Islam can continue to triumph."

Naila listened, watching uncomprehendingly while the women around her murmured approvingly. She looked back to the screen at the front of the room. The camera showed a mullah sitting to the right of the woman on the screen. The mullah placed some papers in front of him and began to speak.

"Leading Muslim women astray is part of a plot by 'the foreign enemies of Islam' to spread prostitution in Muslim countries and make 'our youth forget their duty of fighting for the Faith.' I read this statement on the murder of Anwar Sadat in 1981. The Egyptian Islamic Jihad knew the dead president's 'greatest treachery was the encouragement of sexual license in the country.' The number of full-time or part-time prostitutes in Cairo and its suburbs exceeded 250,000. The treatment of women as the equals of men by the government of President Bourguiba in Tunisia has for years been a source of shame."

Naila listened to the women around her again murmur their approval. The man on the screen stood up and walked toward the camera, his voice strident.

He pointed to a picture lying on the table in front of him. The camera zoomed in to the photo of a young girl's face.

"I will show you a virtuous girl's face." The mullah pointed to the picture. "Sumayah Sa'ad joined the Party of Allah's Sayyedah Zaynab Brigade—the first of several female Shiite commando groups—in 1983 when she had just turned sixteen." He held the picture more closely to the camera and continued.

"Longing to die and to kill, she volunteered for the Entehari, the suicide operation against the American Marines' dormitory in Beirut. She was accepted and trained for that mission. At the last moment, however, her commanders decided that the mission should be carried out by a man."

The mullah then looked directly at the camera.

"But Sumayah's chance to become a Bride of Blood would come. More than two years later, on March 10, 1985, she was allowed to drive a car loaded with dynamite into an Israeli military station in southern Lebanon. It was the fifth confirmed

Entehari attack on Israeli positions in southern Lebanon since 1982. She killed twelve Israeli soldiers and wounded fourteen others."

Naila sat stunned in the back of the dark room as the cassette stopped.

The woman at the front of the room smiled at the women seated before her in the dark, then pulled the cassette out and put in a second. "We have," she said proudly, "received this explicitly for us." Another young woman's face smiled at the camera and then began speaking.

"Women of Saudi Arabia, there are brave women among you, women who struggle to hold to the way of Islam. There are Enteharis among you, brave women who will step forward. The work that began with Johaiman's takeover of the Grand Mosque in 1979 continues. They have killed him, but they cannot kill his words."

The blurred videotape and the static sound filled the screen with a shot of Mecca. Then the screen showed a young man talking through a microphone. His words reverberated through-out the courtyard of the Grand Mosque in Mecca.

"There is no God but Allah! I am Johaiman, son of Muhammad, son of Sayf of the al-Utaibi tribe." His voice raged on.

"The hour promised by our Prophet—blessed be his soul—when Islam shall triumph over impiety has arrived. I and my brothers have been dispatched by the will of the Almighty to put an end to the rule of the corrupt, depraved, and eternally doomed princelings who have brought shame to Arabia and its Muslim people with their corruption, cupidity, and callousness.

"Believers!" Johaiman's voice screamed. "These princelings are interested in nothing but women, wine, money, games, and music. They abandoned Islam long ago, as soon as they saw the golden-haired women of the West and the glittering dollars of Aramco."

The women around Naila applauded while the shot flickered off and a young woman returned to the screen. "Johaiman was killed, but not his spirit," she said. "We held the Kingdom under siege for fourteen days while the Qahtani and the al-Utaibi tribes staged armed rebellions.

"Now," her voice rose as the camera zoomed in, "this was in the past. What are we doing today? How will we succeed now, so that the true Arab world may rise again?" She held up a tape and a book.

"Tapes, books, leaflets are now being smuggled into the country, along the coastal areas. Scores of your Saudi sisters are receiving revolutionary training, courses in terrorist activities. Saudi students in the U.S. and Europe have been recruited for radical demonstrations in Mecca.

"Our leaders will be with us, our headquarters in Mecca—a fitting statement for the rest of the world as the infidel U.S. tramples Arab soil and tries to thwart Saddam's resurrection of a mighty Arab world. We have the means to stop those forces. The plan, the work will unfold from Mecca. We will have cover there as simple hajjis coming to make the pilgrimage. The authorities are used to people from all points of the entire Muslim world streaming in. They will not check, or note our gathering."

She put the tape and book down and folded her hands on her lap. "What is our plan? It remains twofold. We will shut down the country through means which we now have, and we will sabotage the U.S. forces and their plans. We have means to tap into their communications and thus counter their every move. Then the people in the villages, the people in the cities will rise up and revolt in the name of Islam."

Suddenly, the woman standing by the monitor reached over to the machine. She quickly turned off the tape, pulling it out and placing it beneath the cushions of a chair. "My sisters," she said beneath her breath. "There is a policeman close by. Begin to talk as our instructions indicate."

The women began to talk about their children, their families. One began to pour tea.

Naila got up, pushed through the door, and walked quickly, then began running toward the clinic. She pushed open the clinic door. She reached for the telephone and dialed quickly. She listened, terrified, to the click on the other end and then closed her eyes in relief as a voice answered.

"Elaine, I need to come in tonight; please send somebody for me. It is urgent. Please tell Tarek I need to talk to him."

Elaine was waiting for her on the airstrip in Riyadh as the helicopter landed. She listened, stunned, to Naila's story and told the driver to take them immediately to Tarek.

▲▲ Tarek."

Tarek swung around. Naila stood silently in the doorway of his study, Elaine behind her.

Naila, unnerved, her face drawn, began to speak. Tarek became absolutely still as the story poured forth. When she was finished, her body began to shake and she tried to sit down. Elaine stepped forward.

"Tarek," she said quietly, "we need to get a woman back out there to infiltrate, you need to find someone who…"

Tarek shook his head, cutting her off. Elaine looked at him amazed, "But Tarek, this is critical, you need to find a woman who can..."

"We have one."

Elaine felt her body stiffen with apprehension as his gaze turned back to Naila. "Tarek, you can't..."

Tarek leaned toward Naila, his voice low. "Naila, I want you to go to Mecca." She drew back frightened at what he was suggesting.

"To Mecca?" she whispered.

"To Mecca. We will say they need extra house staff in the hospital. The women and children's section of the hajjis' unit."

"And what am I to do?"

"You will report back to me on the women you have seen in that meeting. They will be there."

"How soon would I leave?"

"In the morning."

Naila looked up at Elaine. Elaine remained silent, her eyes full of pain.

"Tarek," Naila whispered, "I'm afraid."

"I know."

Trembling, she stood up to leave. Tarek turned suddenly at the sound of the study door opening behind them.

"Tarek, I..." Her voice caught midword as she saw Said, frozen in the doorway as he saw Naila.

The glass she was holding dropped from her hand and shattered on the floor.

Elaine reached out for her, startled as Said stepped toward Naila, then stopped. "Naila, I tried to reach you so many times..."

Tarek's was stunned.

Said turned to face him, searching for the words. "Naila and

I would often have dinner in Washington. I was surprised to find her gone when I went last..." Tarek drew his breath quietly. "Tarek, I..." Tarek's hand reached out and stopped him midword as he observed the grief in his friend's eyes.

Said faced Naila and then slowly turned and left the room. Tarek stood absolutely still watching Naila's eyes follow him. The silence that Elaine felt engulf the room was now profound. "Naila..." he began.

"We were lovers, Tarek" She whispered finally, shaking. Tarek started to speak, holding his hand out to her. She interrupted him with her next, shocking words.

"Tarek," her voice shook, "I am pregnant."

Elaine's breath stopped in her throat. Tarek's hand stopped midair.

"I am pregnant with Said's baby. Oh, God, Tarek," her voice choked as she looked at him, "I am terrified." Her hand went to her mouth as the terror welled up in her.

He took both her hands in his while the implications of this revelation continued to unroll in his mind, the obvious becoming clear. Said had been in love with her for years.

N.S., Said's folder, "N.S." Naila Saud. Said had been trying to protect her, to move her money for her. His eyes took in her terror. Her assessment, her fears were valid. Musaid would never allow her to leave the country. He would kill her.

He touched her chin and turned her face up to his. Elaine was struck by the utter compassion in the man's face and his voice as he spoke.

"Naila, I can get you to a doctor so that Musaid will never find out."

Naila took his hand and shook her head.

"No," her voice strangled with emotion, "I don't want to have an abortion. I want to have this baby. I made arrangements for an abortion secretly and then realized I couldn't go through with it. In the desert I was going to do it myself, but every day I looked at the calendar, I knew time was starting to run out, but I couldn't make myself do it." Her eyes, desolate, inconsolable, locked with his. "I want this baby. I want Said, I want to live my life."

She looked at Elaine desperately, then at Tarek. "Tarek, I am suffocating here. I am in a cage. My life is at the whim of a brother for whom I have no regard, who can decide where I live, and now whether I live or die, or this baby dies. Tarek, I don't know what to do. I don't want to die but I don't want to live half alive anymore either."

Tarek's hand moved over her ravaged face.

"I can get you out of the country, Naila," he said quietly. "I can get money to you. I will get Said to you. No one else knows?"

She shook her head, her eyes wide.

"Good, say nothing. But Naila, realize if you go, if you marry Said, I can keep you safe. But," he looked at her sadly, "only as long as you don't return. I can't protect you here with this."

"I know."

Elaine watched while he held Naila silently as she cried. "I will arrange for you to leave from Mecca after you finished what I want you to do there." He looked gently into her eyes. "You love him very much, don't you? He is a lucky man. If I had picked a husband for you, it would have been him—you have picked the best, Naila. I am just understanding how much he was protecting you—even from me—at considerable risk to himself."

She held his hand for a moment, unaware of the the second reality he was now absorbing—that his suspicions about N.S. and Nura had been unfounded, a terrible irony.

"Tarek, I never saw my life coming to this, a choice that would force me to go. When I am gone—you and Nura will come to see me, won't you?"

"When you are gone, yes. But," his voice was worried, "be careful." His eyes fastened upon hers as he suddenly became afraid for her. "While you are here, Naila, be careful. Only a few more days and I will have you out, safe."

"I will." The shaking, the tears, had passed. Elaine could only watch the young woman's face, her own voice rendered wordless. She turned to go, then reached out to hold Naila's hand. Naila's eyes held her for a moment and then simply nodded. She watched Elaine go.

Naila then quietly left the room and walked up the stairs. She closed the massive wooden door of the women's quarters behind her and walked down the hall and over to the window. Said was standing by his car. She looked at his face, his eyes, his hand as he reached for the car door. She stood absolutely still, then hurried down the stairs, walking softly to the bottom of the staircase, past the Pakistani houseboy asleep in the hall, and out the door.

"Naila," Said turned around, astonished to see her. "Naila," he closed his eyes for a moment and then reached for her as she moved to him. She opened the door of Said's car and got in. Said's voice, full of love and concern, flowed over her like water in the desert.

"Aren't you afraid?"

Naila shook her head silently.

The desert road stretched through the sand as the outlines of the old ancient city of Dariyah rose up into the night, its crumbling parapets and clay towers like ghosts in the night sky. He drove to an old, abandoned archaeologist's cabin and stopped the car. He looked silently at her eyes, her hair, her mouth. "Naila," he said softly, "I have never known the words, how to tell you how much I love you. I want you, I always have."

She traced her fingers along his face and then opened the car door and began to walk toward the shack. She unhooked the latch and picked up the kerosene lamp inside it and struck a match. The small room of the shack appeared in the dim light, a dusty table next to a wooden chair, an old bed with a blanket on it in the silence of the desert night.

"Said, I have felt like I was dying," said Naila, "like I was slowly suffocating, that everything was slipping away from me, the doors all closing around me. Dreams, night after night, where I am falling, falling, and everyone looks on smiling and I try to scream and nothing comes out. I can't make the sound come out. Another dream where I am trying to climb up a ladder, a stair. It is hanging in midair, and I am trying to climb and I am slipping and there are people and no one will help; they look away as though they don't hear. And, my God," the sobs choked Naila as she relived the anguish. "Said, I love you so…"

He stretched the blanket across the old bed and put the kerosene lamp on the dust of the table next to it and stood there illuminated in the flame's glow. Slowly, gently he drew her to him. He caressed her face with his hands and then brought them down across her breasts and then along her belly as his mouth closed over hers.

She could feel her skin burning as his hand pulled the dress softly, slowly from her body. She stood transfixed in front of him in the glow of the lamp.

He gently, pulled the camisole down from her breasts, the pants to the floor. He stood for one more minute gazing at her, his eyes lovingly wandered over the round, full breasts and the soft mauve nipples. His hand traced the soft rounded belly and the baby within. "You are the most beautiful woman that ever lived," his voice whispered the words. He brought his head down to her stomach listening to the tiny heartbeat inside. She stroked his head as he listened, saw the tears in his eyes at the tiny life within. He looked up at her and seemed lost in her eyes. His mouth moved to her breasts, the beautiful dark hand along her thighs and then gently into the wetness between her legs, gently stroking the softness now on fire, probing gently, stroking until she felt waves flooding her body. She gasped and reached out and pulled his shirt open, reaching blindly for the dark, coarse chest. Searching with her hands for him, feeling him surge and throb as she pulled at his belt. "Oh God, Naila," he said softly, "how I have wanted you."

He pulled her down on the bed. With his mouth, his hands, he caressed her mouth, her nipples, her belly, the wet lips between her legs. Then as she reached for him he came into her filling her with the heat of his body, and her body swam with the pleasure, the pain, as he moved deep inside of her and she cried out. She began to move beneath him as he held her for a moment looking at her in his arms.

"I don't want to hurt you," he said softly.

"No, I want more," she breathed, "I want more."

His body came into hers moving, thrusting, pulsing, as his mouth and hands devoured her until finally she felt her body dissolve, explode beneath him, falling in exquisite pleasure. Falling as she gasped in pleasure beneath his beautiful dark eyes and his magnificent body. And then he held her as she lay breathing against him, in the thousand tiny noises of the desert night.

When they returned to Tarek's house, she held Said for a moment longer. And then she left to gather her suitcase for Mecca.

Musaid watched from his car in the dark.

42

The radio carried the sounds of the BBC Arabic service. "Tanks have moved across Basra heading southeast. Iraqi troops are poised at the Saudi border..." Elaine wrote rapidly and then handed the sheet with the code delineation to the colonel from the Black Hole who was waiting.

"We had one informant from within Iraq when we were tracing their acquisition of trigger mechanisms and other illegal supplies for their nuclear arsenal from London. He has been contacted about 'the bedu,' 'the Palestinian,' 'archaeology.' If he has anything it will be coming back in the code through this broadcast." She continued, becoming agitated but sosunding determined. "I know there is something to this."

The colonel returned shortly. He only shook his head. "There is no code that matches any of yours. It seems to be only the normal broadcast."

"Maybe...," began Elaine.

"Maybe," said Ray walking up behind her, "there is nothing in this broadcast or any others. Maybe he is dead, just like everybody else we touch."

They watched stunned, as Elaine picked up her coffee cup and smashed it against the wall.

Yasmina Tikriti turned off the small radio as the BBC broadcast ended. The sounds of the Baghdad traffic began to fade into the night as the cool river breeze and the low moaning and creakings of the boats drifted through the window. Yasmina leaned on one elbow with the sheets falling from her breasts as Yusif finished telling her the story.

"You came here directly from the marshes?" He nodded.

"Yusif, I am afraid for you." She lay back in bed and looked pensively toward the ceiling for a moment and then turned to him. "Don't go to your apartment. Stay here and leave for Madain Saleh from here, tomorrow, quickly. They are trying to use you."

She got up and began to pace in front of the half-finished painting on the easel. "How, for what, I don't know. But something is wrong. They are trying to use you, now, later, whenever. Trying to set you up with contraband so they can compromise you, get you to deliver information, messages, I don't know what."

"You're imagining things," he said.

"But I know these people, how they work. You must be very careful. It could be anybody here. In the museum, anybody, your colleagues at the academy. They all could be involved; you don't know, you can't tell." She put out the cigarette. "My husband had agents everywhere. People you would never think. They promise you things in your work, pull you in slowly, sometimes over the course of years, then they compromise you." She pulled her long black hair back with her hand. "And then they get you to work for them."

She pulled Yusif down beside her on the bed. "Yusif, listen to me. Yesterday I was talking to one of my husband's friends. He came for the exhibit at the gallery and we went for drinks after. He looks worried, he looks tired. I asked him what is the matter. He knows I don't talk, he has drunk too much. And so he tells me." She closed her eyes for a moment as her hand moved tautly across Yusif's.

"He tells me they are afraid, he says there is a conspiracy in the army. The troops in the south, they fight, yes, but then they pull back. Maybe they are demoralized now after so much time, but maybe too it's something else. There seems to be a pattern, they don't push the offensive. The intelligence they get is not being used well, he says. Points of information they should be coordinating aren't working. In the air they are making the same mistakes, like they can't learn, he says. Or maybe they choose not to. Maybe, he says, it's something at the top; maybe, he says, it's lower down. But something is not right. Maybe, he says, it's the beginning of a coup." She wanted to shake the calmness from his face.

"And you, Yusif, are moving back and forth between the south and Baghdad, somebody nobody would bother as you come and go." She stopped and drew him to her, watching him with troubled eyes.

"Yusif, be afraid. They will devour you. I know."

Slowly she moved her leg between his and moved her mouth to his lips and whispered, "Leave Baghdad, go to Madain Saleh, but whatever you do, don't return to the marshes."

She drew her mouth to his, wetting his lips with hers as he began to make love to her, and breathed again, "Please, do not return to the marshes."

Yasmina stretched in bed while the Baghdad morning sun began to burn off the river haze.

Yusif listened to the news again of Iraqi troops being poised. "Yasmina," his voice was nervous, "do you want to go with me?"

She looked up at him, surprised.

"No, I'll be fine here—it's you I'm worried about. By the time you are back, I will have finished this one," she smiled pointing to the abstract on the easel. She walked over to him as he gathered his equipment and put her arms around him.

"You will stay in the same little hut by the carvings in Madain Saleh? I will call to know you are all right."

She held him for a moment, stroking the back of his neck, and then stood back looking at the painting on the easel.

"You know, I am thinking. Leave me one of your cameras if you can spare one. The small one, the big one, it doesn't make any difference."

She walked over and ran her finger along the edge of the canvas, looking at the tones, then back at him, smiling. "I want to photograph the painting at this stage, before I finish it."

"All right," he said.

"I have an idea for the next one; it will be a series really." She moved the easel toward the light a bit. "It would be tremendously useful to have a copy of this one, at this stage, to move from for the variation."

Yusif picked up one of his portrait cameras. "Here, this one, it's a second portrait-size camera I take along just as a backup. I don't really need it—this should do it for you."

He handed her the camera and rummaged through his canvas bag as he heard the taxi honking outside. He threw her a package of film. "I'll miss you."

He kissed her while the taxi honked. He looked back at the

painting and smiled. "I forgot to tell you. That one's going to be beautiful. I'll call." He waved and went out the door.

Yasmina dressed and stood in front of the painting with her coffee, approving of the way the light played across the deep reds and slashes of blue.

She tilted it slightly to the right and then, satisfied with the angle, she picked up the camera and the film. She looked at the back of the camera, at the sides, trying to figure out how it loaded.

"Ay God," she muttered to herself, "Yusif and his equipment, every one of these things different. I should have had him load it for me."

She pushed one button and a light meter lit up. She began to fumble with another latch. The lens loosened. She tried another and the sound of film rewinding whirred and then stopped.

It must be this other one, she thought, the whole back must open up and you place the film in there. She pulled at the small latch and broke her fingernail.

"Ay God, I hate these things," she swore again softly to herself and picked up the butter knife from the table. Irritated, she pried at the side of the flap door and its latch. Nothing happened. Finally, in frustration, she jammed the knife at the edge of the door just as her eye caught sight of the tiny button to the side. She pushed the button and immediately the door flapped open.

So that was the damn button, she thought. She picked up the film, loaded it in, and started to close the door when she noticed the split in the door flap where she had jammed it with the butter knife. "Oh god," she muttered to herself, "now I've broken his camera."

She brought it toward the light to look at the split in the flap and stared in confusion as something black started to slip toward her from inside the split back of the camera.

She pulled out the black object She looked at it in the light. It was not film, but a marked, black plastic disk. Behind it were two others—black plastic disks, each about three-by-three centimeters. She stood absolutely still looking at them and then she dropped the camera to the table and ran to the door.

"Yusif," she screamed, running irrationally, toward the street where the taxi had pulled away. "Yusif," she screamed again as the people in the street turned to look.

She ran back in the house and began pulling open drawers, slamming them. "Oh God," she cried, "where have I put the number for Madain Saleh, where is it?" She slumped back on the bed and put her head in her hands.

The man with the earphones listened and then pressed the button for Antar's office.

"She knows. She doesn't know what, but she knows something's going on. She opened the sealed back of the camera."

"Did he leave for Madain Saleh?"

"Yes."

"Can she reach him there?"

"There's a phone."

Antar paused for a moment.

"Get her. Now."

The car moved slowly through the streets of Baghdad. At the large iron gate of the prison, the guard gave a signal. The massive electrical circuits shuddered and then opened. They drove on until they reached a towering, black concrete building. The guard turned around to Yasmina.

"Get out."

Frightened, she got out of the car. The guard pulled her by the arm, pushing her inside the door of the dingy building. She stood for a moment and heard the door close behind her. She tried to adjust her eyes to the dim light of the long corridor, taking a step forward.

From the bowels of the building came a scream, then the sounds of low moaning. By her feet, she felt something crawling, then a hand fumbling at her ankle, the sound of some low gurgling, breathing. She saw the bloodied bandaged hand of a man on her foot; he was moaning. The guard looked down, kicked him savagely in the chest with his boot. Yasmina cringed in horror, surrounded by the moans and screams reverberating down the halls of the labyrinth. The guard put the end of his machine gun to her back.

"Go to the right, whore."

She turned down the corridor and then stood still, frozen in horror. Before her lay bodies writhing as though disgorged from hell, some kneeling blindfolded with bloodied feet and legs. Others seemed to be reaching to the sky, their heads rolled back. The guard shoved her with the machine gun again and she started to fall toward the wall, where one of the supplicants seemed suspended, his hands toward God.

As she collided with the man, he gasped and spun slowly around. Yasmina put her hand to her mouth to stifle the scream—the man's hands were bound, he was hanging from a hook, his body suspended above the floor.

"Move," commanded the guard.

Trembling, she moved down the corridor, trying to step over the blood-soaked legs, the bodies tied to radiators, others hung as the first, to hooks along the wall. The guard jammed the nuzzle of his gun into Yasmina's spine while a scream from hell itself rose from some other part of the building.

The guard opened the door at the end of the corridor and pushed her in. She stood dazed before the sea of faces shrouded in black looking up at her.

Below her more than a hundred women, eyes showing from their black chadors, sat cross-legged on the ground, huddled in front of a long wooden plank. The stench of grease choked her nostrils as they spooned soup from the bowls and looked, heads lowered. One woman dropped the spoon, gagged, then vomited. As the stench rose the guard cursed, hit her, then pulled her away from the table. The others kept eating. The guard shoved Yasmina again.

"To the right, go to the right."

The guard opened a door and pushed her toward a cell. She looked at the long dark corridor and the tiny black cubicles that extended like cages through its length. He unlocked the cell door and shoved her into the blackness.

In the instant the cell door opened, a young girl ran out, screaming a name. She began violently banging her head against a wall, smashing her skull at the concrete wall. The guard grabbed her, put his hand over her mouth, and slammed her back into the cell. She fell against Yasmina, then looked at her with strange rolling eyes and sat down. Yasmina stared in shock. The girl sat perfectly still, began to smile, then erupted into hysterical laughter. Just as suddenly she lay down and pulled a blanket over her head.

A voice came from behind Yasmina, whispering hoarsely. "Leave her; she is insane."

Yasmina turned toward the voice and the shadows of five other women wrapped in abayas, huddled in the dim light of the tiny cell. She looked down at the woman speaking.

"She is nineteen. She has been here for three years, her mind has gone. This other one too."

The black shroud motioned to a figure in the back of the cell— a woman's head nodding as she stared at the wall.

"They tortured her with the cables. She tried to commit suicide by setting herself on fire with a kerosene lamp. But," the woman added sadly, "they found her before she died and sent her back here."

The figure in the back rocked from side to side, her head jerked back, then she focused on Yasmina.

"Aunty, aunty," she began chanting, smiling oddly. She lurched to her feet and moved toward Yasmina. Squatting, she brought her face to Yasmina's, looking into her eyes. Yasmina watched the spit trickle down the side of her mouth. She reached out and touched Yasmina's face.

"Aunty, aunty." The smell of urine and excrement rose like fumes from her. Yasmina stood frozen in front of her, recoiling from the food and excrement smeared over the woman's clothes, the burn scars on her face.

"Aunty," murmured the woman as she crawled back in the cell, squatted, and began nodding again toward the concrete wall while she urinated on the floor.

The women in the cell watched her, then suddenly hushed. They listened to the footsteps coming down the long corridor, then looked up, cowering. The guard pulled the door open and peered down into the dark pit. He looked over the women and then focused on Yasmina, pointing the gun at her.

"You, come with me."

chwarzkopf paced the desert, racking his brains for the key to an attack plan that would work. The ticking of the watch on his wrist seemed to pound in his ear. Ray walked behind him, his nerves at the edge.

Schwarzkopf stopped. He stood still, then poked his toe in the desert. "That's it." Elaine looked at him questioningly.

"That's what?" asked Ray.

"This stuff can support trucks as well as tanks."

"Meaning?"

"Meaning that so far Saddam keeps moving his troops toward the Saudi border along Kuwait, to the east. He sees the ships we've brought into the Gulf, our troops over there that the camera crews are filming night and day. But this stuff here," he poked his foot in the sand again. "Nothing to prevent us from moving our people as far west as we want across this while he's not looking. So far you've determined that his air reconnaissance is poor, right?"

"Right."

"So we make a little more noise and show in the east. I'll position the second Marine Expeditionary Force in landing craft off the Kuwaiti coast, get them to practice amphibious landings. All the while I quietly move the troops into the west." Schwarzkopf rubbed his hand across his forehead. "If he gets the information on this you might as well put every man I'm going to send in in a bodybag now. But Jesus," he whispered, "if we can keep him from cracking our intelligence or what we're about to do, we've got him." He turned abruptly to Elaine, "Do you have anything more at all?"

Though Elaine felt her nerves begin to crack, she pulled herself together and answered. "Just something about Mecca, Antar, the plan. But we can't get what, how, or when."

Schwarzkopf closed his eyes and then gave the order. Through the night the troops began moving into the west.

43

Naila felt the plane begin its descent into Mecca. The stunning sweep of the Grand Mosque was a dazzling apparition. Brilliant gold, blue and ivory, a forest of magnificent minarets around the courtyard. At its center the deep black rock of the Kaaba from which Mohammad had ascended to Jerusalem, seemed to rise up before her. She peered down at the winding streets of the ancient town filled with hajjis, pilgrims robed in white, moving toward the Mosque in a circling, chanting, praying, human spiral.

She listened to the pilot calling back to her while he readied the landing gears of the small aircraft.

"Tarek says there will be someone waiting with a car for you."

Naila nodded and slowly put the abaya over her head, while the plane skidded to a halt on the runway. The pilot motioned his head toward the black car waiting on the air strip.

The car drove haltingly through the congested streets of Mecca and the endless stream of pilgrims milling about, crossing in front of the car, as they moved on. Finally, the car arrived at the hospital. Naila got out and the car drove away, leaving her standing there.

Antar watched the guards bring Yasmina into the room. A look of rage, fear, and contempt suffused her face while she struggled for words. She looked about dazed, from the injections, and then fixed on Antar sitting behind his desk. Antar motioned the guards to sit her down in the chair before him. He leaned forward and offered her a cigarette.

"This is most unfortunate really." He dismissed the guards. "We had hoped to avoid this. But Yasmina—you will forgive me, but I feel I know you. Your paintings, and then of course the listening devices in your apartment; one comes to know one. But," he continued, "this unfortunate incident with the camera." he sighed in mild exasperation. "You will, I am afraid, have to stay with us for a while."

Yamina shook slightly and then closed her eyes, drawing a deep breath. She listened to the sounds coming from down the hall, then opened her eyes and faced the sleek, dark-haired man.

"And Yusif?" she felt her voice slipping in fear.

"Ah, Yusif," said Antar sitting back in his chair. "There is a certain irony to it really, isn't there? The Palestinians have been so helpful, so useful to us. And so we have Yusif. Unknowingly so useful. The irony. Perhaps it is incidental."

He looked away bored, then turned back annoyed.

"We had hoped to use Yusif a great deal more. There are great advantages to such an agent, as I am sure you can see. One who moves so freely throughout the Middle East, who is known to be apolitical. But," he waved his hand in resignation, "it is not to be."

"Yusif," she said incredulously, staring at Antar, "is an agent?"

Antar cut her off. "Yusif has never been an agent. He knows nothing. He has no idea he is being used, or for what. It is safer that way." He leaned toward her again, a look of irritation flashing across his face. "Unfortunately, you have interfered.

Unfortunately, he will be useful this once only." He leaned back. "But, 'this once' is critical. We must be certain not to interrupt him." His dark eyes looked at her. "You will, of course, help us."

He pressed a button on his desk. "But forgive me, I have kept you too long after your journey. You must go and rest. We will talk again later."

The door opened and two guards came. "Get up," said one.

She looked at Antar.

"Get up," yelled the guard, pulling her from the chair. He looked at her and spit on the floor, then put the walkie talkie to his mouth and called for the car. Antar watched her go, then walked out of the office.

The voice whispered hoarsely up to Yasmina.

"Sit, sit. Don't attract attention to yourself." Yasmina sank to the ground beside her.

"Why are you here? Do you know?" whispered the woman. Yasmina peered at her through the darkness, at a face in its thirties with penetrating, inquisitive eyes. Fear gripped her bowels as she looked at the other eyes staring at her. She shook her head almost imperceptibly. The woman nodded.

"Many don't know. Others like this one," she pointed to the woman behind her, "they think are politically involved." The woman looked at Yasmina, touched her arm, then her leg and looked again curiously. "They didn't take you to the interrogation room?" Yasmina stared at her.

"Why do you say that?" she asked, shaking.

"They tie you, then whip your feet and legs with cables to make you talk, but you have no marks," answered the woman flatly. "Ah well, maybe they come for you later."

Yasmina looked up as the cell door jerked open. A guard stood there with a sobbing young girl about sixteen, and pushed her into the cell. She sank in terror to the floor, and then lurched screaming, toward the door as he closed it.

"My name is Tahareh, I am not the one. Oh God," she moaned. She turned around, the words running wildly from her mouth in hysteria. "The secret police say I am in the underground. And I said no, I know nothing. I am only in school, I don't understand this. He says," she clutched at her dress, clawed at her arm, "I am to be executed." Her eyes swam in terror. "He says I am guilty. They will execute me."

She began to move about the cell, eyes moving agitatedly as though she didn't understand where she was. Suddenly she grasped the arm of one of the women, her eyes wild with terror.

"Is this true, oh God, will they execute me?" The woman tried to put her arm around her, but the girl broke off sobbing and fell to the floor as Yasmina watched in horror.

The woman next to her whispered again. "Don't try to talk, the microphones," her voice trailed off again as she nodded toward the walls. She whispered again, "the small microphones, the cameras. Some of the guards, they like to watch the women."

She sank back into silence. A scream echoed down the hall. Then the sound of footsteps again. The guard with his machine gun opened the cell door, watching the young girl Tahareh. The women huddled toward the back of the cell as he motioned Tahareh to stand up. She stood up, trembling. He waved her with his machine gun over toward the wall. He walked in front of her and breathed into her face as his hand moved slowly onto her breast.

"You are being called for now. "But before you go," his hand slid down to her skirt as her terrified schoolgirl eyes watched his, "I will make sure you go to hell."

He ripped off her skirt and thrust himself into her with a moan as she screamed and then fainted. He pinned the motionless body to the wall, thrusting until he was finished. One of the women in the back of the cell began to cry softly. He swung backward at the sound, his face flushed.

"So you are sad?" he said, mocking them in a vicious whisper. "Then you must come and watch."

He called out to two more guards who surrounded the cell. They motioned Yasmina and the other women to their feet, then abruptly herded them out into a courtyard. The glare from the sun blinded Yasmina for a moment as she tried to look about. A large platform stood in the center. A frightened man stood in front of him by a machine.

"The machine," whispered the other woman, "they will amputate his limbs to try and make him talk."

The secret police leader brushed a small fly away and ordered the guards to bring the man to the machine. The man struggled back. Irritated, the guard thrust the man's hand into the machine.

With a precise whir, the machine's blade flashed. The man's scream echoed through the courtyard as his hand fell to the platform. He reeled back, retracting the bloody stump in agony. They motioned the guard to bring the girl.

Slapping Tahareh to consciousness, the guard pushed her up onto the platform. He placed a noose around her neck, smiling slightly as her eyes glazed in terror. Suddenly the platform beneath the girl's feet gave way. Yasmina heard the snap as the girl's neck broke, her head jerking up, her feet dangling.

The guard nudged the girl with his rifle to make sure she was dead, then cut the corpse down and threw it behind the platform. He motioned to the women. "Sometimes they make us put the corpses in the bags when they are finished," one of

455

them whispered. "They make us load the trucks."

The women moved obediently to the back of the platform where the bodies lay. They picked up the bags the guards threw to them and struggled, two to a body, to move the heavy dead weights into the bags and onto the truck.

Yasmina looked below the body they lifted and suddenly began to retch. The bloody stump of a hand lay where it had rolled beneath the girl's body. The madwoman from the cell smiled. Mumbling, slurring "aunty, aunty," she nonchalantly picked the hand up and threw it in the bag with one of the corpses. She then wiped the blood from her hands on her dress and began walking in slow circles until the guards herded them back toward the cell, back into the black cubicle, and down onto the floor.

Yasmina shivered in the heat, and waited.

❈   ❈   ❈

The small videocassette came in the night to Elaine. The markings, the code that her old contact within Iraq had used. She delivered it to decoding and the colonel took it instantly from her. He rushed back in. "It says that this was taken in the prison by the guards and there is one woman in whom Antar is particularly interested. She is somehow linked to the transfer of the key materials into the Kingdom."

"Nothing more?"

"Nothing more." Elaine quickly picked up the phone to alert Tarek.

They began playing the cassette and watched a sea of faces appear. The grainy video showed the women in cells, hundreds of them. Others were being marched out into a courtyard. An amputation, a girl's execution. Elaine felt her self becoming sick as the scratchy video played on.

"The faces, one can barely make out the faces," Elaine said weakly as the video ended,

Tarek took the cassette and called Badr to assemble a team: Kurdish escapees, Kuwaiti refugees, Iraqi dissidents. They began to pore over the faces of the women in the prison, about sixty percent of whom could not be made out for identification. By midday they had come up with some identifications—but no answers.

"Oh God," whispered Elaine staring at the cassette, the blurred faces from within the Iraqi prison, the only lead they had, "which one is she, who is she? What is she, why is she important to Antar, the plan? What is the plan, how in the name of God is he going to do it?" The sea of grainy faces simply played on in front of her, Yasmina's lost in it like a speck of sand in an hour glass where the time was fast.

❇ ❇ ❇

The black limousine drove up to the foot of the airplane ramp and stopped. The two men inside watched the plane door open. Yusif emerged and stood at the top of the ramp, letting his eyes adjust to the blinding light of the Riyadh sun, and then began to descend.

One of the men in the car turned to the other one. "That's him." They opened the car door and waited, their white thobes blowing in the hot midday wind.

When Yusif got to the bottom of the ramp, one of the men

walked over to him and put his hand on Yusif's arm. "Ahlan wa Sahlan."

The Minister of Culture motioned to the slight man next to him. "My aide, Majid." Majid bowed slightly and led Yusif by the arm to the limousine.

"If you will be so kind as to give Majid your passport and baggage checks, he will take your things through—without the delay of customs."

Yusif fumbled in his pocket for his passport and tickets, and gave them to Majid, who disappeared with the documents. The minister and Yusif went into the VIP room.

The minister spoke. "We have arranged for a plane to take you north to Madain Saleh," He glanced up at Majid, who had returned and was indicating that all was ready. "We have, I am afraid, only the small guesthouse to offer—you have stayed there before. We hope you will be comfortable. One of the bedu tribes is not too far away, so if you can't get us with your phone, ask them to help. They remember you well from your last visit." He smiled. "They don't, you know, get many visitors. Only a bedu or an archaeologist would find his way to Madain Saleh." He stood up. "Mabruk, we look forward to your book."

The pilot shook Yusif's hand as he boarded and the plane rumbled into the sky.

The pilot smiled through the noise as he watched the liquid roll of the dunes below him. "There is really nothing like it, is there?" He flew shaking his head in admiration at the blue and mauve shadows from the foothills shimmering across the sands below. "In all the years of flying through these wild parts, I am still always struck by the beauty of it."

Finally he looked back at Yusif, pointing toward a faint outline rising against the sky to the north. "That's it," the pilot said.

Yusif saw the ghostly outlines of the ancient temples and crypts of Madain Salah begin to emerge like a mirage bathed in the cold moonlight. Carved out of rose-colored rocks thousands of years ago, it seemed to await patiently, eternally for its world of ancients to return. For one last traveler, one last trader of frankincense and myrrh who had created its wealth and carved its walls, to return to this eternal desert silence. Waiting for an entire world that had vanished, leaving only the columns and rooms of startling rose rock rising from the desert floor in endless solitude.

The plane started its descent, landed, then skidded to a halt. The pilot nodded toward the small wooden guesthouse. Yusif got out, taking his bags. The pilot waved, took off and then headed quickly back toward Riyadh.

Yusif watched him go and stood engulfed in the total silence of the desert. He opened the door to the guesthouse and brought in his equipment.

He brushed the desert dust from the wooden table and sat down for a moment to wipe the sweat and dust from his own face. An antiquated telephone sat on the table. He picked up the receiver and dialed. The phone clicked through to a connection and began to ring Yasmina's number. The phone rang and rang. He wondered where she might have gone, shrugged and hung up. He would try later. He replaced the receiver, stood up, turned toward the door and then stopped with a start. In front of him, in absolute silence, stood two men.

The weathered face of the old bedu chief, wrapped in his flowing black camel's hair cloak, scrutinized him. "Ahlan wa Sahlan, my friend." Behind him the young man in dusty white thobe nodded. The old bedu took a step forward and offered his hand to Yusif.

"My friend, we are glad to have you back." Tarek's grandfather clasped his leathered hand over Yusif's.

"Ma Salaam," bowed Yusif before him.

"In the desert we hear our friends," said the old man softly when Yusif smiled. "We would be honored if you would take your meal with us tomorrow."

Yusif held the old hand, still strong. "I would be honored."

"Someone will come for you then, when it is dark. Ahlan wa Sahlan," said the Tarek's grandfather, then bowed and walked off through the desert.

Antar listened to the report. "Yusif Khalidi has landed in Madain Saleh. The material is in his equipment, all is still intact."

"Excellent. Khalidi still knows nothing?"

The voice confirmed "Nothing. We see no problem so far."

He sat back in his chair. "Bring her to me."

The cell door opened. The guard stood peering through the dim light at the faces watching him in fear. He pointed at Yasmina. "You, come with me."

The woman next to Yasmina put her arm on hers. "God be with you," she whispered as Yasmina struggled to her feet.

Antar watched her walk shakily through the door.

"Sit down."

The guard pushed her into the chair. Antar motioned for him to leave, then extended his pack of cigarettes. She shook her head. He lit one for himself, leaning back in his chair.

"The prisons are very crowded," he mused as though to himself. "It is a difficult time, so many to be dealt with." He blew the smoke slowly toward the ceiling. "A very difficult time. But," he sat back up, "predictably so." Yasmina stared at the dark eyes. He gazed at her absently. "There is something I want you to do."

Yasmina tried to control her trembling while she waited for him to continue.

"We have, we believe, covered your disappearance adequately. Our handwriting men have used samples from your apartment to create notes and such," said Antar matter-of-factly. "However, the remaining loop is Yusif. We do not want him to call and become concerned when you do not answer. Therefore we want you to place a call to him."

Yasmina started. "From home?"

Antar looked surprised, then shook his head.

"You will not be at home. You will be here. We will make the connection. You will say you have gone to Lebanon to discuss a new exhibit. That you will be back by the time he returns."

"This is the case? I will be back home by then?" she asked, hope suddenly flooding her body. Antar pushed a button on his desk.

"You will not be going back home."

She looked up in panic. "What do you mean?"

He leaned his head back, catching the breeze as the fan churned on. "This is all so unfortunate. We did not plan for you to become involved. You, however, became involved. We will, I am sorry to say, have to keep you here for the few days until this mission is completed."

He looked up at the fan for a moment and then continued.

"You will then be found dead in a car accident in Lebanon. The Beirut cells will arrange it."

Yasmina saw the room swimming in front of her. He waited for her answer. She stood up shaking and struggled to speak the words. "Then why should I make your phone call? If I am to be killed anyway?" she felt the scream rising in her throat. "Why should I help you?"

The room spun as she tried to steady herself.

"Because," said Antar with a shrug, "there is torture that is worse than death. There are those who beg to die to be relieved of the agonies one can inflict. Because you have a choice. Yes, a choice." He picked up some papers on his desk. "You may know days that will seem like an eternity in hell. Or you may call, and then die quietly. This is your choice."

He pushed a button. The guard entered to take Yasmina.

"You have until tomorrow to decide."

The guard pulled Yasmina toward the door. Suddenly she jerked her arm free, swung around and faced Antar. She looked at the cold eyes.

"May you rot in hell," she breathed and spit into his face.

Antar watched her go down the long hall and shook his head. He gazed at the TV monitor for a moment, the footage of the American troops on maneuvers in the east. He heard the clock striking and sat back in his chair, pushing the sudden surge of nervousness, once again upon him, back. In the most remote part of Saudi Arabia, away from the eyes of the world, the black plastic, the key to the operation, was about to be picked up by the member of the Royal Family no one had detected. A brilliant plan, really. Antar looked at the clock and waited.

Yusif loaded two of his cameras with film, picked up his tripod, and walked toward the striated deep red of the ancient city. Smoothed and carved from the mountain itself, the grandeur of perfect columns loomed before him. The angle of the sun lit the stones so that they seemed to burn with some deep fire. He adjusted his tripod before the temple and the palace. The sun fell across the imposing entrance of Ionian columns, illuminating the beautiful bas-relief designs, which held at their peak a falcon. With brilliant precision the artist had carved a falcon whose eyes seemed to peer down all sides as its wings spread proudly over the entrance it guarded for centuries.

Yusif moved into the cool, dark interior. The rooms carved from the rock held exquisite carvings depicting the world of the priests and the kings who had ruled it. The intricate story of their powers and lives, prayers and sacrifices stretched along the walls and told of riches from the desert. The frankincense and myrhh, silks and spices from the Far East and India that flowed through their dominion, on to the Romans and the West before this world had vanished. The sound of a falling pebble echoed in the stillness as Yusif photographed.

When the sun finally dropped down in the sky, Yusif made his way back to the small house. A young bedu who had earlier appeared with the old chief stood silently in the door.

"When you are finished," he said, "we go."

Yusif nodded and pulled a clean shirt out of his bag while the bedu waited.

"Yellah," said Yusif. He glanced at the phone, closed the door behind him, and then followed the bedu, feeling the cool of the desert night, hearing the tiny distant clang of the bedu anvils grinding the cardamon coffee.

Tarek's grandfather stood up when Yusif entered the tent. He motioned him down to a woven rug on the sand and handed him the incense burner. Yusif inhaled the rich scent, then passed the incense on to the other bedu. The old man asked after his work, then sat silently for a while before he touched Yusif's arm.

"Come, you are hungry." In front of the tent beneath the clear night sky lay another woven rug and upon it a whole lamb surrounded by mounds of rice and dates. They sat around it and the old chief reached for the best, the meat at the tail of the lamb, and gave it to his guest. They ate, asking Yusif to tell them of the other places he was photographing. Yusif talked late into the night of Hatra where the Romans had built, Ur, Ninevah, and Samarra.

The fire burned low; the old man listened intently. Then abruptly he looked away into the night sky. Listening, he turned back toward Yusif. In a moment he looked again into the dark desert, listening as though he heard something, and then stood up.

"Please, my friend, continue. I will return." He moved silently back into his tent and then out the back way across the desert.

Slowly he approached the guesthouse. He stood still and listened. He moved toward the open door. Hidden in the shadows of the night he watched the back of a person standing above Yusif's equipment. He saw the small black disks being taken from the back of Yusif's camera, disappearing into a case beneath the acquisitor's robes. The old man stood still, amazed that someone would come to this remote outpost, secretly in the night.

Then the person turned before switching off a flashlight. The old man stared at the face illuminated for an istant in the dark—the face of the member of the Family—a face he knew so well.

Quietly the old man drew back into the shadows, away from the door. The person before him set off across the desert.

❈ ❈ ❈

Antar entered Mecca in the night. Inside the tiny room upstairs on a Mecca side street, he scanned the reports coming in from the cells in Mecca, as well as the others positioned throughout Saudi Arabia. He looked up at the tiny monitor he had installed the previous night. He leaned back and thought about his plan just about to unfold.

His mind kept running to the past. Images, swift flashes, like on a tape speeding to their conclusion. Working through the years with Saddam, tightening their control over the country. The boys in the training camps. The endless nights meeting with agents throughout the Gulf, through sixteen years of planting the seeds that would now come to fruition.

He picked up the phone as it rang, listening to the report.

"The materials were received."

"The cells are prepared?" Antar listened for the reply. "Excellent," he said as he hung up the phone, "excellent. Now we begin."

Antar looked out at the Mecca night and then back at the men and women assembled in the room: the young men and women surrounding him. His agent from the Royal Family would arrive in due time. He had picked his mark and over the years he had worked this agent. Slowly, carefully drawing the perfect person in, and now they would perform for him. Antar watched the stars. For a moment Tarek's face flashed in front of him, his face from years past. It came to him for a moment how

465

Tarek must think of him—Antar, a brilliant, tragic figure, a man whose vision had become blurred, whose idealism had become twisted, mired in blood and power. He thought for a moment of that image of himself. Theirs was one of the only real friendships he had ever had, certainly the last. He had a fleeting sensation that startled him; that he missed him. The conundrum flooded his mind—that even as he stalked him, he thought of him with a sense of loss. Antar stood there, realizing how many, many years it had been since he had been able to talk to anybody. The duplicity he had had to use with the U.S., the others, to assemble their arms, the money that would allow them to succeed now. The doors that he had had to close, one by one, as he pursued his ultimate goal. The depths of his isolation suddenly gripped him. For a moment the loss thundered. The revulsion of some of the things he had had to do along the way engulfed him. The pools of blood that had become his life seemed to rage hideously through his brain. Then he steadied himself, slowly, methodically pushing the images back as he sometimes had to in the night. He reminded himself that he was a man who felt nothing when it was imperative to feel nothing.

There was only one goal for him now, nothing else. For a moment, the realization came to him that Saddam had become an animal. And yet, he steadied himself; even that made no difference. The goal, Antar's vision of a brilliant Middle East, was still correct. He pushed the fears, the image of a destroyed country should they fail, back.

He closed the window and went back into the room full of people, hidden in the old street of Mecca. He set the final plans in motion.

44

Naila checked the numbers on the Mecca hospital directory, then proceeded down the hall and opened the door to Administration.

"Yes?"

"I'm Dr. Naila Saud. I was sent for duty in the women's section."

The woman glanced at her curiously, then opened a folder and began leafing through papers. She shook her head.

"No, I don't see anything here about you." She scrutinized Naila, frowning. "Where are you from?"

Naila's breath caught when the woman stared at her. She heard Tarek's words swimming in her head: "Never back up, don't ever change your story."

"I am," Naila cleared her throat, "from the National Guard Hospital in Riyahd. They just assigned me yesterday afternoon."

Fear coursed through Naila while she waited for the woman to speak. The woman said nothing, scowled at Naila for what seemed an endless moment, and then suddenly raised her hand in exasperation.

"Really, I don't know how they expect me to run this place, this is all such chaos. Can't anybody ever do what they are supposed to up there? Simply send us the paperwork on time for once. How I'm supposed to…" Naila stood absolutely still. The woman picked up the phone. "Oh what's the use," she muttered in frustration, dropping the receiver. "Just go on into the women's wing. They'll probably send your paperwork in a few days," she added disgustedly.

Naila nodded mutely and walked down the hall toward the women's wing, remembering Tarek's words. "Do exactly as I tell you and you won't get hurt. I will have people around you. You won't know them, or see them, but they will be there."

Naila steadied herself, aware of eyes upon her, and opened the door. She moved along the rows of hospital beds with the charts the chief resident had given her, stopping to talk to some of the women, looking for the location they had marked as home, searching for faces from the cell meeting. Tarek's words swirled, replaying again and again in her head. "Only contact me," Tarek had said, "when you have something. You need only one lead; remember this, you need only one to find the others."

Schwarzkopf's voice was little more than a whisper. "He's not moving."

Ray and Elaine moved closer to the reconnaissance layouts Schwarzkopf had before him with a questioning look. Schwarzkopf only leaned forward and breathed like a man smelling blood. "He's not moving."

Ray pulled up a chair quickly. Schwarzkopf abruptly turned to him, his mind racing. "Ray, he's taking the bait. Saddam has bought it—the deception about an amphibious landing, that all of our forces are in the east. He keeps moving his troops toward the Saudi border along Kuwait. His reconnaissance, his intelligence hasn't gotten that we've moved all these men into the desert in the west."

Elaine rapidly scanned the sheets Schwarzkopf pointed to.

"If we can keep him from uncovering what we're really doing, we've got him. If we can keep him from shutting down the country as we begin, we've got him." Schwarzkopf stopped as his mind reverted to the leak within.

And then he did something that at that moment was the only thing left to do. He prayed.

arek waited beneath the dim streetlight in the Riyadh souk for the man to appear. He walked up slowly, paused before the closed store window, and lit a cigarette. Tarek turned to the man and asked for a light, then listened to his agent, long stationed with one of Antar's European contingents.

"It will begin within twenty-four hours. An escalation of terrorist activities internationally—bombs, perhaps chemicals, gasses, in London, the U.S., elsewhere. Activated by the cells, no fingerprints. Antar has had us moving the materials into place." He looked at Tarek in the dim streetlight.

"It will be triggered by the operation here. It will begin when the operation in the Kingdom has been successfully completed. But the rest—I don't have it. I'm too far on the periphery. Everything is run too tightly, completely from the inside," his hand gestured upward in frustration.

"I have nothing on who the actual operative is within the Family, how they are going to do it. None of our people in

Europe has anything. But the outlines of the plan are clear. Assassinate Fahd, shut the country down, take over, immobilize, paralyze the U.S. troops ability to act here. A chain reaction is planned for the other countries down the Gulf. The operative is clearly in place, the logistics of the physical shutdown in the Kingdom, they believe, secured."

❊ ❊ ❊

Ray peered at the monitor, Elaine behind him as Tarek joined them in the Black Hole. They watched the masses of people thronging the streets of Mecca.

"Nothing is showing up here," said Ray, dropping the papers back on the desk. "No weapons, no arms showing up in these reports." His eye crooked up at Tarek for a moment.

"Any chance that Naif is covering?"

Tarek shook his head. "I don't think so. Frankly, I ruled him out a long time ago. Even if the man wanted to be some sort of revolutionary martyr, he wouldn't have tried to blow himself up in a car bomb with Fahd before the operation was over, would he? He has all the right access to intelligence, to the interior of the country, the cells—he would have known not to put himself in that car. And it was Naif himself who decided to go along at the last minute."

Ray nodded, looked at the clock, and put in a call through the secure line into the National Security Council and the CIA in Langley. Ray stopped and looked at Tarek. "When do you leave for Mecca?"

"Tonight."

Tarek walked into his office and closed the door behind

him. He leaned closer to Badr, who was monitoring the satellite taps on the Mecca phone lines as he watched the clock.

"Osman's son Abed has left for Mecca?"

Badr nodded his head sadly.

"All right, we leave in an hour."

❈ ❈ ❈

Nura sat quietly waiting as Tarek came in the door. "Tarek, your grandfather called."

Tarek looked at her, surprised.

"He said you won't be able to reach him. He'll try to get through again. He wouldn't tell me what it is about."

"There is something else." She held up a scrap of paper, her voice tense. "It's from the little chambermaid who took care of the women's quarters. She disappeared midday—and left this note." Nura began to read:

> *Mr. Musaid came to see me after Dr. Naila left. I'm so sorry. He asked me if I had seen Dr. Naila with a man. I said no, but he hit me, and he told me he would deport me. I am the sole support of my family in Pakistan. I became afraid and I told him yes. He hit me again and told me to tell him everything I knew. And I became scared and told him I had seen her with a man and that I thought Dr. Naila was pregnant. Please I am so sorry.*

Nura looked up terrified. "Khadija says she thinks Musaid has gone to Mecca."

"Naila knows?"

"Naila knows."

471

Tarek stood still. "What did she say?"

"I could hear her fear on the phone. She couldn't speak at first. Then she only said one thing." Tarek waited. "That she had made you a promise—and that you had made her one."

45

The eerie wailing call beckoning the pilgrims to the Grand Mosque reverberated through the streets of Mecca.

Elaine looked out the window for a moment at Mecca spread below her, recalling Ray's words that she would never see Mecca. She turned back to Tarek in the Mecca headquarters they had set up. He stood beneath the light, scouring the map, the labyrinth of ancient winding streets of the city.

Badr came through the door. "The tail we've put on Abed bin Osman. They've lost him."

Tarek's head shot up "They've lost him? What in the name of God do you mean?"

Badr's voice was agitated. "Something cut them off while they were trailing him, I don't know, some traffic and hajjis came between them." He stopped cold. "They lost him," his voice now dead. He moved toward the map Tarek had in front of him, the maze of Mecca streets.

"Agents are stationed at all of these points, but none of the identified cell members are showing up. They've either pulled them out, knowing they would be identified, or they're too well hidden. And Antar, of course, would never let himself be seen. As far as the taps on the Royal Family members, not one of them has made a move that can be identified as anything suspicious. We're working blind, Tarek."

"Only one, Badr," Tarek rolled up the map. "Only one piece of one trail, one miscalculation, Badr. That's all we need."

"But we don't have it, Tarek," said Badr, his voice weary. "We don't have it."

Naila finished treating her patient and walked to the clinic door. She listened to the call from the Grand Mosque and looked out at the incredible sea of humanity filling the streets. Thousands of pilgrims in their loose white garments and sandals milled through stalls selling Korans of every color and size, while the taxis, buses, and cars ran twenty-four hours a day carrying the pilgrims to the Great Mosque to carry out their umrahs. They moved like a human wave flowing toward the brilliant white marble Grand Mosque. Its ancient, magnificent minarets reflected the sun while the rest of the city, old and new, spiraled around it, teeming with people. The sounds of their voices rose up from the desert floor as they walked toward it chanting, a thunder from the very heart of Islam.

Naila turned to go back to the ward. Behind her a young woman spoke with a nurse briefly and waited to pick up some medication. The voice struck Naila first. She turned to look at her. The young woman glanced absently back at her and then down at her watch, waiting impatiently. Naila turned abruptly. It was one of the women from the cell.

For a moment she felt nothing but fear flooding her, and then, again, Tarek's words, his instructions before she left. "Follow her. Remember these instructions…" Naila pushed the button on the tiny radar locater device in her pocket that Tarek had given her so they could follow her movements should she leave the hospital.

The young woman picked up the medication and began to walk out the door. The nurse looked up, too beleaguered to be bewildered as Naila put on her abaya and left through the same door.

Naila paused, her eyes searching frantically in the crowd that thronged around her. And then her eyes stopped, frozen. Musaid stood only feet away from the woman she was searching for. He stared at Naila, an odd look on his face, and then just as abruptly, he disappeared. Naila looked in vain for the people Tarek had placed around her. Shaken, she moved forward, urgently searching through the throng of people. Then she saw the woman.

Naila moved quickly to follow her through the streets. She dropped back, disappearing into the crowd when the woman turned and spoke to a man. Then the woman continued on toward the Grand Mosque. Step by step Naila followed her as Tarek had instructed. They moved behind the old men, the young men, the women with children, this tide of chanting people flowing toward the Gate of Peace, walking up the wide marble steps to the Holy Mosque like the sea moving to meet the sky.

Naila followed her in the crush of hajjis until they reached the top of the stairs, the Gate of Peace. She removed her shoes and began to follow the steps of the ritual behind the woman.

Stepping with her right foot first, as the Prophet had done, she walked through the gate and stood silenced, awed by the incredible beauty of the vast white marble courtyard of the Mosque, the Haram. The stunning sweep of the courtyard before her held half a million people. The arches and colonnades of white marble above the seven gates soared two stories into the blue Mecca sky while the seven intricately carved minarets of the Grand Mosque blazed in the Mecca sun like poems burned into the universe. Below them sat pilgrims on red silk carpets that flowed across the length of the Haram. Reading their Korans, meditating, they rose as one massive column of humanity, at the sound of the muezzin calling down from one of the minarets. They fell in prostration while the imam led them in prayer. And then slowly they stood and began to move toward the Kaaba while Naila struggled to keep the woman in sight in this human stream. As though drawn to the very center of the earth, they moved toward the massive stone structure at the center of the Haram—the Kaaba.

laine stared at the monitors of the surveillance cameras scanning the courtyard from the tops of the minarets in Mecca. She watched the mass of people begin to circle the Kaaba seven times, chanting hypnotically, "Allahu Akbar, God is most Great." When they reached the Black Stone at the southeastern corner of the Kaaba, hundreds rushed forward to touch it, weeping, to kiss it as the Prophet had done. Suddenly Elaine leaned forward.

"Tarek," she was excited, "it's Naila. I know she's covered in the veil, but the way she moves, the way she walks, the bracelet, Tarek, I think it's Naila." Tarek came immediately to the screen and watched, along with her, the small figure that Elaine pointed to.

Naila's eyes stayed riveted on the young woman. She moved with her, completing the seventh circle. For a moment Naila thought she saw the woman glance back at her curiously. But then she turned back and continued on to the Station of Ibrahim in the Holy Mosque and began two prostrations before God. The eternal remembrance that worship was rendered to God.

Naila followed behind the woman, the pilgrims moving toward the next ritual, the Well of Zamzam and the Mas'a, the Running Place. They surged toward the beautiful marble vault covering the Well at Zamzam with its hundreds of small taps from which the water spouted. She turned at the sound of an old man whispering the story from the Koran to the small boy with him.

"Here," he nodded quietly toward Zamzam, "Here in the plains surrounding Mecca, Hagar and her young son Ismail searched desperately for water. Seven times," said the old man pointing to the hills, "she ran between the hills of Safa and Marwah searching for a well from which Ismail could drink."

Elaine search the monitor, but Naila's figure had now disappeared.

Naila stood behind the woman while she drank from the well, and then followed her out of Safa Gate, moving with her seven times, between the hillocks of Safa and Marwah, until they finished the rituals of the first day of the hajj.

The young woman turned back toward the city, and Naila carefully followed her down the winding streets. She stood to the side of the street as the woman stopped at a house, knocked on the door, and went inside.

Naila looked back at the other hajjis passing behind her in the night along the old streets. Suddenly she looked up and thought she saw Musaid again. Her body froze until the man disappeared around the corner. She tried to control the trembling that seized her and knocked on the door. A young woman peered out at her for a minute and then opened the old door.

"Yes?"

Naila groped for the words that Tarek had given her.

"I, I am here to join the others."

The woman frowned at her. "What do you mean?"

"Antar has sent me."

The woman looked startled, but she opened the door for her to come in. "He has sent you?"

"Yes," said Naila feeling terror well up inside her as she struggled for the words she was supposed to say. "I have been doing work for him outside the cells for some time. I am a doctor based in Riyadh, posted briefly to the border where I collected information for him from the refugees. Now to Mecca. I…"

Naila looked down at the room full of young women staring at her. She suddenly focused on the face of one of the young women from the cell meeting.

"Yes," said Naila abruptly, pointing to her, "she, too, is from the cell there. I saw her one night at one of the meetings. I could not come regularly but I remember her. I was under instructions to keep a distance, so that my postings would not be compromised."

The young woman she pointed to nodded curiously at Naila. Naila waited, begging in the silence for the young woman to speak. The woman suddenly gaped in recognition.

"She was the doctor."

Naila stood frozen.

"The doctor who bowed to the will of God and dispatched the illegitimate child." The woman stood up, as though in a prayer meeting, and began to tell the others of how Naila had ended the baby's life as the Koran dictated.

The leader listened, watching Naila warily. Finally, she took Naila's hand. "Come, you are safe here."

The earth seemed to tilt and spin, as Naila saw her duplicity accepted. She nodded mutely when the leader found her a place, then stood before them all and said, "We will pray."

The entire room of young women, old women, women holding babies, bowed toward the Kaaba, raising their voices in the prayers of Islam. They bent their heads to the ground and prayed. Naila moved to the sounds of the words with them.

Then the women sat down and waited for the leader at the front to begin. She took a small cassette and placed it in the machine. The voice carried through the room, beneath the scratching of the tape. Naila tried to keep her hands from shaking while she watched the soft, gentle faces of the young women, and the older, worn faces, listen intently to the words pouring across the room.

"Tathir...Takfir...some of you have fallen in the past... corrupt kings...the Brides of Blood...true Islam teaches..." the words swarmed through her mind while the voice rolled on. At last, the voice came to the final words. "Deceit to further the will of God is blessed. The means are there. It is only the will." The sound hung, echoed in the room.

They began to file out of the room. A young woman next to Naila smiled. "Come, we eat something before our instructions." Slowly she reached down. "I see," she said softly, "that you are pregnant. I see also that you have no ring; you are unmarried."

Naila felt panic rise in her as the young woman gazed at her belly. "Do not be afraid. I understand," she said softly. "You will give your life to be cleansed. In Lebanon, the young woman Entehari had fallen too. But the fear went, and she took her life and the life of the baby as a gift to god when she performed the mission with the explosives there."

She touched Naila's shoulder. "Do not be afraid," the girl whispered, "it will be over soon."

She reached inside her dress and showed Naila a cheap rumpled photograph of a young man pinned inside.

"My husband was eighteen when he was killed last year. I do it for him. As a gift for Allah. To be with him soon."

The cell leader sitting next to Naila nodded to her. "Stand."

Naila's eyes widened.

"Stand. Stand and tell the others your story. How you have fallen, but will give your life as a martyr to be saved."

Everyone was watching her. She shook her head, terrified, but they only waited, staring. She struggled to her feet, desperately trying to control her voice.

"My name is Naila. I am a doctor. I am, I...I was educated in the West, where I...fell from the true way, from the word of Islam." She stopped, shaking. The women around her nodded and murmured for her to go on. Terror reeled through her. She continued. "I became pregnant."

A hush fell upon the crowd of women. Naila's hands gripped the material of her dress and then moved forward, as though to deliver the lie, an act so totally alien to her. "I returned determined to do the will of God. To give my life, and that of my baby." Naila's voice stopped, unable to go on. The women sat, utterly silent, staring.

Then, as one, they began to applaud. She stood there in terror. One began to weep, another to softly murmur intonations from the Koran. The earnest faces of the young women, a sea of dark eyes, engulfed her in their understanding, their pity, their admiration, their desire to die. Naila's mind struggled, screamed within, searching for how to get out, how to get back to Tarek.

One of the women came up to her. "Dr. Naila, there is something I must ask you."

Naila felt the terror again. The woman looked up earnestly.

"Dr. Naila, we have someone here who is having great difficulty breathing. Could you bring us something from the hospital...go now...and return with it? We are afraid to send others out."

"Yes of course, tell me what you want." Naila took a slip of paper from her.

She left, then raced down the street, bumping into an old man, then a woman. She searched the numbers on the street for the one that Tarek had given her for their headquarters. Finally she reached the door and pushed it open. Elaine gasped in relief.

Naila leaned against the chair flushed and shaking, and began to tell Tarek and Elaine about the cell, the house in Mecca.

Tarek leaned forward as Naila finished speaking.

"Go back."

Elaine turned around, shocked. "Tarek..."

He cut her off. "Naila, go back."

Naila looked up, frightened. Tarek, no. I can't...oh God, I'm so afraid."

He didn't move a muscle. His voice was low, even. Like a bedu training a falcon, his words pulled her in, directed her.

"I want you to go back, be one of them, make them think you're one of them. They have what I need to know. And you can get it for me, you can do this."

She looked down at her hands. The silence after his words seemed relentless, deafening. Then the low, resolute words. Tense, even. Unyielding.

"You must decide, Naila. You must make a choice."

Finally she looked up at him. "Yes." The word was barely audible.

Elaine's eyes searched his for an assurance she knew he couldn't give as fear filled her very being her for the young woman standing before them.

Tarek moved quickly and pulled a small device out of the drawer.

Naila's hand trembled as she spoke, "Tarek, please, I'm so afraid...what if..."

Tarek fastened the small radio mike in the hem of her clothes. "We will be listening all the time. We will have you covered. You only need to return this one last time. When you leave the house in the morning, tell them you must go back to the hospital for something. Then it will be over." He showed her Antar's picture one last time. "This is the man we are looking for, the key to it all."

Elaine put the headphones on to begin monitoring the small mike as Naila looked at Tarek in anguish. He nodded, his head barely moving.

Schwarzkopf sat with his men. The clock ticked toward the time of President Bush's ultimatum to Saddam. The clock's ticking seemed to echo in the night as each man felt the fear gnawing at him. They passed information about targets within Iraq pinpointed by the Special Operations unit, troops, chemical plants, Scud bases. Moving the information by human courier, terrified of the leaks, they reached the Air Force units poised to strike. At the end of the night, knowing they had only forty-eight hours left, they began taking shifts to sleep. The young lieutenant walked down the hall to the small cots set up for them in the tiny room next to the Black Hole. As he lay down, he turned quietly to the other man in the room.

"You know if this fails, we could all die?"

The other officer nodded grimly.

"They still don't have who it is inside, or what the plan is, do they?" he asked. The other man shook his head.

"We could all die," the young lieutenant repeated the words then let the silence fall.

"Do you know what the Saudi soldiers were doing today?" The other man shook his head. "Digging graves, facing toward Mecca."

Schwarzkopf listened to the young lieutenant's words and then placed the connection through to Elaine. She had never heard his voice so quiet.

"Elaine, we are ready. There will be a courier on the way to you with a letter. I want to ask you to please help me get it to my wife. And I want to tell you what a fine person I think you are and that it has been an honor to work with you."

He picked up a pen and paper and went back out into the blackness of the desert. His pen moved steadily in the dark.

17 January 1991

15 minutes after 12:00 A.M.

My dearest Wife and Children,

The war clouds have gathered on the horizon and I have already issued the terrible orders that will let the monster loose. I wish with every fiber of my body that I would never have had to issue those commands. But it is now too late and for whatever purposes God has, we will soon be at war.

As a soldier who has had to go to war three times before, I want you to know that I am not afraid. I know that I might face death but you should know that I am far safer than most of the fine young men and women under my command. Some will die; many could die. I pray to God that this will not happen but if it does and if I am one of those chosen by God to sacrifice my life, I wanted you to know that my last thoughts before this terrible beginning are of you, my beloved family.

Your loving husband and father,
H. Norman

Naila returned to the small house in Mecca, carrying medications and an inhalator from the hospital. The women gathered. They began to chant and pray. "Neither the infidels nor the U.S. can stop us."

They stopped and put on their abayas when the man walked into the room. The women stood up. Naila stared at the man she realized was Antar. A woman next to her whispered.

"Come, we receive our instructions now on how to use the weapons."

Naila followed her.

Elaine and Tarek listened to Antar tell them how to strap

the explosives on their bodies, to wield the knives and use the guns. He was entranced by Antar's final explanation. "Use the knives, the guns, the small explosives to provoke the police in ways that can't be seen by the others so they will turn and fire upon you. Provoke them to actions that will make them look despicable before the world—as though they are killing helpless, innocent people—this will enrage the world watching. Then we will rise up, defenders of Islam, our raison d'être apparent, to end this bloody regime which purports to oversee the holy place of Islam. Remember, deceit and trickery are blessed when used for God. Remember, your deaths will be as martyrs." Tarek listened to the tiny little radio mike on Naila until the women were told to sleep before the morrow.

Badr rushed in behind him with the communiqué from Schwarzkopf. "Schwarzkopf's ready to begin the amphibious landing maneuvers in the east to deceive the Iraqis. His men are simultaneously ready to begin the air attack in the west. He's waiting now only for your clearance, confirmation that you can hold the country."

Badr and Elaine left the room and Tarek quietly closed the door behind him. Tarek's mind turned one last time to the incredible risk of what he was about to do. Everything that had ever been sacred. And yet he knew it was the answer.

In the still Mecca night, Tarek sat alone. The ancient verses seemed to whisper in his head, like a children's rhyme coming back, playing in circles across his mind. He whispered words of the ancient verse of the Koran. "In the Name of Allah, the Compassionate, the Merciful. They ask of you what is lawful to them. Say: 'All good things are lawful to you, as well as that which you have taught the birds and beasts of prey to catch...' "

Tarek moved to the control panel and secretly wired all the commands into his unit. He included every command from the

National Guard, the Army, the Air Force, the Navy, the U.S. military back-up and the U.S. Anti-Terrorist Squad into his own unit. An hour later, when he was finished, he sat back down.

He heard faint footsteps coming closer, now behind him.

"Tarek." Elaine stood there.

She moved closer to him and then stopped, looking into his eyes.

"Tarek," she whispered, again, watching him in fascination, "what are you thinking, what are you going to do?" For a moment his expression, his eyes frightened her.

He drew her down to him, for minutes just gazing at her.

"I want you to go now, just for a while." She looked at him, not comprehending. "It is not good for you to be here with this..." He looked at her "What I am about to do—if they find out they will try to stop me. And yet I know I'm right."

"Tarek?" She stared at him.

"What I am going to do," he said softly, "is to risk Mecca to save Mecca."

She stared at him, stunned, confused.

His voice was soft. "Don't ask anything more. When I am finished, you will know."

He pulled back from her. Confused, she got up and went to the door. When she had gone, he locked it. And then he sat and waited for the dawn to come.

chwarzkopf stood with his troops hearing the clock tick like thunder. Behind him came the aide's voice. "Tarek says begin the decoy amphibious assault maneuvers from the Gulf. Wait for the air attack followed by the ground attack from the west until he tells you."

Schwarzkopf nodded and threw the order. Twenty Navy Seals swarmed onto the Kuwaiti coast, detonating explosives.

Within minutes all satellite feeds from Mecca blacked out.

Schwarzkopf, terrified, told the aide to contact Tarek.

The aide rushed back. "I don't know what he meant. Tarek says he knows. He did it."

Schwarzkopf, now beyond questions, alerted the Air Force to stand by and simply prayed.

46

Naila watched the women in the room breathing in the dawn light. She strapped the explosives and the knives to her body. She stood with the others, waiting. Then the signal came. She prayed that Tarek would come. He had heard Antar's words that the member of the Royal Family had just been there. "He says that all is in place," were Antar's words. She was in the headquarters that Tarek had been searching for. And yet he didn't come.

The call rang out from loudspeakers on the Holy Mosque street, the ancient words echoing through Mecca. Tarek stood on a parapet of an old mosque while overhead the helicopters hovered like fireflies. Naila and the women, followed by cadres of others from houses all over Mecca, began streaming into the streets.

Antar looked down at the boulevard in satisfaction. The cell leaders had done their job; the people were prepared. He watched the masses of people stream from the streets into the boulevard while the muezzin called the words from the Koran. Antar thought of the irony. How Saddam had used religion so cleverly, had actually convinced these people that it was Islam that was threatened here, that he was the new Saladin—the hero who had fought off the Crusaders from the West and saved Islam. Suddenly the nervousness struck him again, that they had all believed so easily. And yet, they were here.

The members of the Republican Guard began to disappear into the crowd. The human wave, the flood of bodies started to flow toward the sound of the Iraqi voice suddenly calling upon them to demonstrate. The call pierced the waiting crowd below.

"Death," he screamed. "Death to the corrupt puppet monarchies, lackeys to the West."

The crowd, prepositioned below him, murmured and chanted back.

"Death," he whispered as others moved toward the crowd and strained to hear, his eyes burning, "to Israel." The crowd stood still before him as they struggled to hear.

Suddenly the Iraqi's voice screamed out in an electrifying sound beneath the shadow of the Grand Mosque.

"Death to America!"

The sound echoed through the Mecca streets. The crowd, whiplashed by the word, roared back with an explosion of hate from the bowels of the earth.

"Death to America."

The voice of the crowd rose up in a piercing cry to meet his, as he raised his arm.

Ray looked at the monitor, then back at Elaine, pacing nervously.

"Christ," he said stubbing out his cigarette, "it's going to blow. I can feel it. It's going to blow wide open." He slumped back in his chair, turned toward the monitors again, and lit another cigarette. "Are our troops on stand-by alert?" The Air Force general behind him nodded nervously.

"The Anti-Terrorist Squad ready to go in to quell a riot?"

The Commander of the Squad nodded tensely.

The blades of the helicopters whirled overhead and dipped lower over the swaying crowd as the voice rose up in a final piercing scream that shattered like an explosion in the Mecca sky. "Death to Israel! Palestine!" The Iraqi screamed, raising his arm in a sign of victory. The crowd roared. He raised his fist once more while the crowd swayed, chanting, repeating the words like a human cobra swaying upward to his call, writhing upward into the Mecca heat. He raised the sign of victory aloft. His voice raged as the crowd roared back and the Republican Guard cells fanned out through the crowd.

Elaine turned as an aide ran into the room with a communiqué from Schwarzkopf. Ray looked up, agitated. "Schwarzkopf says that the amphibious landing has begun but he can't get the OK from Tarek to start the real assault from the west."

Suddenly Elaine, in front of the control board turned pale. Ray looked at her, "What is it?"

"Our whole computer system has just shut down. We don't know why. The Air Force is trying to set up a back-up system."

"Oh God, Jesus…" He turned at the roar from the crowd on the TV monitor to see the Iraqi raise his hand and hold out an American flag. The demonstrators screamed. He spit on it with a smile and raised his arm for victory. Then slowly he took a match and set it on fire, then threw it into the crowd. As the flames consumed it, the screams of the crowd rose in the hot sky.

Then he raised the signal. "Allahu Akbar! Saddam is the Servant of Allah!" Chanting, the cell groups began to form into two human columns and moved toward the Grand Mosque. "Jesus, they're going to storm the Grand Mosque," Ray whispered.

Tarek stood in the control room in Mecca and watched the monitors closely. The Saudi security forces moved cautiously around the crowd. Armored cars stood ready on alert. His helicopters hovered overhead, propeller wings beating the air, each one, per his orders, methodically photographing the faces of every member of the crowd.

Tarek saw the fear written on the faces of the foot soldiers stationed along the way. The helmeted police stood with Tarek's orders to hold the demonstrators before the Grand Mosque. The crowd reached them, chanting and pushing forward. The police warned them back. They pushed forward, hatred written in their faces. The police pushed them back once again. The control board in front of Tarek lit up.

Badr opened the door abruptly after a rapid knock. Tarek looked up at him. "What is it?"

Badr thrust the agent's report just in front of Tarek.

"Arms. The Iraqis have cells of the revolutionary agents amongst their hajjis. They have explosives and knives. They're going to storm the Grand Mosque!"

Tarek scanned the report while Badr waited. He slowly lit a cigarette, and watched the red tip flame.

"Have you given this report to Naif, yet?"

Badr looked puzzled for a moment and then shook his head. Tarek watched him closely. "Does Naif know?"

Badr shook his head again. Tarek watched the monitor. Hajjis in their white robes were surging through the streets of Mecca toward the Grand Mosque, moving beneath the old lattice work wooden balconies, past the stalls of the bazaar like a human fire.

Badr watched Tarek in puzzlement when he spoke the words, "Destroy it."

"Destroy it?"

Tarek nodded slowly, "Destroy the report."

Badr watched Tarek's dark eyes fixed coolly upon him. He heard Tarek's voice low and even.

"I want you to destroy all evidence of this information."

Badr looked shocked and then leaned forward nervously.

"But," he whispered to Tarek, "that is against all regulations…"

Tarek cut him off with a cool, even stare. "Do what I tell you."

Badr stood up shaken and turned to go. Then he turned back toward Tarek, his eyes questioning.

"You will arrange for the arrests?" he watched Tarek's even expression, "you will confiscate the weapons? I should set this in motion from here?" he asked nervously. Tarek's eyes fixed upon him.

"Leave them."

"Leave them?"

Tarek stubbed out his cigarette and looked back at Badr.

"Leave them."

Tarek picked up the alert phone ringing. The officer's voice on the other end sounded desperate. "Our forces need the order to move, please. There is something wrong. We're not getting the order to move."

Tarek hung up while Badr continued to stare at him. The alert phone from the king's office rang. Walid sounded nervous.

"Tarek, all satellite transmissions from Mecca have stopped. Is something is going on? Fahd is worried. Find out what is going wrong." Tarek agreed, then simply hung up.

"Not yet," whispered Tarek, "not yet."

Badr remained stunned in front of him.

"Badr, I want you to continue to technically intercept any communication going to the king from here or any order he might issue regarding Mecca."

"My God," whispered Badr, "Tarek, that's treason."

"Yes."

"Tarek," Badr sounded like a man whose sense of reality is dying, "they are going to try to blow up Mecca, take over the Grand Mosque, kill our troops. This is the end."

"Yes." Tarek looked at Badr with an odd, curious, undefinable expression. "Yes. This is the end."

Suddenly Badr shrank back in total horror as the final possible perversion of reality slowly peeled itself open before his mind. Tarek. the member of the Royal Family they had been searching for. His mind stopped at Tarek's name, unable to go on. He stood staring at the face he had known for so many years. There was a scream from the monitor.

A young man rushed forward at the front of the line of Iraqis. Screaming, "Allahu Akbar." He brandished a knife before a young police officer. Two Iraqis behind him grabbed the officer and threw him back into the crowd. The crowd lurched forward toward the officer, tearing at his clothes, his flesh, his eyes. They flashed a knife, raised it high and held his head back.

The crowd roared as Iraqi hajjis reached down and slit his throat, roared as the warm blood gushed out onto the ground. Once again the man with the knife reached down and this time totally severed the head from the dead man's body. In a scream of victory he held it aloft on a pole before the chanting crowd as the blood began to flow along the streets of Mecca. As at a signal, the knives appeared from beneath the hajjis' robes, rushing, slashing at the poorly armed bedu National Guardsmen. The women from the revolutionary cells moved up with the men, throwing themselves forward to detonate the explosives on their bodies, killing themselves and all those around them.

Raging in the massacre of revolution, shouting Saddam's name, they trampled children and old men. The young bedu guards, struggling to contain, them died beneath their knives, guns, and human explosions.

Naila gasped in terror at the side of the road and ripped at the explosives strapped on her. She dropped the belt of explosives on the ground and began to run. The red light flashed, sirens began. Someone grabbed her from behind. The man put his hand over her mouth. "I'm from Tarek quickly..." He motioned her into the car while the nightmare exploded around them. The radio transmitter blared when he closed the door. "The Iraqis are moving on the Grand Mosque. They are armed with knives, they are firing into the crowd, killing people, burning parts of the city. There are hundreds wounded, some dead already."

They pulled up alongside an ambulance. Naila looked out the car window at one of the doctors in the ambulance, who recognized her.

"Dr. Naila, the women over there," he pointed frantically.

Naila got out of the car. The doctor led her quickly over to a woman lying on the ground. She pulled back the cloth revealing the crushed, disemboweled body. A nurse came up behind her.

"There are many trampled like this, stampeded by the crowd." Naila watched the woman gasp and die before her. She moved to the next woman, who seemed to be breathing. She was very young, with glazed, unseeing eyes. She whispered "Allahu Akbar."

"Yes," whispered Naila, tears coming down her face as she worked frantically to get pressure. The woman's head slowly roll to the side. Naila stood up and wiped her face, quickly looking at the next woman. Silent, lying there dead with a gunshot wound through the head. Numbly she moved on to the next one still breathing. A siren wailed behind her.

They began to carry away the bodies on stretchers. The ambulance driver held one stretcher for a moment while the doctor examined the man on it.

"Is he alive?"

"Yes," said the driver quietly above the blood-soaked body clad in white. "But if Allah were merciful, he wouldn't be."

Naila looked at the side of the head, crushed by a rock, and then watched the orderly place the stretcher on the ground. She watched the remainder of the face she had known for years move unseeing toward some sound. She watched as they lowered Osman's son, Abed, to the ground.

�֍ ✷ ✷

Elaine stood behind Ray as he gripped the phone. "I must get through to Tarek," he shouted. "What do you mean you don't know where he is? It's unthinkable, Tarek would never..." He listened as the voice insisted. "Why is he holding back? We have additional forces we can send in to stop this immediately. We can end this instantly. Oh Christ," he swore and slammed down the phone.

He began to pace the control room above the sirens shrieking below. It was unimaginable, in all the years that he had known Tarek, that he simply wouldn't be there. He looked down at an Iraqi setting a car on fire, at the horrible desecration and destruction taking place in front of him.

Suddenly, as the gun shots rang out below, Tarek's helicopters began descending on the crowds, sweeping the marked ones up in mass arrests. Elaine stared at him while the realization flooded her mind.

"Ray, my God I know what he is doing. Ray," she said, almost holding her breath while Tarek's helicopters swept above them. "Tarek stopped all orders which he knew the king and everybody else down the line would issue to stop these people from gathering, from beginning to storm the Grand Mosque. He's waited, drawing them all out, while his helicopters from above could mark the cell leaders, the members, the houses from which they emerged where they have their communications depots, command connections into the Iraqi military. Tarek now has them all." Ray stared back at her. "Ray, people with the codes. Houses, locations with the equipment, the connections into Iraqi command centers. He can use all this to send false orders, jam the others. All throughout the rest of the world, inside this country, or out. Now Tarek has them."

"Tarek," Ray whispered to himself. "How simple. How brilliant."

Quietly they sat and waited until Tarek's people, led by Badr, brought the material in. Elaine and the Black Hole team began poring over the codes, transmission units, and information that Tarek's men were delivering.

"My god," Elaine whispered, "this is a gold mine. All of their troop plans. Quick, take these to Schwarzkopf. And the rest of this," she looked up shaking her head in near disbelief. "We can transmit them false orders out in the field before they know what's going on. For even twenty-four or forty-eight hours before they find out could turn the war as Schwarzkopf begins his bombing." She handed the other units off to the

Special Ops team for electronic analysis so they would know how to continue to tap into the Iraqi equipment, their transmissions, throughout the rest of the war.

Ray went back to his desk and found the barely minutes-old communiqué he now knew would be there from Tarek. "Schwarzkopf should begin," it read.

Tarek stood quietly by the smoking overturned car, with the body of a dead Iraqi lying draped across the smoldering hood, still clutching his knife. He reached for the scrap of paper sticking out of the man's knife sheath. A picture of Saddam in a hajji robe was printed above the ragged typeface. He read the small print.

"Charter for Revolution...vile and ungodly Saudis...You should not refrain from giving expression to the hatred of enemies."

"And so you have." Tarek whispered to the dead man. He crumpled the paper in his hand. "And led us right to ours."

He dropped the paper to the ground and walked off through the smoke.

General Schwarzkopf signaled the standby alert for the Air Force. Rapidly the men began to load the bombs on the F-117 Stealth Fighters.

47

Antar watched the streets of Mecca, fury raging within him. His aide came in the door sweating, frightened. The man watched Antar nervously, and then spoke.

"Our equipment, our people—they've all been swept up. All of our transmission devices within the country, into Iraq. Should we stop the operation? Or proceed with the final step as planned?"

Antar, seething, closed his eyes and the image of Tarek years ago, moving the pieces over the backgammon board, unfolded across the darkness. He opened his eyes and looked at the phone once more.

"Tarek," he whispered to himself, "you have been clever, very clever. But, my friend, the final element I have planned will now go forward. I will win."

He picked up the receiver and dialed the number. "Proceed as planned."

Yusif finished the photography in the last light of the sun. He packed his equipment and waited for the plane to drop down to the desert. Absently, he turned on the little radio in the old shack. He heard the news of the U.S. amphibious assault. He bent over, straining to hear the words beneath the dusty radio's crackling sounds in this distant outpost. He looked up, startled to see the old bedu standing behind him, listening. The old man was silent. Yusif looked at him curiously and then sat down at the table and picked up the phone one last time. He dialed Yasmina's number. Once again it rang and rang as the desert wind blew the sand into the small room.

The plane descended as Yusif waited on the makeshift landing strip, his equipment slung over his shoulder. He took one last look at the small guesthouse, the deep red of the ancient temple, and boarded.

He watched with surprise as the old bedu chief boarded the plane with him.

Naila entered the Mecca hospital and walked between the long rows of hospital beds. She breathed deeply, feeling the last dregs of strength ebbing from her, and looked down at the broken body. She laid her hand on the patient's face. Osman's voice came quietly behind her.

"I knew he was coming here. I went to see Tarek at your house to see if he knew anything. He wasn't there and I decided to fly my plane in, I was so worried. Nura and Said were worried for your safety and came with me," he motioned back to the melee of people in the Mecca hospital. Then he walked closer to the bed where Abed lay.

Osman heard the small sounds of the machines, the tubes breathing for the young man's body and the fluid seeping from the bottles overhead into his arms. He looked at the bandages that swathed the right side of Abed's head. Osman reached out his hand to touch the even plane of Abed's left cheek and the fine bones above his closed, dark eyes. He moved his hand along the exposed left forehead and then stopped at the bandages covering the rest. His hand stayed motionless, his eye upon the bloody picture of Saddam still pinned to the boy's clothes. The doctor walked up behind him.

"Tell me," said Osman.

The doctor looked at Osman for a moment and then shook his head sadly. "The right side of his skull is crushed, the eye gone. How total the damage will be to his ability to think, to move, to see with the remaining eye, we have no way of knowing now. He is in a coma. We can only hope he lives now."

Osman watched him go, then gently, as the tears began to flood his eyes, bent over and held the silent body in his arms, rocking him softly, whispering to him as though Abed could hear. He nodded silently to the man who came and stood beside him. Said's haggard, taut face gazed at Osman in his grief.

"Dr. Naila," a nurse rushed up, flustered. "Dr. Naila, could you come with me? There is a woman, one of the hajjis, who insists she must talk to you. She says it is urgent."

Naila followed the nurse down the corridor teeming with patients. The nurse opened the door to one of the examining rooms. The young woman with whom she had stayed the past night in the cell stood in front of her. Naila felt a surge of fear pound in her chest.

"Dr. Naila, please, there is someone we are afraid to bring inside who is injured. Please, can you help?"

"Wait here just a moment. I'll get an orderly." Naila turned rapidly toward the door. The woman's hand caught her arm.

"No, we are afraid. It is urgent, she may be dying, please, just you."

Naila hesitated. The woman motioned Naila down the hall, through the chaos of the hospital, toward the back door, opened the door, and nodded toward a clump of shrubs, past the stretchers coming into the hospital. "She is there," she whispered. Naila walked uncertainly toward the enclosure. The woman nodded for her to follow while she parted the shrubs. Naila entered. She looked confused at the empty, shaded space before her.

"Dr. Naila."

Naila turned to find the gun pointing at her. "Dr. Naila," the young woman holding the gun within the white folds of her hajji robes looked steadily at her, "you will come with us."

Naila froze in fear as a second woman came up behind her holding a pistol. "If you make a sound, a movement, we will kill you now."

She placed the black abaya over Naila and held the pistol to Naila's side.

"You will go with us, Dr. Naila, quietly."

The nurse glanced up at Osman, Said, and Nura waiting by Naila's empty office. "She has gone."

"She has gone?" said Nura incredulously.

"Yes," said the nurse. "One of the hajjis came for her, asked her to see someone outside. And then she just disappeared."

Nura stood frozen. "She disappeared?"

The nurse said, "I didn't understand why the woman wouldn't bring the patient inside. In any case Dr. Naila went out with her. Then she was gone."

"Oh God," Nura whispered the words in terror, "oh God, no."

48

Naila followed the woman down the long winding back alleys of Mecca, becoming lost, as they headed toward a different house. She walked up steps into a darkened interior. She stopped. A room full of eyes stared at her. A man, whose head was covered with a hood, motioned. He whispered something to the woman who turned to faced her.

"We know who you are. We know why you were here before." Naila felt her hands quickly pulled and tied behind her. A scream rose in her throat, but she struggled to suppress it.

The man with the hood walked toward her. He took off his belt and lashed out at her stomach. Naila cringed, then fell to the floor choking, convulsed by searing pain. The man stood back as she struggled to upright herself.

The woman, surrounded by the faces in the dim room, continued. "You have tried to interfere with the work of the revolution. You have tried to run from justice, your own fate, carrying a man's baby as you stand before us." The people in the room now joined the woman, calling out, chanting, as they stared at Naila. The words "adulteress," "sins against Islam," "traitor," "spy," swirled around her from voices in the room, an otherworldly cacophony of jargon, scripture, rhetoric, now chaotically hurtling at her. Somewhere in the back of the room, far away, a small radio played, the voice of Saddam thundering, rasping the words of "retribution," "the will of Allah."

The woman turned at the nod of the man in the hood. He whispered again. Naila strained, feeling some faint familiarity in the muffled sound of his voice. The man stopped speaking when he saw her struggling to hear his words. Saddam's voice cried out from the small crackling radio in the distance. The woman spoke abruptly again.

"We will not be stopped by what has happened here in Mecca during the last few hours. No, we will proceed with our plans. The next steps will begin momentarily. Step by step they will unfold over the next hours. You have falsely joined us. But now you will truly be part of our plans. A symbol, a statement of many things abhorrent to the true Islam."

Naila looked at her, desperately trying to understand the woman's meaning.

"Within hours we will begin a series of public executions. They will serve as lessons for those who have sinned against Islam. They will be done publicly in Mecca. You, a spy, an adulteress, will be one of them. They will follow shortly what is about to happen now."

The woman jerked Naila to her feet and led her to a small dark room. Naila heard the bolt on the door slam shut, the radio still playing in the distance.

Elaine, Tarek, Nura and Said listened from Tarek's Mecca headquarters to the sounds of Naila's skirt brushing against the small radio mike. Then quiet. Then the sounds of soft crying. Said buried his face in his hands. Tarek's torment seemed to engulf him. Nura, submerged in a grief that seemed beyond words, simply looked up at him, waiting.

Finally Tarek started barking orders. "Badr, surround the house. Get her out now. Tell Ray to have their Special Operations team positioned as a backup."

Badr hurried out of the room.

❊ ❊ ❊

Ray heard the phone ringing as he paced the monitor room in Mecca, staring at the Iraqi boats swirling around the U.S. ships in the Gulf. Circling, firing in midair, the small black boats swarmed around the U.S. ships. He kept his eye on the urgent messages flowing out of the machine from Washington. Fear now rolled through him undisguised.

Elaine opened the door to say something. Her words were drowned by the eerie wail that came from the mosque. Like echoes in a madhouse the sound began to reverberate from the tops of all the mosques across the city. The crackle of Radio Riyadh flared for a minute. Then came the break and the sound of the woman announcer's voice.

"We will continue. Know that we will win. Know that what comes next is the work of the revolution. We are shutting down the oil fields, the docks, the airports, all communications. The will of Allah be done."

Schwarzkopf's Air Force troops finished loading the bombs on the F-117's and now waited nervously for the signal for takeoff. At 7:15 P.M. the air-raid warning sirens went off over Saudi Arabia. The television crew panned the terrified citizens

504

putting on gas masks. A reporter stood before the camera. Then suddenly, the TV screen went blank.

As Ray and Elaine stood in the room, the lights went out. The phones stopped ringing. The telex ceased. The computer monitors went black. The radio transmissions died. The airflow stopped. The water shut off. Only the eerie wail coming again from the top of the mosque sounded.

Ray listened in the darkened, still room. The sound from the mosque suddenly cut off. He put his head in his hands.

"Oh Jesus, God," he whispered.

N aila listened to the sounds of the radio in the distance, the words of Saddam from Baghdad. Then the radio went dead and the lights all around her went out.

She struggled up, frightened, to the small window. Mecca was black, totally, terrifyingly black and soundless, eerily soundless. She heard the echo of footsteps, people who stopped still, stunned in the dark streets. Naila's heart beat in her throat when the muezzin began to call out from the top of the mosque. "Know that the will of Allah be done." She heard footsteps behind her. The young woman stood before Naila, and two women guards stood behind her.

"Come, we begin," said the young woman. The guards took both Naila's arms and led her down the stairs, then out the door.

At the center of the square, one guard stood waiting while the others gathered confused people from the street to form an audience. When they had formed a circle, they bowed toward the sound of the voice repeating its call from the mosque. They dropped to their knees, praying. The two women guards led

Naila to the front of the circle. The male guard in the center then stepped forward.

"The Koran has told us to know the will of Allah. To do the work of Allah. For too long we have been confused, by the ways, the words of others. But now, the Ayatollah has shown us the way. The way to Mecca, to Islam, to a new greatness. Today in Mecca we begin to create his empire. And to rid the world of those who have sinned against him, spoken against him, lived outside the word as he has told us." The guard fell silent and then motioned with his hand.

Naila felt her vision darken, and her legs give out beneath her. The guards jerked her upright. As they held her, a haggard, blindfolded man was led out.

They pushed him to the center of the circle and removed his blindfold. He was shaking uncontrollably, urine dripping down his leg. The guard pushed him to a kneeling position. He looked up, eyes disconnecting in fear, when the guard handed him a blank sheet of paper and a pen. The guard wrote at the top, "The will of Allah be done, and said to the prisoner, "repeat that until you have filled the page."

The man began to write in wild scrawls, over and over again. The guard looked back to the people gathered in a circle.

"Ibrahim Al Awadi has written books of blasphemy. He has published works that defile the revolution, speak irreverently of Saddam Hussein. Of Allah himself. In the name of the Allah we now offer justice."

The guard bent over and took from the man the paper covered with the hysterical winding scrawls. He held it up, then bent down again, pinning the paper to the front of the man's chest. The guard spoke abruptly while the crowd looked on. "Beg God's forgiveness."

When the man opened his mouth and began to utter the

words, the guard, like taking a lamb before the temple, slit his throat. The severed head rolled back, the blood gushed out. Naila felt the guards jerk her to her feet when she began to faint. Slowly they walked her back into the house.

❊ ❊ ❊

Badr rushed in and bent over Tarek's shoulder. They listened to the sounds of Naila's radio mike.

"Tarek, we have been to the house where she was before. They are not there. It's not the same house they were in—they are someplace else. The radar, computers, the systems are all down, so we can't do a direction finding on the signal from her mike. We can only send men out on foot trying to pick it up. General Schwarzkopf has already sent out two of the men from the Special Operations forces who can recognize her to comb the city, but the chances of finding her are slim."

In the silence of the dark room Naila heard Tarek's voice come across the dimming connection of the slowly ebbing battery in the small radio mike.

"Naila, where are you? Try to identify the location."

A small, broken whisper came back.

"Oh God, I don't know, I don't know." The soft sounds of her crying held in the room when her voice stopped.

Tarek bowed his head in the despair of a man who knows how little possible is left. Elaine's felt the tears coming down her face. Said stared at his hands, too lost in his own inner torment to see.

❊ ❊ ❊

ay's fingers worked wildly to connect the small emergency backup generator for his communication system with U.S. Air Force control in Dhahran. He ripped off the sheet that began to come through.

"Emergency computer systems ready to operate. Sixty seconds, power returns. Systems set to reinstitute power for electricity, communications, water, Air Force and Navy commands."

The hands ticked on Ray's watch, second by second. Then suddenly the lights went back on, and the computers made their whirring noises again. Ray slumped in his chair with wild relief while Elaine stood beside him, breathing deeply.

Then, in exactly sixty more seconds, it all stopped, totally, completely stopped again.

aila looked numbly at the faces around her illuminated by candles, young women and young men praying. She saw Antar, speaking in inaudible tones, giving instructions to the men around him. Across the room, the man in the hood reached into his pocket, drew out a small journal and began to write, first in broad swirls, and then in tight, erratic notes. Naila wondered what words, what beliefs could turn such people into killers.

A woman spoke to Naila. "The Koran has written that the sentence for adultery is stoning. Tomorrow we will lead you to Mina for all of the faithful, the Hajjis to see."

It was then that Naila knew she had lost God. Somewhere in the universe, all that was right, all that was decent had abandoned itself and died. All that was good slowly spiralled down into hell, into death, and now was ending for her, taking her with it. She tried to conjure up Said's face, but nothing came to her except the blackness of the dead Mecca night.

❊ ❊ ❊

Elaine listened to the soft sounds of Naila crying. Suddenly she stood up and ripped the headphone off. She reached over and quickly took Nura's abaya and moved abruptly to the door. Tarek grabbed her arm.

"Where are you going?"

Elaine's voice choked out the words, crying "To try and find her Tarek, to walk the streets, to look to..." she reached for the doorknob. Tarek pulled her hand back, his voice harsh.

"You won't find her like that. My God, do you think if we could, I wouldn't be out there myself?" Elaine looked at him anguished, helpless, knowing he was right. His voice was harsh, brutal. "If you go out there and these people will turn on you. They will rip you limb from limb." And then he moved closer to her and spoke, the words low, deep in his throat while his eyes held her. "I know what you want to do. But this is not your part of the world—you can never be the solution. You can help it, but you'll never be the solution. You must understand that."

She looked at his face, the complex mix of compassion, caring, the stark truth that he spoke. She sat back down the tears now flowing silently down her face.

Said touched her arm then drew back as he heard the soft sounds of the whisperings coming over the radio mike.

"You will never see...; you would have been so beautiful..."

He choked on the words. "What is she saying? Who is she talking to?"

Nura buried her face in her hands weeping for the first

time. "The baby. She is talking to her unborn baby who is going to die with her tomorrow."

Before dawn, the sounds stopped. The battery on the small radio mike sifted down to a final second, depleted, then stopped. Naila's voice hung in the room, a faint whisper, then disappeared.

49

The pilgrims watched the sun ascend in the sky. Naila's eyes rose to meet the guard who came to get her. A woman followed him with a blindfold. She reached forward to put it on Naila, "So she won't be able to identify the house."

The guard shook his head. "It won't make any difference now."

Naila walked out into the deadly silent streets of Mecca. The houses had no lights or water; the people wandered, terrified, in the streets while the calls from the mosques continued to ring out. She walked through a sea of people, lost in the crowd. She was unable to call out, because the cloth beneath her abaya gagged her. She was unable to run—the women on either side held her. They brought her first to the car, and then to the foot of Mt. Arafat.

"Get out."

The hooded man appeared at her side. The other hajjis stared at the hooded man and the woman who emerged from the car, covered in a black abaya rather than the white robes of the hajjis. They stared for a moment as two women stood on either side of this strangely silent black figure. Then they continued, praying toward Mina, losing her in the ever-moving sea of people, forgetting her and the hooded man while they flowed forward mesmerized, chanting.

Naila began to walk, praying softly to herself. She knew that in a matter of hours, when they reached their destination, the horror awaiting her would begin. Then it would end, then she would end, then there would be no more. Slowly she walked, stumbled, climbed in the heat, surrounded by the guards, encircled by the multitude of hajjis, with the hooded man at her side. The miles stretched before them. Below them was the blackened dead city.

Ray and Elaine listened to the reports coming from their squads, searching by foot and by Jeep, every street and house of Mecca looking for Naila and the revolutionary headquarters. They had found nothing.

Tarek turned at the sounds of footsteps behind him. It was Osman.

"Tarek, I am going to leave now. I am going to fly my son Abed back home to Riyadh; the pilot has the plane ready." He stopped. "But before I flew to Mecca I went to your house. I was desperate to find out if you knew anything about Abed…where he might be, whether he was all right. Your grandfather came to the door just as I was leaving. He seemed distressed when I told him you weren't there. He asked me to give you a message. Forgive me, I couldn't tell you earlier. He said to ask Tarek 'whether Musaid will be returning to Madain Saleh again.' Then he left."

"Whether Musaid would be returning to Madain Saleh again?" Tarek stood utterly still. Finally he spoke, "Osman, your plane is here?"

Osman nodded in confusion.

"Your plane has no identifiable insignia on it?"

Osman shook his head.

Tarek turned to Said, who now stared in anguish at the silent board. "Said, stay here in case anything comes through. Osman, I want you to take me somewhere. We will come back for Abed when we are finished."

❇ ❇ ❇

Tarek's grandfather listened to the sounds of the plane approaching. Slowly he covered the top of the incense burner and watched as the embers went out and the last of the pungent desert smoke drifted up into the sky. He stood up and drew his black cloak around him and walked out into the desert to meet Tarek.

"Wait," said Tarek to Osman as he landed, "I won't be long."

He knew the old man would be there. Out of the dark came his footsteps. The old man's feet shifted through the sand, navigating the desert.

Tarek watched his grandfather's face emerge in the moonlight. It was a face of a thousand lines, like parchment. His beard was gray and long; he had withered, bony fingers and a timeless smile visible in the desert night.

"Salaam Alekum," said the old bedu softly.

"Alekum Salaam," murmured Tarek embracing him, kissing one cheek and then the other.

"I have news for you," said the old one.

"I know," said Tarek as the old man drew him off into the shadows and whispered the name.

"I will go with you," said the old man.

He stood up beneath the shadows of Madain Saleh as the

sun began to drop down to the earth. He opened an old trunk and slowly pulled out his gold-edged black cloak. He reached for his ceremonial sword of carved silver, which Abdul Aziz had given him. He picked up the white kaffiyeh for his head and the gold egal to hold it. Then, standing straight, he faced Tarek. "Now, we go." They boarded the plane; Osman handed the controls to Tarek, and the propellers began to pull them into the night sky.

50

Nura listened as Tarek gave her the instructions. She followed him into the car and sat silently while they made their way through the traffic of Riyadh toward Musaid's house.

When they arrived, the servant opened the door and motioned them in, then knocked on the door of the women's quarters. The pale young wife came to the door and looked hesitantly at Nura and Tarek standing before her.

"Khadija," said Nura softly, "I came to speak to Musaid. Is he in?" Khadija shook her head in confusion while the baby cried in the room behind her.

"He's not here."

Nura glanced back at Tarek. "Tarek, can you wait while Khadija and I have a little visit before we go?"

Tarek walked back toward the foyer while Nura walked into the women's quarters. The old servant bowed, then went back to the kitchen. Tarek listened as he closed the kitchen door behind him, then moved silently toward the stairs.

At the top of the landing he stopped and turned the knob of the first door. It opened and he stepped into the room, past the maroon bedspread, toward the chest of drawers. He skimmed over the top of it, opened the drawers, moved his hand through the contents, and then closed them and walked out, proceeding to the next door, which opened on a large marble bathroom. He walked to a third door and tried it.

The lock resisted. He took a small set of surveillance keys out of his pocket and fitted the first one into the lock. With a faint sound, the lock clicked open and Tarek walked into the dark green study. He glanced at the leather sofa, the mounted deer's head above it, the gun racks, and then the desk. It was covered with papers with computations scribbled on them. A copy of the Koran lay next to Musaid's computer and a box of discs.

Tarek pulled the computer around so that the back of the machine faced him. He drew a tiny case of tools from the pocket of his thobe and working quickly, opened the back of the machine and wired a small device in place. He closed the back again and turned the machine around. Then he took the packet of disks from his other pocket. He placed a disk in one of the disk drives. He opened Musaid's box of disks, inserted the first one into the other disk drive, and copied it onto his disk. He moved through the box one by one until all of Musaid's disks had been copied.

He closed the box, repositioned all of the papers, and looked at the old maroon copy of the Koran. He opened it and noted the fingerprint smudges, the small pencil dots that appeared haphazardly throughout the various pages of the long volume. He picked up his disks, the tools, and Musaid's Koran, closed the door behind him, and walked down the stairs.

He stood in the foyer for a moment and then knocked on the door of the womens' quarters. The baby cried again when Khadija opened it and Nura looked at Tarek. She turned to Khadija. "We must be going now. Tell Musaid I'll stop by to see him soon."

Tarek and Nura got in the waiting car and drove directly to Ray's office where Elaine and Ray had flown to from Mecca. Elaine opened the door. The analysts stood waiting. As Tarek walked in the door, they connected the small emergency power unit to the computers.

Elaine put in the first disk and figures began moving across the computer screen. Elaine looked at Ray, astounded.

"Ray, some of these transmissions to Iraq go back for years. 1983, 1981. My god, here's one from 1980. All of these others with the terrorists outfits around the world, Abu Nidal, the others...." She slowly scrolled through the document so Ray could look at.

"They are all the same—numbers, a letter, then more numbers. This one is coming back from Iran. There's one from Tunis." Elaine continued to scroll through the lines. "One from Beirut. Here's one with Gaza; this must be Cairo. Numbers, a letter, then numbers, some with a dollar amount at the end."

Ray looked up as Tarek reached over and pushed the button on his desk, "Send somebody from decoding immediately."

The man walked in. Tarek opened Musaid's Koran to a page with the smudged fingerprints, and pointed to the dots. The man from decoding went off hurriedly into the other room.

Elaine quickly inserted the next disk to check it out. She sat in front of it perplexed as Ray watched over her shoulder. "This one is evidently Musiad's modem control disk. She shrugged as she moved through the command and address data, and then onto the next disk.

"This one is computer operations for the oil fields." She opened a drawer and put another disk on a second computer next to the first one. "See, this is correct; it has the basic commands that run the oil fields. There's nothing out of order here. Same goes for this next one—operations command for the electrical supply for the northern provinces." She looked back at Ray, worried, coming up with nothing. "You know Musaid's work would have legitimately taken him into all this."

She inserted the next disk in frustration.

"Electrical supply operations command in the north again. It's just a repeat, it's..." She stopped suddenly. She scrolled back through the last lines again. "Ray, oh my God." She moved closer to the screen. Ray looked at the lines on the screen as she pointed.

"It's a command to alter operations for a certain time, see here," she pointed again, " and then to destroy the command. This one shuts down all electricity for ten minutes." She looked at him. "The disruptions I couldn't trace. He programmed them so they couldn't be traced in operations." She took out the disk and raced to put another in.

"The water supply—the same thing." She open another document and checked her notes. "This corresponds perfectly to the date and time the water supply shut off for twenty minutes in the south."

She reached for the last disk in the container and inserted it into the drive. It was an unfamiliar program disk. She followed the instructions and operations commands for the countries' communications appeared. The screen rolled through the familiar systems commands. Then suddenly it went black.

Elaine scanned the power lights of the machine still on and pulled the disk from the machine. She punched the recall commands but the screen stayed blank.

"Ray, the memory, it's gone, everything is wiped out." She put in the reboot diskette, rebooted the computer then inserted the program disk. The commands for the normal functions of the oil fields instantly went to black.

"Ray, this is it," she said quietly holding the last disk. "A daemon—a programmed virus. It's a program designed to appear as proper commands to the operator and then to destroy the entire memory of the system before he knows what is happening. If you had cleverly designed daemons and had somebody on the inside able to implant them you could shut the entire country down—water, electricity, communications, air control systems—everything. Everything instantly, and completely."

The decoding analyst hurried into the room and handed Ray some papers. "We're working out the next few lines now." Ray looked down at the sheets and drew in his breath.

He repeated Elaine's words, "He's shut down the entire country, everything, instantly, completely and," he paused, "he's definitely taking his instructions from Iraq."

He handed her the sheets. She looked at the decoding analyst's notes at the top: "First number = page number; second letter = paragraph; third number = word corresponding to that number within paragraph."

She scanned the messages that followed. "God, the organization—Tunis, Beirut, Khartoum, Algiers, Sanaan, Cairo, Dubai—and the money." She shook her head in amazement.

Ray nodded. "It's brilliant really. From the smallest grass roots work in the slums, the camps, the elections, to flamboyant posturing with everybody in the Gulf—the mines, the attacks—and underneath it all the groundwork for the most sophisticated terrorism to finally bring them to their knees. You don't even have to bring in troops, nothing to retaliate against. Just subvert them from inside with invisible fingerprints, cause enough terror, cripple them enough so the people are terrified enough, think the government has lost control, its authority is eroded. The cells rise up, install a new 'revolutionary' government while the whole Muslim world is facing Mecca. At first puppets," Ray looked up, "and then gone. And then it spreads from here right on through the Gulf and across to Lebanon, to North Africa." He stopped.

Elaine spoke quickly. "We need to get people to the computer systems all over the country which are loaded with these program disks. All these systems are going to have to be swept, totally re-programmed. Even a small individual computer system, say the water operation in Najran, could spread it again, any system that connects with any other system has the potential to spread it again when you have something like these 'computer viruses' in the system somewhere."

Ray looked up at Tarek. "Can you trust Abdullah, Sultan? We would need something as widespread as their command units across the country to go to work on all of these machines."

Tarek nodded and Ray knew he need ask no more.

On a hunch, Elaine inserted the modem disk into the second computer and activated the program. She grabbed Tarek's arm. He turned rapidly to catch the message moving across the screen behind her.

"Tarek, it's the tap into Musaid's machine. Somebody is trying to run a message." She pulled up to check the screen. "It's from Iraq." The coding analyst jotted the letters and numbers down.

"MINA. NEXT PLANS FINAL. FAHD, TAREK, MIDNIGHT." Elaine stood behind Ray reading over his shoulder.

"He's going to kill Fahd and Tarek during Fahd's speech to the people tonight on Mt. Arafat."

COMPLETE N.S., MINA.

"N.S." Suddenly, Elaine looked up. "It's Naila isn't it? This is where they've taken Naila. They are going to kill her there while the hajjis look on; then they'll kill Fahd."

51

Somewhere in the back of her mind, she heard sound of helicopters. She continued to walk.

For a moment, in the heat, the faces of all of those she loved seemed to flood in front of her. And then recede, disappearing into nothingness.

She heard a helicopter flying low overhead. In the back of her mind it seemed to circle, dipping lower and lower. She looked back to the top of Mt. Arafat, now miles behind her and then to Mina before her. The hooded man stopped. In a loud voice he called out for the other hajjis to gather.

Lower and lower two helicopters dipped, circled.

Fahd's limousine began moving toward the center of the Valley of Mina. Fahd took the paper that Walid, sitting next to him, handed him. The words from Mecca to the Muslim world. He gazed at Mecca laying motionless before him. The sounds of the muezzins called out, reverberating from the mosques, throughout Mecca.

While the hajjis gathered about her, Naila stood still. The hooded man pulled the abaya from her. He waited for the hajjis to see her thus humiliated and then began to call out to the startled people to raise their stones. They began taking the stones into their hands. Naila bowed her head and prayed one last time, feeling the tiny fluttering of the baby within her.

A man moved forward with a stone. A helicopter dipped toward them; another dropped down now lower to the ground. The hooded man raised the hand that held the stone. She saw his arm draw back and the hood fall from his face—it was Musaid. She felt the final crumbling, hurtling of reality. Her eyes saw images now strangely transmuted, faces from her life now almost over.

The Special Operations pilot in the first helicopter radioed to the second helicopter. "Let's pray to God these people move when they see the blades coming down. I'm coming in on the right."

"Let's pray to God," the second pilot radioed back nervously, "that we don't crash trying to make this kind of hover a few feet off the ground. I'm on the left. Doors are open."

In the last few seconds there was an instant in which she thought she saw Said's face—a man in the white hajji robes walking beside her. There was a moment when she saw another man whisper something into a small microphone he carried, a moment when she thought she saw Tarek's face. She now felt her knees begin to buckle as the world spun. She thought she saw the faces of Nura and Osman emerging in hajji robes from the crowd.

The helicopters dropped down, and seemed to hover just barely feet from the ground. "They could pull us to the ground if we miss by more than a few seconds. Coordinate final descent to the countdown," the second pilot began counting.

Before she closed her eyes, there was an instant in which she thought she saw an old man move up alongside Musaid and take the stone from his hand. She closed her eyes.

Musaid stopped, absolutely still, and looked into the face of Tarek's grandfather. Musaid's people closed around them. The old bedu caught Musaid's arm, the one holding the stone.

Musaid tried to push the old man back. Naila opened her eyes when she heard the people gasp. Now the two helicopters dipped again and hovered only feet from the ground "Nine, eight..."

Naila suddenly saw two knives flash forward from two men in the hajji robes. A scream ripped the air as the two women guards dropped to the ground. The blade reached out and flashed in front of Musaid, Tarek's face behind it.

As the helicopter dipped, the old man and Tarek pulled Musaid into it. "I'm full throttle, habib," screamed the first pilot to the second over the roars of the crowd. "Now it's your turn."

Naila felt the violent wind caused by the huge blades of the second helicopter as it dropped to the ground behind her just before she completely lost consciousness.

A woman and two men pulled her inside the open, waiting door. The helicopter spun up, off the ground, above the screaming, terrified hajjis. The Iraqi guards raised their guns and fired at the helicopter, which lurched as the gunfire hit a blade. "We're all right, we're almost out of here." The pilot forced the gears violently into the maximum ascent. The pull of an updraft rocked them for a moment, and then they soared wildly above the mass of people into the sky.

Naila's head lurched to the side and she opened her eyes. She looked up into Osman's face. The woman who had gotten in first turned to her. It was Nura. Then Naila heard Said's words and she burst into deep sobs.

"It is over Naila, it is over. We will take you home."

There was a moment—it seemed like forever, when the helicopter spun out past Mecca, behind the first chopper, now heading for the Gulf. Naila saw Elaine sitting next to Ray in the front seat and heard his voice on the intercom. "Clear the *Independence* for landing. Clear airspace for a plane to depart with two immediately for Cairo. Have an ambulance waiting in Cairo, the woman is pregnant and suffering severe dehydration and shock. Have someone on board the plane to treat her enroute. Have another plane ready to take them from Cairo to the U.S."

Ray and Elaine listened to the Commander of the U.S.S. *Independence* affirm. Ray turned back to Naila and spoke gently. "Naila, try to describe the house, the street you were on, anything you can remember seeing when you left…"

Naila described the house, and what she could remember about the street of Anatar's headquarters.

The airmen had the lights on aboard the *Independence*. Naila's helicopter hovered for a moment over a speedboat that fired at them, then made the descent swiftly onto the carrier, flagged down by the waiting crew. Nura and Said helped Naila off the helicopter. Said boarded with her on the plane waiting with its engines running. A medical corpsman waited aboard, ready to fly with them. The door was about to close behind her, when Naila suddenly reached out and held Nura's hand.

"Nura," she said, "am I doing the right thing?" She had tears in her eyes when Nura handed her a small brown leather suitcase she had fixed for her.

"Yes," said Nura quietly. "Yes, you are. For now. Maybe later it will be different." She opened up the small case and removed an old photograph framed in silver. In it, their faces when they were small children by the Jeddah seashore looked back at her. Nura handed the photograph to Naila.

"We are yours, my love," whispered Nura. "Wherever you are, we are yours." Said took the picture and carefully placed it back between the clothes, shut the small case. The plane was flagged on. Nura stood with Ray and Elaine watching it move swiftly along the flight deck and into the night sky.

✠ ✠ ✠

Schwarzkopf worked with the programmer now holding Musaid's equipment. "Iraq's planes in the Sudan aimed at Egypt, the others in Libya. Transmit them orders from this equipment that all plans to fly have been canceled." He looked back at the aide. "Tarek got confirmation from Iran on the deal?" The aide nodded. "OK," said Schwarzkopf, "beam this next one to the airfield in Baghdad. They should fly 140 of their planes to Iran now for safekeeping." Schwarzkopf went on to dictate several other orders to Iraqi units inside Iraq, while taking all of the intercepts of their commands that Elaine's team was now handing him on a minute-by-minute basis.

✠ ✠ ✠

Tarek hovered in his helicopter above the *Independence* until the plane carrying Naila and Said took off. Then he ordered his pilot back toward Riyadh. When they were within five miles of the city, Tarek said, "Here." The pilot started to drop down into the desert. The old man nodded. The ruins of Dariyah showed like a deep red outline against the moon on the stretch of desert leading into the old city.

When they reached the ground, Tarek opened the door and pushed Musaid out. Tarek aimed his revolver at him.

"Throw your gun on the ground, Musaid." Musaid took a step back.

"Throw it to the ground."

Musaid's face paled and then a look of hate spread across it. He reached rapidly into his thobe for his gun.

"One of these bullets is for you, Tarek."

"That wouldn't be necessary, if you had succeeded the first time in the desert, would it?"

Tarek fired when Musaid's hand reached his pocket. Musaid screamed in pain. He pulled back his bloodied hand and his gun fell to the ground.

"And," said Tarek, "the other bullet was for Fahd, wasn't it?"

Musaid looked at him, his face contorted in rage. "Fahd lives, Fahd dies, it won't make any difference," he said. "The statement will be made. The world will know that Saudi Arabia is about to make way for a truly Islamic government instead of the corrupt western tools in power. People like me within the Family will ascend. Tonight you will see."

"You and Antar. When did it begin, Musaid? When you met years ago? He was always a perceptive judge of character. And you, so easy. Musaid, you poor stupid bastard, he will chew you up and spit you out like dirt once he's finished with you. The only one to ascend will be Antar, and Saddam. Saddam and Iraq." He smiled. "There will be no message tonight." Suddenly, in the far distance, the city lit up. Tarek watched Musaid's face fill with astonishment, then rage. "We've taken care of the daemons you installed in operations. Over the last few hours they have been pulled out and replaced by Abdullah's crews in the National Guard. Sultan's defense units. Skillful of you to have the daemons made up outside the country and then moved in with the archaeologist's equipment. Shrewd." He left Musaid no time to respond. "We also know how you got the information from the U.S. Embassy. You used daemons to infiltrate their system and program it to send directly to you and Iraq every time they moved." He paused, enjoying Musaid's outraged horror. "But the Royal Council meetings; that was very clever of you to plant a device in Naif's watch. Naif is always in the country, unlike Saud and Abdullah, who travel abroad so you would lose the connection. No, Naif, as minister of the interior, is always within range. He exchanges intelligence with me, you could hear if he had uncovered anything in the provinces or with the hajjis. It was extremely clever of you. All the while feeding Abed out like so much bait to the dogs."

Musaid breathed deeply, "How do you know all of this?"

"Your tape, Musaid, the code on your tape. It has also been very helpful in enlightening me as to who is working with you in this."

Musaid glared at him. "When we have the trial, I will speak. And I will tell the rest of the Muslim world and beyond how corrupt is this government. When they assassinated Anwar Sadat in Egypt, the ones they arrested stood up in the courtroom and told the world the story of how Egypt had been westernized, corrupted below Sadat and his government, and the people throughout the Islamic world listened."

"There won't be a trial," said Tarek. "There will only be an accident in the desert. Stand up."

The old man stood by as Tarek pointed his revolver.

"Pray if you wish. Get on your knees." Musaid dropped to his knees and Tarek raised the revolver to his head.

Suddenly, the old bedu pushed Tarek's hand away. Tarek watched him, startled. Tarek's grandfather bent slowly toward the desert, washed his hands in sand as the bedu had done for centuries, and bent in prayer with the words of the Koran. He then stood up and looked at Tarek.

"It is," he said, his old lips moving painfully over the words, "my right."

With that, his hand moved toward his waist. Suddenly, the sword flashed in the moon, a scream echoed, and then there was stillness. He placed his sword back in his belt. He stood over the pool of blood where Musaid's head lay looking with lifeless eyes at the walls of Dariyah. He bent down to the desert and washed his hands again in the cold sand with the words of the Koran on his lips.

Tarek spoke into the tiny microphone in his hand and whispered the word.

In the next moment a bomb exploded in a house in Mecca. The flames soared into the night. When they died down, the body of Antar was found in the ashes.

❈ ❈ ❈

Tarek radioed to Schwarzkopf. Schwarzkopf's voice was barely a whisper. "Iran has the Shia in the south ready?"

"They've received their orders—the Shia Iraqi soldiers working undercover for Iran will pull out as the maneuvers start—'fail to fight' and pass the plans back on to the rest of the troops."

"And the Kurds in the north?" asked Schwarzkopf.

"Barzani will blow up the chemical plants, the Scud plants in the north.

"Saddam is oblivious?"

"Saddam is oblivious."

Schwarzkopf began the bombing.

EPILOGUE

Elaine closed the shutters of the apartment against the winter sky in Washington. She looked at the volumes that Tarek had handed her as her plane was preparing to leave. Musaid's journals. The flowing script of revolution, God, evil. The erratic scrawlings of salvation and schizophrenia. Computer codes, networks of terror. Antar. The confusions, the longings. She read through the night and then sent Musaid's journals directly on to headquarters.

She sat still for a moment, looking at the calendar, thinking of the two months that had passed since her return. She glanced at the small clock on her desk. The car would be here shortly to pick up the official report. She gazed once more at the papers in front of her.

General Schwarzkopf returned to the U.S., a hero. Yasmina died, one of the thousands tortured and executed in Iraq's prisons. Yusif Khalidi never knew that he had been used or what really happened, and he will never be told. He continues his work in archaeology as one of the heads of the Baghdad Museum. After Musaid was buried, Tarek's grandfather went back to Madain Saleh where for Tarek, he keeps watch, as he always has, along the northern borders, Syria, Iraq, with his bedu.

Tarek bought silence from Naila's fiancé, and the king secretly pardoned Naila, saying that he had given her a special dispensation to marry Said. In fact, he was deeply grateful for her heroic work to save the country.

Iraq rends itself apart now, as the dream of creating a new Arab Empire fades.

She paused for a moment, hearing in her memory the last words of the Koran.

The battle turned out to be the most successful air campaign in the history of the world. By the time it was finished, Iraq had been more heavily shelled than Germany in World War II. The air war was followed by a land battle that was the largest clash of armies since World War II. On the first day, 20,000 Iraqi soldiers surrendered, their morale broken. They used the confusion of the last bombing to escape, walking two, three days to get to Saudi and U.S. lines, fighting ravenously over the food and water their captors gave them. In an attempt to staunch the flow, Saddam sent out execution battalions to shoot Iraqi soldiers trying to desert, but to no avail.

Through the rest of the war, Iraqi communications commands were intercepted, and countermanded. Iraq flew 142 planes to Iran for safe keeping. Iran kept them. They became the first planes of the "new" Iranian Air Force. Throughout the war, Iran prepared the Shia in Basra, Najef and other villages of the south. When the war ended they were ready, staging battles and riots in an attempt to overthrow Saddam. In the north, the Kurds rebeled.

Kuwait returned to the Kuwaitis. In Saudi Arabia, King Fahd emerged from the war stronger than ever—as a result of the high-risk decisions to call the U.S. in.

Elaine picked up her pen to add something, then quietly

put it down. She reached for the letter that had come yesterday. She read it once more. The beautiful handwriting, the elegant signature that simply said "Nura."

Elaine, you have returned to your home in the U.S. But I write to tell you that we think of you always, and hope that you do not forget us. Tarek I know will carry you always in his heart. And you, I believe, will not forget Tarek. He taught you, I feel, how to love again. And Tarek? Tarek has returned to me. I accept what happened. I think that God sometimes moves in ways that we do not understand at the time. I hope as I have been able to forgive, that you too, can forgive—and understand, that day on Osman's boat, the depths of my jealousy, my passion that provoked my action. I think it is unimportant to dwell now on what is pardonable, unpardonable. I ultimately believe Elaine, that God brought us all together in a way that each of us, perhaps not understanding at the moment, walked away with a gift that was profound.

I look sometimes at Musaid's journal, the diary of an assassin, the small volume Tarek saved for me now locked away with my own, and I think of how close, how very close we came to an end. We have taken in his children and his wife, to care for them. It is our wish; our traditions are long and deep. As I write this, Naila sits with me with her son, a beautiful boy. Soon Tarek's grandfather will teach him too, just as he taught Tarek so many years ago and now our son, the ways of the desert and the falcons.

The tragedy of the war remains. The thousands of Iraqis who died, the tragedy of a great country brought to ruin by one man. The people of Iraq deserved better. The fears for ourselves remain. But perhaps one day this child will make the hajj, and remember what happened at Mecca. The day, the moment, and the people who destroyed a revolution and the terror it brought with it. And the truth of what happened there? The truth will never be known. It is better that way.

Elaine heard the car waiting for her outside. The truth will never be known, she whispered to herself. It is better that way.

The little antique clock from the Middle East on her desk chimed. She turned off the light and shut the door.

JO FRANKLIN FILMOGRAPHY

"One of the Top 50 Film Producers in the U.S."
— *Millimeter Magazine*

Following her work as Senior Washington Producer of the MacNeil-Lehrer Report, Ms. Franklin produced and directed **The Middle East Trilogy,** a unique history-making series that aired to rave critical reviews, unprecedented audience numbers, and repeated worldwide broadcasts.

Throughout Operation Desert Storm, **The Middle East Trilogy** was used by General Norman Schwarzkopf, the U.S. State and Defense Departments, and the military to train their personnel for deployment to the Persian Gulf. In an unusual move, the U.S. Military also requested that Ms. Franklin work personally with the Special Operations Forces during the Gulf War — a request she honored and which ultimately became the heart of her novel *The Wing of The Falcon.*

Her eight films have won numerous awards including an Emmy nomination:

I. SAUDI ARABIA (three-part series)

- ⊠ The Kingdom
- ⊠ The Race With Time
- ⊠ Oil, Money, Politics

"One of the finest documentaries on the Saudi move into the 20th Century...it is a literal video-textbook covering Arabian history from the birth of Islam to the birth of massive oil wealth...a stroke of genius!" (*Los Angeles Times*) "A superb piece of television journalism." (*Chicago Sun Times*) "The most extensive and useful look at Saudi Arabia ever presented." (*Washington Post*)

II. THE OIL KINGDOMS (three-part series)

- ✠ Kings and Pirates
- ✠ The Petrodollar Coast
- ✠ A Sea of Conflict

"Fantastic is no overstatement...it is a story of how five small Arab countries on the Persian Gulf struck liquid gold in the form of oil...the issues are formidable." (*Washington Times*) "Incisive, fascinating, a penetrating study of the Persian Gulf's wealth and tradition...a series of Arabian delights and solid entertainment." (*Christian Science Monitor*)

III. DAYS OF RAGE: THE YOUNG PALESTINIANS

"A compelling chronicle of conditions among Palestinians that resulted in the ongoing intifada/uprising...an impassioned testament from people usually seen and heard only in sound bites." (*USA Today*) "The most controversial film of the decade." (Entertainment Tonight)

IV. ISLAM: A CIVILIZATION AND ITS ART

"A panoramic history of Islamic civilization skillfully combining stunning footage of Islamic sites and works of art with commentary by scholars...The result is a stunning and scholarly film that covers the spectrum of Islamic civilization." (The Walters Art Gallery)

All films are available on video cassette. For further information, please contact Pacific Productions, P.O. Box 6601, Malibu, CA 90264.